TRINA'S STORY

HERMANN HARTFELD

IRINA'S STORY

BETHANY HOUSE PUBLISHERS
MINNEAPOLIS, MINNESOTA 55438
A Division of Bethany Fellowship, Inc.

Previously published under the title *Irina* by Christian Herald.
Translated from the German by Henry Wagner.

Copyright © 1980 by R. Brockhaus Verlag Wuppertal, Germany

Copyright © 1983
Bethany House Publishers
All rights reserved

Published by Bethany House Publishers
A Division of Bethany Fellowship, Inc.

Printed in the United States of America

ISBN 0-87123-261-8

Library of Congress Cataloging in Publication Data

Hartfeld, Hermann, 1942-
   Irina's story.

   Translation of: Irina, oder, Die Enkel der Revolution.
   Previously published in English under title: Irina, a love stronger
than terror.
   1. Sokolova, Irina. 2. Nikitin, Alexander.
3. Baptists—Soviet Union—Biography. 4. Persecution—
Soviet Union—History—20th century. 5. Soviet Union—
Church history—1917-   . I. Title.
BX6493.H3513   1983   286'.13 [B]   82-22815
ISBN 0-87123-261-8

Author's Preface

I had not planned to write another book when my first book, *Faith Despite the KGB*, was completed. But I have experienced many difficulties in the West, and these generated an inner imperative to take a position and supply an answer.

Hundreds of letters from readers of the first book could have been combined under one heading, "Dialogue with communism—yes or no?" Here, for example, is an excerpt from one of those letters.

We Christians are duty-bound to see the realization of Christ's teachings in communism. We must start a dialogue with the Communists and convince them that they are our brothers and sisters, for we have the same goal.

I will not argue the fact that the rise to power by Communists has cost millions of lives. In Cambodia alone, more than two million were killed. Yet is it not high time that we Christians extend a hand of forgiveness, saying, "Yes, our dear atheistic friends, blood must flow to secure any goal, and you are bringing what Christ has taught us into realization"? I am convinced that there are many things for us to learn from communism.

So you will not think the writer of this letter belonged to a leftist youth organization, I would like to say immediately that the writer was a foreign missionary from a denomination with many evangelicals in it. While I was reading this letter I again remembered that small group of young Christians in the Soviet

Union who once made this kind of attempt. They tried to persuade the leaders in the Communist Party to call off the ideological war against those "religious vestiges" of their Party's political program. Their story is told in the following pages. These are all true events supported by abundant documentation. The names of the persons involved, as well as names of localities, have been changed so as not to endanger our friends in Russia. The names of government officials and KGB officers were not changed, with one exception.

My theology teacher, Heinz Weber, suggested I devote my practicum to the completion of this manuscript. And the leadership of the Brake Bible School in Germany generously released me from all practical work so that I would be able to give my undivided attention to the manuscript.

The missionary group Friedensstimme (Voice of Peace) obtained many written documents about the persecuted Baptists in the USSR. A number of other missionary organizations aided me in maintaining close ties with the key persons of this incredible but true story.

My stay at the P.E.G. English School in London gave me another excellent opportunity to continue work on my manuscript. I am particularly grateful to the directors of this school, J. Shorrocks and D. Clark, who made the study of the English language possible for my wife and me without cost. In certain London libraries and research institutions I also found very rare documents, which I was allowed to use in my research.

This is not a bedtime story for children, since the tactics employed by the KGB include blackmail, rape, torture, and physical intimidation. Yet the glory of Christ shines through the faith of the Christians. It is my hope that this book will be a blessing for many.

Contents

MAJOR PERSONALITIES

Alexander Nikitin (called Sasha)—Preacher of a registered Baptist congregation.

Andrey Nikitin—Sasha's father; preacher of an unregistered Baptist congregation.

Natasha Nikitina—Sasha's stepmother.

Irina Sokolova—Candidate for a doctoral degree.

Yuri Sokolov—Irina's father; psychiatrist.

Vladimir Sokolov—Irina's grandfather.

Pelagea—Vladimir's wife.

Vassiley Kuznetsov—Russian Orthodox Church priest.

Ivan Nikolayevitch Kuznetsov—Vassiley's father; professor.

Nora—Vassiley's mother; actress.

Tamara—Vassiley's sister; medical student.

Koslov—KGB officer.

Misha Siniszin—Relative of the Nikitins; member of the Central Committee of the Communist Party.

Neverov—Bus driver; believer.

Valentina—Neverov's wife.

Serov—Relative of the Sokolovs; KGB officer.

Lyuba—Serov's wife.

Alyosha, Nina, Svetlana, and Igor—The Serovs' children.

Nikolay Lebedyev—Elderly prison guard.

Ivan and Alexey—Lebedyev's sons.

Zarapkin—Official with responsibility for religious organizations.

Dr. Koshkin—KGB official; psychiatrist.

Ryabushin—Veteran Communist who became a believer.

Samovarov—KGB official.

Lupa—War veteran; worker in a congregation.

Major Lupa—Major of militia; the older Lupa's grandson.

Semyon Anakin—Pentecostal preacher.

Ivan Krebs—Lutheran.

Polevoy—Baptist preacher from Siberia.

1 Catching Up

Alexander Nikitin was seated alone in the train compartment. He was so preoccupied that he barely noted the glorious countryside gliding by the window. He had just been in Kiev, where he had been involved in discussions with several members of the steering committee of unregistered Baptists* who called themselves the "Council of Churches." He was glad to be alone so he could collect and organize his thoughts.

Since he was the preacher of an officially sanctioned—in other words, registered—Baptist congregation, he still had a bit more freedom of movement than his colleagues on the Council of Churches. At least this would have been the superficial impression of an occasional participant in the worship services when he saw the packed houses of worship with their joyous and loving atmosphere. The outsider, of course, would not suspect the battles and power struggles going on behind the scenes.

It was now clear to Sasha Nikitin that these unregistered Baptists, these "schismatics," were not "enemies of the established order," a label the state's propaganda machine tried to attach to them. On the contrary, he had been deeply impressed by the spirituality and clarity of view revealed by

---

*This refers to the unrecognized, in other words, unregistered, congregations which function largely underground. For this reason the overseas secretary, Georgi Vins, established the "International Representation for the Council of the Evangelical Baptist Churches of the Soviet Union" in 1980.

these men in Kiev. He wished he had been able to take notes of all he had heard there, so as to have a permanent record of it. But he knew how much he would have risked by making a record of these conversations. So he merely confined himself to keeping a very accurate mental picture of what he had encountered.

"Of course Lenin was right," one of the brethren had said, "when he insisted that 'the state keeps a hangman around in order to throttle every sign of revolt on the part of the oppressed masses; and the Pope is there to calm the oppressed and to give them false hopes about a rosy future in heaven.' But do we, as Christ's church, really do anything more than that? Do we always and under all circumstances stand up for truth and justice? No! We adapt ourselves to circumstances!"

If this is what the leaders of the persecuted church are saying about themselves, what do things look like in my own church? Sasha thought.

*   *   *

"Hello!" A young woman's melodious voice jarred him loose from his thoughts.

"Hello," he replied absentmindedly.

"Is the seat next to you taken?" the young lady asked.

"No, no, of course not," he quickly exclaimed in order not to appear impolite, and moved over a little.

In spite of that she sat down opposite him by the window, gave him a mischievous look and asked, "Aren't you lonesome all by yourself in this compartment?"

Well, he thought, *this seems to be one of the more affectionate types!* "Absolutely not! Why should I be lonesome?" Then he looked at her a bit more closely and gasped, "Irina Sokolova!"

"Yes, it's me," she said and extended her hand to him. "Isn't this amazing? While I was standing there waiting for this train I suddenly thought, *Wouldn't it be nice to run into a fellow student during this trip?* And here you are, Sasha! How many years has it been since we've seen each other?"

"It's probably been five years since they expelled me from the university. Is it really that long?"

"I would think so. Haven't you gotten over it yet?" she asked compassionately.

"Oh, you know, sometimes it makes me downright ill. I've never understood how anybody can throw someone out of the university because of his personal faith. After all, I was in my last semester. My record was good. Can you still remember the whole episode?"

"Wait a moment." Irina knit her brows and began to think. Looking at her, Sasha began to feel a sudden, wild longing rising within him. Somewhere in his heart an old wound which had never healed began to hurt again.

While they were both still at the university he had felt terribly awkward in her presence. Each time she looked in his direction with her large blue eyes, he got a strange, dizzy sensation. But somehow he enjoyed the feeling and held his ground when she glanced at him.

Occasionally he would run into her during evening discussions. On those occasions he tried to finagle a seat next to her for himself. He then sat silently and observed her from the side, allowing the others to do the arguing while he remained totally oblivious to anything said on either side of him.

Then a well-meaning friend who was not unaware of his smitten state had whispered to him, "She is the daughter of a former KGB officer who is now a psychiatrist. Watch yourself!" Those words cut deeply in Sasha's soul. They still hurt today.

"What *are* you thinking about?"

Sasha was startled. "Oh, excuse me," he blurted. "I've been far away in my thoughts. Can you remember what happened when they dismissed me?"

"I've been trying for quite a while to make it all clear to you, but you're obviously floating far away in the upper regions," she answered, laughing. "It was this way. You allowed yourself to be drawn into a discussion about the relationship between religion and science. According to you, religion and science occupy different spheres of activity. Science confines itself to the examination of natural phenomena as well as the interrelationships within human society. Religion, you argued, concerns itself with the spiritual life of man and with his life after death—in fact, with the entire sphere of transcendental forces. Science is limited, you asserted, in its potential; and the knowledge which science permits us to gain is only relative and is continually modified by new discoveries. Then you continued by saying that if science were to discontinue battling religion and agree to friendly coexistence, she would receive an irreplaceable support from religion. That is approximately what I can recall today."

He was amazed. "You've got a fantastic memory!"

"Not really," she demurred. "At the time, the dean had asked me to take stenographic notes of the entire evening's discussion—so that he could get to know the opinions and the needs of the students better. Naive creature that I was, I fell for it. The notes which I took were used against you later, I am sorry to say. You were declared mentally ill in front of the entire student body. Your philosophic utterances were nothing more than the fabrications of a sick mind, they announced." Irina suddenly began to laugh. "And do you remember what the dean said to you in farewell? 'And I had intended to offer you my daughter's hand in marriage! But with what has happened, all I can say is: Get out of the university!' That old man was certainly funny! He wanted to give his daughter to every male who had anything on the ball."

"She was some beauty!" Sasha scoffed. "I can still see her jumping around the athletic field half-naked! I couldn't stand her!"

"Hey, preacher," Irina said, smiling, "love your enemies!"

"How did you find out that I am a minister?" Sasha said, astonished.

"Oh, excuse me; I should have told you immediately. I have come to a personal faith in Christ and belong to the registered Baptist congregation in Kiev now. I heard about you through friends."

Joy threatened to overflow Sasha's heart. "You've become a believer? That can't be! That's incredible! It's a miracle!"

But what if she had become a Christian only because the KGB had ordered her to do so? The thought stabbed through his heart like a knife. He knew her father. There had often been cases like this, situations when an effort was made to disrupt a Christian congregation by starting arguments and slanders. Suddenly he began to feel utterly miserable. This idea was so horrible, so painful, that it destroyed the happiness Sasha had felt at seeing Irina again. He felt as if he should stop their conversation and then change to another compartment when the opportunity presented itself—just so he would never encounter Irina again.

After he had read *The Traitor,* a book published in France, he had repeatedly discussed the topic with Archbishop Nikodim. And Nikodim had admitted that there had been cases in which a bishop had also functioned as an agent of the KGB. The KGB utilized such "bishops" in order to retain control over the congregations and to steer the patriarchate in the direction that satisfied the Party's wishes.

Irina soon noticed that Sasha was again far away in his thoughts. With feminine intuition she recognized what was troubling this young servant of the Lord.

"Listen, Sasha, I want to tell you a little about myself. You will probably recall that I am an only child. My father did not remarry because of me. I've never known my mother, and I've never seen her. For some reason Father will not talk about her.

"Some time ago the woman who cleans our offices told me that there was to be a meeting of Christian young people near Kiev. So I made up my mind to go and look this thing over out of sheer curiosity. The woman had taken quite a risk by telling me about it. I don't even know why she did it; but she must have had a reason to trust me.

"At the meeting no one seemed to treat me suspiciously,

and I was able to speak freely and openly with many people. Then Joseph Bodarenko began to preach. What he said made such a profound impact on me that I went forward immediately afterward and declared that I wanted to serve God. At the time, of course, I was not exactly certain about what I was doing. After the service some people spoke with me for a long time, explaining the consequences of my decision. But I was so filled with the joy of the Lord that I stuck by my decision.

"Immediately after returning home I told my father everything I had done. He stared at me in utter disbelief and said nothing—as if he had been robbed of his speech. For a long time he sat like that, occasionally blurting out brief phrases like 'Oh, no! How could that have happened? O my God, how terrible! First her mother and now she. . . .' I felt so sorry for him. I put my arms around him, sat beside him on the sofa and begged him finally to tell me about my mother. But he gently pushed me aside and locked himself into his study. Next morning at breakfast he looked so sad that I got really frightened. He did not touch his food, but took my face in his hands, saying, 'I have no one else besides you in this whole world. I gave up my career because of you. But what difference did *that* make? I had lost all interest in it anyway. But I don't want to lose you under any circumstances! You, my child, can count on me no matter what happens to you. I will fight for you!' Then he left for work. Yet something about the whole experience made me very happy: my mother must have been a Christian. You have no idea what that means to me! I am a candidate for a degree in scientific technology right now, and I'm working on my dissertation. You know from your own experience that believers are not allowed into scientific fields of work in this country."

Sasha listened to her soft voice, and his heart warmed to her again. *Surely I can trust her,* he thought.

"Of course I know that. I am not likely to forget it," he responded sadly. Abruptly he asked her, "So you didn't marry Victor?"

"Oh, he gave me no end of trouble. You know that he was the son of the first secretary of the district committee. That made it quite difficult for me to get rid of him. In the meantime, though, he's gone to prison for murder and robbery. He'd always allowed himself to be drawn into all sorts of dusky intrigues, even as a young boy. His father's high-level job had kept him out of having to do time. This time around, however, they did lock him up."

Sasha would have loved to talk to Irina about his conversations in Kiev. Slowly he began to probe her. "What's your opinion about the Council of Churches? I'm getting the impression that because of the work done by these people, we in the registered congregations are getting a good deal more freedom."

"My father says that this freedom will last only until the government has dealt with the Council of Churches. In my opinion the church has been exposed to some good new impulses because of this group's activities. Whether it wishes to or not, the church must now ask itself whether it has the correct understanding of its responsibilities toward society. And whether it is proper to crawl in the dust before the mighty of this world and to lend itself to the defense of the Communist Party's political objectives—which are not at all aimed toward humanity's greatest benefit—and so forth."

Sasha nodded in agreement.

"Above all," Irina continued, "I believe that Georgi Vins and the leaders of his movement stand firmly on the foundation established by the teachings of Christ and the apostles. I am not sure, however, whether both sides did not make some unfortunate mistakes during their arguments and the subsequent attempts to arrive at a common understanding. People became too vehement, feeling insulted by what the others said. Now they have become embittered toward one another. I think this is a deplorable situation. I have written about this to Khrapov, who is in jail. Unfortunately, they tell me my letter never reached him. We might have made even more serious mistakes—who knows? It's not that we make errors that causes the trouble; it's that our congregations are not ready to admit that these errors have been made. Karev was right when he said that our brotherhood is shackled with rustproof chains. We're bound hand and foot. We've been obliged to dance to the conductor's tune—that of atheistic communism—and to do the Party's bidding no matter what is desired of us. Those people don't recognize either the freedom of the individual or the freedom to evangelize others. That is really the way it is. Sasha, we've got to be realistic and acknowledge the existence of these rustproof chains. But just because we're tied hand and foot doesn't mean they've torn the tongues from our mouths. It is all the more reason for us to become the voice of truth and justice no matter what the cost may be to us. I see one danger in all this, that you preachers of the Word dare to say only those things which the powers-that-be allow you to say. That's the crux of the whole matter."

In her haste, Irina did not realize how much injury her words could cause.

Yet Sasha did not feel himself the target of what she had said. Despite the constant control exercised by the authorities, he had continued to preserve his integrity. His views were very similar to Irina's.

"Did you hear that there's now a committee for peaceful coexistence between the church and the government Party?" Irina went on. "We are planning for a dialogue with the government, by means of which the status of the church within society is to be clarified."

Sasha raised his eyebrows and shook his head. "Nobody's going to get me to become part of that. I've burned my fingers with that once already." Seeing Irina's understanding smile he asked, "What are the items on your agenda?"

Irina quickly warmed to the subject. "First we want to make it clear to the Party that a person's philosophy of life is his own private affair, and that the Party has no business sticking its nose into that. In other words, we want to recommend that Marxism cease to proclaim its own viewpoint as the only one mankind could ever have. Those Marxists shouldn't be allowed to say that their philosophy of life is the only one that is correct."

Sasha began to laugh in spite of himself. He cited Lenin: "'All those wedded to such views are cowards and enemies of the Marxist philosophy,' Irina," and his voice gained an unaccustomed urgency that caused Irina to sit up and listen. "With such ideas, you'll all wind up going to the psychiatric clinic in double-quick time. I don't believe that anything sensible will come out of that dialogue of yours. Stay away from it!" Feeling that he might have gone too far he added, "What kind of people are on that committee of yours?"

Although Irina was disappointed by Sasha's reaction, she did not let on.

"All the committee members are academicians. Among them there are Orthodox, Baptists, Pentecostals, and members of several other religious communities. But it's true, isn't it, Sasha, that Marxism disdains every kind of personal freedom? It's enough that Lenin espoused this viewpoint! Now this philosophy is being forced down everyone's throat in this country as if it were a religion. This is nothing else but narrowmindedness and disregard for objective reality in order to lend credence to the concept of a single-class society. That's just another form of sectarianism."

Sasha merely nodded. He knew all about Marxism and was aware that the Party had begun to follow a consciously political course with the aim of totally destroying "bourgeois idealogy," of which religion was a part.

"No," he said resolutely, "the Party will never give up its dictatorial powers. Unfortunately, I can't be part of that, Irina. My view of my job is to prepare the members of my congregation so thoroughly that their knowledge of the Bible and their spiritual armor will be strong. Then they will be in a position to defend themselves against any effort to destroy their spiritual life."

Irina did not give in easily. "But if we don't manage to

convince the ruling men of the state of our view, who will do it for us? We've got to make it clear that the Russian people are basically religious, and that this ought to be encouraged. Only a spiritual renewal can still save Russia. Only the Word of God can influence man in a positive sense and give him inner peace. The Gospel has the dynamism, the power to transform a whole nation."

She looked positively enchanting with her flushed cheeks and shining eyes. Sasha smiled and added, "All right, all right. I surrender! I was told something similar by a member of the Council of Churches. And I think the same way. Despite that, I doubt that a dialogue with the Party on this subject will result in anything. I am much more concerned about the possibility that the Central Committee will listen politely to you and then send you to a psychiatric institution. They've already done that to hundreds of dissidents. But, my clever child, I wouldn't like to see you in there." He looked into her deep blue eyes, suddenly became embarrassed and looked away.

The through train was approaching its final station. The suburbs of the city of Gomel were rushing past the window. Sasha began to gather his books and note pads together and to stuff them into an enormous briefcase. He planned to continue on to Bobruysk, while Irina intended to see a friend in Gomel.

The fact that they would soon have to say good-bye to each other caused both Sasha and Irina to fall silent. Sasha's feelings were in an uproar as a result of this unexpected encounter. He was aware that she had treated him with respect, yet she had also been quite reserved. Suddenly he was overcome with great fear for her future. *They're playing with fire, these silly kids.* He could not think of any way to warn her. If only she would permit it! He looked her straight in the eyes and said, "Irina. . . ." He intended to warn her, to beg her to stay away from this murderous affair; but the words failed to come out of his mouth. Still, Irina looked at him with full understanding.

"I will pray for you all the time," she said simply, as if what she was talking about were something quite obvious. Then she rose and reached for her little suitcase.

Quickly he reached into his own briefcase, brought out a book and handed it to her. "Here is Lenin's *Materialism and Empiric Criticism*. Read through that sometime. It will prove extremely helpful during your talks with the Central Committee. Incidentally, what does your father say to all this?"

She smiled. "He simply says, 'My dear Irina, you are much too naive!'"

The train halted. They got off. Irina waved to him one more time and hurried toward the exit. Sasha began to look for his connecting train.

2 "Flying Dynamite"

Irina belonged to a select group of Christians able to continue work in scientific disciplines. Her father, Yuri Sokolov, was a highly regarded psychiatrist with excellent connections in the outside world. These allowed him to protect Irina from the usual difficulties, at least for the time being. But this was not easy to accomplish and became daily more difficult.

The people in power had not forgotten that he had worked for the KGB at one time. He himself, indeed, remembered it all too well. His former friends wrote to him often if their work didn't take them to foreign countires. They considered Sokolov a remarkable idealist and felt sorry for him because of the tragedy in his personal life. In spite of that, none could accept his decision to remain unmarried for the remainder of his life because of the loss of the woman he loved.

Sokolov had transferred to Irina the tremendous love he had felt toward her mother. He lived and labored for her, taking many inconveniences in stride for her sake. It was his dream to find a good husband for Irina. He frequently fantasized about how he, as an old man, would play with his grandchildren, living out the twilight of his days in the midst of his beloved family.

Sokolov was unafraid of death. He had never considered what might occur in the afterlife. He was an agnostic and viewed militant atheism as something laughable in view of his scientific attitude toward life. He was not interested in the church. Sokolov saw the church as a "miserable reptile" which crawls in the dust before every conceivable regime, and which defends whatever the regime's politics might be, constantly siding with the oppressors.

Irina was unhappy about her father's negative attitude toward Christianity. She was particularly saddened by his statement that he would put no obstacle in the way of her belief in God, but that he himself did not want to hear anything about Him.

Despite all this, when Irina brought home the Council of Churches' declaration about its secession from the Baptist Union, Sokolov read it with considerable interest. But he would never admit that this had actually aroused a kind of grudging admiration in him.

The spirit of revival which had been wafting through Russian congregations brought many headaches to governmental circles. What could the officials do with people who directly opposed the course which the Party had plotted vis-à-vis their religion, and who suddenly had become stubborn enough to say out loud that the KGB had no right to meddle in the internal affairs of the congregations?

To its great dismay, the Party discovered that decades of the most horrible persecution of Christians had had no greater effect than that of a small stone falling into a large body of water. Suddenly there were twice as many Christians as before! On top of that, the KGB was forced to admit that the church had escaped its control mechanisms. Those believers whom they had persecuted because of their faith simply went underground. In certain intellectual circles these underground congregations were referred to as illegal bodies, or as "the silent church." Yet it was this church which had won hundreds of thousands to Christ.

The Party discussed this for a long time, eventually deciding to establish a recognized church which would be obligated to operate under the Party's control.

In the beginning, church members thought there had been a true miracle and that the government had finally conceded congregations unlimited freedom to practice their religion, something which heretofore had never occurred in Russia.

But it turned out to be a fantasy! The Party took another head count of church members and discovered, to their amazement, that Christianity hung on much more tenaciously than they had ever dreamed. As a result of that shocking discovery, the Party hurriedly decided to register only one-fifth of all the church members and to allocate only enough space for worship for this smaller group. They pretended that the rest of the believers simply did not exist.

Since they had created a "privileged" and an "unprivileged" church in this way, the Party concluded that, per Lenin's time-proven method, they could set one group against the other. To make absolutely certain their scheme worked, the government bosses saw to it that some of their most trustworthy people infiltrated the churches, gaining key positions in the new congregations.

One of the assignments of these trusted KGB men was to spread the good word in the western countries that freedom of religion now reigned in the USSR. They reported that those believers who continued to serve time in jails, concentration camps, and psychiatric hospitals had been in conflict with the law and were therefore nothing more than common criminals.

Mistrust settled over the congregations like mildew. Who was genuine and who was not? Whom could Christians speak to, and who had been sucked in as a KGB agent? The resultant bitter conflict among the brethren in Russia was so devastating that it became essential to reform the officially recognized church. The primary task of this reform was to see to it that the KGB could no longer inject itself into the internal affairs of the church.

The reformers did not reproach the government for its measures against religion. On the contrary, they asserted that it was perfectly understandable that an atheistic government would combat religion. But they wanted to make it clear that in their view every servant of the Lord in the church should stand up for the Word of God and for the church—even if it cost him his life—rather than function as a puppet manipulated by the KGB and thereby injure all of Christendom. The government, on the other hand, took steps to sabotage any brotherly conversations which might have cleared the air between the two factions in the church.

Because it agreed to exclude young people from its fellowship activities, the officially recognized segment of the church received greater freedom than it had before. Within the persecuted church, however, young people enjoyed complete freedom. Young people were permitted to meet, conduct Bible studies, attend worship services, and perform missionary functions. The brethren in leadership positions took this responsibility upon themselves. The preachers in the persecuted churches agreed that "the government consistently issues decrees whose objective is the slow choking off of religious life. For this reason, it is our duty to preach the crucified Christ all the more faithfully, even if it costs us our lives." They took the young people under their wings, while the whole congregation gave them its backing, prepared to sacrifice whatever was necessary on their behalf. As a result the government once again lost its control over a large segment of the church.

Irina Sokolova had accepted the responsibility for setting up contacts between the young people of the various congregations. These contacts became a life-or-death necessity for the young people. Although by government decree young people were prohibited from establishing Bible study groups or holding meetings on their own, the ministers who led registered congregations—and who had agreed to obey the government decree—were powerless to prevent young people from gathering on their own initiative.

The ministers found themselves between a rock and a hard place. Either they turned their backs on the idea of having a youth group spiritually alive, full of their own ideas and initiative, and ready to serve God with eagerness and total commitment, or they came into conflict with the law. The upshot was that whenever they made attempts to stop their young people, they merely succeeded in driving them into the "underground," into unregistered congregations who considered such government restrictions unbiblical.

Initially the government had no alternative but to close its eyes to the existence of such young people's groups—to pretend that they weren't there—until it could be in a position to destroy the underground church. Then the Party could focus on dismembering the official church. To prevent this from happening the young believers considered it essential to create a consultative body that would provide a forum for discussions with the Party about the status of the church in the USSR.

Irina had returned from her visit to her friend in Gomel in high spirits. The visit with her friend had not been her only goal for the trip, for she had also participated in organizing an illegal gathering of young people in one of the forests in White Russia. There had been other earlier meetings like this, earning the ministers of official congregations one "beating" after another from the ministry for religious affairs. After all, they hadn't been "alert enough" and had not "notified the right people in time."

*   *   *

After Irina had settled down in a bus in Kiev she suddenly realized that she would have to return to work the next day, and her mood became quite subdued. She really loved her work in the research center, but in recent days her enjoyment of her work had been spoiled by the clumsy and importunate advances of her supervisor. Koslov hounded her constantly and recently had begun to babble about his love for her.

What made the situation particularly delicate was the fact that Koslov had been placed in charge of the research center by the KGB. Irina's father had alerted her to this, urging her to be careful; for as far as scientific matters were concerned, Koslov was totally ignorant.

Koslov did seem to have an irresistible capacity to attract women. Irina could not think of a single female in the whole center who had been able to resist his magic. Women raved about him, and their husbands were jealous of him because their wives didn't even make an effort to conceal their passion for this man.

All of them were aware of the fact that Koslov was married and had two children. So what? Whenever one of their co-workers vanished into Koslov's office for more than an hour, emerging later with her dress and hair rumpled, but with starry eyes, she was openly envied by the other members of her sex! No one had the slightest doubt about the purpose of the wide couch in Koslov's office, but they all remained silent. The husbands did so in order not to jeopardize their own careers.

No one could understand Irina's unyielding attitude toward her boss. Her fifty-year-old section leader, a woman named Makarova, once whispered, "You're a fool. Why do you behave this way toward him? I've run across many men, but one like this doesn't come around very often."

"I am a Christian," was Irina's annoyed answer, "not a lady of easy virtue."

It would have been better if she had not said that, because the Makarova woman got up on her high horse and said, "So I'm a woman without virtue to you!" Real trouble was brewing, but his majesty the boss happened to appear on the scene just at that moment, and Makarova disappeared.

Koslov also busily pursued women tourists from other countries. Once he took his vacation with a young woman from East Germany who had a doctorate in theology. When he returned he said to Irina rather insolently, "Well, you theologians are pretty sociable people. I've discovered that eternal life is not your only concern!" Irina turned away in contempt.

Recently Irina's father had again warned her, "I've made a study of Koslov's technique with women. Be careful of this man. If you allow him to trap you, I won't be able to help you."

Irina knew where her father had obtained his insight. But she could not quit her job in the research center until her dissertation was finished and she had received her doctorate. On top of that, this man was so repellent to her that she thought herself strong enough to beat back his advances.

Lost in her thoughts, Irina unlocked her front door, hung up her coat in the small vestibule and walked into the kitchen. Her father loved to have everything in order. The dishes had already been washed; but apparently he had been in a big hurry, because the dishes had not been put away.

How orderly he is, she thought.

She would have liked to tell him right then how thankful she was that he kept the apartment in such wonderful order and made her life so easy for her. How very much she loved him! In the future, she decided, she would have to arrange to spend more time with him.

She went into the living room, intending to put on a record. She loved music, especially Beethoven, Chopin, and Liszt. She and her father had often attended concerts of the Philharmonic together. Her father was especially fond of Tchaikovsky.

Suddenly she heard the words, "Good evening, Irina!" In her shock she recoiled a few steps. Koslov arose from the sofa. She had not noticed him when she entered the apartment.

"What are you doing here? What brings you to my apartment?" Irina stammered. She was so shocked that her whole body shook and her voice sounded strange.

"I've been waiting for you, Irina. Yuri Vladimir [her father] received a phone call. He had to hurry back to the clinic, and he gave me his permission to stay behind since I absolutely had to speak with you. He told me that you would be coming in this evening." Koslov lowered his voice and looked intently at Irina. "I'm so happy that I did not have to wait for you in vain."

Koslov had Irina's diary in his hands. She tore it away from him and said angrily, "What gives you the right to look at my diary? I kept it in the dresser drawer in my bedroom!"

Koslov eyed her calmly. She looked even more attractive with her face flushed in anger. "I'm interested in everything about you, Irina dear," he said to conciliate her. "I am your supervisor. Furthermore, your diary was not in your dresser drawer but was standing right here on this bookshelf." Koslov pointed to the enormous bookshelves Irina's father had built to accommodate his library of specialized books.

"You have no right to read the personal papers of strangers, even if they were on a bookshelf." Irina was so upset she was ready to cry. Her eyes filled with tears, and her voice shook.

"You might as well stop remonstrating with me, Irina. It won't get you anywhere. Sit down next to me so we can get to the point." It was obvious that he felt himself to be the master of the situation.

Irina pulled herself together, replaced her diary on the shelf and sat down in her father's easy chair. Koslov resumed his seat opposite her and threw her one of his impertinent, wooing looks. He was well aware of his charms.

Yet none of this had any effect on Irina. She had been exposed to his techniques too often. She had resisted them and had learned to see through his devices. Of course she had often had to pray hard in order to remain steadfast. In turn, he was consumed with desire for her.

Koslov was the first to break the silence. "I didn't know you were a Christian." Naturally this was a lie. "I wonder why a girl like you is religious, Irina. I was just talking with your father about your dissertation."

This blow struck home. Koslov had reached Irina's most sensitive area. Her doctoral dissertation was already written and merely had to be typed and paginated. She gritted her teeth and showed no reaction.

He observed her intently. "You will have to choose between your faith and your career, Irina. We cannot tolerate scientists who are Christians in our Communist society. We can't stay on the sidelines where science is concerned."

"You talk about 'Communist society,' but we haven't erected a Socialist structure here. What we have is state capitalism." Suddenly she became indifferent to whatever was to happen next—to her career, to her dissertation. Her heart stopped pounding. She gazed firmly at Koslov and said, "If that is all you wanted to say to me, I must ask you to leave now. We can continue our talk tomorrow at the office." Suddenly she realized how weary she was. "And one more thing, Comrade Koslov. I must request that you refrain from visiting me when my father is not at home."

Koslov had risen from his seat but showed no indication that he was ready to leave. "Irina, I'm in love with you. You know that. Don't reject me when I try to help you!" There was an imploring tone to his voice.

Since he realized that despite his begging she was showing no reaction, he suddenly seized her by the arm and pulled her toward him. Irina had not expected that kind of assault and lost her balance. He caught her as she fell and carried her to the sofa.

She defended herself desperately against him.

"I love you," he whispered hoarsely. "Don't make me miserable! I am ready to leave my wife for you and marry you! You know how serious I am about this!"

Later Irina would be able to listen again to these words on the small tape recorder Koslov had left in the apartment in the heat of action.

Now she was really afraid. She motioned toward the door. "Get out of here, Koslov! Or else I will scream for the police!"

This seemed to make no impression on Koslov. He pulled her toward him and wildly began to cover her with kisses. She desperately tried to beat him off, but Koslov was much stronger than she was.

As if he had lost control of his senses he ripped her clothes from her body. But he had not counted on so much resistance. Still struggling, they both fell to the carpet. Irina screamed and called upon God to help her. Koslov busied himself with removing his own clothing with one hand while he clamped the other over her mouth. What then happened he would never be able to explain to himself later.

Like a stroke of lightning from a blue sky, a well-directed blow struck him with such force that he slammed into the corner. He saw before him a furious young woman waiting only for him to fall before she struck him again. Blow after blow rained on him until he flew into the hallway and was hurled against the entrance to the apartment. The door gave way, and before he was able to do anything he tumbled headfirst down the stairway, clattering noisily down the steps.

Moving quickly, Irina slammed the door shut. She had been taking judo courses for years. Her appearance showed that she had been physically active, but no one would have suspected that it was this particular skill. Those who trained in judo in the Soviet Union had to be listed in an official register. The authorities were never able to explain why Irina had not been registered.

Normally Koslov would have been able to defend himself, since he knew judo just as well as Irina did. But the attack had come with such ferocity that he had been knocked down before he realized what was happening. By that time he was on his way home. He was so angry that he did not even feel the pain. As he picked himself up, little boys and girls were jumping up and down around him, taking turns offering their assistance.

"Look at you, you poor man," an inquisitive little boy named Lyosha, the son of a professor, said to him.

Koslov had been caught so much by surprise that he hardly realized what was going on. He began to button his trousers and to dust off his jacket.

"Here, mister," said little Lena, "I'll help you!" With childish eagerness she began to dust off his trousers. Koslov reached into his pocket, felt for his pistol and discovered that it was no longer there. That on top of everything! He could not recall where he had left it. But he had to get away from there! Away from there at any price! Away from those inquisitive, nosy brats who were having such fun trying to help him and to inspect him from all angles!

He muttered, "You've got a really slippery staircase in that house of yours." He accepted his wallet, identification papers, and Party membership card from the children who had picked them up where they had fallen. Little Misha insisted that he, Misha, had never fallen down those stairs! The staircase was not slippery at all, he declared. But Koslov wasn't listening. He hurriedly whispered, "So long!" and ran to the nearest taxi stand as fast as his legs would carry him.

It had been his luck that everything happened so quickly no adult had seen him in the staircase. But the taxi driver certainly was not tactful. He looked at Koslov sarcastically and said, with all the insight of a constant observer of humanity, "It didn't work out this time, did it?"

"Shut your trap!" exploded Koslov. "Start driving, or I'll break your neck!"

The driver shut off his motor and calmly said, "I won't be insulted by you, citizen. Kindly get out."

Koslov pulled out his KGB card and held it under the driver's nose. The next day the taxi driver was arrested and had to spend two weeks in jail for "insulting the dignity of a Soviet citizen." The poor man was so upset by this that he accused the judge of being prejudiced, and he promptly received a one-year sentence on top of everything else.

The children drew their own conclusions about the stranger's fate. They told their parents about the totally dishevelled man who suddenly had fallen down the stairs. Little Lena told her story to Irina, too, reporting that the strange man must have been in a hurry to leave the bathroom since he didn't even have time to button his pants.

Irina was still in a state of shock. For a long time she simply sat on the floor, unable to pull herself together. The room was in chaos. The easy chair was overturned, the magazine rack lying on top of it. Newspapers and books were scattered everywhere. Suddenly Irina saw a tiny tape recorder. She reached for it instinctively. It was still running. She had never seen such a small tape recorder. She inspected it eagerly from all angles, pressing down on the tiny button which stopped it. She soon discovered how to turn it on, reversed the tape and began to listen. First there was the discussion with her father. Then came the sounds of the struggle with Koslov, his heavy breathing, his passionate whispering: "Please don't be so foolish; I love you!" With revulsion she stopped the machine and took it into her room.

When she had changed her clothes and straightened out the apartment, she called the priest, Vassiley Kuznetsov. She told him about the incident and asked for his advice on what she should do.

The youthful clergyman listened to Irina's report with evident glee. At various times he interrupted her with statements like, "Boy, you certainly are doing all right! You sure gave it to him, didn't you, daughter! . . . You can believe me, for this heroic reaction you'll be pardoned all of your sins! . . . We've got to make you into a saint in my church!"

"Very funny," said Irina, annoyed. "Why don't you quit talking like that, Vassiley? You're forever the little boy. I'm asking you seriously whether I have to move away from where I'm living, and you tell me jokes."

"I told you to move away some time ago. The KGB is making a real psychological pursuit of you. I'm really afraid for you." He sounded worried.

Although Irina was not part of the official leadership of her church, she was very well liked there. People respected her and listened to her. In addition to that, she was an academician. In short, the KGB saw in her someone who could influence her Baptist congregation in the right direction. What is more, people like her could be useful in Russia as well as in foreign countries.

Vassiley Kuznetsov knew his way around the KGB's machinery. He had every reason to be concerned about Irina. Several times in the past, the KGB had attempted to enlist the young Orthodox priest for subversive activities in the West. He, too, filled their requirements exactly: from a good home, his father a scientist and professor, his mother an actress, he himself talented in several areas. But so far, Vassiley cleverly had resisted all of their enticements. "I am not interested in moving up the professional ladder," he would answer them. "What I want to do is to proclaim the Gospel of Jesus Christ to our Russian people. They have a greater need for that than for your Utopian ideologies!" Already he foresaw that he would not get away with this without some punishment. But his hour had not yet arrived.

The point now was to come to Irina's assistance. During his telephone conversation with her, he could not hide his honest admiration. This delicately built young woman certainly had handled herself adroitly and courageously. "I would like to see you present during our discussions with Bishop Pitirim!"

"Why?"

"Because this bootlicker says that the Christian education of children is nothing but a rape of their souls. It would be nice if you would use a few of your jujitsu holds on him!"

"You really are still a baby," Irina replied peevishly. "I'm not in the mood for joking around."

"Do you really think that of me? I'm deadly serious! If you had studied the report from the All-Union of Baptists by Shidkov, in which he insists that nobody in the USSR is persecuted because of his religious convictions, you would be sick! You would not only want to shoot Shidkov to the moon by rocket, but also all the others who print those kinds of lies, even in foreign countries!"

"All right, Vassiley. We can talk about that later. Now I've got to call Koslov's wife before Father comes home."

She said good-bye and hung up. Then she dialed Koslov's private number. As usual, Koslov's wife appeared unmoved.

Nevertheless Irina managed to drag out of her the fact that Koslov had come home, changed clothes quickly and driven off again. She gave Koslov's wife the information that she was changing her place of domicile.

When she had finished with this call she busied herself and got dinner ready.

Shortly thereafter her father arrived home. He embraced her and gave her a fatherly kiss.

"I felt very lonely without you, my daughter." He stroked her hair.

"I missed you too, Father," Irina returned. His presence restored her sense of security. She always felt safe in his presence. All of a sudden her eyes filled with tears.

"What's the matter, my child?" said Sokolov, and examined her probingly.

She lowered her eyes and replied evasively, "Dinner is ready, Daddy. Shall we start?"

Sokolov put his arm around her and walked to the kitchen with her. He soon began to suspect what had happened but was unwilling to prod her. During dinner he said casually, "By the way, the children in the building told me that some man had slipped on the stairs and had fallen all the way down. From their description it must have been Koslov."

Irina said nothing. Sokolov did not object when she said grace out loud. He sat there and waited for her to finish. Irina began her prayer but broke off in the midst of it and began to sob.

Sokolov rose, helped her get up and gently pulled her to him on the bench in the corner. She wept heartbrokenly. Bit by bit the whole story came out. The only thing she did not mention was the manner in which she had gotten rid of Koslov.

"Why did you leave him alone in the apartment, Daddy?" she sobbed.

"I had no idea that he had it in for you and not for me. And I know that the KGB leaves no stone unturned in its search for facts. I wanted them to know that I had nothing to hide. But if I had only known...." Sokolov fell silent. To him, it was a clear case. He knew that now he would have to fight for his daughter with all the means at his command. He wiped Irina's tears away with his handkerchief. Then he said, "Come, child, let us eat now before everything gets cold. Afterward we can talk about everything in peace and quiet."

They ate in silence. Finally Sokolov shook off his somber premonitions and began to inquire about Irina's trip to Gomel.

"By chance I ran into Sasha Nikitin on the train," Irina said. "Why didn't you come to his aid when they tried to throw him out of the university because of his religious beliefs?"

Sokolov's face clouded over. "Oh, Irina, not again. You know perfectly well that it wasn't in my power to help him. Please don't bring that up again."

There were occasions when Irina could not understand her father. She surmised that he might have known Nikitin had fallen in love with her and might have found it convenient for Sasha to be forced to leave town. But why, of all things? Was he jealous of him? Of course not! So why then? Was it because Sasha was a Christian as her mother had been?

She did not intend to ask her father about it again. She knew of no one who was permitted to ask so many questions at home as she. This asking of questions had been abandoned in Russian society because of the existence of so many spies. People kept their eyes open, listened carefully, and pondered ideas. Ever since the KGB had begun to keep tabs on everyone and to interrogate people all night long in order to get the answers it wanted, people no longer asked too many questions.

Sokolov's short laugh shook Irina out of her thoughts. "Excuse me—you really did a masterful job of removing Koslov from the apartment!" He laughed loudly.

Irina stared at him, dumbfounded, her mouth open. "How did you know about—?" she stammered.

"Should I not know about it when my dear daughter

possesses ways and means for getting rid of pickpockets and thieves?" He got up, walked into his study and brought a letter back with him. He handed it to Irina. "This was addressed to me in error. That's the reason I opened it. Please excuse me." Again he broke into laughter. "Excuse me, flying stick of dynamite!"

Irina reddened, pulled the letter out of the envelope and began to read. "Flying stick of dynamite! I send you greetings. You know from where. Yesterday I talked with a man who had been sentenced to prison for robbery. We spoke about Christ's teaching about not resisting evil. We talked especially about the sentence 'Whoever strikes you on the left cheek . . . then turn him your other cheek.' 'You Christians don't obey the rules of Christ at all,' the thief said. Guess what else he told me. Once he waylaid you after a worship service and demanded your watch. You meekly gave it to him and told him about Jesus while you did it. He must have listened to you very carefully, because he found you so attractive that he decided to drag you into some bushes in the park. But you—contrary to the teachings of Christ—hit him with such a lightning-fast blow that he lost consciousness for twenty minutes, only to wake up in a police station. He is very angry at you. He didn't get sentenced because of you but because he robbed a store; but he still blames you. I comforted him that love must also suffer sometimes. In prison camp the prisoners regale each other with stories about you, calling you the 'flying stick of dynamite.' "

"I keep wondering," Sokolov stated, "how these prisoners manage to smuggle mail out of the camp time and time again. Our camps have been designed according to Hitler's examples. Nothing receives so much attention as the prevention of leaks of even a single syllable to the outside, and still these guys manage to do it."

The telephone rang. Irina picked it up. It was Koslov.

"I just wanted to tell you, don't do anything stupid, my dear; and keep your mouth shut. What's more, it would be a good idea if you asked for your dismissal. And bring my pistol and tape recorder with you tomorrow—the things you stole from me."

Irina didn't even have an opportunity to make up her mind whether or not to be indignant at this impertinence when Sokolov tore the receiver from her hands.

"Oh, it's Casanova! Are your ribs still in place? Your skull's not broken? Wonderful, so they don't have to operate on you. Otherwise I would have been delighted to switch your brain with that of a donkey! Aren't organ transplants 'in' today? Or does the gentleman require the services of a psychiatrist? I stand ready to serve you at any time! And don't forget this, dear friend: do that one more time and you're going to have to reckon with me!"

Sokolov slammed the receiver down. In his excitement he didn't realize that he had alternately addressed Koslov with the personal pronoun and with the respectful form of address. He put his arm around Irina and they went to wash the dishes. They didn't go to bed until midnight. Irina could not sleep until dawn.

3 Night Attack

When Sasha returned from Bobruysk he found in his room a note which his mother had left for him. "Dear Son: Zarapkin, the official in charge of religious cults, asked me to tell you to call him as soon as you returned." Sasha sighed and turned the piece of paper over. "We're visiting Aunt Nyura until next Friday," it said on the other side. Sasha grinned. He would have to take care of his own needs for a whole week.

He walked into the living room and dialed Zarapkin's number. Zarapkin answered immediately, saying, "Hello, Nikitin. How are you doing, old man? Listen, tomorrow we're going to be running some informational meetings all over town in collaboration with the All-Union and the people from the patriarchate. We decided in the Gorispolkom [the town's executive committee] that you really must be there."

"Listen to me, Zarapkin," protested Sasha, "I would be acting against my own father if I were there. I certainly can't do that!"

"Don't get so excited, old pal! We've invited quite a few comrades from the All-Union* and asked them to explain the relation between church and state to the citizens. We agreed that it would be to your advantage if you took part in that.

*The All-Union is an abbreviation for the government-approved leadership of the registered Baptists and other Protestant churches sanctioned by the Soviet government. The patriarchate is the leadership of the Russian Orthodox Church.

37

We're running these meetings in fifty different places in the city. I'd like to see you make an effort to be at the factory housing development tomorrow at seven. See you then, Sasha." And Zarapkin hung up.

Sasha stood there thunderstruck, with the receiver still in his hand.

Before Sasha's election as minister of the registered Baptist congregation, his father and 150 people who shared the same convictions had seceded from the congregation. With this act, Sasha's father and his fellow believers registered their protest against the congregation's collaboration with the secret police.

At that time Sasha had been in charge of the young people in the congregation and had been busy setting up illegal Bible studies in private homes. In these groups the youths were to be equipped to fulfill the Great Commission of proclaiming the Gospel. The congregation's minister knew nothing about any of this. Sasha had made every effort to prevent a split in the youth group, which had approximately a hundred members. He considered it unnecessary to make a public break with the All-Union. What headquarters in Moscow wanted to do meant nothing to him. His concern was only that the local congregation continue its strict adherence to the Bible.

When the congregation split, the minister refused to continue to serve. Thereupon the congregation decided to elect Sasha as its preacher. The young people obviously had played a large part in getting him the majority of the votes.

Sasha thought about the matter and prayed about it for an entire week. After that he accepted the call. Zarapkin merely had to confirm his candidacy.

Zarapkin had spent a long time in the ranks of the KGB. Yet somewhere along the line he had done something wrong and had been transferred to "retired status." A rumor had circulated in dissident circles that the KGB had fired Zarapkin because he had been unsuccessful in enlisting a French diplomat as a subversive.

However, Zarapkin had no desire to remain idle and began

to get himself involved in antireligious propaganda. With remarkable skill and cleverness, he managed to gain the trust of Christian believers. As a result he had been named as official in charge of religious cults.

He confirmed Sasha's role as preacher of the congregation as soon as he was informed about it. During the next session of the first secretary's district committee he had reported, "I find Nikitin's election as the Baptists' minister an extraordinarily favorable development. His father is a schismatic, and it will be child's play to set them at each other's throats. We soon will see the usefulness of this development."

Needless to say, Sasha knew nothing about these deliberations. Yet he had the distinct impression that he was expected to denounce his father before the tenants of the factory settlement the following night.

The next evening Sasha was seated in the front row of the auditorium in the housing development's palace of culture. Each speaker did his utmost to present clearly his opinion on the subject of religion. All the speeches and statements had obviously been checked out carefully and were simply read aloud before the audience. A smattering of applause followed each set of remarks. The speakers demanded that the "splinter group members" be treated like enemies of the people and "removed from our city." They were to be "chased off Soviet soil"—but no one indicated just where they were to be sent.

Sasha had to smile as he thought of the statement Khrapov made during his trial: "Our Bible tells us that our soil isn't Soviet soil at all. The Bible says, 'The earth is the Lord's and all that is on it!' "

Sasha continued to listen. The Party secretary in a furniture factory demanded, "We must take the believers' children away from them and send the believers to the North Pole!"

A young woman who was the leader of the factory Komsomol organization called "Red Ray" demanded heatedly that "the splinter group should be branded with irons, then strung up and shot." She stormed on angrily, saying that for centuries the church had stuck its nose into politics and eliminated all who dissented. From now on there was to be no place for religion in this land of socialism. "While our country guarantees the freedom of religious conviction, this applies only to those organizations who join hand in hand with the Communist Party's movement toward our wonderful future—which is communism! Long live communism! Down with the bourgeois bastards! Down with the followers of mind-numbing religions!"

Sasha looked up at the flushed, red face of the young woman and prayed softly for her. Next to him there was an empty seat; and when she climbed down from the podium he rose and offered the seat to her. She looked at him with some surprise, obviously not realizing that he was a minister. Filled with hate, she glanced at the Orthodox priest seated next to Sasha.

"What's your name?" whispered Sasha.

"Yelena Lobova," she replied just as quietly.

Sasha squeezed her hand and said, "You spoke with great conviction. Thank you very much!"

She didn't reply, and listened to Zarapkin's litany about Soviet laws relating to religious cults: "The Party must exert strong controls over the church. . . . We must hinder with every means . . . the infiltration of the church by anti-Communist tendencies . . . etcetera . . . etcetera.

"And now people such as Andrey Nikitin, who currently is minister of an unregistered congregation, make a point of insisting that the Party is not to interfere in the internal affairs of the churches! And the totally discredited Council of Churches demands the same thing!"

Suddenly Sasha had to think back to his conversation with Irina. It became hard for him to concentrate on what was going on.

"Understand this, comrades," Zarapkin went on. "Our laws guarantee the freedom of religion—but only so long as neither church nor religion interferes with the rights of Soviet citizens! As long as they do not draw citizens of our nation into their circles! As long as they do not rob them of their Marxist understanding about the creation of the world! The notion of a transcendent world is totally foreign to Marxist philosophy, and we Communists will never make peace with religion! And this Andrey Nikitin has the nerve to insist on the right to make religious propaganda! Freedom of religious conviction isn't enough for him! This is open defiance of Soviet law and order—which forbids every kind of anti-Soviet agitation. These schismatics, with their idealistic philosophy of life, are a serious danger to Soviet society!" Zarapkin had become so enraged that he bellowed to those assembled, "If there are any followers of this splinter religion in this hall, let me say to you here and now: Soviet society itself will destroy you, and we won't move a finger to aid you! May the avenging hand of the Soviet people sweep you from the face of the earth!"

He spat out the last words like a rifle salvo. Zarapkin's face, contorted with fanaticism, looked like a mask. Thunderous applause shook the hall. Yelena Lobova clapped her hands with special intensity. Sasha looked at the flaming red palms of her hands and whispered to her, "That hurts, doesn't it?" She was suddenly self-conscious and embarrassed.

It was really quite comical. The priest seated next to Sasha was applauding with everyone while simultaneously casting anxious glances toward Zarapkin, who was surveying the entire audience's reaction from the podium. Sasha bent his face toward him and whispered, "Bravo, colleague; right on, Father!" The cleric looked at him with a bewildered expression and stopped applauding.

"Long live communism!" were Zarapkin's closing words.

The priest jumped up as if he had been stung by a bee and shouted, "Hooray!" clapping as if he had lost all his senses. The rest of the audience also clapped as if their lives depended on it.

"Father Miron of the Orthodox Church has the podium,"

announced Zarapkin, climbing down from the speaker's stand. Father Miron stepped to the podium. He was visibly upset, casting anxious glances in all directions, giving the impression of a scared rabbit. Suddenly the audience appeared to be overcome by embarrassment. People averted their eyes from the sorry creature on the speaker's stand.

"Comrades!" cried Miron, "I promise you we will do all in our power to deliver a mortal blow to religion!"

Loud laughter followed that statement. The young people in attendance were howling with laughter. "Bravo! Bravo, priest! Long live Father Miron!" they yelled derisively. Sasha began to feel a deep shame for his "brother in Christ."

The cleric opened his mouth one more time as if he had something else to say, but shut it again. He almost crawled down from the speaker's stand and shuffled toward the exit.

Not this time. A sturdy woman about thirty years of age threateningly stepped in his way.

"You traitor!" she hissed. "You disgusting hypocrite! You dreg of humanity! You have sold Christ out once again!" Her voice rose to a shrill scream. She began to beat Father Miron with her fists, scratching his face, and tearing at his cassock.

The police rushed to Father Miron's aid. The young people in the audience booed and whistled. Someone was cursing. The hall was in chaos. Eventually the police seized the young woman and began to drag her toward the exit. After a while order was restored, and Sasha climbed up on the podium.

With a sad voice he began to speak slowly, "Friends, I have listened to the accusations which have been brought against my father." The hall became so quiet one could have heard a pin drop. "I cannot deny that I have listened to Lobova's accusations with particular interest. When she announced that she wanted to brand my father with irons, as well as hang him and thereafter shoot him, I even fell a little bit in love with her." There was laughter in the hall. Sasha's voice rose anew. "You can see, comrades, how far irrational thinking can lead you. There is a great danger in this, and not for

Soviet society alone. My father spent many years in prison during the Stalin years. He had been convicted of 'anti-Soviet activities.' Yet his entire crime had been that he served the church. Finally he was pardoned. A special committee of the Supreme Soviet decided on that. You see, my father does an honest day's work. He would not dream of making anti-Soviet propaganda. Do you know what he taught me about the state when he was bringing me up? He often impressed the following on me: 'Sasha, the government has been established by God. It is your job to obey the government because of your love for the Lord.' He lived every moment in the conviction that God so loved us that He gave His only Son in order to draw us to Him. He came not only to save us but so that we would demonstrate the same love He showed us and be ready to give our lives for our fellow human beings if that is called for. My father had a habit of saying, 'We must love the authorities as Christ loved them, even though He Himself was the highest of all authorities.' My father often said, 'Certainly Christ is of greater authority than any earthly power, and He must take a place above all others in our hearts.'

"Do you know, when Yelena demanded my father's death, this is what was going through my mind: *Dear Yelena, dear Communists! How glad I would be to give my life to persuade you to stop wishing the death of your neighbor! I would be ready to take on the worst tortures to cause you to cease your hatred of mankind and your wish to pursue to the death anyone whose convictions disagree with yours.*

"It is true that we have survived the days of Stalin and of the Nazi occupation. Is it your intention, my Communist comrades, and yours, dear Yelena, to march across millions of corpses all over again on the way to your goal? Haven't we all seen enough corpses? If, on top of everything else, you destroy totally innocent people who love you from the bottom of their hearts—or even if you only wish them dead—isn't that inhuman, to put it mildly?

"I am ashamed of my own congregation, which split into

two camps, because of this: the government interferes with the church's activities in a way which shows it has no conscience. Not a single one of those who sincerely believe in God can tolerate a man such as Father Miron, who has become a lamentable puppet.

"I'd like to declare before all of you here that Zarapkin counted on me to declare war against my father today. But as a servant of a registered Baptist congregation I share my father's views from the bottom of my heart and forgive all those who wish us dead." Sasha turned directly toward Zarapkin, looking straight at him.

The hall was deathly quiet.

"Now listen, Nikitin," whispered Zarapkin threateningly. But by this time, applause had already begun to fill the hall. Everybody was clapping. Sasha stepped down from the podium and began to push people out of his way so he could reach the exit. Those inside the hall rose to a man and followed him out, still applauding. Zarapkin made another desperate effort to get himself heard, but nothing could be done.

Sasha started to make his way to the house of worship, where about twenty young people were meeting in prayer. As he entered the bus and sat down, deep in thought, he did not realize that the young woman who sat down next to him was Miss Lobova. They both remained silent. When the bus stopped and Sasha got out and began to walk briskly toward the house of worship, he heard a young woman's voice behind him calling, "Wait a minute, Nikitin!"

He whirled around and saw it was Lobova, who stopped in front of him, a bit out of breath and somewhat embarrassed.

"Excuse me, Nikitin, but I've absolutely got to speak to you." She looked down at one of her shoes, with which she was digging a hole in the lawn. "I want to ask you to accept my apology. . . ." Her voice wavered a little.

"But please, Lobova, I wouldn't dream of being angry at you," Sasha reassured her. "In addition, we Christians are to restrain our feelings of hatred toward our enemies. And you aren't even my enemy; you are my neighbor, whom I am told to love as I do myself."

She gave him a shy glance and said, "You know, I have a fiancé whose name is Fedya. He is an engineer. We have been arguing about just what love is for months. Would you perhaps be able to tell us what your opinion is about this? This would certainly be a help to us."

Sasha smiled. "I'm at your disposal any time." He tore a slip of paper out of his little notebook, wrote his address and telephone number on it and gave it to Yelena. "If you would both like to speak with me, just call me."

"Thank you," Yelena said, "and please send my regards to your wife."

"My deepest thanks," Sasha quipped. "I promise you that if and when I marry I will transmit your greetings to. . . ." He bit his tongue and said, "I mean—I'll be happy to tell my wife of your greeting as soon as I'm married."

Miss Lobova smiled and put out her hand to say good-bye. "So long, Nikitin, and thanks again." She turned around and ran to the bus stop.

Sasha looked after her. "That's the way things go," he muttered to himself and walked into the building shaking his head. The young people inside were already impatient. He reported to them about the evening's activities. They continued to talk together for a long time, praying for Lobova, for Zarapkin, for Father Miron, and for all those who had been present at the various propaganda meetings that evening, as well as those who spoke at them. They didn't stop until after midnight. Finally they separated. Most of them went home on their bicycles and mopeds, while the only group with a car offered Sasha a ride. He refused it, preferring to walk home in order to be able to go over the events of the evening one more time.

The night was pitch dark. On the streets with lights lovers were strolling along. In one of the buildings someone was playing a Russian harmonica. In the distance a dog howled. Sasha decided to take a shortcut. His walk took him down several poorly illuminated back streets. He was thirsty and on the lookout for a drinking fountain. When he finally found one he bent over, depressed the lever and eagerly began to drink the water.

Suddenly he was given a tremendous blow from the rear and collapsed on the ground. A blanket was tossed over him. Blows began to rain on him from all sides. He felt boots kicking him. Someone beat him especially vigorously. "Now this is for you, you good-for-nothing cleric!" a voice hissed. "If you don't stop making your propaganda we'll put you away for good!" For some reason Sasha thought of Sisov, the superintendent of Kirgisia. Then he lost consciousness.

4 Discoveries

Actually the dialogue with the Central Committee of the Communist Party had been Vassiley Kuznetsov's idea. In all seriousness this youthful priest thought it possible to convince the government, after fifty years of Communist dictatorship, that the teachings of the New Testament are in no way aimed against the state. That on the contrary, these teachings call for compliance with the laws and faithfulness toward authority. And that for these reasons Christians should be allowed to live according to their beliefs and to proclaim the Gospel freely to the rest of the people.

Vassiley and his friends sensed similarities between communism and Christian teachings. After all, the message of Christ and His apostles stressed that all earthly and spiritual possessions are the property of God and of those who follow Him—in other words, of all mankind. In the same way as God had created righteousness, church and government should also strive for righteousness.

The young people clearly realized that the Communist "religion" employed a rather peculiar logic when it came to the distribution of the world's goods. At the outset it suggested to its adherents that "everything which belongs to *you* is *ours.*" This created a paradox: all possessions now belonged to the state while individuals were expected to believe that all things were public property and therefore belonged to *them.* To be sure, they had to win them back by means of hard labor in order to be able to regain the use of a tiny portion of those things which were once "mine" and which were now "ours." In this way one could regain the bare essentials of life by the sweat of one's brow.

The intelligentsia had thought much about this curious confusion of terminology. Vassiley, too, had often argued with his father, Professor Ivan Nikolayevitch, about this. Yet such issues stuck in his father's craw, and he did not want to discuss them anymore. "Don't think so much about Communist ideology," the professor told his son. "Nothing good will come of it." Although Vassiley could not miss the warning tone in his father's voice, he could not bring himself to purge his mind of the subject. When he brought the matter up again he was told even more pointedly, "Your life is better than that of most other people; so why not just keep your mouth closed?"

Vassiley's grandfather had died in the infamous prison camp on the Kolyma Peninsula. His parents never said anything about his grandfather. Vassiley had learned from his sister, Tamara (who had heard about it by sheer accident from an acquaintance of her parents) that the grandfather, Nikolai Kuznetsov, had been a well-known theologian in the thirties. He had been arrested and had never returned from prison.

Ever since Vassiley discovered this he had been interested in the subject of religion. When he visited the Lenin library in Moscow with a group of students, he chanced upon his grandfather's works. He was allowed access to them because he was the son of a well-known scientist.

The many paradoxes Vassiley encountered at home and at the university, and those few but very impressive things which he heard about his grandfather, eventually contributed to his entering a theological institute after completion of his studies in law. Yet when he discovered that KGB informers had wormed their way even into his theological courses, he was upset and repulsed.

He noticed that the KGB was particularly adroit in luring foreign students, generally from friendly countries and from the Third World, into its nets, and that these visitors had often been converted into some of their most trustworthy collaborators. He soon stopped getting upset about these matters. He had, in fact, decided against becoming a servant of the Orthodox Church because he had concluded that this church had fallen away from Christ's teachings.

Just at that time he ran into a preacher of the Word from the western Ukraine, and this caused him to change his mind again. This preacher had been in contact with the spiritual renewal movement within the Roumanian Orthodox Church. Something so totally unique transpired there that Vassiley, too, was fascinated. The members of this church met in private homes after their worship and studied the Bible together. It was quite natural for these men to consciously place themselves into the service of the Orthodox Church. Their spirit of the pietistic movement had begun to permeate the Orthodox Church and gained ground rapidly. The renewal had a special impact upon the young people. For them, the idea of being disciples of Christ gave their lives and thoughts a wholly new dimension.

Vassiley changed his opinion about the priesthood as the result of these discoveries. When he concluded his studies he asked to be sent to the Ukraine. Here he was also ordained into the priesthood.

He had married while still a student but had lost his wife soon after that as a result of an automobile accident. It was one of those often mysterious accidents which one accepts at the outset but about which one gains some explanation later as the result of a chance encounter. Vassiley had difficulty in accepting his loss. He threw himself into his work even more deeply, which soon caused him to be put on the KGB's blacklist. It was their view that he was much too active in his work. And he proved himself to be much too devout for his ecclesiastical superiors. He had to use every trick and cleverly manipulate events to remain in his post at all.

The KGB increased its surveillance of Vassiley when he began to get in touch with the Council of Churches of the

Evangelical Baptists and to discuss the idea of joint Bible studies with them. This increased surveillance began to get on his nerves so much that he undertook to convince the Communist Party of the fact that considerable parallels existed between what Christ had taught and what the Communist Party preached. "Why should we fight each other when your ideology seeks earthly well-being, while we Christians merely seek eternal joy after earthly well-being?" he once said to the philosopher Mitrochin. Only much later, when he was able to consider all of these things in peace and quiet, did Vassiley begin to wonder at how simpleminded he had been. But this occurred many years later as he sat in solitary in prison.

Vassiley had discovered more and more young people from various denominations who shared his convictions. Since the persecution and public denunciation of Christians continued, he built up his contacts. Although young in the faith he developed a fine sense of discernment that helped him ascertain whether or not the people he spoke to were sincere believers in Christ.

Whenever he heard that a Christian was on trial somewhere, he made an effort to get there. This brought him at one time to his home city, where his parents were still living. One night he was on his way to their home. The next morning he had to locate a Baptist preacher who had been caught in the KGB's trap. He was a former member of the Council of Churches and had often visited Vassiley's Bible studies when he was still a student in the city.

Vassiley had visited one of the "informational" meetings in the Lenin section of town. The government had succeeded in inciting the town's population against everything for which Christ stood. Despite the fact that the purpose of these meetings was to awaken hatred against the "unregistered" believers, the hatred would spill over and be turned against all of Russia's Christians.

The fanning of hatred against Christians resulted in criminal activity against them. Auxiliary policemen whose anger had been aroused would beat Christians until they died. These crimes were never investigated by the police or by the attorney general. As a result these auxiliary police became bolder and bolder, launching a reign of terror with their break-ins, rapes, and other forms of violence.

On his way home Vassiley walked down a narrow back street. Suddenly he heard groaning. He stopped and listened. The groaning was very close.

"Is there someone here?" Vassiley called out. The groaning stopped. Vassiley took out his flashlight and shone it in a circle. A man was lying on the ground a few feet from a water fountain. *Obviously a drunk,* Vassiley thought as he walked over and shone his light on the man.

"My God," he exclaimed, "he is bleeding!" *Has he injured himself while he was drunk? Of course not; he couldn't hurt himself that severely while falling down in a drunken stupor. What can I do?* Vassiley put his flashlight away and tried to move the unconscious man into an upright position. *I must call an ambulance!* Yet, without knowing why, he decided to carry the severely injured man to his parents' home. He struggled and got him onto his back. The man was now clearly unconscious and no longer made any sound.

Vassiley had walked for about two hundred yards when he heard voices behind him.

"But we left him at the drinking fountain!"

Vassiley turned the corner hurriedly with his heavy load and continued to listen.

"Don't use your light, man!" another voice ordered.

"Listen, he's gone!"

"What a mess! We didn't beat him up enough if he's still able to walk."

"That's impossible," the first voice said defensively.

They inspected the entire area near the drinking fountain. "Look, see the pool of blood! Zarapkin told us not to kill him but to teach him a lesson this time. Most likely somebody took him to a hospital."

"Let's move! We've got to get to the orthopedic hospital.

Zarapkin must be told his medical status." Once again they swung their flashlights around the entire area. The beam of light traveled from the drinking fountain to the empty street beyond. Vassiley, meanwhile, was crouching with the injured man behind the fence of the corner building at the end of the street. If only he wouldn't begin to groan again! When Vassiley heard Zarapkin's name he realized that he was carrying on his back the victim of an antireligious persecution.

The men vanished as quickly as they had appeared. Vassiley dragged himself and his cargo to 12 Mitchurin Street as fast as his legs would carry them. The garden gate was locked. He rang the bell. Suddenly he heard an ambulance siren.

"For God's sake," groaned the sick man, "not to a hospital!"

"Be quiet," Vassiley whispered. Someone inside the building turned on the street light.

"Who is there!" a girl's voice called out.

"It's me—Vassiley! Turn off the lights!" The light went off and Vassiley's sister, Tamara, came running to the gate.

"Vassiley, who's that?"

"Please—no questions now. Just be quiet." He entered the house with his burden. "Please, would you make the sofa bed ready for him?"

She quickly went about getting bedding out of the closet, opened the bed and spread a sheet on it. Vassiley laid the man down with great care. He was unconscious again. Vassiley began to remove his blood-soaked clothes.

"What's going on? Tell me!" said Tamara, still not daring to speak normally.

"I don't know myself." Vassiley began to examine the man's battered body. Tamara put a kettle of water on the stove. Suddenly the stranger opened his eyes.

"My name is Sasha Nikitin. I am a minister in the Baptist congregation, . . ." he said, then groaned and lost consciousness again.

"What a clumsy oaf I am," Vassiley grunted. He had been trying to cut the man's matted hairs from his head, and his scissors had accidentally come into contact with the wound.

This was truly an unusual way to run into a friend from his youth. His hand had slipped with the shock of hearing Sasha's name.

"Come on, let me do this." Tamara took the scissors from her brother's hand. Deftly she cut the cloth and hair away from his wounds and began to disinfect them with alcohol.

"Who did this to him?"

"Most likely it was a bunch of rowdies who were told to do this by the man in charge of religious cults," Vassiley said grimly.

Tamara shook her head in disbelief.

"That couldn't happen! It sounds like a tale out of a book of horror stories!" She was in her fifth semester of medical studies and had already gained considerable experience in the treatment of wounds. She put bandages on all of Sasha's injuries, then gave him an injection of camphor. After this she held a bottle of ammonia under Sasha's nose so that he would come to.

Eventually his eyes fluttered open briefly. "Please inform my parents," he whispered. He had forgotten that his parents were out of the city. Vassiley was already busy leafing through Sasha's notebook. He discovered the telephone number of Sasha's parents and started dialing. Sasha suddenly remembered that no one would be home. "They're not home," he said almost inaudibly. His head fell sideways and he dropped off to sleep.

Tamara sat down next to him and took his pulse. Vassiley was about to hang up when a woman's voice answered.

"Are you Sasha Nikitin's mother?" Vassiley inquired.

"Yes; has something happened to him?" the woman replied anxiously. "I've already waited four hours for my son and for my husband, and they haven't arrived."

My goodness, Vassiley thought, terror-stricken, *what if they've tapped Nikitin's telephone?* He knew that they already were listening in on his own parents' telephone.

"I would have appreciated being able to speak to him," Vassiley said into the receiver. "Would you kindly remind him that he is to call Zarapkin?" He hung up.

"What in the world did you tell his mother?"

"I was afraid that their telephone is tapped."

Vassiley rehearsed the events of the day for Tamara. When he was finished she said with a smile, "Oh yes, we were told that we were expected to be present at these meetings. But I was excused by the secretary of my Komsomol group. I had *such* a headache last night."

She never was in the mood to attend that kind of meeting and usually developed a convenient headache or stomachache on such occasions.

Vassiley knew about her tactic and laughed. "You haven't changed, little sister," he said. He kissed her on the forehead. "But this won't do at all. You will have to go to the Nikitins and tell them what has happened." Tamara grimaced. "Come on, you've got to help me. I'm convinced that they've surrounded Nikitin's home in order to learn where Sasha is to be found. I would prefer not to be seen by these people. Go on, take your bike." All of a sudden he was afraid for her. How would she explain to the police her bicycling around at night? But Tamara had already put on her jacket.

"Komsomol Lane, number two, right? That's where a friend of mine lives. In number thirteen!" With that she was gone.

5 The Arrest

Sasha had no way of knowing that his parents had learned of the informational meetings ordered by the Party and had interrupted their trip to hurry home. The mother then remained home while Andrey Nikitin went to the meeting in his part of town in order to find out what the accusation was against him and his congregation. He had, however, said nothing publicly the whole evening. He simply refused to defend himself. He was seated next to the district superintendent and conversed quietly with him. This brother had formerly belonged to an unregistered congregation. After five years in jail because of this, he became a member of a registered congregation. He immediately was given the position of district superintendent.

"Is it worth it to defend oneself and try to prove that we aren't enemies of the government?" asked Nikitin.

"The ideological section of the Central Committee began this whole campaign to immunize the general population against religion. They plan to provide theoretical freedom of religion but only on the condition that the church's activity serve the development of a Communist society in Russia and throughout the rest of the world. What this means to us is that if we want to be legitimized under the constitution we must work against ourselves. Kuroyedov called me at home yesterday and told me that ten houses of worship per Soviet republic were going to be registered. 'But see to it that the activity of these churches is directed toward the well-being of the Communist Party,' he warned me. 'You've got to educate your believers in the spirit of communism. Otherwise we will close your churches again some day.' I was so distressed that I could have wept aloud. But let them do their thing, Andrey. We must continue to live according to the Word of God. Yet it is getting harder and harder to do so."

At this point the superintendent was asked to mount the speaker's podium and denounce the splinter group. Instead he simply stood up and said, "How could I do that? They are, after all, my brothers!" With that he rapidly walked out of the hall.

Lupa, a friend of Andrey Nikitin and a member of the congregation which Sasha served as preacher, was seated next to Andrey. He nudged Nikitin and said, "Let's get out. Let the atheists play their crazy games without us."

They rose and hurried toward the exit. Behind them formed a chain of Christians who had made up their minds not to listen to any more insults.

"Hey, you Fascists, where are you going?" yelled one of those functionaries who had organized the campaign.

Nikitin smiled and turned. "Soviet law forbids insulting the sensibilities of Soviet citizens. You can see for yourself, my friends, that Soviet law does not apply to Communists and their militant methods."

One of the Party members in the front row, who obviously had had one drink too many, jumped up and bellowed, "One more word and I will bite your head off!"

Nikitin and his friends did not respond, but left the hall. Lupa then invited the brethren to have a cup of tea.

Ironically, Lupa lived in a large apartment house in which the police also were headquartered. In the basement were a detoxification tank and some interrogation cells. The examining judge and other members of the police had their offices on the first and second floors. The remaining apartments were for the policemen's families.

Through the good offices of his grandson, old Lupa was given one of the apartments. His grandson, Major Lupa, was well known for conscientious work. He honored the name "Lupa" by making a painstaking examination of all details before rendering his decisions—as if he were using a jeweler's magnifying glass. ("Lupa" in Russian means "magnifying glass.")

Because Major Lupa was so successful, the authorities conveniently overlooked the fact that his grandfather had spent many years in prison, especially in view of the fact that meanwhile he had been rehabilitated. And Major Lupa's father also had been decorated as a "hero of the Soviet Union."

Old man Lupa had had to suffer principally because of his too-free tongue. He couldn't keep his mouth shut and was forever telling jokes. Naturally some of them had political overtones. Thus when he returned from the battlefront after the Second World War he regaled his friends with a joke about the relationship between the Third Reich and Stalin. After the nonagression pact between Soviet Russia and Nazi Germany had been signed, he said, one of the men in the government had stated that this treaty should not be compared to a marriage of love but to a marriage of convenience. A Jewish teacher reportedly replied that even a marriage of convenience could result in children. That was the "joke," and for that, old man Lupa had received twenty-five years in prison. Forgotten was the fact that Lupa had distinguished himself by his heroic conduct at Stalingrad and during the capture of Berlin. Three years after the victory over Germany, the heroes of the war had the temerity to make jokes about Stalin and to criticize him!

Not too long after Lupa's arrest and imprisonment, his wife got herself a divorce. After all, who could guarantee whether he would ever return? And even if he should come back, what woman could be happy with a husband who had been branded an "enemy of the people"?

On top of that, Lupa had begun to believe in God during his term in prison. The district committee of the Communist Party asked him one day, "Why do you believe in God?"

The old man replied, after giving it some thought, "Well, if God hadn't given the Russian people the strength to carry the yoke you have laid on them, what fool would still tolerate you?" He was thrown out. But since de-Stalinization had just begun to sweep the country he was spared further persecution.

When Lupa had volunteered to go underground with Andrey Nikitin, the minister had urged him to stay in the registered church. "I don't want my flock to be endangered by your sharp tongue," Nikitin had said. The two men, however, remained friends for life.

Old man Lupa still longed for his wife, who had remarried soon after the divorce but had been widowed and had gone to live in Moscow. Her second husband, a colonel in the Soviet army, had died in an automobile accident. Lupa urged her to come back to him. He assured her that he still loved her and that he bore her no resentment. But she had no desire to live with a Baptist and didn't want to lose the pension to which she was entitled as a result of her second husband's death.

Lupa's apartment was quite roomy by the standards of that day. He had a large bedroom, which also served as his workroom, as well as a huge kitchen where he received his guests. He had a large convertible couch in the kitchen, and a large round table which had been "requisitioned" from the estate of a Count Nowicky. The estate had been converted into a children's home by that time. A former natchalnik (boss) in the police had given this table to Major Lupa, and he in turn gave it to his grandfather. "Why don't you take this thing? What should I do with this huge piece of furniture? I don't know where I could put it!" his grandson said.

The grandfather was overjoyed. Now his kitchen looked exactly like the outrageously oversized office of a Party functionary! Somewhere along the line Lupa had helped a natchalnik furnish such an office. And when he saw an upholsterer tacking some red fabric onto an easy chair he commented, "This fabric would certainly look good as a tablecloth on my new table!"

The natchalnik—may he live forever—then ordered, "Give the old man as much of the fabric as he wants!" From that time on, the red tablecloth lay in magnificent splendor on Lupa's table.

In addition, Lupa's apartment had a roomy pantry with no windows. This had become a highly useful room. Lupa had managed to turn it into a respository for a number of Bibles, New Testaments, and other Christian literature, all of which came from outside Russia. From here they were conveyed forward with the unwitting assistance of the ever-ready-to-oblige police.

Customarily all the important concerns of the congregation were discussed in this apartment. Today was no exception. The brethren sat together in this room, drank their tea, and went over the events of the evening. Andrey Nikitin was about to speak about a publishing house named "The Christian" when the phone rang. Lupa picked up the receiver.

"Oh, it's you, grandson. . . . Yes, yes. All right, I'll do it. So long."

That was all that was said, but one could see that the old man was deeply disturbed by what he had heard.

"What a bunch of nonsense!" He looked at Andrey. "You allegedly beat up your son. The police are on the way to the place where the crime was committed." They were all shaken.

Nikitin grew pale. "It certainly seems like somebody is up to some dirty tricks. Father and son serve congregations that compete against each other. Now the object is to insinuate that they're at each other's throats. I hope nothing serious has happened to Sasha."

He was lost in thought for a few moments. The rest of them were at wit's end, unable to make up their minds about what to do. Finally Nikitin pulled himself together and said, "Excuse me, my friends. I'm going to hurry home. Natasha is probably going out of her mind with anxiety and worry over the two of us." He shook hands with each of them, asking them to pray for him and his son.

*   *   *

Natasha was watching the activities of the police from her window, her face pale. She smiled happily as she saw her husband returning to the house. Her pleasure was clouded by the thought, *Perhaps this is the last time I will see him!*

"Aha, there he is!" called Zarapkin when he saw that Nikitin had arrived. "And where is the son?"

Without a word Andrey went up to his wife and embraced her. Later on he would write to a brother in Christ, "At that moment I felt such deep pain in my heart! I could have howled like a dog over my powerlessness, my inability to prove to these militant atheists that what they were doing bordered on insanity. But I merely stood there, saying only, 'May the Lord forgive you!'"

Zarapkin was very suspicious. He concluded that Nikitin knew something about Sasha's fate and that this prompted him to say, "May the Lord forgive you." Yet Zarapkin was wrong. Nikitin only had a premonition about what might have happened. This was depressing enough. He was well aware that even those who served registered congregations could be beaten up by the police at the behest of the KGB, and he suspected that something like that had happened to his son.

Suddenly one of the militiamen noticed that a young woman was looking into the building. He rushed outside and yelled, "Halt, or I will shoot!" But he was too late. The young woman had already vanished into the darkness on her bicycle. The militiaman returned to the house, cursing. At that moment Zarapkin ran out of the same door and nearly knocked the militiaman over.

"Did you catch her?" he yelled.

"No, and I didn't really get a good look at her."

"You boob!" scolded Zarapkin.

"I hope that this remark was not intended for one of my subordinates!" growled Major Lupa angrily. He walked past Zarapkin and told the Nikitins that the militia had collected eyewitness testimony that Sasha had been severely beaten, after a meeting during which much had been said against the schismatic Baptists, and had been left on the street unconscious. Two witnesses claimed to have seen Sasha's father and another unidentified man assaulting Sasha. They reported that before they were able to call the militia and an ambulance, the victim and his tormentors had fled into the night.

The Nikitins listened wordlessly. Sasha's mother wept softly. At first his father was unable to say anything. Then, noticing the confusion in the room, with open boxes and suitcases lying around, he asked grimly, "You weren't by any chance looking for my son inside these suitcases, were you?"

The militia had now completed its search of the house. The soldiers stood around in the kitchen and waited for their orders from the officers. Major Lupa and Zarapkin completed the written search forms and asked Nikitin to sign them.

Then the major stood up and announced, "I am sorry to have to trouble you, Andrey Semyonovitch, but you will have to spend the night in the militia station until everything has been cleared up."

Lupa went over to Zarapkin and whispered, "Can't we leave this old man here? He's not about to run out on us."

Zarapkin, however, was in no mood to comply with Lupa's wishes and show leniency. He shook his head. "He's got to know where his son is. He might be able to create trouble for us because of what has happened tonight."

Andrey prayed quietly with his wife. Then he raised his head. "I am ready to go with you. God be with you, my dearest!" He kissed her one more time and followed the militiamen out of the apartment.

*   *   *

Vassiley waited for his sister's return. For him the dramatic events of the evening had not been surprising. Frequently students who had refused to denounce someone else were found hanging in their living rooms or bathrooms. They usually prepared their friends for this by saying, "If something should happen to me, I want you to know that I did not want it to happen and had nothing to do with it. Someone did it to me."

There were occasions when ministers, after interrogation by the KGB, died as the result of automobile accidents. On such occasions Vassiley's friends would say, "If you want to stay alive you have to become an informer or a double agent, for the good of the church and to benefit the KGB. Of course you can do that only until you are discovered."

Vassiley had fallen asleep in his chair and did not hear Tamara's return. She did not wake him until she had made his bed.

"Come, Vassiley, go to bed!" she said, shaking him.

He stretched himself and murmured, "I am terribly tired. Did you tell Sasha's parents what was going on?"

"No. There's a house search in progress." She looked down at the sleeping Sasha. "When he wakes up I have to give him an injection for his pain." She thought for a moment. "He can't remain on this couch. Let's carry him to my bed, and I'll sleep here. Somebody could walk in here and see him."

She went to her room to get the bed ready for Sasha.

"Where are our parents?" Vassiley called after her.

She called back, "Father is away on business; I think in Tchelyabinsk." She came back in. "Something went wrong in the Institute there. Silitch, the engineer in charge of the research team, has associated himself with Sakharov and wants to emigrate to Israel. He is a Jew, you know. His requests are constantly turned down, and the KGB has started an investigation. They are afraid to let him go because he knows so much about our atomic energy activities. Father feels he knows nothing that isn't already known to the West. Now they are making things difficult for Father because he has taken Silitch under his wing."

"He must stay out of that Silitch affair or they'll throw him out of the Institute."

"I told him that too. Once when Father came home he appeared to be all confused. 'My child,' he said to me, 'they want me to become a Party member.'

" 'And so,' said I, 'why not? Your first concern anyway is science, not communism.'

"That night he drank so much wine at dinner that he wound up singing a drinking song. A few days later he came home with a guilty look on his face and said, 'Little daughter, I've become a Communist!' Tears were streaming down his face.

" 'What do you mean, Father?' I asked.

" 'But, child, I am a man of science! Why do I need a Party membership?' Then he said very quietly, 'It's all a big deceit.'

"I didn't know what he was driving at, so I asked him, 'Wouldn't you have joined the Nazi Party, too, in order to be able to keep your position?'

"He screamed at me, 'Go to the devil or I'll whack you one!' He had never screamed at me like that—ever! I was deeply hurt and went to my room. An hour later he came into my room, asking me to forgive him. He was really crushed. It took me the entire evening to calm him down. Ever since then, whenever he has misplaced his Party membership card, he says, 'Where are my bread ration coupons?' On one occasion he so forgot himself that he referred to his Institute identification card as a bread ration coupon too. Well, the secretary of the Party committee let him have a piece of his mind! I know that Father is merely tolerated there nowadays."

Tamara walked to the couch where Sasha lay. "He's sleeping like a rock. I'm really sorry to have to disturb him." She sat down on a chair next to Sasha and looked at his face.

"He's a good-looking fellow. He is the spitting image of his mother."

Vassiley smiled softly. "Some time ago someone told me that she is not his real mother."

"What difference does that make?" Tamara shrugged.

"By the way, you haven't told me anything about *our* mother."

"Didn't she and her friend visit you?" Tamara asked, astonished.

"Why should she have visited me?"

"Oh, she and her new boyfriend wanted to go to a sanatorium. They intended to visit you on their way there. She was very eager to introduce you to her new friend."

"A new one already?" Vassiley asked disgustedly. "How can Father put up with that? Why doesn't he throw her out? Are all actresses prostitutes like our mother?"

"Don't talk like that, priest. Sasha's making faces because of what you just said, even while he's still asleep. Her new boyfriend works at the Central Committee of the Communist Party, get it? He's a young career man about your age. Maybe a little older than you are. His father works for the cabinet. He's absolutely crazy about Mother, and she's even more insane about him. And don't call your father names. He loves Mother and overlooks all her escapades. Sometimes I think this might be because of his work in the atomic field. Maybe he cannot really live with a woman anymore, do you understand? He forgives her everything for that reason."

"But Mother's fifty-five already!" Vassiley replied indignantly.

"You are so stupid! You ought to be ashamed of yourself. You, a man charged with serving people spiritually, see very little of what is actually going on inside them. But let's get going! Let's carry Sasha into my room, and then let's go to bed ourselves. I can see daylight outside. I'm going to wind up falling asleep during all of my lectures today."

They went to work. Sasha's eyes opened and he tried to get up, but he sank back exhausted and groaning.

"Lie down, you hero," growled Tamara, lifting him up under his armpits as Vassiley lifted his body. Together they bedded the injured man down in Tamara's bed. Soon after that, both Vassiley and Tamara were asleep. But Sasha lay awake until the morning.

6 Memories

Vassiley did not have time to speak with Irina before he left the city, because a few days after the Koslov incident she had gone off to see her grandfather. On the morning of her departure she received a letter from him. "I am worried about you, dear child!" wrote the old gentleman. "Please come to visit me as soon as you can arrange it."

The letter came as if she had prearranged it. Irina read it to her father and then quickly made her decision. Her father intended to arrange personally for her resignation and at the same time apply for his own transfer to Minsk.

Irina had seldom visited her grandfather. Her work left her with little time. Nor was her father very happy to see her go to visit him. He probably feared that the old man would disclose some parts of the carefully covered up family secret to her. Under the circumstances, however, her trip was the best that could be done.

As soon as she arrived, the grandfather proudly took her for a walk along the waterfront. He introduced her to some of his acquaintances and blithely attempted to take her by the arm and toss her into the Black Sea. Considering the fact that he was almost ninety years old, he was unable to do that. They usually ended up venturing too close to the water, winding up with sopping wet clothes. They headed for home, to be scolded by a good-humored Pelagea, his wife.

It was bruited about that the old man was by no means ninety years old, that he had simply added one or more decades to his actual age. Vladimir Sokolov merely chortled at that. He paid court to all the elderly ladies of his large circle of acquaintances and patiently accepted Pelagea's intolerant attitude toward these activities. She was thirty years younger than her husband, but one would never have guessed it when first seeing them. She was his fifth wife. He had survived four wives, having been on excellent terms with each one. He sometimes told Irina that God had given him good health and a long life so that he could make Soviet womanhood happy. "Look, we had an excessive number of women as a result of the war. Somehow, someone had to take care of them," he would say. The conscientious Irina refused to indulge in such witticisms.

During the long evenings he devoted himself entirely to his recollections. At those times the years of his work alongside Professor Pavlov came up again and again. He called Pavlov his master and a scholar without compromise. He himself had worked in the field of psychology. But he had made no important discoveries and remained a candidate in the medical sciences his entire life.

Pavlov had been a wonderful Christian, Sokolov told Irina. He had been a truly God-fearing scientist in the twentieth century. He compared Pavlov's spiritual attitudes with the posture of the leaders of the present church in the Soviet Union and said derisively, "These puppets of atheistic and Utopian communism simply don't know anything about the true message of Christ. They've sold Christ for thirty pieces of silver all over again!"

Irina had heard these stories over and over again. What she didn't know was that the old gentleman would have loved to talk about another subject; but his son had ordered him to silence, and Vladimir Sokolov was a man of his word. Still, each time Irina visited him, the memories came crowding back again as they did today.

"Leave me alone for a while, Irina. I want to lie alone in my chair. You go swimming!"

That suited Irina fine. "Don't snore so loudly that the waves start rising up," she teased, and walked off.

Irina, what really happened at that time? he thought as he started reliving the scenes.

*　　*　　*

"You are Vladimir Sokolov?" a captain named Volin had asked him. The officer stammered, "I don't know how I can tell you this . . . but. . . ." He fell into an awkward silence.

An evil foreboding caused Sokolov's stomach to knot up and he yelled, "Why do you keep silent? Say something! Has something happened to Yuri?" Volin had been one of his son's closest friends. Both of them had worked in counterespionage.

Finally the truth emerged from Volin like the shot from a cannon. "Your son's fiancée and her parents are under arrest. Yuri has been removed from his post and sent to the front lines." Having said this, Volin spun around and ran from Sokolov's apartment without saying good-bye.

Vladimir had just lost his second wife. He lived in a quiet little street in Moscow during the war years and worked at the Institute. He wanted to run after Volin and ask him for more information. So Yuri had a fiancée? Why had she been arrested? And why had Yuri been removed from his position? But Sokolov was unable to move after hearing the news. Instead he remained seated as if he had taken root and brooded about this unanticipated news.

His Siberian cat then jumped onto his lap, rubbing its head against his chin. He hugged the cat close to himself, then rose and telephoned his supervisor. He told him of Volin's visit and asked for his advice.

The professors at the Institute lived in constant fear that they would be jailed for some inconsequential matter. Hardly any of these scientists had escaped the purges of 1937 and 1939 untouched. When the war broke out, many of them had been freed again. But while the large majority had asked to be sent to the battlefront, the committees in charge of wartime manpower allocation had resisted this move and often turned them down. Instead they sent the scientists to the research centers and institutes, where they normally would be employed more usefully. There were no guarantees that they would not unexpectedly be put behind bars again as a result of some trifling incident. In fact, there might be no obvious reason at all. Sokolov had a great advantage in that the director of the Institute was a friend of his, and the director's brother was an important functionary within the KGB.

"Vladimir, I will make every effort to find out what happened and to help out your son. Wait for my phone call," his supervisor now said soothingly.

Several months earlier this supervisor already had helped Sokolov out of a very ticklish situation. On that occasion the leader of a large organization in Leningrad had been involved. His death sentence had been commuted into a "disqualification" because of the director's personal intervention. The man's name was Borisov. At the time, Yuri had begged his father to put in a good word for the man with the director. And now it was Sokolov himself who needed the good turn.

He could not have said how long he sat there waiting for the return call. Finally the telephone rang, and the director reported that Yuri had fallen into disgrace because of a love affair. He had fallen in love with the daughter of the very same Borisov. The girl's name was Natasha. Borisov and his family had happened to hear a traveling preacher, and all of them had been converted soon afterward. After this Borisov had turned in his Party membership card. The next day he and his whole family were arrested and eventually sentenced to ten years in prison.

"But what did Yuri have to do with this affair?"

"There was every indication that your son was engaged to marry Natasha. I also learned from my brother that Natasha is expecting your son's child. Yet they sentenced her to ten years without taking that into consideration. After all, this is war, and there is no mercy. Your son knows nothing about any of this. They immediately sent him to the battlefront because he had been involved with 'enemies of the people.' "

"But what brought Yuri to Kuibishev so that he could even become acquainted with the Borisovs? He'd been spending his time in Leningrad these last few months."

"I can't tell you anything more about that. It's also irrele- vant. The only thing we must concentrate on right now is the child. We've got to save your son's child." They continued to talk about this for a long time. Sokolov did not close his eyes at all that night.

A month later a letter arrived in his mailbox. At first he thought it came from Yuri, but he was wrong. He tore open the envelope and saw a strange handwriting. He began to read. "Dear Grandfather Vladimir: You are Yuri's father, and I continue to love Yuri to this day. Yuri has told me many things about you and has lovingly called you his 'Grandfa- ther Valdimir.' This is why I use this appellation too. I am the daughter of the man named Borisov whom you saved from execution. You never knew it, but I had been engaged to marry Yuri after we met in Leningrad and had been meeting with him off and on in Kuibishev whenever he was sent there on official assigments. We planned to get married with- out waiting for the war to end. But something unexpected occurred. I accepted the Lord. Please don't tear up my letter now; keep listening to what I have to say! I have studied philosophy. I've read much, beginning with the Greek philos- ophers and all the way to Marx. Again and again I tried to discover the reason for evil, why it arose and why humanity is unable to stamp it out. Why are there wars and why do human beings hate one another? At any rate, while I was taking a late walk with my father one evening we happened upon a Baptist house of prayer.

"The door was open and we went in. There were several elderly men sitting inside listening to an address by a young man in military uniform. He had been sent home from the battlefront because of an injury. As all of us know, during the war Stalin consented to the reopening of a few churches. No one noticed our arrival. The young man spoke about Saint Augustine, whose story already had fascinated me during my studies. He said that according to Augustine all evil, the root of sin, is transmitted genetically from parent to child, and that we—that is all of humanity—come into the world with the seed of sin within us. This evil grows inside us and turns us into egotistical and envious human beings. War, misery, poverty, and exploitation are caused by the fact that we carry this original sin within us. Wars, therefore, cannot be stopped by the use of weapons! Those high moral principles which permit us to end all wars can be found only in Christ. Yes, not in the church, but in Jesus Christ Himself. This is the gist of what the young man had to say.

"This young man spoke very forcibly. One could tell that he spoke with deep conviction. Quite obviously, he had thought much about the topic during his days at the battle-front and had arrived at his conclusion there. Father and I left the house of worship without being noticed, since I had to get back to work in the hospital. Later I spent many hours searching for the writings of Augustine in the libraries of friends. Finally a member of the clergy lent them to me. In these books I found the very same ideas the young man had spoken about on that memorable evening. His message pursued me and my father everywhere we went. As a result, one night at dinner our whole family converted to Christianity. I turned in my Komsomol membership card, and Father his Communist Party membership. This was enough for all of us to be named 'enemies of the people' and to be sentenced to a ten-year term in prison.

"I wanted so badly to see Yuri one more time. I wanted to tell him that I could do nothing else. Unfortunately this was not possible. I ask Yuri to forgive me because I have caused him real difficulties. Most important, I want to inform you,

Grandfather Vladimir, that I am expecting a child by Yuri. I am in my fourth month of pregnancy. Yuri knows nothing about this. I am of delicate health and fear that I will not be able to carry this baby to term. I became a Christian a month after my last meeting with Yuri. I beg you to let him know that I continue to love him. Good-bye, Grandfather Vladimir! I will throw this letter into the street from the prisoners' van. My sentence does not permit me to send or receive mail. Your Natasha."

So this was his son's secret love story. In the meantime, no letters arrived from Yuri. He was obviously in combat somewhere at the front. Perhaps he wasn't even alive any longer.

Sokolov and his friend, the director, began to make plans on how to save Natasha's child. First they tracked down the prison camp where Natasha was serving her sentence. Then they established contact with the camp's natchalnik and were able to persuade him to transfer Natasha to light duty. She gave birth to her baby, a daughter, in the prison hospital. The director and Sokolov traveled to Siberia and took custody of the child. Sokolov considered himself responsible for his son's baby. He did feel sorry for the child's mother, but not enough to intercede on her behalf. She was told simply that the baby had died. Sokolov, in turn, lost contact with the young woman since caring for the child took all of his free time. He was forced to hire a housekeeper—a kind-hearted woman who had lost her husband in the war—to care for the little girl. Since she had no children of her own, the housekeeper showered all her love on Sokolov's little granddaughter.

He did not hear from Yuri until the war was over. When Yuri finally appeared at his father's apartment one day, Sokolov did not recognize him. Bearded, mature, somehow turned inward, Yuri stood in the middle of the room and said, "Well, Father, don't you recognize me anymore?"

They quickly embraced. Vladimir could not see because of his tears.

"Gramps, gramps, you told me that men don't cry, and

now you're blubbering yourself!" The child, who had been observing both men from her place at the table, looked at Yuri with undisguised curiosity.

"Who is that, Father?" Yuri asked.

"It's your daughter."

The child jumped off her chair, walked around Yuri and scrutinized him from all angles.

"No," she said, pouting, "my daddy doesn't have a beard!" She ran into her room and brought Yuri's picture back with her. She then alternately looked at the picture and at the man before her, shaking her head pensively as an adult might. Eventually Vladimir motioned his son to sit down on the couch and introduced his third wife, Lilya, the former housekeeper. He then brought the letter from Natasha out of a drawer and handed it to Yuri.

Yuri began to read and turned pale, occasionally looking at the child. Finally he tore himself away from the letter, asking, "Where is she?"

"She is married."

Quietly Yuri rose and walked to the little one, crouching down before her.

"So I don't look like the picture of your daddy, eh?" The little child backed up a couple of steps.

"No. My daddy hasn't got a beard. And he is an officer. You are only a soldier."

Yuri began to laugh. He had been a major. He picked up his reluctant daughter and announced, "I'm going to shave right now and then you'll see that I am your daddy!"

That evening father and son sat up for a long time. They spoke about Yuri's past and his future. After that, Natasha was not mentioned again.

Yuri intended to rejoin the KGB, but his father was definitely against that. It took a long time before Yuri was ready to go back to the university to study for a new career. His free time was spent with the child. They became such fast friends that the grandfather began to feel jealous. It might sound ridiculous, but he had become more attached to the child than to his own son and felt that he would not be able to survive the departure of both of them. But things had not quite yet reached that point. Yuri began the study of medicine. He often took his daughter to class with him. She soon was completely spoiled by the students. His parents urged Yuri to marry. His answer was a shake of his head. Finally the constant badgering got on his nerves. He burst out, "For goodness sake, leave me alone! I have no intention of ever living with another woman!"

The small child eventually began to ask questions about her mother. It seemed impossible to break her of that habit until she discovered that it was not always possible to get an answer for every question in other families either. One had to think things through very carefully. Irina learned that early in life.

*   *   *

The sun had moved so much that it began to shine down on the old man. He began to roll around until he found another spot. The sun's rays were too strong for him. He settled down to enjoy his rest again.

He suddenly felt drops of water on his forehead and cheek, and even on his shirt. He looked up to discover that Irina had changed and was wringing out her bathing suit over him.

"What's come over you? Get out of here, you wild brat!" he shouted at her. There was to be no more of the rough play of former days. Now she put her hand out for him and helped him to his feet. They headed home at the customary pace. Tomorrow Irina would travel to Minsk in order to begin work at her new position.

Yuri Sokolov had been unable to find an apartment in Minsk and gladly accepted his cousin Serov's offer to stay with him for the time being. The Serovs owned a large, beautiful home on the bank of the River Ptitch. They had

enough room for both of the Sokolovs. Irina would certainly
be able to do a number of things with the children. She
would benefit from living in a large family with children
with whom she could go boating and swimming and play
tennis. Nevertheless, Yuri would have to warn his daughter
to be careful, for Serov held an important post in the KGB.
All telephone calls from the house would be under surveillance. Serov himself was away on official trips most of the
time, so that his family rarely saw him. The Sokolovs also
would have few contacts with him.

Irina again had a position in a research institute. For the
time being she could not give any thought to her dissertation.
Her father worked at an outpatient clinic.

She tried to force all memories of the incident with Koslov
from her mind.

7 Disturbing News

The KGB had no documentary evidence against Sasha. They had been bluffing, putting totally fictitious material in front of his father to really scare him. It became quite apparent that Sasha was slow in recuperating completely from his beating and would continue to be subject to fainting spells. His condition was described in a most anxiety-provoking manner to Andrey Nikitin, who was still in prison. The authorities hoped the father would be willing to do whatever might be necessary to prevent his son from going to jail.

The elders of the congregation counseled Sasha to take a leave of absence for a few months and to spend this time vacationing at the Black Sea. A visitor from the United States had brought a thousand rubles on behalf of a missionary group, and the elders had decided to use this gift toward Sasha's recuperative leave.

Irina heard about this from Vassiley, with whom she had been in touch regarding preparations for the conversations with the Communist Party. She immediately telephoned Sasha; and since his voice sounded a bit distressed, they arranged for her to pay him a visit on the following weekend. On the short journey from the train station to the apartment of a surgeon named Fedin, Irina attempted to persuade Sasha to spend his vacation in the Crimean city of Sudak, where her grandfather was living. When Sasha finally agreed, she called the old gentleman from Fedin's home and asked him to rent Sasha her former room with its view of the sea. This room had been set aside by her grandfather for Irina when he purchased the house. He wanted her to know that she was always welcome—that this was her home, too.

"Are you certain that this Baptist preacher isn't some kind of informer from the KGB?" growled old Sokolov over the telephone.

"Oh, do me a favor and stop suspecting every worker from an officially recognized congregation!" As she said this she winked at Sasha to keep him from getting the wrong idea.

"All right!" her grandfather said. "But you're not going to persuade me that Archbishop Nikodim isn't a KGB puppet!"

"Listen, Grandpa, I'm not a millionaire's daughter; so I can't afford to discuss these subjects on the telephone. Do you want Sasha to have my room or not?"

"Of course! Naturally! Tell him to come ahead! But make it clear to him that he is not to make propaganda for his religion here. My beliefs follow the ways of Pavlov and are not like those of the Baptists. By the way, I'd like to know whether you and Sasha aren't actually already engaged. And when are you coming down here?"

"Well, Grandpa," and her voice took on an edge, "you certainly are getting on my nerves with this interrogation! I am not coming!" Irina was ready to hang up.

"Wait! Please wait, granddaughter!" old Sokolov called out. "Don't be so impatient with an elderly gentleman! I must discuss my will with you. In addition to that, I am worried that something else might happen to you. Would you please come—please, my love? I've got so many things to tell you!"

Her grandfather's voice was pleading, but it also sounded sad and somehow full of concern. Irina's heart melted. "All right, I'll come! But right now please lie down and get some sleep, Dyedushka. You must have your rest!"

"I'm on my way, Irinushka! Until then."

Irina put the receiver on the cradle and remained silent. It was getting close to midnight. Her eyes met those of Sasha, who was seated in an easy chair opposite her. She turned away quickly. Sasha sensed that he meant more to her than she was prepared to admit. Ever since their unexpected meeting in the railroad compartment he had had to think about her again and again. Until now he had had no opportunity to seriously test his feelings toward Irina.

They had come to see Fedin, who was a member of Sasha's congregation, because Sasha wanted to have another physical checkup before he left on his trip. Fedin had also promised to give him some medicines and some advice on what to do during his recuperation. But Fedin had suddenly been called to the clinic, and Sasha and Irina were forced to wait for him. Around midnight he finally reappeared and said he was at their disposal. His wife wished them all good night and withdrew.

"Irina, how did you find out that M. is cooperating with the KGB?" Fedin asked. "Are you certain this is true?"

Irina, who had been seated by a desk until then, moved to sit next to Fedin on the sofa. She had not counted on that kind of question so late at night. But she gladly gave him the information.

"When my grandfather was still living in Gorky," she explained, "some writers, poets and other artists regularly met at his home. Often I was present for these soirees and participated in the discussions. For example, we spoke of what had become of Russian literature. Naturally our discussions during these evenings were quite frank and critical about the fashion in which the Party managed to steer all of Soviet literature in the direction it desired. We were quite open, as a matter of fact, and did not mince words. Well, one day M. appeared at Grandfather's. They had become acquainted during the war. Grandfather trusted him even though he knew that M. had been a Baptist and a preacher on top of it. During one of these evening discussions M. paid exceptionally close attention, taking notes diligently as several of the writers spoke. This aroused no curiosity, since everyone took notes during these discussions. But this time the consequences were quite tragic for my grandfather and his guests. Soon after this, all those who had been present during these conversations were summoned to the KGB, and you know what kind of 'conversations' take place on those occasions. Two women authors were brought to Professor Koshkin. He interrogated them and admitted them to a psychiatric hospital. They were guarded closely as they were taken to Moscow from the western Ukraine and put into the Serbian Institute. No one knows what has become of them. My grandfather experienced some unpleasantries as well and made up his mind to discover who had been the informer. He gave his investigation the code name 'Operation Red Hair.' He devoted several years to this with little success.

"Then one day M. suddenly professed great interest in our dialogue group. Since we did our work in total secrecy, not allowing any information to reach the congregation, there was no way in which any outsider could learn anything about it. We hoped to make things safer for all this way. We would be able to proceed without being disturbed, and no one in the congregation would be endangered. To put it all in a nutshell, M. had been completely informed about every detail of our activities. We decided to speak to him about it. We prayed about this conversation for an entire month. We were afraid to accuse him without cause. In the resulting conversation M. revealed that he was working hand-in-glove with the KGB. My father had warned me about him some time ago. When Grandfather heard of our finding he said, 'You can't change the natural color of red hair.' This became an axiomatic expression among us, and we repeat it whenever we speak of M.'s hopeless situation."

"Is his position really so desperate?" Sasha asked. "Is he never going to be able to free himself from the KGB?"

"Well, he could do it all right," Irina replied. "When his cover was removed at a meeting of the Council of Churches, he could have sent an open letter to every church in Russia. In this note he could have confessed that he had fallen into the KGB's trap. But he was too afraid of the consequences. As a result, the Council of Churches excommunicated him. M. deeply resented this. He then 'publicly confessed' his sins in connection with his 'relationship with the Council of Churches' before the national congress of the All-Union of Baptist and Evangelical Churches. Naturally he was forgiven in the spirit of generosity and was again accepted into the ranks of the All-Union."

"I see," Fedin murmured, rising from the sofa. "Take off your shirt," he said to Sasha, reaching for his stethoscope.

After he had listened to Sasha's pulse and had taken his blood pressure he commented, "Your heart still isn't acting quite right. You need a lot of rest. Try to get plenty of fresh air when you get down there. Take a half–hour walk every morning. And at night, before you go to bed, take another walk by the seaside. I have arranged to get some medicines for you and have written precise instructions about how you are to take them." Fedin handed him a small package and looked into his eyes thoughtfully.

"All right, children, now to bed! Irina, you sleep in Yelena's room. She won't be back until the day after tomorrow."

"I'd rather go back home, Ignaz Petrovitch," Sasha said. "Isn't my bicycle still downstairs in the hallway?" Some weeks earlier he had lent his racing bike to Fedin so he could participate in a bicycle race. Fedin had come in second.

"Shouldn't I accompany you?" Fedin asked.

"No, no; many thanks," Sasha replied. He shook hands with Fedin and Irina and left.

*   *   *

Sasha had always loved his father. But when he thought about it during the train ride it occurred to him that they had always kept secrets from each other. Somehow the mistrust between the registered and unregistered congregations, though always in the background, had also intruded into the relationship between him and his father. Thus they were rarely of one mind when they discussed congregational activity. As a result these conversations often ended in silence. His father had been particularly strange, withdrawn, and morose following his fourteen-day stay at the KGB headquarters. Sasha had the clear impression that since then his father was a broken man. What actually had happened? Suddenly fear enveloped Sasha and he wished he had remained at home.

*   *   *

Where did this nagging sense of unease come from? He had not been particularly disturbed when his father's congregation suddenly had received a room for its worship services in one of the suburbs and had become a registered congregation. On the contrary, this had made it possible to organize many joint meetings between the youth groups of the two churches. Sasha had made frequent use of this opportunity. The young people from both congregations often made trips into the forests together. There they would look for an appropriate site to have their games and Bible studies and to sing songs together. At these times they witnessed to each other about their spiritual experiences with the Lord at work or at school.

Zarapkin, the head of the ministry of religious cults, had watched these joint activities with distrust for some time. He refrained from taking legal action against them because under certain circumstances he could lose control over both congregations at the same time. After being taken to court, the congregation could reject its registered status and go underground. This was precisely what Zarapkin did not want.

Sasha knew his opponent's Achilles heel and adroitly made use of his knowledge for the benefit of both congregations. But would his successor be equally adroit? Would he gain the confidence of the young people? Was he knowledgeable vis-à-vis the KGB? Not only were these questions of real concern to Sasha; but he was also worried that even though the congregation had confirmed the selection of the new man, many of its members continued to view him with a certain degree of distrust. Before all members of the congregation would be ready to accept him without misgivings, the new leader would have to demonstrate that he followed Christ unreservedly and that he had spiritual authority.

The train slowed down suddenly and came to a stop in open country. Apparently there would be a delay of considerable length, for the train's crew was soon standing and talking beside the train. One could hear compartment doors opening all around. Sasha decided to step outside to stretch his legs. He began to look at those who had stepped off the train and discovered a familiar face—that of an elderly gentleman name Golev. Sasha walked over to him and greeted him, "We know each other, don't we? My name is Nikitin. You must know my father."

Golev looked at Sasha's face searchingly. "Nikitin, you say? Oh yes, of course I know him. You are his son? That's wonderful! Which car are you traveling in? Would you like to join me in my compartment, or would it be better if I came to yours?"

Golev had little luggage with him; so they agreed that he would change to Sasha's compartment. This elderly preacher was a member of the Council of Churches and had only recently been released from custody. He was on his way to a meeting of the Council. As soon as Golev was seated opposite Sasha, the train began to move again.

"How is your father?" Golev inquired. "I was told that you were beaten up by rowdies one night. You don't look well, young man!"

"Serge Terentyevitch," replied Sasha, "none of that is very important. I am doing much better now. But I am worried about father. You know him well; so I would like to ask you to help him. I cannot rid myself of the sensation that something is torturing him, that he is not at peace within himself.

You know, after that night when he was taken into custody for two weeks by the KGB, he was hardly recognizable. He is subdued and has a constantly worried expression as if—well, as if he had a bad conscience."

"Do you think he might have declared himself ready to work for the KGB?" Golev asked cautiously.

"No," Sasha said quickly, startled to hear an idea expressed which he had not yet been able to entertain himself. "No, not that—but, perhaps yes?" Sasha fell silent.

The elderly man seemed lost in thought. "You know, I can recall that a colonel in the KGB told one of the brethren on the Council that they now would begin to destroy the Council's fellowship from within. After all these years we certainly know how they accomplish that. They sow discord among the ministers, create disagreements by artificial means, and with all kinds of intrigues attempt to create enmity among these people. It did not take them too long to sign on the old preacher by the name of M. And now they are starting to do it with others. Well, if you're carrying a load on your back it's hard to pretend you haven't got any. Still, no matter what, we shy away from condemning those who have delivered themselves to the KGB monster. In my opinion we should not be trying so hard to unmask them in public as to help them free themselves from these devilish traps. Yes, we stretch out our hands to such people and offer them our help. But many of these men have become so deeply enmeshed that they are afraid for their lives if they stop going along with the KGB. These days we have more problems with the shepherds than we do with their flocks, my dear brother."

The train stopped. Golev looked out of the window and hastily reached for his possessions. "Farewell. May the Lord guide you safely on your journey, dear brother. I will pray for you and for your father." He gave Sasha a firm handshake and got off the train.

Sasha had no inkling that just a few weeks after this encounter Golev would be arrested by the KGB during an ordination ceremony. It was his fourth arrest. Sasha never saw him again.

In Cherson Sasha alighted from the train directly into the bear-hug of his friend, Neverov.

"You've gotten thin," Neverov said in amazement. "It's quite appraent that something is troubling you. Clearly, it is high time for you to find your own dearly beloved and to get married!"

"Come, come, don't make such a scene! People are beginning to notice us!" Sasha grinned. "Let's get out of here quickly."

"We're going, we're going, dear friend." Neverov shifted into gear. "My wife has baked some pirrogi especially in your honor. Absolutely delicious, as you will soon see for yourself!"

8 Secret Mission

Sasha sat at the table with the Neverovs and observed his friend closely. The two men had known each other since childhood. Neverov had not been a Christian for long, yet already had done much on behalf of the persecuted congregations.

Sasha felt at home during his visit with these hospitable people. Neverov's wife was a quiet, unassuming person who reminded Sasha a little of his own mother. She may have appeared a little innocent, but she was a strikingly beautiful woman. She plied Sasha with all kinds of delicacies while her husband looked on lovingly, praising her freely. She protested gently, with an embarrassed smile. Sasha looked on in amusement but said nothing.

After dinner Sasha's friends insisted that he lie down for a while. He accepted their suggestion with thanks and quickly dozed off.

"Get up, my friend; it's already seven o'clock!" He heard Neverov's booming bass voice, which had awakened him.

Sasha was ashamed to have slept so long. He quickly washed himself, had a quick bite with his hosts and hurried off with Neverov at eight.

Hmmm, Sasha thought, wondering about the coughing and rattling of the bus's engine. *The bus certainly appears heavily laden. How peculiar!* They were rolling down a smooth asphalt street, yet the engine continued to make a terrible racket.

"I'm not heavy enough to cause this motor to labor when trying to get up some speed, am I?" he said to Neverov.

His friend merely grinned and said, "I am carrying a precious cargo, my dear friend, which weighs more than the thirty-six students I have to pick up. You'll soon see what I'm talking about. Don't ask so many questions now."

Sasha's curiosity got the better of him, and he examined every seat in the bus. Yet he couldn't find anything, and he sat back down next to his friend, shaking his head in amazement. "You are and always have been a partisan, Neverov!" His friend smiled and concentrated on his driving.

Suddenly Neverov saw a black Volga automobile in the rear-view mirror. The car obviously was following them. He drove close to the curb as if to signify to the driver of the Volga that he could pass. But the black car's driver had no intention of passing. Neverov became uneasy.

"I don't like this Volga that's trailing us," he said. "If we're asked for our papers, you just tell them you're the minister of a registered congregation, which is what you really are. Let me take care of the rest."

Sasha looked back. The Volga was still following them. At a fork in the road Neverov said, "We actually ought to make a turn here. Now, however, we have no choice but to continue straight ahead."

Finally, about three miles farther down the road, the Volga passed the bus and came to a stop. A man got out and motioned to Neverov to pull over and stop by the roadside. As Neverov and Sasha had anticipated, their pursuers were KGB operatives.

"Your passes!" demanded one of the four officials. Neverov and Sasha handed their passes to him, and Neverov also handed over the manifest of his employer.

"You're driving to Feodosia?" the official asked.

"That's right," replied Neverov.

"And what are you transporting in your bus?"

Neverov smiled. "Just the seats on which my young passengers will be seated when I drive them back to where I came from."

"Are you by any chance transporting Bibles in here too?"

one of the members of the secret police inquired.

"Before I can transport Bibles they have to be printed," replied Neverov with reproach in his voice. "You allow us to print only a few thousand every five years, and these have to be enough for millions of people."

The officials merely smirked and proceeded to search the bus. They could not see a trace of a Bible anywhere and finally permitted Neverov to drive on. The Volga remained at the side of the road.

About half an hour later Neverov left the expressway and drove into the nearby village. There he turned off his lights, told Sasha to stay inside the bus and vanished. A few minutes later he returned and continued driving without turning on his headlights. When they reached a small forest he stopped the bus again and said to Sasha, "How would you like to lie down on the rear seat and take a little nap? We'll stop here for about two hours."

Sasha didn't question him and accepted the inevitable. Neverov vanished again. Sasha lay down on the seat but was unable to fall asleep. He got off the bus and began to look at the stars. Suddenly he heard whispering in the bushes. "I've got to unload immediately—tonight," Neverov whispered in his unmistakable bass voice. "You see, someone must have betrayed me. The KGB is hot on my heels."

"This friend of yours, isn't he the minister of a registered congregation?" another voice asked. "Maybe he turned you in."

"No way! We have checked Nikitin out; he is totally trustworthy. Irina Sokolova is a friend of his and even recommended him for our work."

In the darkness Sasha felt his face turning red. What right did Neverov have to call Irina his friend? He hadn't even mentioned her!

"All right," the other voice replied, "wait here. I'll come back with a car." The two voices stopped. Sasha hurriedly climbed back into the bus and lay down on the rear seat.

Shortly thereafter Neverov got in and made himself comfortable on one of the front seats. Soon Sasha heard the quiet, regular breathing that indicated Neverov had fallen asleep. He had learned to sleep in all sorts of positions and at any time of the day so as to have enough energy for those frequent occasions when he had to remain awake for an entire night.

Eventually Sasha apparently had dozed off too. But some noises woke him up again. When he raised his head he saw men taking stacks of New Testaments and concordances from under the seats and handing them out the windows. Others then packed them away in the trunk of an automobile.

When another car arrived, Sasha was asked to get up. He stepped out of the bus without asking questions. Neverov patted him on the shoulder and indicated, "We'll be done soon. Why don't you take a little walk? We won't be long."

The roosters were beginning to crow, and the sky in the east had begun to turn grey. When they had completed unloading, Neverov called to Sasha and asked him to come back. They got into the bus. Neverov said a brief prayer and they drove on again.

They had gone not quite thirty miles when another Volga sedan passed them and ordered them to stop.

"Where did you vanish so suddenly, Neverov?" one of the KGB operatives asked menacingly. "Why did you leave your planned route?"

"Why?" asked Neverov innocently. "We stopped in a forest for a few hours and had a little sleep."

The men walked around the bus and looked at the springs. "And how do you explain that the bus is much lighter now than it was yesterday?" one of them asked Neverov.

Sasha thought his heart would burst inside him—it was beating so wildly. He held his breath and waited for Neverov's reply. He quietly prayed for his friend.

Neverov looked calmly at the KGB official. "You know, you judge this bus's weight by the springs, but I am guided

Sasha had, of course, not mentioned anything about the books. Trick questions such as this were always asked to catch one off guard. Sasha simply looked at the man in amazement. For a few moments neither of them said a word.

"I find it amazing that no one seems to be interested," Sasha said eventually, "in who was shooting at Neverov. Were you the ones who made this attempt on Neverov's life?"

The civilian rose from his chair and yelled in agitation. "You're forgetting yourself, aren't you, Nikitin? Do we have to give you a lesson to remind you?"

The interrogator had said too much. A lieutenant colonel in the KGB happened to walk in just in time, ordered the interrogator to leave the room, and turned to Sasha. "Allow me to apologize for my co-worker. Nikitin, you're our man because you're young and you've already begun a brilliant career with the Baptists. You're only thirty and yet you've been a successful preacher for many years. I understand that my Moscow comrades want to recommend you to the Moscow leadership. You will be able to perform many good services for us there.

"You know, time and again religious books are being smuggled into our country. We cannot permit the distribution of these volumes because among them are the public statements of Solzhenitsyn, for example, which have been published in foreign countries, as well as other anti-Soviet literature. This is subversive writing which turns the people against the Communist Party and against the policies of the state. We've known for a long time that Neverov cultivates relationships with foreign countries."

"I'm awfully sorry," Sasha interjected, "but I really cannot be of help to you. I would be overjoyed if my congregation had at least one Bible per family. If the state wishes to prevent the smuggling of Bibles from foreign countries, then it must allow a sufficient number of Bibles to be printed in this country to fulfill the need. And it must allow Bibles to be sold at any book counter."

"Sure! Are you crazy?" the lieutenant colonel roared.

"We're waging unconditional war against all religion! And you want us to allow unlimited publication of Bibles and thereby support these religions on top of it? We do permit the printing of a few thousand Bibles every five or six years, and that ought to be more than enough."

"Yes, you do permit that," Sasha retorted, "but half of the Bibles go to the atheistic propaganda people. Another batch goes to foreign countries for propaganda purposes. Finally only a few hundred Bibles remain for the use of several million believers. And these are seized again during your house searches. Under these circumstances, is it any wonder that we welcome it when people bring us Bibles from outside the Soviet Union?"

"Aha, so you're in cahoots with this group. Now I understand everything. I can see now that your father has succeeded in diverting you from the right path and is leading you astray toward an anti-government attitude—to disobey the government."

"You're wrong about that. My father hasn't had the slightest thing to do with it," Sasha said. His heart ached at the very thought of his father. What could it mean? Why did he feel so miserable every time his father became the subject of a conversation?

"If you have no further questions to ask me in regard to the attempt to murder Neverov," Sasha announced, "I'd like to leave." The officer let him go after again warning him to report to the KGB as soon as he returned home.

Sasha set off on his journey again. When he had located the families of believers in the town and had told them what had happened to Neverov, they promised to take care of the injured man. After lunch Sasha returned to the hospital to visit Neverov. This time he was not asleep. He looked pale and worn out, as if he had just come through a rough fight in the boxing ring. But he brightened when he saw Sasha enter.

Sasha squeezed his hand and inquired, "Well, how do you feel?"

Neverov grinned and answered in a whisper, "Think how

much joy there would be in heaven if the would-be murderer repented!" Then he fell asleep again, a smile still on his lips. Sasha gently replaced Neverov's hand on top of the covers and quietly walked out. Outside on the street he ran into the local congregation's youth group, which had come together to pay the sick man a visit. Sasha, however, urged them to come back a bit later. He remained in Krasnoperekopsk overnight and waited for the arrival of Neverov's wife. Then he took the train to Sudak.

*   *   *

Once in Sudak Sasha had no trouble in finding the home of Irina's Grandfather Sokolov. But his trip had taken a lot out of him and he could hardly wait to retire for some much-needed rest. So when Sokolov and Pelagea saw just how exhausted their guest was they showed him to his room without much ado, brought him a cup of tea, as was the Russian custom, and left him alone. He fell asleep immediately.

He awakened to the sound of a stubborn knocking on his door. He sat up, rubbed his eyes and staggered to the door. Sokolov stood outside, a telegram in his hand. Sasha tore the envelope open with trembling hands and read the words, "Father dead. Please come at once. Mother." The color drained from Sasha's face.

Old Sokolov said quietly, "I'll call a taxi for you. If you show this telegram at the airport, they will allow you to skip the normal procedure and will sell you a ticket."

Sasha nodded gratefully. His eyes brimmed with tears. Conflicting emotions swept over him: a mute sorrow for the deceased person; sorrow for his mother; a deep regret at not having been present during his father's last hours. But he also felt a sense of relief which he was unwilling to acknowledge even to himself.

Just three hours had elapsed when Sasha stood at the door of his home embracing his weeping mother. "Don't cry,

Mother," he consoled her. "Father, you see, now has escaped all danger. He is with the Lord, of course. But we must still face many a battle."

Natasha looked at him, her eyes filled with tears. "I still have to tell you a great many things, my boy."

He nodded wordlessly and walked with her toward the table on which they had laid his father. He stood with his arm around his mother as he studied the deceased man's face for a long time. In death Andrey Nikitin had a solemn, almost triumphant expression on his face. It appeared to Sasha that at the very end his father had scored yet one more important victory. He could not move his gaze from the dead man. His entire childhood, his whole life was tied inseparably to that of this man. Suddenly Sasha sobbed. He let his head sink down onto his mother's shoulder and wept. She stroked his head silently.

"Oh, Dad," he whispered, "how little of you I understood. . . ."

The house began to fill with members of Christian congregations. Sasha began to make preparations for the burial. In Russia it is permissible for the deceased to remain at his home until the day of interment. Customarily friends and acquaintances come to help with the burial preparations.

On the day of the funeral nearly a thousand people gathered in the Nikitins' courtyard to accompany the dead man to his final resting place. Members of the registered congregations as well as of the unregistered congregation were present. They stood together in harmony, mourning a man whom they had all loved and respected. This man's death seemed suddenly to reconcile them.

Oh, Lord, how did Satan succeed in turning us against each other? Sasha thought, full of grief.

9 The Signature

What had happened to Andrey Nikitin? Why had the KGB kept him under detention for so long a period?

This would have remained a secret had it not been for the notes he covertly made before his death. Sasha and Vassiley held back their emotions with great difficulty as Natasha read her husband's diary aloud. The events did not follow each other in chronological order. Apparently he had made notes during his imprisonment.

"They arrested me. But this did not shake my composure. I've been expecting it all the time. Something inside me broke when I learned they had beaten up my Sasha that night."

At this point Nikitin interrupted his personal narrative and inserted the draft of a sermon about the lost son, based on the fifteenth chapter of Luke. The thoughts expressed were so profound and the content so gripping that the three were unable to tear themselves away from it. Andrey seemed to be speaking about himself, about his own journey home. Natasha found it difficult to continue reading. She got up and put on a kettle of water for tea.

"It will take a long time," she said. "I think we ought to read through everything in order."

When she returned she read on, "I was detained at the militia station for an hour. Around midnight they took me to a KGB detention cell, where Captain Samovarov spoke with me. He was very polite. We had tea together. He indicated that he, too, was worried about Sasha's fate. Zarapkin had gone far beyond his assignment when he attempted to accuse me of having beaten up my own son merely because he was the preacher of a registered congregation. 'But you must understand our side of this too, Nikitin. We are afraid you will attribute the incident involving your son to us. For this reason we have to detain you here until everything has been cleared up. We have had a bed put into one of our own private rooms. Surely you can spend a few nights there.'

"I shrugged my shoulders in amazement. It seemed like a fairy tale, this polite, agreeable, almost gentle tone and this cozy atmosphere. I knew all my protests and objections would get me nowhere, and I followed the captain. We rode to the first floor from the interrogation cells. There Samovarov made me wait in the hallway and entered room 87 alone. He emerged with a key and motioned for me to follow him. We rode up to the fourth floor. Soft carpeting in the hallways and the stairways silenced our footsteps. The captain opened the door to a room which bore no number and asked me to step inside.

" 'Make yourself at home, Nikitin. We've prepared two rooms for you here. One is a bedroom and the other will serve as your workroom.' Samovarov smiled as he said that. He showed me a bathtub with a shower-head and a toilet. Never had I even dreamed about a place like this. There was an enormous radio in one corner of the bedroom. On a table next to the window there was a tape recorder. At the right of the window was a wooden bed which I had not noticed at first. The captain walked over to the table and turned on the tape recorder. I heard religious music. I couldn't trust my own ears! An orchestra was playing 'Silent Night, Holy Night.' The fact that this was a Christmas recording did not seem to bother them in the least.

"Still smiling, Samovarov walked toward the door and said, 'Sleep well, Nikitin. We will explain everything to your wife and calm her fears. We will make a tape recording of our conversation with her; you can listen to it afterward so you won't be concerned about anything. Have a good rest, Andrey.'

"I felt a pleasant kind of lethargy. I could not make sense out of the series of events. The religious music and the pleasant surroundings made me sleepy and took my mind off the realities of my situation. I was soon sound asleep. I cannot even recall taking off my clothes. Yet when I awoke I was in bed, undressed. A kind, gentle voice said from the adjoining room, 'Andrey, breakfast is ready!'

"I heard soft footsteps next door and the sound of a door being pulled shut. Still confused, I began to get dressed. I hardly recognized my suit. It had been cleaned and neatly pressed. I opened the window. Swallows were circling the house, and starlings sang merrily in their tree house. I did momentarily wonder who had built the birdhouses.

"After breakfast Samovarov reappeared. 'Well, how did you sleep, Nikitin?' he asked. I was unable to think clearly. I was ashamed of enjoying my stay. Christian melodies continued to come out of the tape recorder. I had the distinct impression that nothing ususual had happened. In fact, I thought I was in the seventh heaven. I couldn't even get my mouth open to answer Samovarov.

"He seemed to understand my condition, sat down on the couch and started talking casually. 'Zarapkin told me that your congregation will be registered in the next few days and will function independent of the Council of Churches. You can do as you please. He even told me that you can now travel to foreign countries.' He rose again and added, 'I would like to ask you to have lunch with me at a restaurant.'

"Silently I shrugged my shoulders. I seemed to be half asleep, although I felt really good. He smiled and left me alone again.

"An hour later there was a knock on my door. A civilian stepped inside. He smiled reassuringly, extended his hand and introduced himself. 'Siniszin is my name. I'm visiting from Moscow and decided to look you up here in the prison.'

" 'Who are you?' I inquired.

" 'I work on religious matters, Nikitin. I work in the gov-

ernment office with responsibilities in this area. I was told
about the incidents that have occurred here and expect to
stay until everything is cleared up.'

"Siniszin regarded me silently for a long time. Something
familiar about him caused me to stay on my guard. Yet for
some reason I was unable to think clearly. It was as if my
brain had been paralyzed. I could concentrate only on the
things around me in the apartment. I was unable to think
about my wife or my son. I was not even surprised that this
man addressed me as if he were a close friend. I felt as if my
reasoning powers had been taken away from me. It was
horrible how pleasant this was.

"Eventually Siniszin said, 'Well, Andrey, have you totally
forgotten me? I'm Lena's brother!'

" 'Lena's brother?' I exclaimed. Lena was my first wife,
Sasha's mother. My mind went into high gear. My head
buzzed with memories. During the war Lena and I were taken
into custody as 'enemies of the people' because I was a
preacher. Lena was pregnant. Though we were jailed in different camps we were located in the same village. Prisoners
who were trustees and therefore permitted to move freely
outside the camps took my letters to Lena and returned with
her replies. Under these circumstances she was really very
courageous. Then the time came for her to have her baby. She
died during childbirth, but our little son remained alive.
Natasha had her baby at the same time, but her child died
soon after birth. So when I requested that Natasha breast-
feed my son, I was given this permission. I was not allowed
to go to Lena's funeral. That's why Sasha was raised by
Natasha. . . ."

"Mother," Sasha suddenly interrupted, "is this what you
have been trying to tell me?"

"Yes, Sasha, that's it."

They were alone. Vassiley had quietly left the room.

*   *   *

Vassiley had intended to stay at his parents' home only for the weekend. Sasha thus called him up the following morning to tell hım how much he wanted Vassiley present when they read the rest of the diary.

Vassiley came gladly. He found Sasha unusually clearheaded and felt that Natasha was also more relaxed than usual. They sat down in the same places they had occupied the night before. Natasha returned to the diary.

"A few years later my son was put into a children's home. Natasha and I were released from prison on the same day. I asked her to become my wife, and she agreed. We were married, got Sasha out of the children's home, and moved to this city.

"Now I finally was able to remember this man Siniszin. Yes, he was Lena's brother. But—hold it! Hadn't he also been an evangelist in those days? Of course! Again I tried to recall the past. Now I remembered. He was the reason we were all taken into custody! Churches still were prohibited in those days. A bit later Stalin allowed a church or two to open again. Let's see if I can remember those days.... Ah yes, we often assembled in my apartment to read the Bible and to pray. Then Misha Siniszin turned up—accompanied by the militia. That put an end to everything. Everyone who preached the Christian religion was arrested. Only the officially 'blessed' evangelist in our district—Misha Siniszin—was not arrested. Everyone except me perished in the prison camps.

"O Siniszin, Siniszin! And there he sat across from me now, grinning.

"Like a shadow, a thought crossed my addled brain. I tried to seize hold of it. My head buzzed as though I were a teakettle. Now I had it! *Serge Gratchov, the Kuibishev preacher, lies on his deathbed. We are all assembled around his bed. He gazes at each of us, one after another, and asks, 'Have you forgiven him?' No one asks who is to be forgiven. Everyone is silent. 'Forgive him,' Gratchov whispers with his last ounce of energy, 'as Christ has forgiven you.'*

"In my mind's eye I saw another scene. *The preacher Golo-*

vatzky is on his deathbed. He has been starved in prison. His death-struggle is horrible. But why? Normally the starving die so easily. 'My brethren, tell him that I have forgiven him. . . .' And Golovatzky dies. These are his last words.

"I saw a glass of water and an aspirin on the table. At least I thought it was an aspirin. Just as on the day before, I reached for it, swallowed it. Funny, but this stuff didn't work like aspirin! I began to feel so light and so happy!

" 'Did you all forgive me?' Siniszin suddenly asked with great seriousness.

" 'Naturally we did! And how have things gone for you, Misha?'

"Misha drummed on the table with his fingers. 'I was so young in those days. I had to go to the front lines and fight. I was decorated as a "hero of the Soviet Union." I joined the Party. Now I'm working in the ideological division of the Central Committee. I've been thinking about you. Above all I'm interested in Sasha. I don't have any children myself. My wife fought on the front lines too.'

" 'What is her name?'

" 'Nina Perepelova.'

"As an eighteen-year-old girl, Nina Perepelova had been in charge of the choir of the congregation in a neighboring town.

"Siniszin continued, 'We volunteered to go to the front. After the war we attended the university together.'

"Captain Samovarov's arrival interrupted our conversation. 'Men, it's time for lunch!' he exclaimed brightly. 'Let's go; we'll drive to a restuarant!'

"Samovarov took me by the hand like a small child and led me outside. A Volga limousine was waiting for us in the inner courtyard. We drove through the entire town. I looked out through the windows eagerly in hopes of seeing someone I knew, but I saw no one I recognized. We came to a restaurant in the woods at the edge of town; I had no idea such a fancy restaurant even existed. We were shown to a reserved table by a window. Samovarov did the ordering. In my entire life I have never eaten like that! Samovarov told all sorts of interesting stories while we ate.

"My thoughts revolved around Siniszin and my son, Sasha. Samovarov seemed to guess it, for he suddenly said, 'Your son is out of danger, Nikitin. We've spoken with your wife. She knows where he is but will not tell us. Reportedly she was told nothing more than that he is all right. We have taped everything. She sends you her greetings. We told her you will go free as soon as all of the accompanying circumstances have been cleared up.'

"The captain then turned the conversation to all kinds of jolly events, most likely because he wanted to divert me from my thoughts about my family.

"After the meal Siniszin suddenly disappeared. Samovarov drove me around the countryside and we took a long walk. During our chat he kept dropping tidbits like, 'I can't for the life of me understand why some of our people have tortured members of your congregations, like Moiseyev or Chmara, to death. In my opinion the state should not stick its nose into religious affairs.'

"I was surprised but accepted everything at face value. We spoke of the status of the Christian faith in Russia. Occasionally he changed the conversation to discuss the All-Union Council. He opined that this body was engaged in highly useful activity. He said it was indeed praiseworthy that the leadership of the All-Union supported the liberation movements in Africa. He praised our brothers in the All-Union to the skies.

" 'We probably went too far by compelling the leadership to follow our instructions. But the legislation which has just passed prohibits us from dabbling in the internal affairs of the church anymore.' He said all this casually, shifting on easily to another topic. He conveyed Natasha's warmest greetings. She had heard my voice on the tapes. Naturally she had to agree that she would never mention this to anyone else.

"During the following days I became quite friendly with Samovarov. We were able to discuss the Bible for hours on end, a book which he knew better than I did. He expounded the Bible eagerly, spoke of the imminent return of Christ and things like that until I began to wonder why he was working for the KGB.

" 'We Communists know very well that Christ existed,' he said. 'We also know He rose again! It's your liberal theologians who deny the divinity of Christ, not us. We know that a human being cannot rise from the dead by himself. It must have been a supernatural power that awakened Christ. You call this power "God," while we simply don't know what name to give it. Historical sources corroborate the fact that Christ actually did rise from the dead. Those of our scientists who have studied this express no doubts about it. The so-called atheists have to deny it in order to bring about a reeducation of society. To do this they quote mainly from the statements of certain western theologians.'

"I could not understand why he was saying all these things. On one occasion he hurried into my room and said, 'Zarapkin has made the material being used against your son available to me. It is evidence that your son set up Sunday schools and Bible study groups for young people and for women.'

"He threw the statements from the witnesses on my bed. By that time I had already spent fifteen days in the KGB building. I began to read the statements. Everything dealt with the facts as I knew them. There was even a doctor's testimony to the effect that Sasha would not be able to survive detention in a prison. . . ."

"Evidently he did not notice that this was a fake and that such a doctor's certificate is never issued," Vassilley commented, irritated.

Natasha read on.

" 'We must do everything we can to keep your son from being imprisoned,' Samovarov said very quietly. I looked at him in amazement. 'Siniszin was particularly insistent about this,' he continued. 'Sasha is, of course, his nephew. I am very concerned as well. Actually, if Siniszin hadn't been my good friend, the case of Sasha would have been laid at your doorstep and you would have been sent to jail for five years for doing bodily harm to another person!'

"I listened to him with my mouth open in surprise.

" 'It's time to get you back home, Nikitin! Please forgive us for attributing your stay here to resistance against the rightful government. Your son is well cared for.' With that he departed.

"I was led to an office where they put my discharge document in front of me and asked me to sign it. I was so glad to finally get away that I did not consider the document very long—did not read its contents but simply signed it. Samovarov shook my hand firmly when I left. In my own mind I was already home."

At this point there was a new outline for a sermon entitled, "The Joy in Heaven at a Sinner's Repentance."

Natasha had some difficulty in reading all of this again. This report about her husband's sufferings made his death and the parting from him even more painful.

The three of them looked for more documents which would supply additional information about Nikitin's contacts with Samovarov. They wanted to discover everything they could about possible pressure tactics which might have led to a change in his personality. Finally, after reading all the way to page 96, they found some clues.

"He who does not understand the soul of a Russian cannot possibly understand this nation," Nikitin had written. "It is possible that no other people have ever, despite their highly sensitive natures, permitted themselves to be betrayed, persecuted, and treated so badly. This unique characteristic of the Russian people helps them to find positive elements even in the present government, despite its political adventurism! A Russian might even identify with those in power without acknowledging their deceptive ways. Perhaps he simply does not want to see things as they really are. If this people were actually able to launch another revolution, they might well only exchange one dictatorship for another, and that a vastly more cruel one."

What did he mean by that?

"Here's yet another notebook." Natasha handed it to Sasha. "I've given it a quick look, but he wrote in Latin script, probably in the German language, which I could not understand. So I put it aside again."

The two young men eagerly devoured the material in this notebook. Oh, how wise Andrey had been to use Latin script on these pages! A half page was indeed in the German language, and his wife could not read that; but the rest was in Russian.

"Well, I'm free again. Sasha is recovering slowly but still needs much rest. My congregation has been registered in its new suburban location. We are attempting to keep up good contacts with Sasha's congregation. Zarapkin has promised not to interfere with our internal affairs.

"Sasha has left to join his friends in the Crimea. I imagine he may want to resign completely from his congregational duties. He has become very withdrawn. On one occasion he told me it is important to start Bible study groups in all the congregations. That way Christians can gain sufficient biblical knowledge to resist atheism and to be prepared for periods of isolation from other Christians.

"Samovarov visits me again and again. He is kindhearted and sympathetic. Today Natasha and I accompanied Samovarov and his family on an excursion. We really enjoyed ourselves. I believe that the Lord may still draw this man to Himself. Samovarov and I discussed the Bible a lot, and his wife listened attentively. Shenya and Lonya, Samovarov's sons, asked me to play the guitar and urged Natasha to sing a psalm for them."

At this point Psalm 121 was inserted in the notebook.

Andrey had copied it all down, underlining "He will not suffer your foot to slip, . . ." and the verse preceding it. Then he continued his report.

"Samovarov visited me in our house of prayer. He brought me medicine for my heart, which has given me trouble in recent days. These drugs have the same effect as those so-called aspirin tablets. They take away the feelings of stress from which I normally suffer."

After inserting a new date Andrey wrote, "He was here again. He always manages to come when there is no one home to see him. Today he told me that the Council of Churches had exposed an informer named M. Imagine, M. actually had succeeded in becoming a member of the Council's leadership! Samovarov said that M. had been recruited by Siniszin. He was really angry that M. had been exposed. The KGB feels it absolutely must discover the underground publishing house! Why? Our brethren merely print Bibles. Why not let them print them? But no, everything has to be crushed and destroyed."

Two days later: "Samovarov tells me the government is inclined to give me permission to travel to Canada. It is very important for the Christians of Russia to begin contacts with the Mennonites of North America. 'But what will happen when I tell them I spent ten years in prison because I was a preacher?' I asked.

" 'All kinds of people were in prison while Khrushchev and Stalin were in control. You can talk about whatever you want,' he responded. This sounds very fishy."

A day later: "Zarapkin asked me to come to his office. He wanted to speak with me. I did as he asked.

" 'Samovarov has already told you we would have no objections if you were to visit Mennonite churches in America,' he said. I agreed. Zarapkin went on, 'Outside Russia, people still believe Christians continue to be persecuted in the USSR. But you yourself surely know we are concerned only with those who encroach upon the honor and dignity of

Soviet citizens. You must hold meetings in America and make it clear to those people that this is merely slander, that you have been in prison yourself in the past, but that today no one is hailed into court because of religious convictions.'

" 'Well—well, . . .' I interrupted. 'Hundreds of Christians of various denominations are in prison today; yes, even today. Besides, you still have not stopped your campaign to cleanse the Soviet mind of these religious anachronisms. All I can say in a foreign country is that you tolerate religion on paper only.'

"Zarapkin sneered sardonically. 'What are you trying to do now, Nikitin? You have signed an agreement to work for us under the cover, "the holy one." Why are you being so pigheaded at this time?'

" 'What?' I exclaimed. 'I am supposed to have signed a paper which says I will work for the benefit of the KGB and your ideology? Never! That's nothing but a lie!' Suddenly I was clearheaded. I was able to follow events and to reason clearly. And I was much too grateful for this gift to tolerate even the slightest befogging of the facts.

"Zarapkin stared at me wildly. 'What? You're going to tell me Samovarov hasn't mentioned anything to you yet? When you were released you signed a document in which you obligated yourself to work for us!'

"Now I really began to feel sick. Despite that, I was sure I had signed nothing but my release papers. Zarapkin disappeared, returning in ten minutes. He placed a paper bearing an official seal before me. This declared that I had obligated myself to work on behalf of the KGB and the ideological department of the Party inside Russia or in any foreign country. Yes, they had given me the nickname 'the holy one.' Suddenly I became very calm and said, 'You really led me by the nose—me, the simpleton. You shoved this under my nose instead of the release certificate. That ought to be a good lesson for all believers in this country. As for me, I certainly will leave no stone unturned. I definitely will tell my congregation all about this today.'

"Zarapkin grinned wickedly. 'So we haven't worked you over enough, I understand. All your struggling, however, is useless, Nikitin. If you refuse we'll simply throw your son into prison.' He had struck my most sensitive spot. I rose without another word and went home."

Natasha interrupted Sasha and Vassiley as they were reading. "When he returned home he embraced me and whispered, 'O my dearest, my love! The sons of darkness are really more clever than the children of the light!'

"He walked into his room and made these final notes. He then asked me to look for Golev's address because he wanted to write to him. But at that moment Samovarov entered the courtyard below. Andrey saw him and reached for his heart. I caught him before he fell and helped him to sit down as gently as I could. Yet even before I heard Samovarov's knock, Andrey had died."

10 Bible Study Cells

His father's death shook Sasha more deeply than he was willing to admit. At home he discovered that the preacher Golev had been arrested again. Clearly Golev had not had an opportunity to speak with Sasha's father after his release.

After the funeral Sasha invited the preachers and elders of both congregations to his home. He attempted to establish an open exchange of ideas with these friends of his father. In addition, he had set himself another goal. The congregation he had served for the past few years still considered him its spiritual leader. This discouraged the new preacher even though it was flattering to Sasha. When one of the younger brethren brought this to Sasha's attention it made him realize how difficult it was to divest himself of the responsibility for the congregation without taking on an equally important task elsewhere. He definitely would have to help the new preacher gain the trust of this congregation.

The new preacher was an older man who had experienced many difficulties during a period of poor health. Sasha suspected he would have difficulty withstanding the pressure exerted by the official in charge of religious cults. He had already forbidden the church's young people to take part in the Saturday evening Bible study, a source of great dissatisfaction among the young. A group of them had moved over to a neighboring congregation, which Sasha's father had served until Zarapkin had assigned this congregation space in the suburbs. Sasha had decided to discuss this prohibition with his successor in private.

Natasha was finding it difficult to cope with the task of putting Andrey's written estate in order.

"Look, read this!" With these words Natasha showed Sasha one of his father's old diaries.

When Sasha read this diary he was again deeply disturbed. He was unable to explain why his parents never had spoken to him about this matter.

When he glanced up from the document and saw his mother he was suddenly aware how much he loved her.

"I am sorry, son," she said, "that we never talked to you about this. I couldn't find it in my heart to do that. I loved your father. But the old wound never seemed to heal over. I also didn't know what you would think, while still a boy, of a mother who brought an illegitimate child into the world and then married your father, the preacher."

Sasha embraced his mother.

"I do understand, Mother. Everything is so unexpected, and I've got to absorb it, but I know what you mean. During the last few weeks I have had so little time for you. All that is going to change now. First of all, you are going to Sudak with me. I've been offered a position there, and if everything goes well we will move there." After a brief pause he continued, "You have been a wonderful mother to me, and I will not leave you uncared for." He gently stroked her graying hair.

When Sasha's friends finally arrived they found the young man and his mother in animated conversation, already discussing the details of the move.

Sasha asked that his friends follow him into his father's study.

"I've had this burden for a long time," he began, "and I want to discuss it with you. You are well aware that the laws covering religious practices are not designed merely to inhibit Christian activities but to achieve the gradual destruction of everything that is Christian. In other words, all our hopes and beliefs have been officially condemned to death.

"Jesus Christ told us to evangelize the world, but we are preoccupied with only one idea: how can we survive? Stalin knew very well what methods to use in attacking religion. After all, he attended a theological seminary himself. As a result, the noose is being tightened further year after year. We can be grateful to the leaders of the Council of Churches for the fact that we aren't already dangling in it. But it won't be long before the government enlists us in the battle against the Council's leaders. At the same time, it is clear that the government is afraid to exert too much pressure on us now. They are afraid we might move over to the Council's side and thereby escape the direct control of the KGB. They want to avoid this; that is why they aren't tightening the noose too quickly now. I do know, however, that the KGB is using all its resources to undermine the Council of Churches from within. Those who lead the persecuted church are guilty of mistakes as well. And when the KGB succeeds in sowing the seeds of disunity among them the KGB is the winner. For that reason we cannot afford to be neutral observers in this struggle. We must plan how to make our ministry more fruitful. This is why I invited you here. We are clearly not to work against government laws. There is, however, an alternative approach and that is Scripture. I urge you, my brethren, to invite all Christians in our city, regardless of church affiliation, to join in community Bible studies to equip us for the times when we will be isolated, and for the severe persecution we can expect."

Twenty pairs of eyes stared at Sasha in undisguised amazement.

"Should this be modeled after the ecumenism of the World Council of Churches?" old Lupa asked. Sasha was grateful that Lupa had come with the rest. They needed courageous old men like him more than ever before. Lupa was simply irreplaceable.

"I anticipated this question," Sasha replied. "But I am thinking about something quite different. If we begin to make contacts with leaders of other Christian groups in this city and in the immediate suburbs, and if they accept our suggestion to meet for Bible study at a predetermined time—

perhaps once a month at the outset—then we would be able to meet in private homes. If no more than two representatives of each of the twelve or so Christian congregations were to become part of such a Bible study, it would then have approximately twenty-four members. Joining together in the reading of the Bible will help us understand one another better and recognize special needs and problems of our brothers and sisters in other congregations. These groups should be restricted geographically so that no one who takes part would have to walk very far."

Sasha stopped to give the new preacher a chance. He could see he was opposed to the plan before he opened his mouth.

"But such a plan would be against the law. We would be inviting trouble with the minister for religious cults."

Sasha had to admit he was right. "Of course. And we would get into trouble not only with them but also with the KGB. But that is only half as bad as not finding a way to broaden the outlook in our groups. We are in danger of becoming totally isolated from the larger body of Christ.

"It will not be easy to bring all believers of different movements under one roof. It will be even more difficult to make it clear to our friends that they are not to force their personal views on people with different convictions. We will read the Bible together and then we will give every person an opportunity to share briefly his insights about the part we have just heard."

"And what is supposed to be the result of this?" one of the oldest members of the group asked.

That was precisely what Sasha had taken such great pains to explain during the past few minutes. So he began all over again.

"We must gather around the Word of God in order to discover what it tells us about the times we are living in. We must find how together we can withstand the tricks of the devil. We can no longer afford to use our gatherings solely for the purpose of debating theological ideas. These will fall into place when we listen together to what the Bible has to say."

The new preacher got up and declared, "No, brethren, this is against the law and I cannot agree to it."

Old Lupa stared at him with raised eyebrows. "Oh, no!" he thundered, "this is *not* against the law! This is against the noose they've drawn around our necks—around yours, too." He moved toward the preacher, his finger pointed straight at him. The preacher recoiled in obvious fear.

"My friends, I cannot agree to this proposal by Nikitin. It is against the law!" the preacher persisted. Then he left the room.

Everyone was silent.

"Oh, Sasha," sighed Lupa, "why did you leave us?"

After a brief period Sasha said what he never would have expressed were his successor still in the room.

"After that terrible night I simply couldn't carry the weight of this job any longer."

"Are you afraid they will totally—?" Lupa did not finish his sentence. He looked at Sasha inquiringly.

"No, no. That's not it. Look, my brethren, I had a full-time job as a bookkeeper in the Institute besides my work as a preacher. The dean's office kept playing all sorts of games with the money. I just cannot go along with such shady deals. I was just barely able to avoid having to falsify entries on the balance sheets, but I know for certain that I cannot continue to do that. I tried to find another job here in this city but could not find one. I cannot in good conscience live off the congregation. Now I've been offered a job in the Crimea. I feel—and my mother thinks so too—that I ought to take it. My mother will go with me. It is up to you to help the new man. He will need your aid."

Dr. Fedin, who had not spoken for a long time, interjected, "The laborer is worthy of his hire. You would not be a burden to us."

"That may be true, Fedin. But you yourself don't know

how much longer they will tolerate you in the clinic. I have heard that the KGB knows about your contacts with the Council of Churches. They'll fire you sooner or later."

"Then I'll work as a street cleaner," was Fedin's calm reply. "My family will go along with it. My wife assured me months ago of her support. On top of that, we've consciously been cutting down on our needs so that eventually we will have the financial resources for more important things."

"Let's get it out in the open—it's for the publishing company!" one of the brethren growled unhappily.

"And so? Do you have anything against that?" Fedin responded quickly. An awkward silence followed.

"How lovely, how beautiful—," was heard suddenly from Lupa's corner. Fedin roared with laughter.

"You are made of pure gold, Lupa. Too bad you're so healthy. I'd be glad to visit you more often."

"That time will come, my man," the old man consoled Fedin.

The discussion continued until midnight. The brethren concluded that Sasha's suggestion could be implemented if it were done with caution and wisdom. No one was under any illusion that this was going to be an easy task.

*   *   *

Behind prison walls, Christians of various denominations did not get into debates about various theological fine points. Each had just one desire: to possess a Bible and to talk with the others about the Christ they had in common, to think about Him and to commune with Him. Shouldn't it be possible to have this kind of unity outside prison walls?

That turned out to be a tough struggle. The local ministers created the most difficulty with their continual references to the law. Others were afraid of run-ins with people who had different ideas, and of getting into bitter theological disputes. Some were afraid of losing their "sheep" to other congregations. It certainly was not easy making these people understand that millions of Evangelical, Orthodox, and Catholic Christians could not read the Bible because they simply had none and that because of this they had no idea what Jesus Christ expected from them. This was why Sasha continued to believe God would bless these small cells. He was certain God had called him to do this work, though he knew that sooner or later it would result in imprisonment.

When Sasha later described these plans to Grandfather Sokolov the old man muttered, "That's exactly what I've been saying—you are determined to turn me into a Baptist!" Hundreds of other Christians, when they first heard about this scheme, reacted the same way.

Sasha's answer to all was, "No, but I want you all to become thoroughgoing, consistent Christians who know the Bible and read it daily—if you have one—and thereby learn to discern the will of God."

He had less difficulty with members of the intelligentsia. Later he was to find that true in the Crimea as well. There he succeeded in turning Vladimir Sokolov into a skillful and devoted leader of such a Bible study group. The elderly man began by reading the Bible himself and then putting what he had read into practice. He then shared his love for God's Word with a former member of the Tscheka (secret police) who was converted through this witness. In time Sokolov gathered a group of about thirty persons, most of whom belonged to the educated class in the population.

Despite his literary and his more recent religious interests, Sokolov had plenty of time to think about the events of the past. When he did so, he was reminded again and again of the kidnapping of his son's daughter. This was a memory he would dearly love to straighten out before he died.

*   *   *

During all those years Natasha had never known what had happened to her former fiancé, Yuri Sokolov. After she was told—as Sokolov had ordered—that her little daughter had died, she had tried to repress this memory.

When she was released from prison she was told that Yuri had died "while performing official duties." Some time later someone had denied this. Yet whatever actually might have become of Yuri, Natasha was certain of one thing. She could never, as a Christian, spend her life as the wife of a KGB functionary. God had led her to Andrey Nikitin and to his son, Sasha, and she was satisfied with that. In order to avoid having to divulge family names to the KGB, members of her congregation called each other by their first names only; and so it didn't occur to Natasha to ask Sasha for Irina's last name on those occasions when he mentioned her. As a matter of fact, there were almost as many Sokolovs in Russia as there were Nikitins.

Yet it was peculiar that somehow Natasha kept thinking about Yuri again and again after she and Sasha moved down to the Crimea. They were living close to the elder Sokolov; and his wife, Pelagea, often stopped by for a little visit. Something about the old man kept reminding Natasha of those old times. Every once in a while Pelagea mentioned something about Irina and her father, who apparently was an agnostic and someone important in the field of psychiatry.

Natasha enjoyed herself in the Crimea. Sasha had a job as a bookkeeper in one of the villages near Sudak. He also was enjoying himself. On weekends he was frequently away visiting Bible study groups he had organized. There, too, he succeeded in building good relationships between members of different denominations. He even won the confidence of a Mohammedan mullah, who began attending the Bible studies regularly.

Yet despite all these successes Sasha had to face the reality that groups who met in homes to study the Bible were forbidden by Soviet law and that sooner or later he would wind up having to answer in court for this kind of activity. The local KGB authorities could not understand why he so consistently flouted the law. They attempted to understand what he was doing. The Party wheelhorses carefully analyzed every thought Sasha expressed and came to the conclusion that someone had made a fateful error in this young man's treatment. At any rate Captain Sosin, in charge of the investigations division of the KGB on the Crimea, wrote in his report, "Alexander Nikitin, the founder of numerous Bible study groups, has considerable influence over the young people and over several groups of highly educated people. We'll have to write him off. In my opinion, the reason he is so active is that we put such strong moral pressure on him. He should not have been tossed out of the university, nor should he have been beaten up."

When Sasha later saw this entry in his file he grinned. No indeed! This was not the reason for what he had been doing!

*   *   *

The Christians in Russia, in their hunger for spiritual nourishment, uncritically swallowed everything offered them by tourists from "the golden West." An especially poisonous tidbit was the so-called modern theology. Christians who never had enough Bibles—many of them had never even seen a Bible—accepted everything as unvarnished truth. Here and there Christians began to question the Bible's authority, which in turn led to the secularization of the church. Sasha began to notice that some of the young prospective preachers who had studied in England, East Germany, West Germany, or Sweden returned with radically new viewpoints about the person of Jesus Christ and about Scripture. In discussions these men said straightforwardly that Jesus was not the Son of God, that He was nothing more than a religious reformer, that not all the words of Jesus in the Bible were actually the words of Jesus, and that therefore they should not be accepted uncritically. Sasha clearly recognized that this could lead to a fatal development: Christians who knew neither the

Bible nor Christian doctrine might be persuaded that believing in Christ was not worth the cost, and therefore they might turn away from Him.

Sasha's greatest concern was for young people, with their burning desire to understand the Bible better. He understood the logic of their argument: if Jesus is indeed not the Son of God, as some western theologians—as well as Communist propagandists—maintained, why should one suffer because of belief in Him? Didn't it make more sense to be concerned about the here and now? Why suffer losses, insults, and distress because of belief in Christ if He was nothing more than a good democrat? Young people everywhere were beginning to ask what the Bible's answer was.

Something else motivated Sasha in starting these Bible study groups. Many believers in the various denominations did not really know why they followed one religious practice or another. The Adventists happened to observe the Sabbath, the Pentecostalists happened to pray in tongues, the Orthodox worshiped icons. Some baptized infants, others adults. Wedding ceremonies were conducted in certain ways simply because the people who had brought individuals to Christ happened to do things that way. Many Christians simply did not know what the Bible had to say about these practices.

That was why Sasha kept saying, "We must get back to the source of our belief! Back to Holy Writ!" That was the goal of this young servant of God. Yet the path was strewn with thorns. Those in authority were confused by it all. Some of his best friends were skeptical and could not understand what he was trying to do. And why should anyone become involved with other denominations? When Vassiley invited Sasha to the Ukraine to preach in the Orthodox churches, Sasha's Baptist friends were totally nonplussed. There, too, Sasha emphasized his theme of "back to the Bible" and founded two Bible study groups.

But wasn't he unnecessarily provoking the powers-that-be? The early Christians had no Bible either; yet the church didn't go under. Instead it survived all its persecutors and all of the tyrants!

Sasha took all these objections seriously, replying, "If you've read Paul's epistles to the Thessalonians you know that Paul sent Timothy, his friend and fellow laborer, to Thessalonica to carry his letter there. And Timothy went there, actually risking his life. Paul attached that much importance to the task of informing the believers of that city about the resurrection of Christ. Paul himself was not concerned about the fact that he was being persecuted constantly. He sacrificed himself in order to preach the Word of Christ everywhere, in order to solve the prickly problems that came up in the congregations he visited. We must do the same today."

Sasha was no longer the cautious—even a bit reticent—young preacher of earlier days. Instead he had become a zealous fighter for the cause of the Bible. And for that reason he would not remain unmolested for long.

11 Dialogue Preparations

"**M**insk, August 17. Oh, dear Sasha, if you only knew the many questions for which I need your help! But you are far away from me and I cannot come to see you at this time. We're up to our necks in work. Thus it will not be possible for me to embrace my grandfather and your dear sick mother. You write that she resembles me very closely. Could it be because we are both women? (Forgive my attempt at humor!)

"You write that you want to know how Georgi Vins was released from prison. Mere words could never describe that event. He and his family mean so much to me! We must not draw him or anyone else from the persecuted church into the preparations we are making for the dialogue with the Party, so that nothing can be pinned on them if things go wrong. Even you do not want to become involved in this matter. I happen to agree with you that it would be better for your service for Christ if you kept out of it.

"In Leningrad I spoke with a representative of the Baptist World Congress visiting our country. He referred to the action of the Council of Churches as 'fanatical rigidity.' That hurt me a lot. You know I belong to a registered congregation and I am well aware how difficult it is for our preacher to remain true to his calling. But these naive gentlemen from the West do not have the slightest idea about how brutal and stealthy the KGB is. With our western guests present our preacher asked our people to bring their children along to the next worship service. Imagine that! The following Sunday,

118

however, with our foreign visitors safely out of the way, teachers and the militia were posted all around our house of worship to prevent a single minor from attending our worship service! I asked our minister why children were allowed to be present when the guests were there but at other times had to fight their way through the militia to get into the Lord's house. He responded, 'That's what the authorities decreed. You were the witness of a propaganda exercise which our Communists put on for visitors from the western countries. They want these innocents to believe that religious freedom reigns in our country.'

"Oh, Sasha, I am so tired of these deceptions! There are lies every step of the way. The KGB wraps all these people around its finger. This organization of two and one-half million functionaries will someday put the whole world under its thumb! May God help us to be true to Jesus Christ. Injustice is gaining the upper hand. And things are going to get worse until our Lord comes again. Excuse me for being so melancholy! Please write to me; I wait for your answer. Irina."

*   *   *

The Sokolovs decided to move again. It had become increasingly clear to Irina's father that they could no longer live with the Serovs. Their house was under constant KGB surveillance. Serov himself worked for the scientific section of the KGB, but he was home so rarely that his wife and children completely lost touch with him. Still, Sokolov felt the state's eagle eye observing him constantly, and he resolved to find another place for them to live.

They found a small house in a little village five miles away and made themselves comfortable there. Because of his former occupation and because of his services to his country, Sokolov could retire long before other members of his profession. So he put in an application for early retirement. He had no intention of remaining idle. His plan was to spare no efforts to keep Irina out of any difficulties she might face.

Sokolov learned about Andrey Nikitin's death. It was no secret to him, either, that Irina was a close friend of Sasha Nikitin. He noticed that their relationship was becoming more and more intimate.

Now that Sokolov had discovered that the young man was not Natasha's son by birth, he did nothing more to interfere with this developing relationship. But he was worried. He was concerned about Irina, who certainly would face a life of struggle and uncertainty should she marry Nikitin.

Irina was totally unaware of her father's inner struggles. She had completely immersed herself in the preparations for the dialogue and had no time for anything else. Would the Christians receive a proper hearing from the government? Would something definitive be accomplished during these talks? These concerns took up her days and nights and left her no time for other problems. She had written off her academic promotion long ago.

Eventually, after many letters and inquiries, Irina's group received a response from the Central Committee of the Communist Party. The committee declared itself ready in principle for such a conversation. But it would be necessary to arrive at a date. Irina and her friends decided that they should go to Lupa's apartment once more in order to go over the questions to be taken up by them before the Central Committee in Moscow.

Old Lupa was overjoyed and made the necessary preparations for receiving the young people. He still lived in the militia headquarters building. Lupa was a do-it-yourselfer and made all kinds of toys for the neighborhood children. As a result he attracted scores of the militiamen's children whenever he appeared on the street. Occasionally he invited them to his apartment, supplying them with sweet rolls and cups of fragrant tea. In addition he always had a surprise for these "adopted children" of his, as he called them. But he did not indulge in that more than once a week, since he also did a lot of work for the congregation—something the young friends were not allowed to see.

Irina had asked Lupa to make copies of some important papers. As was his custom he went to purchase several items for his toy-making activities, then asked for several reams of paper. Everything was put into his suitcase. Normally Lupa dragged this load to his building, using up every ounce of his strength in the process. Then, totally exhausted, he asked one of the militiamen he encountered to carry his suitcase upstairs to his apartment. The men were always happy to do it, even if they groaned a little under the load. They did not get upset because they knew the old man made such wonderful toys for the children!

The chief of police once had asked Lupa to bind some prisoners' files for him. Lupa gladly agreed to do it. Needless to say, this indicated the police chief's complete trust in Lupa, who took great pains not to disappoint the official. He did the work skillfully and with great care. He still had the strength to do that. Naturally his curiosity occasionally got the better of him and he leafed through the files before passing them on to the examining magistrate or to the archives.

Through no fault of his Lupa occasionally saw some secret documents. He did not pass up those opportunities, copying the key points of "witnesses' depositions" by informers against clergymen. Then he warned the preacher or priest of the danger he was in.

One day Lupa happened to see the testimony of the bullies who had beaten up Sasha. He could not trust his own eyes! One of the two bullies was actually a member of the congregation and had worked as a part-time helper of the militia for quite some time. Lupa was afraid to inform the new preacher of that. That unfortunate man might blab to the authorities about it, with negative results.

No, Lupa thought, *I will take this character to task myself!* Which he did.

Lupa bought a lot of groceries for the young people's

gathering. He also had copies of the letters to the government made and arranged for the removal of the thousand brochures about Christ's resurrection by Dr. Beletzky. The conveyance was, as usual, a militiaman's car. The driver happened to be going in the same direction Lupa was going, and he took the elderly gentleman along. Everything went well until Lupa wanted to get out. Then the driver insisted on carrying his suitcase for him. It took a lot of arguing to persuade the sympathetic militiaman to go on his way. Once he was gone Lupa called up Fedin, who lived two blocks away, and asked him to pick him up. Fedin arrived a few minutes later, accompanied by his son. Together they took the precious cargo to his house.

That evening Lupa sat on his old sofa, dead tired but satisfied. He poured himself a cup of especially strong tea, then waited for the arrival of his friends. He had already informed his grandson that he wanted to be left alone that evening. Some friends were coming, he said, and they wanted quiet so they could pray together.

"Pray, dear Grandpa, pray," the major replied, "but don't beat your forehead in; we still need you around!" The major was thinking of the way in which Orthodox Christians prayed, kneeling and bowing down several times, touching their foreheads to the floor.

Vassiley was the first to arrive. Lupa let him in and warmly embraced him.

"Well, have you done penance for praying to icons, you young greenhorn?"

"Look, Grandpa, if you say things like that to me I'm going to cuff you on the ears!"

"Listen, with all the fasting you did—or did you maybe fall in love?—you've shrunk down to a shadow of yourself. In your condition you wouldn't stand a chance trying to beat me up!"

Lupa poured his guest a cup of steaming tea. The doorbell rang again. Outside stood a Pentecostal preacher named Semyon Anakin from the Pentecostal congregation of Kasachstan. Lupa was ready with yet another one of his old jokes. "I haven't heard any foreigners talking for a long time. Please do me a favor and have someone translate for me if you should be speaking in tongues."

Anakin laughed. "You haven't changed, Brother Lupa! You may have a sharp tongue, but you are some man! Come here; I'll kiss you in Russian." He kissed the elderly man on both of his cheeks and lifted him off the ground. "Well, are you going to make fun of us anymore?"

Lupa screamed and kicked. "Let me go immediately or I'll call the militia!"

"Don't let him go, Anakin," Vassiley said. "First make him give his word of honor. . . ." At that point the doorbell rang again. Anakin had to set Lupa down whether he wanted to or not.

"Why didn't you do that sooner?" the old man growled and stalked to the door. Ivan Krebs, a Lutheran, and Sudakovitch, a Catholic, stood outside.

"The Lord be praised!" Lupa greeted them solemnly. When they looked at him in amazement, he explained, "Well, I can say that because the Catholics are beginning to make their peace with Luther."

They all went to the kitchen, sat down on chairs or on the floor, and waited for Irina.

Irina finally arrived quite late. She had been shadowed, finally shaking off her unwanted escort by doubling back and forth through Minsk's back alleys. She was forced to take a taxi to the nearest suburban train station or she never would have caught up with her train.

Irina did not ring the doorbell but opened the door quietly and was suddenly standing in the apartment. "Well, did I scare you or didn't I?" she asked Lupa, who was taken aback.

Somewhat bewildered he asked her, "How did you get in here?"

"You recently gave Sasha the key to your apartment, didn't you? You remember that, don't you? Sasha put it in my purse and told me, 'Why don't you give the old man a scare, but don't forget to greet him for me.' "

Tears sprang to Lupa's eyes. "Oh, Sasha, the rotter, he left us high and dry!"

"I'm going to start crying along with you," growled Vassiley. "At least he's doing something, while we're just treading water. He stole my congregation away from me, even though he preached in my church only once! They liked him so much that they went over to the Baptists."

"Bravo!" cried Irina, clapping her hands.

"What do you mean, bravo? Do you think it's fun preaching to an empty church? You just wait. . . ."

"Well, why don't you go out and do some mission work? Just ask the people in off the street. Remember, there are plenty of Communists in your village who can be brought to Jesus."

"You must be crazy! Cut the talk or I'll eat you alive!" Vassiley showed his teeth threateningly. It made him look so funny everyone had to laugh.

Polevoy, a Baptist preacher from Siberia, wanted to get to the point, weighing in with the usual preacher's voice, "All right, my beloved, let us now thank the Lord for our safe journey here. Vassiley, would you lead us in prayer?"

"How can he pray when I have no icons here?" teased the irrepressible Lupa.

Vassiley rose. "Quiet. I'll manage without an icon! Let us all rise." He prayed, "We thank You, our heavenly Father, for Your constant protection and help. We ask You to be present here in the person of Your Holy Spirit. Give us Your peace, Your love, and the ability to understand each other. Amen."

The discussion that evening was wide-ranging. The main reason for their get-together was the impending dialogue with the government, but it was also enormously important for them to share openly about the stresses and strains they were experiencing. Despite government prohibitions, hundreds of priests and preachers were ministering to children and young people. Even Catholic priests could lose their freedom. Baptist preachers definitely could count on the administrators for religious cults removing them from their positions sooner or later, replacing them with preachers of their choice. Alternatively, the Baptist preachers were harassed in hopes they would voluntarily give up their congregations.

After all members of the group had gotten their problems off their chests, they spent an hour in concentrated prayer fellowship. Then the plan for the dialogue was discussed and specifics nailed down. The group finally broke up after midnight.

Vassiley's parents were home. He had already told them that he would be bringing friends to spend the night with him. His mother and father were so glad to see him again that they promised to wait up for him and his friends.

Every room was brightly lit and a table was set in the kitchen when Vassiley arrived with his friends. Professor Kuznetsov, Vassiley's father, greeted them all affectionately. Vassiley embraced him. "Thank you, Dad, for waiting up for us all this time."

"Well, we haven't seen you for a terribly long time, you young parson. We've been looking forward to seeing you. Mother isn't asleep yet, either."

Vassiley introduced Irina and the two preachers, Klim and Polevoy, to his father. His father embraced the guests and called, "Nora! Tamara! Where have you gone?"

"I'm coming!" Vassiley's mother called, her melodic voice floating into the room.

"Aha, so this is the young lady Sasha mentioned so often during his high fever!" Tamara exclaimed, squeezing Irina's hand. "Now I understand why he couldn't fall in love with me!" Irina flushed red. Tamara greeted both men and sat down opposite Irina. "I don't know where you've got your eyes, Vassiley," she said to her brother. "You should have stolen such a beauty from Sasha long ago. Then I could have

Sasha for myself!" She said it so seriously that everybody broke out in laughter.

At this moment Vassiley's mother entered the room. Vassiley rose and greeted her. "Well, Mother, you never seem to get older!" he said as he kissed her on the cheek.

"Now, now, you didn't really come to reproach me, did you?" she said, her whole face radiating a smile as she greeted the other guests. Vassiley did not reply. His father threw him a pained look, attempting to let him know that he should keep his tongue under better control.

Before they began to eat, Vassiley asked, "Father, do you think you will be fired if we pray in your presence?"

"Of course not; please do pray!" countered the Communist, ashamed at his embarrassment.

Vassiley nodded toward Klim. "Would you lead us in prayer, please?"

Klim rose and said, "We thank You, creator of all things, for blessing this home so richly. Bless us with Your presence tonight."

Tamara smiled at her parents.

"Do you always pray before you eat?" Professor Kuznetsov asked.

"Of course, Dad!"

"Petya Subov has told me," the mother said, "that the Central Committee has devised new ways of combating religion. He says they will administer the death blow to all of you very soon."

"Why don't you shut up about your Petya?" her husband said, annoyed.

"Who is this Subov?" Irina inquired.

"Oh, he's one of Mom's friends," Vassiley explained. "She is an actress and associates with people from the Central Committee."

Irina gave Vassiley's mother a searching look. No wonder Vassiley was never willing to answer questions when asked about his parents.

"You're home so seldom these days," his father reproached him. "You've really buried yourself in that church of yours."

"I apologize, Father. I've got so little time! In addition, I don't want to endanger your reputation. You're members of the intelligentsia, after all, and you are both Communists. So you can ill afford to have a son around who is a priest. Have I caused you any problems so far?"

"My colleagues sneer at me and tell me I don't have to go to church since I've got my own private pope. That's about all."

Tamara was just serving homemade pirrogi to her guests. All of them praised the delicacy while eagerly listening in on Vassiley's exchange with his parents.

"We've got an Adventist working for us as a cleaning woman," the professor reported. "She's got five children. The courts took away her right to educate her children according to her convictions. When the court-appointed guardians came to pick up the children they hid wherever they could. One was under the bed, another in the cellar. One of them actually crept into the oven. They were chasing the kids like rabbits! But they finally found them all. They even dragged the one out of the oven, covered with soot. They took him along with them, as dirty as he was, telling the neighbors who stood around on the street, 'There, look how these people treat their children! They let them live in the most horrible filth. And when the government decides to take them away they make a big row and denounce the Soviet authorities.'

"The Adventist woman's husband was not a Christian. So the KGB tried to force him to divorce his wife, after which the courts were going to let him have the children. He wouldn't go along with that. He lost all of the children. He could not reconcile himself to that and finally hung himself in his bathroom. The woman was blamed for that, too. It shook her up so much that she did not show up for work for several days. I was ordered by the workers' committee to dismiss her. But I still haven't done it. . . ."

Irina listened with tears in her eyes.

"Aren't you going to get into trouble because of your stubbornness?" Tamara asked.

"I don't think so. I still have a few fairly important discoveries to fall back on—a kind of job insurance. Sakharov continues fighting for human rights and isn't afraid to risk himself. After all, why should I dismiss that poor woman? Yesterday she stepped into my office and said, 'Many thanks, Ivan Nikolayevitch, for not dismissing me. God will reward you for that.' "

"But how are we to react when these Christians insist on bringing their children up according to their religion?" asked Vassiley's mother. "If the Party is against that, they will have to obey."

Vassiley grimaced. "Imagine what you would say if you lived in a country which takes children away from their parents because they are bringing them up as Communists. Wouldn't you protest that, too?"

"Oh, my goodness, no. I just wouldn't bring you up as Communists! Who wants to lose one's children because of illusory dreams about another life in the future?"

Everyone laughed at her naive openness.

"At my instritute we've got two Baptists. They're brother and sister," Tamara related, "and they refuse to join the Komsomol."

"You Baptists are so well organized," said Professor Kuznetsov to Klim. "The Party fears you more than anyone else because your congregations continue to expand explosively despite the prohibition against evangelization in any form. I understand they're allowing you a little more freedom for the time being because you have such powerful opposition within your church. How did that split of yours ever come about? Why did the other side reject Moscow's direction? And why are the illegal church's members pursued so brutally?"

Preacher Klim began to explain to Kuznetsov how the split occurred. It happened when the director of religious cults began to interfere with the congregation's internal affairs. He told how the KGB manipulated both openly and covertly and how this caused a lot of trouble for preachers.

Nora, the lady of the house, listened attentively and finally said, "What would happen if all of you, whether Baptists, Orthodox, Catholics, or whoever, simply told the government, 'From now on we refuse to live under such diabolical coercion; from now on we will obey God more than man'? That was said by someone in the Bible, wasn't it, Vassiley?"

Vassiley nodded. "Hm-hm, that was the apostle Peter." He gave Klim an insistent look, gesturing to him to respond to his mother's statement.

"Of course something like this could be done if all the Christians were of one mind," Klim indicated. "But they are too afraid of having to go to jail. Furthermore, they do not agree on what the relationship between church and state should be. There are many different opinions about that. Of course if all those who believe in Christ in all of Russia—that army of several million members—if each of them declared to the government *to a man* that we will obey the state in all matters affecting the government without any conditions except in the spiritual area, where we will obey the Word of God alone, they certainly could not toss us all into jail! The church surely would blossom during that period. But we will not be able to achieve that unity among the people of God. Dissension tears us apart and we are also too cowardly. The KGB increases our conflicts constantly by intimidating our clergy, as well as by bribing and provoking them."

"The KGB doesn't use any different tactics with us scientists, either," the professor said pensively. "I took the side of an engineer in my office. This man, Silitch, wanted to emigrate to Israel. Right away they hustled me off to KGB headquarters and held me there for a good eight hours. I think we're headed back to Stalinism."

Dawn was breaking when hosts and visitors finally wished one another a good night's rest. It was certainly high time to go to bed if they wanted to get a couple of hours of sleep, but it was difficult for them to go their separate ways.

Toward the close of the conversation Nora asked, "Do they take away Baptists' children too?" They were overcome by a sudden sense of helplessness.

Klim explained, "I have spoken with representatives of the council of the prisoners' dependents and was told that in recent times children are more and more frequently being taken away from their Baptist parents. So far, about fifty families from all denominations have been affected by this."

Nora remained silent. Suddenly Kuznetsov asked, "And who will pray with us to close the evening?"

The young people looked up in surprise. There was a brief pause. "I will," said Vassiley, getting up. He said a brief prayer for Silitch, for his hard-pressed parents, for the preachers and, yes, also for scientists who had been caught in the government's net. Then he thanked God for His aid. Everyone began heading for bed.

The elder Kuznetsovs were already in bed when Nora suddenly embraced her husband and buried her face in his shoulder. He stroked her hair gently. Tears were in her eyes when she looked up at him.

"Forgive me, my dear," she said. "Can you forgive me? It is so terrible to lose one's children. . . ." They talked softly until daybreak.

12 A Secret Printing Press

When the Council of Churches decided to start its underground publishing operation the Soviet government was really perplexed about what to do. The KGB assured the Central Committee that it would not be long before this publishing house was discovered and "turned upside down." It was inconceivable that anyone could go on printing for months on end without being discovered.

Obtaining paper in the large quantities required would be a great risk. Anyone who bought more than fifty kilos (110 pounds) of paper would arouse suspicion immediately. "Why are you buying so much paper?" they would be asked. "Why don't you give us the address of the organization buying this paper?"

The transportation of paper over any distance would also involve many problems. If anyone were to transport the paper on a train inside a suitcase, this would automatically arouse the attention of the militia and the train's passengers. And few Christians owned their own automobiles. Any fortunate enough to own cars were also "fortunate" enough to be shadowed by the militia, both openly and secretly. The transporting of all the equipment associated with printing would also create difficulties.

Because of these factors the KGB's experts predicted the quick destruction of this illegally spawned and born "baby." As its first step the KGB ordered heads of paper supply houses across the nation to report larger purchases of paper to

131

the militia. Next the KGB collected all the names of those members of Christian families who were experts in printing. All lathe mechanics, locksmiths, and technicians were placed under secret surveillance. The shadowing of members of the Council of Churches was intensified. Andropov promised the members of the Central Committee that all employees of the publishing house named "The Christian" would be picked up in a few months and brought to justice.

An open letter from the Council of Churches told the government about the founding of the publishing house and gave reasons for such a publishing house. The letter referred to the constitution of the USSR, which guaranteed freedom of the printed word.

The government's only reply to this letter was an intensification of the repressive measures against the persecuted church. One year—two years—passed, and the KGB still had not tracked down the publishing house. Whole New Testaments were being printed and distributed in the churches. The KGB ground its teeth in impotent fury and again tried to infiltrate the leadership of the Council of Churches. That misfired as well. The man was unmasked immediately. Though he was not expelled from the church he quickly was removed from the leadership of the Council.

Now the authorities embarked on another tactic. The KGB offered up to ten thousand rubles to any member of the church who was even remotely knowledgeable in printing if he would help them track down the publishing house. When these attempts failed, the KGB began to lash out with its accustomed brutality. This is why Neverov was shot at by an agent of the KGB. The KGB allegedly "knew" that Neverov somehow was involved in the diffusion of New Testaments. Unfortunately Neverov's wife, of whom he was terribly proud, was the one who had been intimidated so much that she told the KGB everything her husband had been doing for the persecuted church. It was she who told them Neverov was not driving an empty bus to Feodosia the day Sasha had traveled with him. But both Neverov's wife and the KGB were wrong. Her husband had had absolutely nothing to do with the publishing house. Some Bibles and tapes that had arrived from the West urgently needed to be moved from one village to another. And this thoughtful, goodhearted bus driver accepted this assignment without even suspecting that his own wife had betrayed him. She had received two hundred rubles, more than a month and a half's pay, as an advance. She was to receive another five hundred rubles if her information led to the exposure of Neverov as a Bible printer. She also received a promise that her husband would not be sent to jail. This made the KGB's disappointment all the greater when it turned out that Neverov had duped them.

During the time Sasha left the bus in Krasnoperekopsk the KGB's experts had searched the bus from stem to stern without discovering any secret compartments. Then they shadowed the bus day and night on each of its trips between Moscow and the Crimea after, of course, replacing the window which had been shot out by the rifle. Imagine their surprise when they discovered that none other than the director of the bus company in Cherson was transporting stolen grain in this bus! He drove to a kholkhoz one day with his mechanic, loaded his bus with several bags of that collective's best grain (with the consent of the head of the kholkhoz) and then drove it back into town. The KGB officials who had followed the bus ordered the militia to arrest the thieves. The militia got there but, to their astonishment, were unable to find any grain in the bus.

The KGB demanded that the bus be dismantled and searched until the grain was found. The bus firm's mechanics began doing this under KGB supervision. Eventually one of the mechanics could no longer restrain himself. He began to cry like a baby, begging, "Please leave this vehicle alone! I have labored on it for many years, even to the extent of putting some secret compartments into it; and now my highest achievement is going to be torn apart!" He pushed a small lever located under the steering wheel and started the engine. Some of the seats moved to one side and the floor opened to reveal a secret compartment below. The KGB operatives gaped open-mouthed at the grain shipment.

During the investigation that followed, the mechanic protested that there was no way Neverov could have learned of the secret compartments. When Neverov himself was interrogated he merely smiled and said, "Comrade investigating magistrate, what could I possibly have to do with all of this? Someone rigs the bus with secret compartments and absconds with the property of the Soviet Union, and now you ask me whether I knew anything about these secret compartments. He who isn't caught red-handed isn't a thief! That's a Russian proverb, and I will tell you no more."

No matter how long they interrogated him they could not extract the truth from him. That is, until he told his wife about it one day and she passed it on to the KGB. Neverov had seen the bus firm's director, who had once been a mechanic, and his mechanic, who had then been a bus driver, puttering around with the bus on their days off, putting in the secret compartments.

Obviously those were not the only obstacles placed in the publishing house's way. The KGB put considerable effort into drumming into the Christian preachers' ears the message that undercover production of reading material was illegal and therefore a criminal act. They went on to say that all criminal acts are in opposition to the teachings of Christ and of the apostles. They made the registered congregations' preachers apprehensive by repeating over and over, "If you distribute illegally printed New Testaments and songbooks in your congregation you're headed for big trouble with us!"

A few of these preachers did permit themselves to be buffaloed to such a degree that they preached from their pulpits that no one was even to touch material published by "The Christian." A preacher in the Ukraine went so far as to say, "Even the word 'God,' illegally printed, is to be equated with anti-Soviet propaganda."

Yet the majority of preachers, even those from the All-Union and the Orthodox Church, placed a great deal of hope in this new effort to print and distribute Bibles in the USSR. Mitrochin, the philosopher, wrote that if foreign countries continued to furnish Bibles as they had been doing, and if the publisher of "The Christian" continued to print its editions, one could assume that not only would all believers receive Bibles of their own but that it would soon be possible to give every nonbeliever one also.

These prospects distressed the government no end. The KGB, certain of victory, declared after one print shop had been discovered that the illegal printing of Bibles had been permanently halted. Andropov must have been beside himself with anger when soon after the arrest of people who had been employed by the publishing house he received a letter from "The Christian" demanding that all repressive measures against this publisher be stopped immediately. They were going to continue issuing and diffusing their printed material until the government committed itself to allow the printing of Bibles throughout Russia as well as their distribution in bookstores and newsstands. This letter was printed on the same kind of press which had just been confiscated in western Russia. When another branch of the publishing house was discovered and destroyed, a similar letter was received.

The KGB's anger was the reason why a young Christian soldier named Vanya Moiseyev was murdered by KGB functionaries. Sasha had known Moiseyev personally.

Those responsible for this publishing effort refused to disclose their secrets to other critics of the regime when they turned to the Council of Churches for help in starting a similar publishing operation. The Council did not want to supply the government with evidence which would enable it to accuse the Council of political activity. And should the KGB succeed in infiltrating the ranks of the dissidents with an agent of their own, this would make it easy for them to destroy "The Christian." The Council was willing to furnish Bibles to those who needed them, but they categorically refused to become associated with the printing of any kind of political material.

Christians from registered as well as unregistered congregations gave spiritual and material support to the publishing effort. This mutual concern brought the young people from registered and unregistered congregations into closer contact with each other, and they learned how to look past potential disagreements.

The KGB viewed this new development with growing uneasiness. With increasing zeal they attempted to effect a split between the two groups. Once they were started, however, it proved impossible to stop the cooperative ventures. The younger generation of Christians no longer saw the validity of the split between registered and unregistered congregations. And since the government tended to allow the registered congregations a bit more operating room, it was no longer essential for the young people to go underground. Joint youth gatherings, combined field trips, song festivals, baptismal ceremonies, and Bible evenings brought them together. This development only created more problems for the already oppressed preachers. They became the targets for more and more abuse from the authorities and the KGB. However, many remained steadfast in spite of the harassment.

A young man in Moscow, for example, started three Bible study groups for young people. He told a western visitor that the government demanded that his preacher exclude him from the congregation for engaging in illegal activities, but the preacher had the courage to refuse the request.

The main target of the attack continued to be the unregistered church. Efforts were made to force preachers like Andrey Nikitin, who had served time in prison, to join a registered congregation. Or their congregations were speedily registered and attempts were made to exploit them in combating the persecuted church. This complex campaign against Russia's spiritual renewal had taken on heretofore unheard of dimensions.

The young people could not be bothered by these quarrels. "Let the old folks fight each other," they said. "We want to learn about Christ!" Those were their watchwords. Tourists from the West could find no rhyme or reason in what was happening. How could there be functioning churches serving children and young people, and at the same time persecuted congregations whose members met secretly in the woods and whose pastors spent most of their time in prison camps? Was the governing board of the churches justified in obstinately insisting on retaining an illegal status? Of course the western visitors had no idea what the KGB was actually up to. Russia needed a healthy, strong opposition to the formally recognized church.

Sasha had recognized this while still a minister with the registered church. Now that he was free of pastoral responsibility he could be, as it were, a neutral observer of the contradictions and disagreements between the two church brotherhoods. As a result his resolve strengthened to do his part toward spiritual renewal. The longer he was active in this role the more he concentrated on only one thing: the promotion of intensive Bible study and the resultant impact on the lives of believers as the only appropriate preparation for the continuing struggle against Soviet ideology.

This joint study of Scripture led to an acute awareness among members of various denominations that many areas of their daily lives still needed changing. What the Bible refers to as a renewing of the mind began to take place.

Such study of the Bible had a wide-ranging, somewhat surprising effect. In some of these Bible study groups participants began to ask one another seriously whether it was not time to break down denominational barriers and simply live according to the principles of the Bible.

For the moment Sasha was without a job. The head of the kholkhoz where he worked as a bookkeeper had received strict orders from the regional committee of the Communist Party that Sasha was to be let go. He had run himself ragged in the search for another job, but it was hard to find any work in the Crimea. His last hope was the old mullah, who had good contacts with a Tatar who was the director of a large factory. The mufti promised to help Sasha. So day after day Sasha waited for news about a job. In the meantime he had visited the Neverovs and invited the whole family to come to the Crimea for a visit and a vacation at his place. Neverov really needed some time to relax and recuperate. He no longer mentioned the bus trip and his bullet wound, which was still troubling him. He felt that the less he said about this affair the better he would be able to carry on his church duties in the future.

The Black Sea climate did wonders for the Neverov family, with the children becoming livelier each day. Natasha, who was a marvelous hostess, showered them all with love.

*   *   *

One day Irina again turned up at her grandather's. Natasha invited her over. When Irina arrived, Natasha held out both of her hands to her and said, "How wonderful to see you here, Irina. Come in, come in, my dear!"

Irina embraced her and looked at her closely. *It is odd,* she thought, *she does indeed look like me! Her blue eyes, the wavy hair, her mouth.* Her heart was moved as it had rarely been moved before.

"I'm happy to get to know you, too, Natalia Petrovna!"

"Do come in! Sasha will be here shortly. He went to the beach with our guests. The Neverovs are visiting us at the moment."

"The Neverovs?"

"Yes. I'm going to call them right away and ask them to come in. Now won't you please sit down?"

Natasha went outside. Irina stayed behind, suddenly feeling oddly depressed. She could not get rid of the ominous feeling that something bad was about to happen to the Neverovs. Since she had heard what was being said about Neverov's wife, Irina did not know what to do. What she had heard might possibly be merely a rumor started by the KGB to destroy Neverov's family. But she kept thinking back to her grandfather's statement, "You can't change the color of red hair."

Sasha rushed inside ahead of the others. He was all smiles. "Well, finally! Your grandfather and I were beginning to think you had completely forgotten about us! Always excuses . . . that you have no time. . . ."

Irina looked at him wordlessly. Their eyes met as he talked, and it was as though each was looking into the other's soul. Sasha, suddenly speechless, continued to hold Irina's hands. Only the arrival of the rest of the group broke the spell.

Neverov's greeting was vigorous. "Aha! I ought to spank you for letting your grandfather wait for you this long!"

Irina smiled and said, "Now hold your tongue, you hero! We have been waiting for you to come down for an important discussion, but first you had to get over your wounds in the hospital."

"Now listen, Irina, they were just scratches, that's all! I'll catch up with everything. I'll be there for the next gathering."

A deep sadness seemed to cloak Mrs. Neverov. Real fear appeared in her eyes. This only made her more beautiful than ever.

It wasn't until Irina saw Natasha busily running back and forth setting the table that she remembered the message she was to bring to her. "Excuse me, Natalia Petrovna, my grandparents have invited everyone to dinner at their place! Pelagea has everything ready and told me specifically not to let her wait too long. Her table is already set for everyone!"

Natasha did not have to be asked twice. She looked forward to seeing old Sokolov and his wife again. As they started out she took Neverov's two youngest children by the hands, chatting with Valentina and walking ahead of the others. Sasha, Neverov, and Irina followed slowly. Some things still needed discussing; so they were in no hurry to catch up with the rest of the party.

"Who besides you knew what cargo the bus had on it?"

Neverov looked at Irina thoughtfully and said, "No one besides my wife. Naturally she may have spoken about it to some relatives. I will not question her about it. After the attack on me she has been looking guilty and sad, and I don't want to make life even harder for her."

Irina remembered the advice of an elderly member of the Council of Churches, Shalashov. He had told the ministers to spare their wives trouble and tell them as little as possible about assignments. She shared this with Neverov.

Neverov nodded. Shalashov could be right.

"You belong to a registered congregation," Sasha said to Irina, surprised. "How do you know about this kind of thing?"

She put her finger on her lips. "Ssshhh! It's premature to ask me about that." Then she turned to Neverov again. "You're not taking enough care of yourself. You're just skin and bones!"

He smiled and said, "Let me walk ahead and catch up with the ladies. Mitya seems tired. I'm going to carry him for a while."

Sasha and Irina were suddenly alone.

"Have you got some time for me?" Sasha began. "I'd like very much to talk with you about things which affect only the two of us."

She laughed at the way he expressed himself, took his hand and said tenderly, "Come, let's catch up with the others. We'll talk about our personal problems later!"

Irina caught up with the others, picked up little Anya, and joined in the conversation.

Grandfather Sokolov greeted his guests warmly. He kissed every one of them on each cheek, according to Russian custom, then led them to the table, which was set beautifully. The smell of roast beef made their mouths water.

"Let's sit right down to eat, dear ones," Sokolov said. "Otherwise Pelagea's pirrogi will be cold!" He showed the guests to their places at the table. Natasha was seated to his right, Irina to his left.

The conversation around the table was spiced by Sokolov's inevitable anecdotes. Only once did he become serious. This was when talk turned to Bible studies. Sasha had won him over completely. Sokolov's work with the Bible study groups totally absorbed him. He was unafraid about the reaction of government functionaries. When he learned that it was the persecuted church which had organized these illegal Bible study programs in many places he asked, "Can't I be an evangelist too?" He could. He became an evangelist despite his earthy sense of humor, or perhaps because of it. Most important, his work with the Bible attracted young people and the top levels of society in the area.

They met once a month. At first the sessions resembled the usual discussions about literary issues. But the old gentleman skillfully steered the conversation away from current literature and the writers of the past century and onto spiritual subjects. As time passed everyone became more and more engrossed in the study of the Bible. It was this that drew the largest numbers of participants. But Grandfather Sokolov did not like to speak about that, since he did not wish his work to receive too much attention. He permitted himself no reckless or extravagant behavior. In addition to his great clarity of mind, the biblical knowledge he had pursued with such zeal since his conversion helped him greatly.

When Sasha and his mother came to live nearby and both began to attend his Bible study evenings, Sokolov became even more careful. "I would prefer it," he said to Pelagea one day, "if they threw me in prison rather than Sasha."

But now, with everyone seated at the table, Sokolov could not resist letting loose a barrage of his latest anecdotes.

It seems a student had come to Sokolov one day saying, "Did you know that our Orthodox patriarch is an atheist?"

"But how can that be?" Sokolov had asked him.

The student had replied, "Well, when Gagarin returned from his Sputnik flight around the earth Khrushchev received him and asked, 'Yuri Alexandreyevich, did you see God in outer space?'

" 'Yes, Nikita Sergeyevich,' said Gagarin.

"Khrushchev paled and whispered, 'That's exactly what I suspected.'

"After his audience with Khrushchev, Gagarin was received by the patriarch, Alexey, who asked, 'Did you see God in outer space, my son?'

" 'No!' replied Gagarin.

"The patriarch became very reflective and said, 'I knew it! There is no God!' "

While telling this story the grandfather periodically glanced at Irina. She was rumpling her nose and raising her eyebrows. Suddenly she blurted out, "You're not making any bones about how little you think of Alexey, are you?"

Sokolov did not answer her, but instead concentrated on his food. He hardly ever needed his glasses, and had all of his teeth—and that at ninety years of age! Only in recent days had he begun to complain about stomach trouble. The surgeon Fedin, who had spent his vacation with the Sokolovs, had urged him to chew his food more carefully. This is what he was doing now.

Irina broke the silence again. "Grandfather, you read all of the Samisdat* publications. Well, what is your opinion of Roy Medvedyev?"

Sokolov looked at her from the side. He waited for a time before he replied.

"Let's talk about the patriarch Alexey first. He and I played ball together when we were both small. I've kept a careful eye on him during his rise in the church hierarchy. We were on a first-name basis to the very end. The Party couldn't praise him enough; they even decorated him. So it's quite certain on whose behalf he has been functioning."

"Listen, Grandfather! What are you saying? You must have completely forgotten. . . ."

*Unauthorized anti-government publications.

"Excuse me—oh excuse me, my child; I didn't think of *that.*"

They had agreed to watch their step carefully when in the presence of Valentina.

"As far as Roy Medvedyev is concerned," Sokolov went on as rapidly as he could, "let me say that everyone who has read the works of Marx and Engels considers himself to be a Marxist. Recently a student said to me, 'Did you know, Sokolov, that whoever has studied Marxism is a Communist, but he who *understands* Marxism is an anti-Communist?' Roy Mevedyev plays the role of one who, judged by his published writings, has understood Marxism and has stayed with it nonetheless. He himself probably is aware of the contradiction this represents. On one hand he opposes the use of force. On the other he grants science the right to experimentation. What this means is that the millions of victims of the revolution from its inception until today have been merely part of a scientific experiment. He must therefore be a little clearer why we are to condemn Hiroshima and Nagasaki; for the Americans, too, might explain quite simply that the atom bomb was also a scientific experiment! So I cannot understand why the Soviet government considers Roy Medvedyev a dissident. He is one of them. They simply haven't understood him correctly. They ought to make him a member of the Academy of the Sciences, and the Samisdat people ought to throw him out. Every experiment on living human beings is an expression of sadism and barbarity. But Medvedyev does not share this opinion. In addition, he considers any human being who views Marxism differently from the way *he* does as a psychopath. In that he thinks exactly like the Central Committee of the Communist Party, which views everyone who disagrees with it as a schizophrenic. For that reason I think all of you who are taking part in that experimental dialogue will eventually be stuck into mental hospitals."

He had whispered the last sentence. At the same time, the sadfaced Valentina was being kept so busy by her lively brood that old Sokolov was sure she had not heard anything of what he had just said.

"Couldn't we change the subject?" interjected Pelagea. "If everyone has had enough to eat, we could give our thanks and adjourn into the living room."

How Irina loved that particular living room, which also served as her grandfather's study, with its shelves crammed with books he had collected over these decades! There were the Marxist philosophers next to the ancient philosophers, with the modern literature available in Russia, as well as biographies and books about Party policies. These volumes filled the shelves all the way to the ceiling. On two shelves, too, were Sokolov's Bibles, a few commentaries and whatever one could get hold of in spiritual books.

Students came and went in Sokolov's apartment. They arrived with questions when they could find no other place with answers. To them he was a walking encyclopedia. It was clearly a miracle that Sokolov one day had turned to the study of the Bible and that he should continue it with such unbelievable intensity. He had read the Bible earlier on, before he had become a Christian. But he had considered it nothing more than a code of morality. Now it had become a wellspring of saving knowledge for every man. When he discussed the Bible, such gems of spiritual wisdom came from his lips that one could listen to him for hours at a time without getting tired of it.

Only Sasha, Neverov, and Irina had followed Sokolov into the living room. The others were in the kitchen busy with the dishes.

"I can understand Medvedyev when he fights for democracy in our country," Sokolov continued, "and when he strives for the founding of opposition parties and the creation of opposing factions within our Communist Party. But will someone please tell me how that can be reconciled with official Marxism? This form of Marxism advocates the use of force not only as a legitimate means to gain and hold power, but also as a way to compel everyone to agree to its way of thinking. Yet according to Medvedyev this is how things are. The experiment with Marxism has cost millions of Russian victims. In the years of the Soviet 'housecleaning' between 1937 and 1939, the government executed half a million people, of which 120,000 have been pardoned posthumously. Surely it is a sign of weakness that the Party will not tolerate an investigation of what happened. Following that line of thinking, national socialism would also have to be viewed as an experiment. The Mafia ought to be included when talking about such experiments. Marxism is a punishment for the apathy of those who believe in democracy and freedom and yet remain indifferent to it. But one cannot consider something that is in effect a slow death an experiment!"

"Why, then, is Marxism so popular in the western countries?" asked Irina, her question based on discussions with students from western countries.

Sokolov thought about that for a while, then answered, "You know, Marxism did not germinate on Russian soil. It was imported into Russia. Even people like Herzen and Bakunin went to the West in order to absorb its theory. The West dropped this rotten apple into our basket as an experiment. It is true that Russia provided excellent terrain for such experimentation. And we have turned out to be Marxism's best guinea pigs. But there are two sides to that. To Russia, Marxism represents the past and the future. For the West it is only the future. These countries have no idea how Marxism works in actual practice. Believe me, in those countries Marxism will bring forth greater monstrosities than it ever did in our country. At the moment, the West accepts our dissidents. The day will come when we will accept the West's dissidents—that is, if the poor suckers are allowed to escape from the West's experimental terrain if and when Marxism finally takes hold there."

"That's a grim picture you're painting, Grandfather."

"Don't ever forget, my child, that the Bible says we are to lift our heads up high when disaster strikes, for our redemption draws near. For you young Christians and for us old ones one certainty remains. Jesus is with us now and He will come again! Ever since I made this startling discovery, the horror which surrounds you and me and which touches us often doesn't affect me very much. I felt I had to say these things to you before you take part in that dialogue of yours. Based on everything I have experienced and seen, your experimental dialogue is pure Utopia. It may, in fact, turn out to be a very tragic Utopia, my dear one! But I suppose you have to go through it yourself. If I am still alive when it's over and done with, I hope to be able to help you as best I can."

Irina embraced the old man, kissing him on his cheek. "Thank you, Grandfather. I thank you for everything."

The old man wiped away a tear. He turned to the others and said, "Did you forget the ladies in the kitchen? Please ask them and the children to come in here!"

Neverov, who had been listening to the old grandfather as if transfixed, jumped up as if he had awakened from a beautiful dream and went into the kitchen to get the women.

Sokolov's penetrating gaze took in Irina and Sasha. Irina began to feel uneasy, for one could never be sure what kind of trouble was brewing in the old man.

"What's the matter, Grandfather?" she asked. But he did not answer and merely continued to inspect the two of them silently. Expecting the worst, Irina began to rummage desperately in her mind for something with which to divert him. Then he dropped his bombshell.

"Well, you two, when are you going to celebrate your engagement?"

"Grandfather! How could you?" Agitated, Irina jumped from her chair.

"As far as I am concerned we could do it today," Sasha quickly responded. He stepped over to Irina and said quietly, "I love you, Irina, and I would dearly like to ask you to become my wife."

Poor Irina—she who was strong enough to throw a man like Koslov down the stairs with a judo blow—paled.

"You are a bungler, Sasha. That's not how you do it! First you must ask me for the hand of my grandchild!" grandfather said, and smiled at Irina, who totally lost her nerve and ran out of the house. Natasha was just entering the house when Irina slammed the door shut as she left. Sasha stood in the middle of the room as if he had been struck by lightning and didn't know what to do.

"What have you men been up to with Irina?" asked Natasha.

Instead of answering, the grandfather snapped at Sasha, "Don't stand around like a statue! Run after her. I'll keep the rest of the people busy here in the meantime."

Sasha found Irina standing next to a lilac bush, looking out at the beach. He stepped close to her, took her hand and softly said, "Come!" She obeyed him as if she were a child. Hand in hand they walked silently down toward the water.

Irina had recovered. "Come on, let's go swimming!"

"Did you bring a bathing suit with you?"

She ran back to the house and was soon back carrying a beach blanket and her bathing suit. The beach was jammed with people screaming in delight, playing ball, sunning themselves. But Sasha did not want to remain there. Now that he had finally confessed what was in his heart, he wanted to get the whole matter cleared up. So they went walking along the shoreline for about half an hour. Finally he put the question to her again.

"Would you like to be my wife? You haven't given me an answer."

She stopped walking, looked him in the face and asked gently, "Don't you have any eyes? Haven't you sensed that I am in love with you? Oh, my Sasha, promise me—please promise me—not to bring this up again until the right time has come!"

He couldn't understand that at all. "But when will be the right time?"

"You ought to know that. I have waited for the trip to

Moscow for such a long time. I've worked so hard for it. I know that the Lord has a plan for the two of us. But right now I cannot think of my own personal happiness. Can you understand that?"

"Well, why not think of *my* happiness?"

"What egotists you men are! And I had talked myself into believing you are different. All right now, let's get into the water!" She jumped into the surf.

They did not return home until nearly evening. The guests had already departed. Old Sokolov sat reading on the veranda. He looked cheerfully at both Sasha and Irina but said nothing.

Sasha did not think everything was so cheerful. "God will show us our future path," Irina had told him. "Let us pray for each other in the future as we have in the past." He certainly wanted to do that. And certainly he did not intend to thwart the plans which the Lord had for them both. But was "the dialogue" really part of the Lord's plan? Sasha had an ominous feeling that Irina was chasing a mirage.

13 The Youth Meeting

Irina had returned from her visit to the parents of Vanya Moiseyev, a young soldier murdered by the KGB. She had spoken with Vanya's parents for a long time and was trying to assimilate Vanya's thought processes. To give her father some idea of what they were, she played a tape containing Vanya's personal testimony. The tape included Vanya's discussion of the miracles he claimed to have witnessed.

Her father merely shrugged his shoulders and said, "I don't believe in miracles, my dear. The young man may have been in some sort of ecstatic trance. Of course this does not necessarily imply that he had a psychological illness. Undoubtedly the KGB authorities were afraid visions like these might attract the attention of nonbelieving young people, and for that reason dispatched him into eternity." That's how this former KGB officer reacted.

Irina trusted her father implicitly. She knew she could depend totally on him. And since she was intellectually on the same level as he was because of her academic background, he no longer made any effort to shake her convictions. Thus when the KGB functionaries indicated to Sokolov one day that, as a Communist, he ought to put pressure on his daughter to stop "running to the Baptist prayer-house," he simply said, "She is a scientist herself and is superior to me in scientific knowledge; so she ought to know what she is doing."

He did not beat about the bush when he asked his old

friends still in the KGB to leave Irina alone. Despite this they began to persecute her with the zeal of hunters. Yuri saw clearly that she was in real danger. He had warned her of this when they were still living with the Serovs and she pestered her father's cousin with questions.

During that time an entirely new series of legal proceedings had been launched against the dissidents.

"Why does the state treat these dissidents with such cold-blooded brutality? Why this severity?" Irina had wanted to know.

Serov had simply evaded her questions with statements like, "Those dissidents ought to be grateful they aren't being shot as they would have been in the days of Stalin!"

Irina had not allowed herself to be put off like that. "In other words you are implying, if I understand you correctly, that it is an especially humanitarian act of the government to throw perfectly healthy human beings into psychiatric asylums or to hand them prison sentences of ten years or even more! Is that what you meant by that statement?" she had retorted angrily.

After an even earlier exchange Serov had told her, "You know what, Irina? You ask too many questions. If you keep this up you may very well land on the blacklist before you know what's happening to you."

Now things had reached that point. And as Sokolov was forced to discover in Minsk, Irina was being shadowed there, too. He spoke to her quite candidly about it, offering her his help.

Irina gratefully accepted his offer. After that, Yuri began to initiate her into all the subtleties of the KGB's methods. He made it crystal clear to her that if she was convinced of the lawfulness of her activities as a Christian and intended to continue them, she would also have to study her opponent's methodology and techniques. Otherwise whatever successes she might anticipate would be doomed to failure right from the start.

Yuri began a rigorous program of training. For example, he simulated an actual KGB chase, giving Irina the assignment of losing her pursuers. This turned out to be anything but a simple task. But they trained tirelessly until Irina was able to recognize quickly even a very sophisticated pursuit and to rid herself of it.

It was more difficult to teach the young woman the art of unmasking a spy or informer. Yuri offered his services to the Baptist congregations in the area when they made plans to hold a youth rally in a forest.

Organizing such an event was exceptionally difficult since youths under the age of eighteen were prohibited from taking part in any of the church's worship services. Someone with sharp instincts was needed. Yuri, who no longer objected to the church itself except for the faithless behavior of its servants, flung himself with great zest into the task of preparing a strategy for such a youth gathering. Irina submitted his recommendations to the young people's committee as her own, since no one was to suspect that these excellent plans emanated from her father. They were, in fact, so outstanding that no discussion was needed before their adoption.

The planners knew that eventually the militia would hear of these plans and would initiate counteractivity immediately. Experience had also taught Yuri that no responsible group of leaders in the Soviet Union could function without the presence of an informer in its midst. He made certain Irina checked out her friends to see who it was.

Irina arranged to meet with each member of the youth leadership and tell him, after receiving strict assurances of secrecy, something confidential previously known only to her. Among other things she described the status of the congregation's library.

For a long time the militia had been extremely eager to learn the location of this library. They had never succeeded in discovering its location. In the meantime the house in which it initially had been secreted had been sold, and the books had been moved to a safer place. Irina told one of her friends she knew where this library was located, without telling him that the books had long since been spirited away from there. And, would you believe it, two days after that the militia appeared on the scene with a search warrant, much to the discomfort of the retired air force colonel who now lived in the house.

Thus Irina unmasked the man who, much to his own regret, had become an informer for the militia. However, it would have been unwise to remove him from the young people's committee. Instead Irina let a few trustworthy friends in on the man's activities and they agreed to give the informer the job of finding an appropriate spot for the youth gathering. While he got busy looking within a fifty-kilometer radius of the city for a clearing large enough for the meeting, the rest of them decided on a completely different site, about which the informer naturally was not told.

All the youth leaders and their groups were told to assemble at a location about fifteen kilometers from the ultimate meeting place. From there everyone was to proceed to the final destination by foot. The informer was the leader of a youth group from the suburbs. One week before the gathering he told his people where and at what time the youth meeting was to take place, naming the spot where they were to join the others beforehand. He drove there early that morning only to find, to his surprise, that not a soul was there to join him. The leader of the choir had told the young people secretly where the meeting was really going to take place and had later conveyed them to the actual meeting site.

The informer concluded that he was tardy and that the members had marched off without waiting for him. He got into a bus and proceeded to drive in the direction of the meeting place he had selected. After that he had to walk ten more kilometers. When he finally arrived at the spot he thought they had selected, there was no one there. Suddenly he realized what had happened, and fear almost paralyzed him. Simultaneously a genuine feeling of shame threatened to overwhelm him. He slipped to the ground, crying like a baby.

Soon he began to hear some noises. This was the militia preparing to chase the young people away and to arrest their leaders. But after the militiamen had surrounded the meadow they discovered they had been duped by the same informer who had already sent them on a wild goose chase when they looked for the congregation's library.

The militia major now complained bitterly to Major Lupa about the rascal who was constantly turning in false alarms. Then he turned on the unfortunate cause of his misery, saying, "What did you think, anyway? That you could play cat and mouse with us? Are you making fun of us?"

He didn't bother to listen to the weeping young man's explanations, ordering one of the militiamen to hustle him off to the station and to place him in custody for further investigation.

About two hundred militiamen stood around the forest clearing in small groups. Some were smoking peaceably and talking quietly. Others, who normally would have had the day off if they had not been called for "Operation X," cursed softly under their breath throwing hateful glances toward the informer. The young man knew full well that during the interrogation the irritated militiamen were going to beat him until he was unconscious. In his desperation he resolved to take his life while still in the holding cell.

What he did not know was that Major Lupa had placed him under constant surveillance. Old man Lupa had initiated this as well. Irina, worried about the unhappy informer, had told the old man her secret and had asked him to find out how many militiamen had been dispatched for the operation.

Old Lupa went straight to his grandson's apartment. The major received the elderly gentleman with his customary heartiness, but the old man could tell that there was tension in the air.

"What's going on?" said the old man affably. "Are you off

on a big operation again? It looks to me as if you are getting ready for a major battle! Is some gang planning to rob one of the office buildings?"

"Gang, you say?" the major grimly contradicted him. "It's some of those Baptists of yours! They don't seem to have learned a thing and are planning one of these meetings in a forest again. So we have to do our duty! And I was just about to go fishing with my wife. I've been looking forward to it so much! But no! The Baptists will not give us any peace!"

"But, dear Grandson," the grandfather quickly said, "don't get all excited before it's time. Maybe the whole thing is a fabrication? What are they supposed to be up to? A meeting in the forest?"

"We've received information from a reliable source," the major stated, "and now I've got to get going. Why don't you stay here and console my dear little wife?"

"Make sure your 'source' doesn't cause you problems. What if it turns out that he led you astray?" the elderly gentleman asked casually. "How many men are you going to be using?"

Major Lupa gave the old man a searching look. "Now listen, you're not keeping any secrets from me, are you? Two hundred militiamen are going to be involved in this. And if the fellow put one over on us, my boys are going to have his head!"

Old man Lupa soberly looked into his grandson's eyes. "So they're going to put him out of his misery, eh? I imagine he can live through a beating from your men's fists, but he might just hang himself later out of pure shame and misery!" The major examined the old man's face without a word, threw on his coat, and stalked out.

When he reached the clearing he knew at once that his grandfather had been right, and he immediately ordered his lieutenant personally to put the young man into his cell and to have him watched carefully.

While all of these things were taking place, Serov's four

children were riding up the River Ptitch in a motorboat. Their mother was busy in the house and their father was away on one of his interminable official trips. The children intended to visit their maternal grandmother in the "October housing development" and had brought along candied fruits, smoked ham, and homemade bread for her. The grandmother was quite old and frail. She could hardly walk, but her mind had not yet been affected. The children were looking forward to their visit to the elderly lady. They looked forward to sitting in front of her little house and listening to her tales of the old days. They especially wanted to hear about their grandfather, who had served in Budenny's cavalry during the civil war. Grandmother told all these stories so excitingly that the children soon forgot about what time it was.

When the children finally realized how late it was, it was already late afternoon. They should have been under way long ago! They had promised their mother to stay no longer than two hours, and four hours already had elapsed! Grandmother haltingly accompanied the children to the river. They got into their boat and waved to grandma one more time, calling, "So long! We'll come to visit you again soon!" The old lady waved back and slowly hobbled home.

The oldest Serov child, Alyosha, started the motor and guided the boat to the center of the stream. The girls, Nina and Svetlana, pulled off their blouses and let the sun brown their backs. The youngest child, Igor, dipped his hand into the river so that the girls were splashed by the water. They screamed and demanded that he stop.

They had gone a few kilometers when the engine began to cough and finally stopped. Alyosha fussed with the engine, trying to start it again. Finally he remembered to look at the gas tank. "Well, isn't that something? We've got no more gasoline!" he yelled.

"That's all right!" Nina retorted. "We'll just start rowing, that's all. You and Igor can man the oars, and we'll be the passengers."

Alyosha laughed and reached for the oars.

Suddenly Igor began to listen intensely to something. He asked, "Can't you hear it? Somebody's singing out there!"

Svetlana looked at him contemptously and teased him, "You're hearing ghosts again!"

Igor tapped his forehead. "You're spinning tales again! Can't you hear the singing?"

True enough, a beautiful choir song could be heard from the forest. Alyosha stopped rowing and listened. Then he said, "Those are Christians singing. Probably our Irina organized something for her fellow believers again."

"I don't like these Christians," said Svetlana, pouting. "Christians are uneducated and ignorant people."

"You're not going to tell me," retorted Alyosha, "that our Irina is uneducated. She has finished her doctoral dissertation. The Christians can't help it if our government often hinders them from getting higher education. Anyhow, I think it is unfair to act this way toward those who think differently from us."

"I can see why father says Irina has too great an influence over you," countered Svetlana waspishly.

But Nina told her, "Aw, stop saying these things! Aloysha, would you row us to the shore? I'd like to see what these Christians are doing in that clearing. Did you pack your camera in your rucksack?"

Alyosha nodded and steered toward the river's edge. Svetlana objected at first and complained, but her inquisitiveness eventually got the better of her. Soon she was straining her neck to see what was taking place in the forest and where the singing was coming from.

The children got out of the boat and tied it to a young tree, then began to search for the singers. They crept through the underbrush very carefully, hoping no one would notice them. Finally they saw a large, grassy clearing where young people stretched as far as the eye could see.

At the precise moment when they reached the clearing, a

young preacher began to speak. His sermon about the evidence of the power of the Almighty in creation was delivered in such simple language that anyone could understand it. And the longer Svetlana listened to him the more strongly she felt she could trust this man with her life. After a few moments the children overcame all their reservations and began to listen raptly. Man could not justify himself with anything, said the preacher, if he denied God's existence. All of creation witnessed powerfully to the presence of its creator, who had made everything for man and for his wellbeing. Man's task is to hold faithfully in trust the earth and all that inhabits it.

The young Serovs were amazed at how well the preacher presented his subject and how convincingly he spoke. No, surely this was no uneducated, ignorant human being as their leader had attempted to persuade them in school. By no means! He had now spoken for fully half an hour, yet the children wanted to hear more. They could not get enough of what they were hearing.

Suddenly the preacher turned directly and personally to each member of his audience. "If you have not given the glory to the earth's creator up to this moment, if you have not given yourself to Him yet in order to live for His Son, Jesus Christ, then you can do it this very minute. Say to Jesus that you are sorry you have been so far away from Him, and give Him your heart! I ask all those who wish to do so to come forward."

Alyosha gave a quick glance toward his brother and sisters. For a moment he thought he was dreaming. Svetlana and Igor were rising from their tree stump and walking forward hand in hand! Nina followed behind them. Alyosha's heart was in his throat. As the oldest, he knew the deep significance this step would have for all of them. He hesitated for a fraction of a second; and then he, too, went forward, following the irresistible yearning of his heart.

The preacher repeated his invitation one more time. About

a hundred young people began to gather around him. Then many assistants came forward. They began to speak with each individual. Serov's children were taken by Sasha. He took them to a more secluded part of the forest in order not to be disturbed, and there he prayed with them. When they gave him their names he was startled, for Irina had previously told him about the Serovs. To his relief she herself soon arrived on the scene. She kissed all four of her cousins and asked them how they had happened to get there. Alyosha told her the whole story, adding, "We are so happy that we chanced on this. We don't care any longer about the fact that mother will scold us for being away so long."

Irina turned serious. "We'll look for fuel for your boat right away so that you can get home. Your mother permitted you to go away for two hours and now you've been away from home for five hours. Sasha, would you explain to them how to behave as Christians in their home? I'll start looking for gasoline for the boat!"

Irina disappeared. Sasha sat on the grass with the children and began to explain to them what could happen under some circumstances if their parents or classmates discovered that they had become Christians. The children listened attentively. They did not appear uneasy about the possible consequences of their decision. Thus when Sasha told them emphatically that it would be extremely important for them to read the Bible every day, Svetlana responded, "Why don't we all read the Bible together, Alyosha? You could then explain something I don't understand."

Alyosha simply nodded. It might not be too difficult to find a place and time in the early morning, he thought. But Svetlana, who always liked to sleep late, might not get up early enough.

After a while Irina reappeared in the company of a young man who was carrying a metal container. "Let's go. We'll get your boat going again and you can go on your way home!" Irina ordered.

"But Irinotchka," Nina begged her, "can't we stay with you for at least another hour?" Some of the young people had begun to play their musical instruments.

Irina shook her head. "Alyoshka, you're already sixteen. You certainly understand by now what a difficult situation we are in. If the militia were to strike suddenly, and if they found you here, then my friends and I would be sent to jail just for your presence alone. Besides, your mother is waiting for you."

Alyosha understood her and got up.

"Come on!" he said to his brother and sisters.

Sasha and Irina accompanied them to the river, refilled the boat's gas tank and readied the boat for their departure. After that they said good-bye to the children and stood waving for a long time until the boat disappeared around a curve in the stream.

Irina still behaved as if she had been struck by lightning. In her mind she could see with terrifying clarity the possible consequences of the fact that, of all people, the Serov children had turned to Jesus Christ at this young people's gathering! When the preacher asked her about these nice children she had just escorted to the river, she said, "They are relatives of mine. But believe me, the less you know about them the better it will be for you. We have to pray for them very hard," she added a bit helplessly.

Her mind was in a turmoil. *What will happen now? Will the children tell the whole story when they get home?* The possible consequences of that could not even be guessed at. What was she to do?

The others about Irina were baffled. She appeared totally absentminded, far away in her thoughts. Only Sasha and Vassiley, who had come to join them that evening, were able to understand what was going on inside her.

Mrs. Serov had been waiting for the children for several hours. Again and again she looked for them down the river. Why hadn't they come back yet? She hoped nothing had happened to her elderly mother. At long last they arrived and stormed into the house, tired but excited. Their explanations and stories tumbled out as they told why they had gotten home so late. For the moment they mentioned nothing about any youth meeting. They had returned enormously hungry and made short work of the food given them.

At the table the mother told them, "Do you know what? Dad telephoned and told me that he will be home in a few days."

At that Alyosha became reflective and said, "Mother, we haven't told you everything."

The other children suddenly grew silent. The mother looked inquiringly at her oldest child's face. Her heart told her that some misfortune was about strike. Alyosha remained quiet for a moment, then began to tell his story. "When we had run out of fuel we rowed toward shore and stopped there. We heard singing. We were curious about who would be singing in the midst of a forest and began to follow the singing to its source. There we ran into a large number of young people—at least a thousand, if not more. One of their preachers had just begun to speak. After we had heard his sermon, all four of us decided to become Christians." Alyosha became quiet and looked at his mother, saying, "Please, mother, try to understand. You must also help us explain the whole thing to father."

The mother sat there, pale and silent. The enormity of what she had just heard had made her speechless. Finally after a long pause she said, "Was Irina there, too?"

"We didn't run into her there until the very end," Nina said hurriedly. "Just a short time before we got under way again. She had nothing to do with it!" Because there had been talk in the past of Irina's bad influence over the children, all four of them made strenuous efforts to absolve their dear Irina of any complicity.

"Good. All right, children," said their mother finally. "Finish eating your dinner. I'm going to my room to think about all this. Right now I cannot think clearly about it." The children knew her well and realized she would not make a scene or try to talk them out of it.

Mrs. Serov believed that the children had acted in a rush of enthusiasm and that everything would get back to normal soon. But how could she explain all this to her husband, who would be certain to let loose a torrent of invective in reaction to the situation? Above all, this would really hurt Irina if Serov finally heard about it.

Mrs. Serov locked herself inside her husband's study for a long time and thought things through. Then she reached for the telephone and dialed the KGB department where her husband worked.

The duty officer was at the other end of the line.

"I've got to speak to Semyonov," she said. The duty officer suggested that she try to reach Semyonov at home.

He was at home when she called, and after listening carefully to all she had to say he said, "Many thanks. Please don't worry about anything. I will talk everything over with your husband. And we'll smoke these Baptists out of that forest!"

In that way the KGB finally learned where the young people were meeting. Semyonov alerted the militia again and in addition ordered reserve detachments to report to the area to aid in the chase of the young people. Everyone got ready for action again.

Irina had foreseen what would happen. After the children's departure homewards she swung onto her motorcycle and raced to her father, after telling Sasha her worst fears.

Yuri had gone fishing for a few days and was actually in a spot only a few kilometers from the meeting site. He had caught a goodly number of fish and was in the process of cooking a robust fish soup when Irina arrived, completely out of breath. She looked so pale and stricken that he immediately sensed something serious had gone wrong.

"What happened?" he asked, full of concern. His daughter told him what had occurred. He sat speechless and merely shook his head.

"The militia won't be coming any more tonight," he finally stated. "It's getting dark already. They won't come for you at night." He smiled a sad smile. "Isn't it awful? First it was she, then you, and now even my cousin Christen's children! Serov won't be able to take that, just as I couldn't in those days. He will take revenge on you. And on me, naturally." Sokolov resumed an oppressive silence.

"Dad," Irina said impatiently, "time is passing. What are we going to do?"

Her father brushed against his forehead as if to wipe away his somber forebodings and said, "Doesn't your Bible say that the angels in heaven are glad when a sinner repents? That is coming true now, isn't it? So perhaps the angels are really joyful, but you and I are caught on the horns of a dilemma and we're unhappy."

"That's not the way I feel," Irina interrupted him. "I'm very happy. But we've got to get busy planning a way out of this situation. It would be a pity if the young people had to break up their gathering prematurely after all the work it took to get them together. While we're sitting together here, my friends in the forest have broken up into groups and are praying for a positive result from our talk here."

"You didn't tell them you were coming to see me, did you?" asked Yuri, alarmed.

"Of course not! I simply told them I was going to see someone who would advise me about what we are to do. My friends never ask me nosy questions anyway."

Her father calmed down again and said, "Now eat some of the fish soup, and while you're doing that I will look at the map of this area." She was certainly hungry, so Irina attacked the soup with vigor. Meanwhile her father disappeared into the hut which he had built for himself out of bales of freshly mown hay.

Some time later, smiling from ear to ear, he left his hut and suggested, "What would you say to a change of site for your friends this very night?"

"And how are we going to accomplish that?"

"It's certainly possible," Sokolov explained. "As soon as darkness falls, your young people must break into groups of two or three and, keeping some distance between groups, they must migrate to the other forest—the one in which the militia looked for you in the first place. Do you understand? You've got to shift to the very place where the informer sent the militia on a wild goose chase in the first place. No one will notice a large number of young folks going for a walk in this enormous forest if they are in pairs or in small groups. After all, this is a weekend; and who knows how many people are headed for this forest right now? The partisans were able to hide out in the forest during the war, and you will succeed as well."

"But there's a distance of fifty to sixty kilometers between the two forests!" cried Irina.

"That is correct," said Sokolov, "but the night is long, and you will be able to bring it off. Suppose the young people, in small groups as I've stated, walk into some of these little towns around here. There's no big problem with that. The buses continue running fairly regularly at least until midnight. So everybody could cover part of the journey by bus. Of course, by hook or by crook, everybody will have to do at least twenty kilometers on foot. Either you change to another location, or you have to cancel the meeting. Because tomorrow morning, I'll guarantee it, the militia will be there!"

Irina's father concluded his advice, making it clear that he had nothing more to say.

Irina hurriedly kissed her father and ran back to her motorcycle, which she had parked some distance away.

"I'll stay here until morning and see what happens," Yuri told her as she departed.

Irina returned to the meeting area at top speed and immediately began to discuss the matter with the preachers and her close friends. They all agreed to the idea of changing locations. The rest of the young people were told of the plan.

They all bowed their heads in prayer once more, and then they began to drift apart in small groups. Vassiley had some additional matters to talk over with Irina and rode with her on the motorcycle. Many others had brought their bicycles, and they took along as many as possible of those who had come by train. Soon the entire youth gathering was on its way to the new site.

The next morning the militia combed the entire forest, but once again without success. Major Lupa ironically asked his boss, "And now whom are we going to punish for a false alarm?" The other man did not reply. Of course the trampled grass left no doubt that the young people actually had been there. Everyone attempted to figure out whether the Christians had returned home or had merely changed their locale. The militia colonel gave orders over his radio that all the militiamen were to return to the city, but he also ordered the traffic-control helicopter to start scouring the countryside. The place where the young people had regathered was discovered within a few hours.

Once again the furious militiamen were drummed together. Yet as the troops reached their destination, the Christian young people were already departing for home. The militia threw themselves upon the Christians in blind fury, pinned their arms to their backs and threw them into the Black Marias* waiting for them. The militia were so incensed that not a single one of them had any desire to adhere to regulations in dealing with the young people. They broke the arms of two young boys, who had to be taken to a hospital. Many of the Christians were severely beaten right where they were discovered or on the way back—wherever there weren't too many "impartial observers."

Many of the young people served fourteen-day sentences and returned home happy and blessed. The militia was unable to identify the clergy responsible for the gathering.

*Police vans.

14 A Surprise Attack

The sky had been overcast the entire afternoon, and it rained off and on. It wasn't until dusk that the sun finally showed its face, only to disappear again shortly behind some clouds. It was getting dark already. Those walking along the streets had to put up their coat collars and pull their jackets more tightly around their shoulders because of the penetrating cold and the humid wind beginning to blow from the north.

A young woman deep in thought meandered through the city park. She seemed oblivious to the cold air and to the approaching darkness. The wind tore at her light summer dress, baring her shapely legs and knees so that she constantly had to tug at her skirt and smooth it.

Every so often she bumped into a passerby, made some quick excuses, and again resumed her deep brooding. She apparently was concerned about something very important and disturbing, for her finely sculptured face had an almost melancholy expression.

Eventually she realized that people were looking curiously at her; so she decided to sit down on one of the benches. At this point she finally became aware of how cold it had become and of the fact that her stomach was growling. She glanced at her wristwatch and realized to her dismay that it was already six o'clock. She apparently had been walking around here for four hours. She looked around her and spotted a small restaurant in one of the streets which butted up against the park. Above the entrance gleamed a sign with the name "The Lilac Bush."

The young woman stepped inside, took a seat by a table next to a window, and ordered dinner for herself. The waitress examined her from stem to stern and asked, "Aren't you freezing in such a thin dress in weather like this?" The young woman looked at her distractedly and shrugged her shoulders.

She ate her meal, put some money on the plate, and headed for the exit.

"Stop! Stop, citizen!" the waitress called after her. "You haven't even paid me!" The young woman gestured toward the money without saying a word and walked out.

She had covered several blocks when suddenly a feeling of imminent danger overcame her. She began to run, hurrying through the entrance door of a large building. Behind her she heard the screech of brakes, the shattering of glass, and the dreadful screams of an injured person. She whirled around and looked into the street. The driver was hanging out of the car's door, and he was covered with blood. He seemed to be wedged inside the badly damaged automobile. The man in the back seat apparently was injured also and was yelling at the top of his lungs.

The young woman hurried toward the driver and tried to pry him out of the smashed car. He was bleeding profusely. His right arm had been torn away and lay alongside him on the pavement. The young woman tugged at him with all her strength, but he was so firmly wedged inside that she could not budge him.

"Why don't you do something?" A curious mass of humanity had begun to gather around the horrible display but no one seemed to be able to do anything. She cried desperately, "Don't just stand around! Help me!"

Two men and a woman emerged from the crowd. The woman was a nurse. The men attempted to open the rear door. They struck at the car's windows with stones from the pavement and tried to pull the second injured man out of the car through the window, but to no avail. He, too, was firmly wedged inside the automobile.

"What is keeping the police and the ambulance?" the young woman asked. She walked over to the side and observed the carnage once more. The car had hit a telephone pole, knocked it down, and then struck the building into which she had run for refuge. She shivered at the thought that she probably would no longer be alive had she not acted as quickly as she did.

"Why don't you step inside and wash yourself?" said a friendly woman's voice. It was one of the cleaning women who scrubbed the floors of the building's offices. Only now did the young woman notice the sign on the entrance door: 5. *Headquarters of the Construction Ministry of the Republic.* She followed the older woman inside the building as a doctor and hospital orderly were just beginning to try to remove the injured men from the wreckage.

The cleaning woman, obviously friendly, held a towel in her hand as the young woman washed herself. "I was just looking out of the window back there and I saw you running," the older woman said. "At that distance I thought you were my grandchild, Sima. I expect her at any time. So I went to the entrance door to unlock it for her, then returned to cleaning the windows. All of a sudden this car came racing down the street. The man in the car pointed his finger out of the window at you. You were already quite close to the entrance door; so I realized that you were not my granddaughter. Everything seemed so peculiar. Think what you wish, but it looked to me as if the man in the car was trying to run over you!"

The young woman smiled weakly. "Oh no, why should anybody be trying to kill me?"

"Irina Sokolova!" Someone in the street was calling that name.

"Irina Sokolova! Please come forward immediately!"

The young woman gave a start.

"Among you there must be a citizen named Sokolova," said the militiaman to the crowd. "Irina Sokolova, I urge you to come forward immediately."

The assembled crowd looked at each other questioningly. No one came forward.

In extreme anguish the young woman grasped the old woman's hands. "Grandmother!" she whispered imploringly, "I am a Christian and will pray for you to the end of my days, but please save me right now! Please unlock the rear door of this building for me so I can get away from here without being noticed."

Wordlessly the old woman took her by the hand and led her through an unlit passageway to the rear entrance. Before she let her leave she kissed the young woman on the cheek and whispered, "Hurry, my child, but be careful! Gogol Boulevard begins right behind this building, and you must hurry across it and turn into the narrow Sverdlov Street. It's dark there, so that no one will notice your soiled dress. Here's the key to the garden gate. Throw it over the gate into the grass after you've gone through the gate. My grandchild will look for the key tomorrow." She looked at the young woman one more time and added thoughtfully, "My husband was a priest. He died in prison."

The young woman quickly embraced her and vanished into the night.

In the meantime, some people had told the militia that the person they were searching for might possibly have entered the building with the cleaning woman. Two of the militiamen marched to the main entrance. At that moment the elderly woman was talking with her granddaughter, who had arrived a bit late.

"A young woman was seen entering the building with you," bellowed one of the militiamen. "Where is she?"

The cleaning woman gave him a wide-eyed look and stated innocently, "Where is she? Why she's standing right before you! She's my grandchild, my golden treasure! She's studying at the medical school," she added with great pride.

"And what are you doing here?" blurted the other militiaman to the young girl.

"Oh, I'm helping my grandma," she said quickly. "I came a little later than usual tonight because we had a Komsomol training session. I arrived right after this terrible accident. I wanted to be of assistance," she said in explaining the blood on her dress.

The militiaman pulled a photograph out of his breast pocket and held it up against the girl. Then the two militiamen left.

After a while the curiosity seekers left the scene. The injured, unconscious men were taken to a hospital. The state inspector's vehicle came by and loaded the crushed automobile into a truck. The street was swept clean of the chunks of cement dislodged from the building's facade. Then everything resumed its normal daily grind. Only the large hole in the side of the building, which went unrepaired for a long period, told of the accident that had occurred there. Each time she passed it the cleaning woman quickly made the sign of the cross and whispered, "Praise God, she is still alive!"

The young woman never saw the elderly lady again. After a short while the local newspaper, in a brief report on the very last page, noted that there had been an automobile accident on Lomonossov Street, during which both the car's driver and its passenger died.

Irina reached home safely even though the city's entire militia had been searching for her. She could not understand why they had chosen that day to look for her. She was to be in Moscow in two days, for she and her friends had finally received permission to conduct their discussion about the affairs of the church with representatives of the government's Central Committee.

Several weeks earlier Irina had succeeded in persuading an elderly preacher from Siberia to take part in this dialogue. She was awaiting his arrival on this day. But he had not come. She and her father lived outside the city, and their apartment was difficult to reach by public transportation. Only during the rush hours in the morning and evening did one streetcar per hour make a trip there. The rest of the time a bus left the city park for their district only once every three hours. This is why she had had to stay in the city.

Irina was worried. Ryabushin was in his eighties and recently had been complaining about chest pains. Would he be able to survive this long journey at all? She reproached herself for having drawn the old gentleman into the whole affair.

When she finally reached home she made an effort to be quiet so that her father would not notice her arrival and see what condition she was in. While looking inside she had noticed that her father was seated at his desk in his study. She succeeded in creeping inside the house without being noticed. She took off her shoes, reached for a few of her things in her room, and slipped into the bathtub.

When her father heard the water running he called from his study, "Irina! I've got a telegram for you here."

Irina turned off the water. "Who is it from?" she answered back.

"From Ryabushin. He's letting you know that he made a stopover during his trip and will be arriving here at the airport tomorrow."

"Thank you, father!" Irina called out, suddenly breaking into tears. Her father heard her sobbing and, filled with concern, came to the bathroom door.

"What's the matter, child?

For a long time she was unable to reply.

"Later, father!" she finally said chokingly, "I'll tell you everything later!"

She sat in the bathtub for quite a while, sobbing quietly. The tension inside her had been too great; and now when she learned that she had been worrying needlessly, she inwardly collapsed. After a long while she calmed down and began to pray quietly. She thanked the Lord for Ryabushin and for the fact that he was all right. Then she recalled all the people with whom she had come in contact during this day. She had made it a habit at night to think of everyone whom she had encountered during the day and to pray for them. And now she was praying for the two men who had been in the accident, for the good cleaning woman, for the woman's grandchild, and for the militiamen.

Then she attempted to recapitulate how she had gotten back home. She had run into Gogol Alley, looked all around and then crossed over into Sverdlov Street, which turned out to be a very narrow, unlighted passageway. But what direction should she follow then, and how would she manage to get out of the city without being noticed by anyone? Obviously she could not avoid running into someone during her long walk, and whoever she met would notify the militia of her presence, even if only because of the bloodstains on her dress.

For the moment she hid behind a vegetable stand. After her eyes had become accustomed to the darkness she suddenly noticed a telephone on the vegetable stand's wall. Trembling, she picked up the receiver and dialed a number. Her colleague, an engineer named Boyko, had been a member of the committee for human rights for many years. Irina also knew that he recently had inherited his father's automobile.

"Misha," she spoke into the mouthpiece excitedly, "this is Irina. I'm in Sverdlov Street at the moment and urgently need your help!"

"Woman, really!" Boyko almost shouted at the other end, "I've been looking for you all day long! I'll drive to the vegetable stand. You hide someplace nearby in the meantime! There'll be a night watchman there after ten o'clock, but you don't have to worry about him. He is my grandfather. I'll explain everything later! Stay well!"

Boyko hung up. Soon Irina heard footsteps. She slid into the night watchman's cabin without making a sound and squatted on the floor next to the chair without moving. Two men slowly sauntered by her hiding place.

"I can't understand it," one of them said. "Why are we to catch her on the street and arrest her? That's really nonsense! If she's committed a crime, she can be arrested at her home. Can you make sense of it?"

"Naw," the other one replied, "but what can we do? That's what the colonel ordered." The voices became softer and eventually faded away.

Some time later Irina heard an automobile engine. It was Misha's car. He came to a halt and opened his door. Irina hurried from her hiding place, jumping into the car's back seat.

While driving, Misha reported, "I am informed by a reliable source [i.e., a friend whose name he would not disclose] that the city government made a decision to keep the young Christians' dialogue in Moscow from taking place." They feared that certain illegal steps they had taken toward the Christians would be disclosed during these talks and would cause difficulties for them. Misha's friend was employed in the ideological section of the district committee of the Party and had told Misha that if they were unable to kill Irina inconspicuously she was to be arrested somewhere on the streets. Misha had already been under way all day long in order to warn her of this.

Irina could not grasp what she was hearing. Her mind refused to accept it. The people in the city government must have taken leave of their senses. Not in her wildest dreams would she think of complaining about the city authorities to the government! Every child knew that in 1929 a law was passed which legalized illegal proceedings against Christians. The Christians themselves knew well that all the violations of laws committed against them had their basis in this law. For this reason the Council of Churches had implored the government repeatedly to replace this inhuman law with another more democratic one, a law which would confer the same rights on them as those enjoyed by the militant atheists.

As she now sat in the bathtub thinking back over the day's events, Irina felt such a soothing warmth, and her inner tensions had been so great that she dozed off without expecting to. Her father waited for her in his armchair. His heart was full of dark foreboding.

*   *   *

Ryabushin, meanwhile, had interrupted his journey at Perm. His sister and her children lived there and he wanted to visit them. After that he asked one of his nephews, a taxi driver, to drive him to the Symyansky district.

During the trip there Ryabushin reminisced about the old days. More and more often lately he thought out loud, which could at times be dangerous for him.

As a youth he had thrown himself full tilt into the Soviet revolution. The Russian tsar's court had sent him into exile on numerous occasions, and so it happened that he was forced to celebrate the 1917 October revolution in Siberia. On his triumphant return to Petrograd (today's Leningrad) he was given the task of eliminating the "religious scum" of the nation. After that he operated as a partisan in Siberia.

He had always had a lot of luck, this Ryabushin. While a Social Democrat, and subsequently as a Communist, he was so fanatically loyal to his party that he was spared even during the worst days. This included the terrible years of 1937 and 1939, when all sorts of reprisals and mass executions of the innocent as well of the guilty, of Communist as well as non-Communist, were the order of the day.

Misfortune seemed always to make a detour around Ryabushin. Was it because he enjoyed shooting others so much? In 1940 he wrote to his wife that his "activities" gave him an unusual tingle of delight. Naturally he did not mention that his assignment in Kattowitz had been to shoot ten thousand Polish officers.

This secret operation of the Soviet government could not have been entrusted to a better man. Ryabushin had performed his duties extremely conscientiously, so that one could read the following in his notes. "They were all enemies of socialism and therefore my personal enemies. One of the officers had begged me to spare his son, who was still a nursing baby. But I shot the baby in full sight of its mother—she was a peasant. How could I allow any of them to live? The child would grow up, his mother would tell him about me, and the fellow would take his revenge on me. So I wiped them all out."

Ryabushin did not know what it meant to have a guilty conscience. "Does a shoemaker have to be ashamed if everyone is satisfied with the work he has done?" This is what he often said at home. "One's job is simply one's job."

On top of that, Ryabushin was a very pleasant man to work with. He had asked the Party for no preferential treatment for his family. He even built a house for his family with his own hands. He constructed all the furniture by himself, for on top of everything he was an excellent cabinet maker.

Blessed with a constitution that seemed indestructible, he had outlived Yeshov, Stalin, and Khrushchev and had the habit of saying, "Well, maybe I will even outlive Brezhnev." Should any member of the government pass away or be removed from his post, Ryabushin wept sincerely for him.

His wife frequently became upset at this and scolded him, "Well, what are you blubbering about now, old man? Didn't Beria deserve getting shot?"

"It might be that he deserved it," retorted Ryabushin, "but he also did his duty for socialism. Good or bad, the man fought for socialism!"

His philosophy of life got on many people's nerves and caused many to become angry at him. But in the district committee of the Communist Party the officials only smiled. Why, this man was irreplaceable! Someone high up always held a protective hand over him so that nothing would happen to him. Socialism was an absolute mania with him. When the Second World War broke out, Ryanbushin's amazement knew no limits. "Are the Germans crazy? We'll twist all their heads off if they don't maintain the peace!"

He immediately volunteered to go to the battlefront. And how he fought! When his infantry company was surrounded, he vanished into the Bryansk woods and became a partisan again. He was wounded nine times—they were merely scratches, he maintained later.

His ninth wound was a different matter, and thereby hangs a tale. It was inflicted on him by a three-year-old by means of a pocket knife—straight in his seat. This happened in the village of Gomel. There lived a man named Makarov, who was an invalid and therefore not drafted into the service. When the Germans occupied Gomel they asked Makarov, who had studied history, to take a position as a teacher. He agreed.

Ryabushin learned of this and, in the company of two other partisans, paid a "visit" to Makarov. They held a kangaroo court and sentenced Makarov to death, shooting him in the presence of his wife. At this point Makarov's little son, Misha, stabbed Ryabushin in the rear with all the strength of his three years, crying loudly in the meantime, "Daddy! Dear Daddy, please don't die!"

Ryabushin was so surprised by the child's action that he allowed the little one to remain alive. Misha later became a preacher in the Ukraine.

After Ryabushin had accepted the Lord the two of them, the murderer and the son of his victim, met on several occasions. They both reminisced about the old days. Ryabushin cried every time, and Misha consoled him. Then the two of them prayed together.

Ryabushin worked as head of several concentration camps during a period of fifteen years. He himself had been an inmate of one of the so-called death camps at Auschwitz during the war. There he had decided that it would not be a bad idea to deal with the enemies of socialism in a similar way. Thus when the war was over he volunteered as an employee in one of the gulags (the network of concentration camps in the USSR).

Upon his arrival in Perm this time, Ryabushin was drawn to the camp he had served as director before he was pensioned off. In those days the camp was filled with political prisoners who were forbidden to correspond with the outside world.

In Yakutsk and in Taishet, where he had also served as camp leader, he had become acquainted with many of the Christian prisoners. He chatted with the prisoners as if they were his people. No one suspected that he was an unscrupulous murderer with thousands of killings on his conscience. Often he listened to the speeches given by the Christians. The camp's inhabitants were not afraid of him and called him "the good master." A prisoner named Serge Gratchov once predicted that Ryabushin would one day meet another "Good Master" and that he would become His follower. Ryabushin merely smiled at this prediction. But after returning to his office he called in his operations officer and gave him a terrific dressing-down for permitting the camp to be run too loosely and for failing to prevent the gatherings of "the enemies of the people." Those prisoners whom Ryabushin did not like, or whom he considered dangerous, he removed according to his own methods.

Now Ryabushin was seated in his nephew's car, and his memories—oh, those memories!—of all those things he had done in the name of socialism began to surge through his mind. He sighed deeply over and over. He was aware that he stood at the threshold of another world, of eternity. He was drawn once more to the camp which he had ordered run over by tanks.

The prisoners had started a revolt, but they had been, of course, unarmed. Ryabushin's notes read, "This was the happiest day of my life! I had just been informed that my son had triplets. And then what did I discover?—that these Fascists had begun a revolt!

"I was beside myself with fury. For the first time in my life I lost control of my emotions. I called up Beria, since I personally knew him. 'We'll just let a couple of tanks loose on them,' he said. 'Why shouldn't we make short work of them?'

"The tanks began to roll. I didn't really have any at my disposal; they had to come from Uralsk. The drivers from Perm refused to shoot at their own countrymen; so we had to dispose of a few tank drivers first. The drivers from Uralsk were prepared to do the job and get it over with. They were mostly Kirgiz and of Turkish origin. And they shot their guns—oh, how beautifully they fired them! The prisoners raised their hands to indicate that they were giving up, but the Kirgiz didn't understand their gesture and simply wiped them off the face of the earth. Some of the Christians knelt down to pray. So two tanks simply rolled over them. Only about two hundred Mohammedans were left. When the tank drivers saw them throw themselves down to pray, these drivers also jumped out of their tanks and started to pray alongside their fellow countrymen. They couldn't shoot their own people. When the Kirgiz officer saw this he pulled out his revolver and drilled a hole through his head. I couldn't prevent it. So the Mohammedans were still alive when it was all over. We dispersed them to various camps with instructions to get rid of them as quickly as possible."

Ryabushin wept as he wrote these lines. In place of the former camp there was now a wheatfield. He walked along the field for a great distance, oppressed by the memory of his terrible past. His nephew could not understand his uncle's strange behavior but waited patiently for him in the car.

Ryabushin finally grew tired and sat down on a tree stump at the edge of a forest, pulled a notebook from his briefcase, and began to write.

"I am sitting for the last time in a spot where there was once a Communist extermination camp. My days are numbered, and it will not be possible for me to come to this place again.

"I am guilty of the murder of several thousand innocent human beings, I could not even find the names of their relatives in order to tell them what I inflicted on their dear ones. We were in pursuit of Utopia, and in the process we destroyed the lives of millions of innocent people. Who will honor the memories of these dead in the future?"

Ryabushin suddenly gave a start. A young rabbit sat at his feet, observing him with frightened eyes. Initially the old man was pleased at the sight of the sweet little animal. But the fearstricken, sad look of this creature confused him. What had it been like in those days . . . when hundreds . . . thousands . . . of eyes had looked at him with equally frightened, equally imploring expressions as he pointed his machine gun at them? . . . Ryabushin sighed and closed his eyes. A wave of inner agony shook him. Oh, those merciless recollections! Then a stabbing pain in his chest under his shoulder blade caused him to sigh out loud. The rabbit jumped up, frightened, hurriedly scooting away toward the wheatfield and vanishing there.

Slowly Ryabushin picked himself up and walked with small, labored steps toward his nephew's automobile. Along the way he stopped once again and looked all around. No one could suspect that there ever had been a death camp here where the wheat now stood in orderly rows. *I wish everything which happened in those days had been nothing more than a bad dream!* thought Ryabushin. He was unable to tear himself away and sat down on a small hummock.

"What should we Christians do to prevent this from ever, ever happening again?" he wrote in his notebook. "Are we really praying for quiet, untroubled times? No! Instead we assist others in the killing of more people. With our contributions we give support to so-called freedom movements and thereby the murders of millions of human beings throughout the world. Marxist hangmen cause the deaths of thousands of innocent Christian people of various nationalities and we even lend support—both moral and material—to these criminals.

"O you church! I am ashamed of you as I am of my own past. I am as afraid for your future as I am of my own past! You are a miserable puppet in the hands of these Marxists, and you allow yourself to be exploited by them in our land and in other countries. And you justify this murder and spilling of blood with the argument that the church is obligated never to discriminate against anything.

"To the last argument I, too, say, 'Yes and amen.' It is our duty to denounce injustice just as Jesus Christ did. But where were you, o church, when I was gunning down the innocent? Why did you remain silent then, and why do you remain silent now? Why do you convict those Soviet individuals who demand the freedom of their thoughts and battle for the right to confess their God freely, branding them as criminals at international congresses in foreign countries?

"You've become enslaved, my church! A slave to the might of the world. Oh, how ashamed I am for you! You've become a shameless liar, an inciter of murders. There can be no justification for your deeds, just as there can be no justification for the murders I committed. Future generations will cite our names as examples of dishonor! Yes, you too! You are bespattered by blood and will not accept a cleansing for it. In our country you have sunk so deeply into slavery that you no longer can free yourself of it. If I were not convinced of the existence of God I would burn you at the stake."

Ryabushin arose. It was beginning to get dark. Suddenly he was overcome by fear of those things he had written. He started to leaf through the notebook once again and to read what he had written, in order to think about every single word he had committed to paper.

In the midst of this he burst into tears. As a child distraught over its actions, he began to sob uncontrollably. If only he were a little younger! Maybe around forty years of age! He would arrange his life completely differently. "O Lord, have mercy on us sinners!" he whispered.

His nephew had left the automobile and was striding toward him. Ryabushin turned away and wiped his eyes with his sleeve. He then turned toward the young man and said, "Listen to me. I want to tell you about something. Please write it down when you get home. Attempt, if you will, to listen closely and to remember all the details. But let's go to the car now. It's getting cold."

The two of them did not return home until around midnight. Two days later the nephew presented his resignation to the Communist Party at the local headquarters.

*   *   *

Irina wrote from Moscow as follows.

"Dear Father: I want to write to you quickly so you won't worry. My friends and I have already been in Moscow for three days. We were received by the Central Committee after lunch, and our discussion lasted three hours. I want to let you know the fundamental questions which we laid before the government's representatives.

"First: why are Christians only permitted 'the practice of their worship as a cult' and why is their voice not to be heard outside their church buildings and houses of prayer? The discussion of this topic took at least an hour. Andropov made it clear that the intrusion of the church into the spiritual life of our country's citizens cannot be permitted. It was his feeling that the government confined the activities of Christians to their buildings in order to protect its citizens from the 'opiate of religion.'

"To this Ryabushin interjected, 'Please tell me, my dear man, how something like that can be possible. In times past I fought for socialism hand in hand with priests and other Christians. In those days these people seriously believed that the revolution was the will of God. Without the religiously prepared populace the revolution would have been defeated. Surely these believers fought for a Socialist society in those days. But they surely did *not* fight so the right to preach their

God outside their churches would be taken from them. These Christians had in mind a society free from exploitation, a society in which one could practice one's belief in God freely, as Lenin had promised. Believe me, an old fighter in the revolution, not a single one of these Christians would have remained on the side of the revolution if he had suspected that all this would happen. According to this it seems that we totally defrauded the Christians, didn't we?'

"Ryabushin used the word 'we' because he counted himself among those who had persuaded the Christians to fight on behalf of the revolution. He himself, of course, has known for a long time that everything was a fraud. His contribution to this discussion was absolutely topnotch.

"Simin posed the second question. 'Our constitution permits antireligious propaganda. But to Christians it grants, as has been stated before, only the practice of their worship activities and not the right to recruit new members. Not only are individual atheists permitted to initiate antireligious propaganda, but this propaganda actually is carried on by the state. The programs of study of secondary and academic institutions are riddled with antireligious propaganda. Every believing student is forced to act against his conscience and to deny the existence of God if he wishes to receive his diploma. Can we continue to refer to this as freedom of thought? Do we, as believers in Christ, do any harm to socialism when we openly speak of our convictions? I personally was expelled from the university as the result of my beliefs.'

"Ustinov made a face and remarked, 'We have struck upon this issue several times before. I really cannot understand why you are so locked into religion. You are alive here and now, and not in heaven.'

" 'Comrade Ustinov,' I interjected, 'it happens to be a fact that we are Christians. And we do indeed wish for peaceful coexistence with the state. You know perfectly well that the church inflicts no damage on society. The teachings of Christ incorporate lofty rules of moral behavior for family life and for life within society. The New Testament calls upon every human being to place himself on the side of justice and the good of all the people. You, as Communists, also fight against alcoholism, drug addiction, robbery, murder, and other crimes; and this corresponds precisely to the demands which the New Testament makes of us. On what basis, therefore, have we no right to exist? You frequently bring up the shady nature of numbers of church servants who allegedly supported all sorts of injustices in the past. But it was precisely these men who did not act according to the principles of Christ but stomped on them with their feet instead. . . .'

" 'Things are working out smoothly with the leaders of the cults we have recognized officially,' said Andropov before I could continue. 'Their activities are sanctioned by law. They even function in various international organizations.'

"To this Ryabushin stated, with a faint smile on his face, 'My dear man, you can surely recall what you told me once when you and I were still very close and when you worked for the Central Committee and not the KGB, "We've got to make use of the people who are active in the area of religion in order to improve our relationships with western society. We've got to persuade the Orthodox Church and the Baptists to join the World Council of Churches so they can act on the behalf of our political system." Now that you've become head of the KGB you undoubtedly are aware of the outstanding services our representatives at the World Council have rendered for you. If you're going to use the church to achieve your political goals, you could surely make the appropriate freedoms available to it—such as the position within society to which it is entitled. What is the reason for our not having the right to print Bibles and other reading material if we find it necessary? Why are those students who believe in Christ not permitted to go without an examination in so-called scientific atheism? Why are we forbidden to express our side of a controversy when we are denounced falsely in newspaper articles? And what comes of it all? You aren't blind, and you know quite well that such harsh measures have forced Christians to set up illegal printing operations, as the Council of Churches is doing, and to smuggle in Bibles from foreign countries. Only very seldom do you allow us to print Bibles and to import them legally from outside countries. Yet this is merely à drop in the bucket! There are millions of Christians in Russia who do not have Bibles in their possession this very day. At the same time, they are flooded with atheistic propaganda! Can this be called justice? Is this the freedom of conscience?'

"Ryabushin stopped. We did not intend to escalate this discussion too far. After an hour-long discussion it became obvious to us that the government was not prepared to move away from its viewpoint that religion was nothing more than a form of drug addition. But no one was able to give us an example of Christ's teachings actually doing harm to Soviet society. At the end of our talk, Andropov asked as if in passing, 'Does the patriarch or the All-Union Council know of this meeting?'

" 'No,' I replied. 'We did not want to disclose our plan to meet with you so that they would not run into difficulties with you. You have turned these poor men into such obedient serfs that if, on top of everything, this discussion were blamed on them, they would become totally confused.'

"Andropov grimaced again. 'We have turned nobody into our vassals,' he stated. 'The people of whom you speak are honorable citizens of our country and are pulling at the same end of the rope as we are. They are not like those splinter groups of yours from the Council of Churches. By the way, does the Council of Churches know about these conversations we are having here?' He looked at me with undisguised curiosity.

" 'No,' I responded without embellishment. And with that we went our individual ways until the next day. What awaits us tomorrow I do not know. What a pity, dear Father, that you couldn't come along! Now I'll say good-bye. I've got to pop this letter into the mail quickly. Tomorrow I'll report to you about the next part of the talks. Your Irina."

*   *   *

Ryabushin sat writing at a table in his hotel room. Vassiley, with whom he shared the room, was reading a newspaper article about a foreign correspondent's interview of Archbishop Nikodim. Again and again Vassiley broke into enraged laughter.

"Man, this guy lies like a rug!" he said between snickers. "Boy, oh boy! How can anybody lie so obviously?"

"Will you stop?" said Ryabushin irritably. "You're disturbing me while I'm writing."

"Well, read for yourself what lies this man manufactures about religious freedom in the USSR!" Vassiley held the foreign newspaper under Ryabushin's face. But Ryabushin pushed it away.

"If I were in his place," Ryabushin explained calmly, "I would have lied, too. Can you imagine what would happen if he told the whole story about our church in another country? They would just stage an automobile accident for him as they tried to do with Irina. The man is lying because he can do nothing else."

"You miserable Baptist," said Vassiley, flying into a rage, "don't you know it is a sin to tell a lie?"

"Oh, leave me alone," the old man said disgustedly. "We're all big heroes as long as no one touches us. My best friend, the late Mr. Shalashov, always said, 'He who criticizes another too often finally commits the same crime as he whom he has criticized.' Instead I suggest that you try to find ways to help the archbishop stand up for the Lord's work rather than worry about his lying. And write to him in such a way that the KGB won't be able to use your letter against him, for all letters to Nikodim are first read by Andropov."

Vassiley sat down and started writing a letter to Nikodim.

While he was doing this, Ryabushin made a record of the day's events in his notebook.

"*One day later:* It was perfectly clear to me at the outset that the idea that we could achieve a state of coexistence between the church and the Soviet state is simply unrealistic. But it is difficult to persuade the young people of this. A completely different set of people took part in our conversations with the government today. Apart from Morosov, I did not know any of them.

"The Central Committee people have made it abundantly clear that we never will accomplish what we wished to achieve with them. Time and again they came back at us with examples of the church hierarchy supporting oppression and of church intervention in state affairs.

"We attempted to prove to them that such occurrences are contrary to Jesus' conception of the relation between church and state.

" 'We are not here because we want to suck the blood out of people. We are not even interested in proving that human rights are being violated in the USSR. You are well aware that our country's history has quite a number of dark spots. Perhaps they even outweigh the positive and happy memories any of us have. No less than a million Christians have been sent to prisons and concentration camps since the Soviet government has been in power. But we are not here to tell you about this, because you yourself planned these purges with Stalin and Khrushchev. We are here to see that a line finally is drawn through this dark past to indicate that it is over. We want to achieve that status by which Russia's Christians will receive the right to speak out about theological subjects, to print as many Bibles as they want to, and to have the opportunity to spread the Gospel without being afraid of being put into prison for it. We want to see to it that our priests and preachers no longer need to be ashamed of their churches when they travel to foreign countries and that the KGB does not force them to lie about them. We ask you to employ only the weapons of ideology in your struggle against us and give us the opportunity to defend ourselves, if not in the official press, then at least in our own. Legalize the publishing arm of the Council of Churches. Make it possible for the Council of Churches and the All-Union to be reconciled to each other so that jointly they can do God's work. You deliberately are preventing such a reconciliation by setting each side against the other! You employ whatever means you can in order to put an end to the illegal church so that you can get a total grip on the official recognized Orthodox and Baptist churches.'

"Naturally, only Irina Sokolova could have given such a fiery speech. I am sorry for this young woman. I am afraid for her. Nothing will come of her requests. But I am here to protect her in whatever way I can."

Suddenly Ryabushin felt ill. He put down his pencil and put his notebook aside. His breaths became short because of the great pains he felt in the area of his heart. Painfully he got up and tottered toward his bed.

Vassiley jumped up, frightened. "What's the matter, do you feel ill?"

Ryabushin, pale and unable to speak, merely nodded. He motioned toward his night table, where he had a small bottle of medicine for his heart. Vassiley hurriedly put some drops of the medicine on a spoon and handed this to the old man along with a glass of water. The elderly preacher swallowed the medicine and stretched out carefully on the bed.

A few moments later he whispered, "Please take my notebook and write what I am about to dictate to you. It looks like the end is near for me. . . . Why aren't you writing?" he asked in surprise as he realized that Vassiley was staring at him with his mouth open.

"Surely you aren't going to die on me so soon?" Vassiley was close to tears. Ryabushin looked at him firmly.

"Now write," he ordered. "We don't have much more time. I will continue.

"Our church leadership finds itself in a serious crisis. Karev said it correctly at one time, 'We are shackled hand and foot with rustproof Communist chains.' We will not get rid of these shackles through a 'dialogue.' Our government is well aware that if it confers on us the right to preach Christ without restrictions it will lose about sixty percent of the population to our God. No one among us wishes for a Capitalist regime, yet the Communists see a potent rival in us nevertheless. They wouldn't dream of considering the possibility of friendly coexistence with us. You know they have used every means at their disposal since as far back as I can remember to combat the church, manipulating us to achieve their ends. I am afraid for you, my beloved church. Farewell until we see each other again in the presence of the Lord."

Toward the end Ryabushin's voice had become almost inaudible. After the last sentence he fell into a deep sleep.

He did not awaken again. He gently slipped away in his sleep.

Vassiley telephoned Irina and the others and told them of Ryabushin's death. They came to the hotel as quickly as they could. Irina sat beside the deathbed for a long time crying softly and stroking the dead man's already cold hand. Klim and Polevoy surreptitiously wiped away tears as they silently looked at the physical shell of the man who had been more than just a teacher to them.

Valentin Relin, Krebs, and Sudakovitch also had arrived, and they sat glumly on Vassiley's bed and quietly discussed what they should do next.

Vassiley placed the notebook with the comments of the dead man into the drawer of the night table and discovered a folded piece of paper in the drawer. Absentmindedly he unfolded it and read, "In the event of my death, please notify my son by telegram and call the following by telephone." Among the numbers listed were the number and address of a colonel in the air force, Ryabushin.

Silently Vassiley left the room and began to look for a

telephone. He dialed the number which had been written down. "Nina Ryabushin," a woman's voice said. Vassiley explained who he was and what had happened.

"Grandfather is dead," repeated Nina Ryabushin in a flat voice. "My father and I will be coming immediately."

Within an hour the hotel had been turned topsy-turvy. Hotel employees ran every which way. But the colonel, who had just arrived, did not pay any attention to the commotion and sharply inquired of the desk clerk, "What room is he reposing in?"

Two women, the older one clearly the colonel's wife and the younger one the spitting image of the older, rushed after the colonel. When they reached the room the colonel stepped toward the deathbed of his father and knelt down next to it. He grasped the dead man's hand and kissed it. "Forgive me, Father," he said softly, "for thinking your Christian work was just another crazy idea in the name of socialism."

Vassiley and Irina, who stood slightly apart from the newly arrived group and who had seen what happened, looked at each other. The colonel stood up, stepped over to the night table and pulled out the drawer. He grabbed the notebook and the other papers in it, pushed them quickly into his briefcase, and handed it to a newly arrived officer who so closely resembled the colonel that he was obviously his son. The colonel snapped, "Go." The young man nodded and walked out.

"Why isn't the ambulance here yet?" asked the annoyed colonel of the people on duty at the hotel.

"We called it over an hour ago! But it hasn't come. I don't understand what's the matter, either."

Finally the doctor arrived. The colonel received him angrily, complaining about the delay. But the doctor did not have the time to reply, for immediately behind him KGB agents burst into the room and began to search the entire room. The colonel looked on, a mocking smile playing on his lips.

After the search was completed, one of the agents showed

the colonel his identification card. "May I ask you to see me at ten o'clock tomorrow?"

The colonel coolly nodded his assent. "I'll be there," he said. The KGB agents disappeared as quickly as they had arrived.

When the door had closed behind them the colonel looked at Irina with a conspiratorial smile on his face and winked at her.

"You saw nothing and know nothing, right?" He gave everyone a probing look. "That's the situation, am I correct?"

They all nodded eagerly. The maid who was present did not look very bright, and she looked uncomprehendingly at the colonel, then trotted off.

In keeping with his final wish, Ryabushin was buried in Siberia. He had written to his son about that even before his arrival in Moscow. But Irina and her friends were not able to be present at the funeral. For one day after Ryabushin's death, following two hours of further conversations with the KGB officials, they were arrested and placed into solitary confinement at Lefortovo.

*   *   *

Author's note: At this point we must ask the reader's indulgence for recounting all of the main characters' conversations as well as the complete contents of Ryabushin's diary. It could be done in such detail because Vassiley had carefully read the reports and reconstructed them from memory, since he had shared his hotel room with Ryabushin for five days.

All those who took part in the so-called dialogue took stenographic notes and will make their notes available to the public when this will no longer be dangerous to their lives and when it will be of maximum benefit to the Christians in Russia. Our task is to convey to the western reader—but also to the reader in the Soviet Union—some idea of the experiences and hopes of those thousands of Christians in Russia fighting for the freedom to proclaim the Gospel. They serve the cause of freedom in silence, yet with great loyalty to God, in the process risking their lives constantly.

Very often in the USSR even the closest relatives are not aware of the role their own brothers or sisters or fathers or mothers are playing. Because of the great danger to all concerned, servants of Jesus Christ must carry out their missions in strict secrecy so that nothing can come to the attention of the KGB. In this report we have taken great care not to endanger these Christians.

One final word to the enemies of Christendom. The stenographic notes made by the main personalities in this book are in the good care of western friends. It would be totally useless to search for them at the homes of the people who took these notes or even at the home of the author of this book.

15 Revelations of a Coptic Priest

On more than one occasion Irina and her friends had asked themselves what the nature of Serov's activities actually was, but an impenetrable veil of secrecy covered his work. Even those closest to him in his family knew nothing definite. It was known that he was constantly on the move on official trips and that his business often took him to foreign countries. There was also a vague impression that he somehow was busy in the area of religion and on behalf of the KGB. But no one was told exactly what he did.

Serov loved his work and performed all his assignments with skill and genuine cleverness. His work meant a great deal to him, if not everything. But because of the cloak of total secrecy which had been placed over everything he did, he had become completely isolated. And despite many significant successes he had become a lonely person.

It was a coincidence, or whatever one calls such an accident of chance, which brought Serov on the young people's trail.

A young preacher named Pyotr, because of family relationships, had received permission to leave Russia and was pursuing his studies in a Bible school in the West.

During his practical internship in Graz, Austria, Pyotr was looking for one particular issue of the Soviet newspaper *Isvestia*, which carried an interview with a man named Shidkov, the leader of the officially recognized All-Union of Baptists in the USSR. Shidkov had loudly trumpeted the religious freedoms enjoyed in the Soviet Union, and Pyotr was extremely anxious to read what had been said in this interview.

To his great disappointment, that particular issue was already sold out. So he returned to his trolley stop without achieving his objective. On the way there he passed an ice cream parlor. He stepped into it because the day was unusually hot. Suddenly he noticed a man in a cassock reading the very issue of *Isvestia* for which he had been searching for so long.

He observed the priest with mixed feelings. On one hand he was not at all keen on running into an Orthodox priest from the USSR. He knew they had to give the KGB a complete account of everything they had encountered during their foreign journeys. A conversation with Pyotr would surely provoke interest at the headquarters of the Soviet secret police. Yet there was no other way he could hope to read this newspaper. Since he was alone, he could send no one to the priest to offer him three times what he had paid for the newspaper. The priest had a face like that of an Arab. But he easily could have been a Georgian or an Armenian, too, since the inhabitants of these Soviet republics had similar facial features. Pyotr determined not to let the priest get out of his sight.

Suddenly the priest turned to Pyotr and asked, "Excuse me, but I am a stranger in this city. Could you tell me where I could have lunch at a reasonable price?" He spoke fluent Russian, but his accent clearly was not that of someone who lived in the Soviet Union.

Pyotr restrained a smile.

"I'm confused," he countered. "Is the same lunch available at different prices in Russia? And why are you speaking to me in my mother tongue?"

"I'm not from Russia," the priest answered with a smile, "but from Egypt. And we have expensive as well as inexpensive places to eat lunch in Egypt. In addition, I happened to overhear you asking for *Isvestia*."

Pyotr asked several additional questions which the man evidently didn't appreciate. But when he saw the longing with which the young man glanced at the newspaper he laughed and said, "No, no, I really am not from the USSR. But I know the Russian language and read Russian newspapers as often as I can in order not to forget the language."

This finally reassured Pyotr, and he invited the man to have lunch with him at the "Lobster's Basement." His new acquaintance immediately accepted his suggestion, and ten minutes later they found themselves comfortably seated at a table, conversing in low voices.

Pyotr reached into his briefcase and felt that he still had a copy of the book which had just been published in the West. He pulled it out and presented it to Abdullah, who opened it immediately and began to read it with great interest while Pyotr occupied himself with *Isvestia* with equal intensity. Eventually Abdullah pushed aside his reading material and casually said, "Oh yes. I've also attended the theological academy in Leningrad."

Pyotr's interest in his new friend suddenly intensified. The bowls of soup in front of them had long ago gotten cold. The waiter arrived at their table with a tray, ready to serve the meat course. They began to spoon up their soup rapidly.

"It is certainly interesting that theologians from western countries studying at theological academies in the USSR are almost always targets of the KGB."

"Did they work you over as well?" asked Pyotr casually.

"And how!" Abdullah said, laughing. "Especially when they learned that I had connections with the cloister of Saint Catherine. After that, they didn't give me any peace because of the valuable manuscripts which are kept there."

Interesting, thought Pyotr.

"Did Archbishop Nikodim put pressure on you as well?" he asked aloud.

Abdullah smiled jocularly, saying, "Ah, that poor man, Nikodim! All officially recognized Russian priests are directly under the thumb of the KGB! Otherwise they couldn't maintain their ministry."

Pyotr looked at him sadly.

"Back in those Leningrad days I became good friends with Professor Serov," continued Abdullah merrily, "who was very interested in old handwriting. But I couldn't help him much. My brother, who is a monk in the cloister of Saint Catherine on the Sinai Peninsula, was able to supply him with much more valuable information."

It is difficult to explain why Abdullah did it, but he told of his encounters with Serov and of the consequences of these encounters.

Abdullah had been born into a non-Christian family. As young men he and his brother chanced upon a Coptic worship service. Afterward they were invited to a young people's Bible study by one of the girls. A young priest explained Jesus' genealogy to the group, referring to historical sources.

This so fascinated the two young men that they began to attend the Bible study regularly. Eventually they asked to be baptized. Abdullah's brother, who was an engineer by training, became a monk; Abdullah decided to study the history of ancient civilizations. Originally he planned to go to Moscow for his studies. Instead he was invited to Leningrad Theological Academy.

He attracted attention very quickly because he was unassuming, had no woman friends, did not go on drinking sprees with the rest of the students, and did not smoke or attend dances. He spent his free time reading the Bible and in prayer. One day Abdullah was asked to come to the director's office. The director introduced him to an important-looking man and left the two of them alone. The new acquaintance was extremely polite and obliging. He asked Abdullah a few questions relating to his family and mentioned that he was interested in ancient history. Abdullah felt flattered by that. He found the man an excellent conversational partner and exceptionally knowledgeable in ancient history. He began to meet with him regularly. The man's name was Serov.

Serov was neither pushy nor was he excessively inquisitive, and he and Abdullah soon became the closest of friends.

Serov often took Abdullah along on trips to the Crimea or the Ukraine and on all sorts of other journeys. He began to play a significant role in Abdullah's life. Abdullah trusted him and always turned to him when he needed help.

A few years later Abdullah returned to Egypt. At the time, he was working on his dissertation and had to travel to Rome in order to find some information at the Vatican library.

One hot summer day Abdullah heard someone call his name as he was on his way to Saint Peter's Church. He whirled around and was amazed to see Serov, who headed toward him with open arms. They embraced each other and agreed to meet that evening at a restaurant to eat dinner together.

At this time Abdullah was badly in need of money. One of his sisters suffered from leukemia, and her treatment already had used up the family's entire savings.

Thus as Abdullah and Serov sat together in the restaurant at the appointed time, the young clergyman told his "dear friend" about his financial troubles. His family was in debt to the tune of ten thousand dollars and he, Abdullah, was considering interrupting his work on his dissertation in order to earn money.

"But really, Abdullah!" exclaimed the aghast Mr. Serov. "You must not say anything like that! You are a scientist. Theology is your life's work; so you must go on working on it!" Serov rested his head in his hands as if deep in thought. Finally he gave a confident smile as if the right solution had just occurred to him. He asked Abdullah to excuse him for a few minutes and disappeared. Soon he returned carrying an important-looking briefcase in his hand.

"Some time ago I was in Africa," he began as if speaking to himself, "and saw what wonderful work is being done by the missionaries there. They are bringing civilization to the African people. They give them education, raise their cultural level, study and master the language spoken by the people they are visiting, and translate their religious works into that language. Yet they often do not have enough money to do that! I have already spoken with Archbishop Nikodim about helping these missionaries through the World Council of Churches so that they can carry on their work more effectively and more purposefully. You see, we cannot spread Communist ideology among Africans if the missionaries do not first teach the black people how to read and write!"

Abdullah saw no contradiction in the idea of first converting Africans to the Christian faith and then to communism. He shared Archbishop Nikodim's conviction that the Christian faith and communism had many things in common.

As a result, Serov could converse quite freely with Abdullah about his ideas. In order to be successful, he said, communism would have to be transformed into a sort of religion. In this way communism would be able to satisfy the spiritual needs of the people. Abdullah himself had had similar thoughts. When he thought of his beloved sister and of how his family had been brought to the edge of financial ruin by "capitalist blood-suckers" in order to get her leukemia treated, he became particularly enraged. He gritted his teeth in anger and announced that he could gladly choke these "exploiters" with his own hands. But since no more effective medicine or treatment seemed to be available in Russia or in the East Zone, he continued to be dependent on the West for her treatment.

That is why Serov offered Abdullah ten thousand dollars. Abdullah accepted the money gladly, as one naturally would from a real friend. He simply signed a receipt for the money, and with that their get-together was over.

When he accepted the money, Abdullah suddenly received a complex assignment for which he was, of course, very well paid. He was to develop personal contacts with liberation movements, especially in South America. He became very concerned about Catholic theologians who preached revolutionary theology, visited them regularly, and passed on what he learned to Serov.

When Serov one day vanished from the scene, Abdullah's next contact was a bishop in Alexandria. Abdullah delivered his reports to his new intermediary and also received his payment from him.

Pyotr suddenly realized that he had heard about Abdullah before. Vassiley Kuznetsov actually had studied with Abdullah for a time. It was Abdullah, in fact, who induced Vassiley to come up with the idea that a dialogue with the Party could serve a useful purpose. But they had also met after their student days at the academy. Each time Vassiley thought back to that occasion he had a pained expression on this face. It was Abdullah who had declared himself willing to escort Vassiley's young wife to her relatives. It was he who had caused the accident. She had died of her injuries, while Abdullah had emerged without a scratch.

Abdullah went on to tell how he had tried to draw his brother into the Party's activity. But not only did his brother indignantly reject the whole idea, but he also told the entire family what kind of activity Abdullah was involved in and where the money for his sister's treatments had come from. Yet nobody could have proved that Abdullah was a Soviet spy. He was a theologian and a scientist specializing in early antiquity, living an exemplary life in keeping with his personal convictions. That is, if one could overlook his furnishing of information to the Soviet secret service! However, his brother, his sister, and the rest of his relatives despised him after hearing of his ties to communism. His sister refused to accept his help and returned to Egypt. Yet when she lay dying she asked to see Abdullah one more time. The confused theologian, who had become enmeshed in his own distorted philosophy, stood weeping next to his sister's deathbed.

"She lay there, pale and fragile," he now said to Pyotr, "and looked at me in deep sorrow. While she was in America, Bishop Ramadi had visited her and told her of my activity. 'You are caught up in a terrible network of error,' she said to me. 'You know that no way of life on earth, even the most ideal one, is able to free mankind of hatred, envy, and meanness. For that reason, human beings continue to destroy each other. In fact, isn't it those very same Communists who tell the world of their lofty morality but continue to kill each other? They hate, envy, and persecute their own comrades if these people depart even minutely from their doctrine. You are well aware of that. And when communism has achieved its aims, then evil will not be extinguished, but the opposite will happen. In a material sense, those who live in poor areas may actually have a better life under communism. But in return for this they will be spiritually brutalized. They will plunge into chaos because they have broken off their relationship with God. Oh, Abdullah, my brother, you travel along a dangerous path. May the Lord forgive you.' At that point she fell back on her pillow, exhausted, and closed her eyes. She died minutes later. I fell on my knees and prayed."

"You no longer have any contact with Serov?" Pyotr asked.

"No," Abdullah answered. Immediately after his sister's funeral he had traveled to see Bishop Ramadi, who had asked for him. There Abdullah discovered that he had long been viewed with great concern because of his activities with the Soviet secret police. The clergy wanted to help him and to show him how contradictory his activities had been. At this time he had also learned that Serov, on returning to Moscow, had been surprised by the news of the conversion of his four children to Christianity. "Serov considered this a terrible blow. He felt as if fate had mocked him. This was more than he could handle, and he died from a heart attack in his boss's office."

"What?" Pyotr couldn't believe his ears. "I heard that he had taken his own life."

Abdullah insisted that this was nothing more than a rumor. But Serov's death had allegedly precipitated the arrest of Irina Sokolova, Vassiley Kuznetsov and all the others who had taken part in the dialogue with the Central Committee of the Communist Party in Moscow.

"So what are you doing in Graz at this point?" asked Pyotr at long last.

It appeared that Abdullah had radically changed his life-style after his talk with Bishop Ramadi. He had repented bitterly and recorded his experiences on paper as a warning to others. That evening he had an appointment with his brother to visit a historic monastery. He had just about two hours until his train was to leave for Vienna when he ran across Pyotr.

"I would like very much to hear what has become of Serov's children," he said pensively. Pyotr could help him on that.

"They were placed into a special boarding school for children of highly placed Communist officials."

Abdullah listened to that open-mouthed. He blurted, "How do you know what happened to that family?" But at that instant the waiter arrived, and Pyotr had no more time to answer Abdullah's question.

Pyotr paid the bill and hurriedly said his good-byes to Abdullah. He still had to deliver a sermon that evening and wanted to fill in a few gaps before then. They exchanged addresses and went their ways.

Pyotr never saw Abdullah again. Abdullah wrote to Pyotr while he still lived in Austria, telling him that he had spent some very pleasant days with his brother and that he had returned happily to Egypt. But what Abdullah did not know was that within himself he carried the same disease which had killed his sister. He died in Cairo, and his notes vanished mysteriously. No one knew where they disappeared to, and his brother eventually lost all hope of ever being able to recover them.

16 Impressions, Impressions . . .

The daily routine in Lefortovo prison, the atmosphere in the prison as well as its unwritten laws, stood in crass opposition to the kind of life Irina was used to. Up to a certain point she found it interesting, in fact, to be in jail.

Vassiley Kuznetsov, who had been completely taken in by a high government official with whom he had a conference at the time they were all arrested, told Irina before they were all assigned to separate jail cells, "He is an extraordinary man. I'd like to know how he managed to stay in the government during all these horrible years."

The jail guard interrupted him at that point. "Stop talking with each other." He did not yell at him, but spoke in a friendly manner as if giving fatherly advice.

This elderly man with his snow-white hair had spent his entire life working inside various prisons and felt as if he were at home there. He had performed his duties as a prison guard for fifty years and still did not want to take his pension. Klim, the elderly preacher from Siberia, simply called him "Grandfather White Swan" because his name was Lebedyev. ("Lebed" means "swan.")

Lebedyev no longer had a family. His wife and two children vanished at the start of the Second World War. They had gone to visit Lebedyev's brother when the war broke out. One of the first German bombs to hit the village in which he lived struck his brother's house. That was the last Lebedyev heard about his family.

The loss changed his personality entirely. He became quiet,

closed in, and devoted entirely to the "care" of prison inmates from then on. When he still had a family he had considered his duties nothing more than a "job" with which he was able to earn a living, a series of duties just like any other. But afterward he seemed to become aware that this might be a sort of calling and began to consider it his life's work.

He hated anyone of German origin. He "served" German officers with deliberate neglect and had put poison into the meals of several of them in order to "assist" in the execution of justice.

The German-language-speaking Russians who wound up in Lefortovo prison had no idea of the bitter and dangerous enemy they were meeting in Lebedyev.

When Irina and her friends were brought in, Lebedyev was in the process of reading the prosecuting attorney's decision regarding their detention. The duty officer entered the room without recognizing a single person.

Curtly he asked Lebedyev, "Theologians again?"

"Yes," he said, handing the officer the papers. Two more officers entered, threw inquisitive glances toward the detainees and sat down at their respective desks. The duty officer gave the order to escort the detainees away.

"That one's pretty as a picture, isn't she?" said one of the officers, moving his head in Irina's direction.

"She is their leader," retorted the duty officer. "They made a special call from Lubyanka for us to place her in strict solitary detention."

That was all Irina was able to hear.

Not one of the Christians was afraid. Rather, they were amazed. Why had they been arrested? They had been having this peaceful discourse with the government! They had shown the government tolerance, accepted its jurisdiction over them and respected it. Their only interest was securing equal rights for Christians within the Communist society. They simply could not get it through their heads that they would be put into prison for having these peaceful intentions!

Of course they did not yet know that the same night in

which Ryabushin died, Serov's life also had ended. A letter to Serov's sister revealed Serov's personal distress. It was written while he was still in a Moscow hotel.

"I still have not seen my family," he wrote, "and hope to fly home tomorrow. Yet I am altogether too depressed by what I have heard. My friends have shared with me that my children have become Christians. I am well aware that my children's views would change if I were to devote myself to my family more in the future. Up to now, that simply has not been possible. Can you imagine? I've been fighting religion all my life and have been quite successful at it. When the Sokolovs moved in with my family, I was so happy! I had hoped to gain some influence over Irina, who was my family's favorite. And now in my absence this misfortune had to happen! It won't be easy to erase the ideas about God the children have picked up.

"You see, normally we don't have very much difficulty in converting these Christians into puppets of ours. We do it by employing the Bible's teachings (of which they are none too knowledgeable because of the shortage of Bibles) to our own ends. But it has not been possible to reeducate such people and turn them into genuine atheists. You are right in stating that it is extremely difficult for man to accept that his life span is limited to the time he spends on earth. He searches for a transcendental life and lives in the expectation that his life, once ended here on earth, will continue into eternity. It is certainly obvious that such a concept would have a comforting effect on the human soul. If a human carries this concept within him he possesses a final goal for his personal existence. You are right to say that our Communist ideology must incorporate religious characteristics. We must expropriate everything that is absorbing and useful from the religious way of life and incorporate it into the festivities of communism. We must impress on people's minds that it is their sacred duty to live for the good of future generations and to labor to the end that future generations will forever honor the memory of their labor. A new form of religion must take the place of the old one. I consider what happened to my children as the reaction of fate to the work I have been doing."

There were a lot of rumors and speculations about Serov's death. Irina did not learn of it until after her release from prison.

No investigation had been initiated against any of them. Everyone was imprisoned in strict solitary confinement, and each one was kept from knowing anything about the others. But after a week's detention the preachers from Baptist congregations were taken under guard to the Kasan railroad station and sent home without a single word of explanation.

Irina was escorted from her cell one night. Lebedyev opened the heavy steel door and ordered, "Get dressed; you are being taken somewhere else."

She had, as a matter of fact, been unable to sleep anyway and had been thinking about her father. Once outside, she greedily inhaled the wonderfully fresh night air after spending nearly two weeks in the sticky closeness of her cell. The air seemed like a priceless balm to her.

Without a word of explanation she was pushed into a Volga automobile and driven to a location somewhere in Moscow. She had no inkling of what time it was, whether early evening or already past midnight. The windows of the car were covered with heavy curtains. The ride seemed to take forever. Finally the car halted in front of a horseshoe-shaped building complex. The man wearing civilian clothes who had accompanied her opened the car door and asked her to follow him. The driver remained seated in the car.

They walked up to the fourth floor. An eerie silence pervaded the building. Irina made mental notes of every detail as she walked along. Her companion led her down a long passageway with doors on both sides. At the end of the passage he motioned for her to take a seat in a chair and said softly, "Please wait here."

Irina could see no guards anywhere. Yet she had the impression that invisible eyes were following her every movement. She had no sensation of fear, only human inquisitiveness. While she waited—for what, she did not know—she rested her elbows on her knees, covered her face with her hands and began to pray.

The door across from her opened. She raised her head. The same man waved her into the room. She rose and entered a large, brightly lit room. In the corner opposite the door stood a small table with an outsized samovar on it. At left she saw a couch and a desk. Some chairs stood along the wall.

A young woman entered the room and extended her hand to Irina in a friendly greeting.

"Good evening, Irina. My name is Vera. I have heard much about you and am pleased to have the opportunity to get to know you." With a disarming smile she pulled Irina down with her onto the couch. Irina was sorry she kept being surprised, but permitted herself to be conducted to the couch without resistance.

"You are truly a beautiful woman! And such beauty has to languish in Lefortovo prison! That's really too bad!" Vera said as she stepped to the samovar and began to make tea.

Irina wondered about Vera's slight accent. She was very deft with the samovar. When she was finished, she magically brought out some cookies and chocolate and put them on a little table in front of the couch. Then she poured some tea for Irina and gestured toward the plate of cookies.

"My dear, do help yourself. But first let us say thanks." She began to say a prayer. Irina did not know what to make of it. After praying, Vera handed Irina the plate of cookies. "Don't be surprised at my prayer. I happen to be a theologian. I come from East Germany and have received my doctorate in theology. But perhaps Koslov has told you about me by now. I spent one of my vacations in his company. He is a fine man."

Irina nearly dropped her glass of tea.

"Did you by any chance realize that he is married?" she asked.

Vera laughed lightly, a clearly pleasant, bell-like laugh. "You are simply too naive, my dear! That doesn't mean a thing. Love knows no governmental, ideological, or whatever-you-will boundaries!" she added as if she were teaching a child. But she quickly changed the subject. "You don't seriously think the Communist Party has any intention of stopping its battle against religion, do you?"

Irina shrugged. "That's not a matter of personal opinion," she countered. "We are involved with logic. The Party could very well cease fighting religion and thereby free up a lot of energy to be used for more productive enterprises. Of course this can take place only if Communist ideology does not insist that it takes the place of religion in the consciousness of people. If, however, this is its aim, then to renounce the fight against religion is, of course, impossible."

Vera sat there deep in thought, examining her fingernails. She looked bewitching in her fashionable dress and beautifully coiffed hair. Irina looked at her admiringly from the side.

"Why am I allowed to be here at this late hour?" she asked Vera.

Vera rose again and walked toward the samovar. "I am involved in working out the relationship between Marxism and theology," she answered, pouring herself some more tea. Then she sat down opposite Irina and crossed her legs. "I'm also interested in your—you will excuse my expression—Utopian action. We in the West also are engaged in efforts to reduce theology and Marxism to a common denominator and have many contacts with Marxist movements for that reason. You must understand that the Bible does not provide a political program for a just society on this earth. The Bible is, if you will, a plan or program for the achievement of moral perfection in man, while Marxism points the way toward socialism. There is no doubt that religion can coexist with Marxist doctrine. Or, to be even more precise, religion and

Marxism supplement each other. Either one would be unsuccessful without—."

"Excuse me," Irina interrupted. "Christ through His teaching has told us very clearly how we are to behave within our
families, in society, and in life in general. His parable of the
Good Samaritan, His discourses about loving one's neighbor,
about marriage, and about other interpersonal relationships
are crystal clear for everyone. If we live according to His
teaching, we will have a just society. The fact that representatives of the church often have acted in ways inconsistent
with these principles does not indicate that Christ's teachings
are incomplete and need to be perfected by Marxism. All we
ask, if Marxism is not prepared to completely cease its offen-
sive against us, is that the authorities at least resort to only
ideological weapons instead of continuous physical harassment. In this century more Christians have been killed at the
hands of Communists or in the name of communism than in all
the centuries preceding this one by every enemy Christianity
has known, including the Roman emperors' persecutions."

"But, my dear Irina," Vera interjected, "we Christians are
asked to forgive our enemies!"

Irina smiled. "What do you think we are constantly doing?
If we did not continually forgive you, we would not be able
to sit at the same table with you and have a peaceful conversation with you! Love does indeed forgive all things, but I
cannot sit by indifferently as one after another of our preachers is thrown into prison. At the same time those who serve
the church and are ready to make compromises are exploited
to ideological ends in the name of policy! Just one more point,
Vera. If we forgive murderers simply without insisting that
they repent, we will lose credibility. We become partners to
their guilt and no longer can preach repentance."

Once again Vera changed the subject and pretended to be
most concerned about Irina's future. "My dear, you absolutely must continue your studies. Yes, yes, you lack a theological education! You must devote yourself to the study of

Bultmann, Karl Barth, and other important theologians. That's absolutely a 'must.' The prosecuting attorney has guaranteed that if you agree to attend a theological school in East Germany you will be released today and be allowed to travel to East Germany with me next week!"

"No!" exclaimed Irina, thoroughly alarmed. "I do not intend to study theology. My professional goal is research in scientific technology."

Vera took a pack of foreign cigarettes from her handbag. She lit one and said—no, she spit out venomously, "Why do you stick your nose into alien territory?" Her voice had lost all its loveliness and now had the ring of steel. Irina noted in amazement that even Vera's exterior was undergoing a very odd transformation. Her face and her entire appearance appeared to assume a harsher texture. Her bewitching smile had disappeared. Seated opposite Irina was now an icy person with cold eyes and a hard mouth. Irina was so fascinated by this transformation that she stared at Vera wide-eyed. But this open, artless look appeared to get on Vera's nerves. She began to dig into her handbag and finally held up a photograph. She glanced at it contemptuously for a moment, then threw it toward Irina. Irina took it, and as she looked at it her cheeks reddened. Taken during her battle with Koslov, the photo had really turned out well. On it could be seen an almost naked Irina lying on the carpet alongside Koslov while he passionately embraced her.

The memory of this ugly encounter struck Irina with such force that she almost broke into tears. Again she began to feel like that little girl who used to run to her father when she had been treated unfairly and to seek comfort on his lap. But her father was nowhere near her, and she was no longer a little girl. She sighed deeply and returned the photograph to Vera.

"What do you want from me?" she asked.

"That you stop this idiocy about a dialogue once and for all and that you come to East Germany with me!" Vera was almost screaming. Then she got hold of herself a bit and added, "You would be doing us a great service if you were to work alongside us."

"Who do you mean by the word 'us'?" asked Irina sarcastically, "your theologians or the KGB?"

Vera jumped up and disappeared into an adjacent room. Alone again, Irina began to pray softly and soon regained her calm. Suddenly Koslov stood directly in front of her. Grinning broadly he extended his hand and said, "Well, you didn't expect to see me, did you?"

"I am a prisoner of the KGB," retorted Irina softly, "and with that I have to be prepared for anything."

"The picture came out pretty good, didn't it?" said Koslov with a nasty laugh.

Irina did not reply.

"My friends took these pictures from the building on the other side of the street!" he bragged, pulling out a whole packet of them from his breast pocket. "Here, look at them!" He threw them on the table in front of Irina. The photos indicated how Irina had been seated on his lap, how he was covering her with kisses, how he threw her down on the floor, tore her clothing from her. Yet, oddly enough, not a single photo was shot of her in the act of throwing him out of her apartment.

Irina pushed the photographs away. "Take this garbage and do whatever you want with it. But above all, please give the order to have me taken back to prison. By the way, did you get the German theologian into your power the same way?"

Koslov stared at her furiously but did not reply. A few moments later he said, his voice icy, "I'm still looking for my pistol and my tape recorder. Where are they?"

Irina knew where the tape recorder was, but she had no idea where the pistol was. She was unaware that her father had discovered this weapon underneath the sofa and had carefully hidden it. So this question confused her.

"I know where the tape recorder is, and you will get it

back," she said, a bit at a loss, "but I know nothing about the pistol." She said this in such an honest manner that Koslov, who had a lot of experience in the interrogation of people, believed her.

At that moment the telephone rang. Koslov picked up the receiver. After his conversation he told Irina, "I've got to go now, but we will see each other again. Think carefully about what Vera has told you. And mark my words. Should any part of your conversation with her seep through to the West, we will make these photos available to the western press. They happen to love sensationalism." He disappeared as suddenly as he had come.

The man in civilian clothes who had brought Irina to the building now came in and indicated that she was to follow him. The Volga automobile's driver attentively opened the door for her. After they had entered, the car door was locked from the outside. *A prison on wheels,* Irina thought.

At the prison Lebedyev welcomed her with a friendly smile and conducted her to her cell. She felt totally washed out, and when the lock closed her in she sank down on the bed and broke into tears. The stress had been simply too great. Then she realized someone might be watching her through the peephole. She pulled herself together again, wiped away her tears, took off her clothes and got into bed.

Every cell had an electric light bulb that was on day and night. Irina pulled her covers over her head, then put her hand underneath her pillow, as was her custom, and pressed it against her face. She felt something hard. She sat up in bed in amazement. A slip of paper had been put inside her pillow cover. She pulled it out with trembling hands. "My dear daughter," she read, her heart beating rapidly, "be of good cheer and don't give up! I am doing everything in my power to see that you are freed again. Sasha Nikitin also has been arrested. Don't hang your head! With kisses, your father."

Irina pressed the piece of paper to herself and whispered, "Dear Dad, don't do anything foolish."

Her heart was filled with deep gratitude for this message, and her thoughts turned away from her current situation. She began to think about her friends and about Sasha Nikitin and started to pray for them all. While doing so, she fell asleep and slept soundly until the morning.

*　　*　　*

Neverov's wife was cleaning her apartment when she heard a knock on the door. Her visitor introduced himself as an examining magistrate in the prosecuting attorney's office. Valentina was used to such visitors, for they normally came to see her when her husband was at work and her children in kindergarten.

This visitor did not wait for an invitation, but sat down immediately on the sofa. The Neverovs had just moved into a new, comfortably furnished apartment. This, too, had been a result of Valentina's activities, although her husband did not know that. He trusted her so completely that he was not a bit suspicious of anything she did. More recently he had even let her attend all meetings of the elders responsible for the congregation. These gatherings always lasted for several hours, and the brethren gratefully accepted her offer to serve them with a meal and something to drink.

Valentina was generally considered a reliable co-worker among her fellow Christians. She was, too, up to a certain point. She was absolutely essential to her husband's work for the church. But she worked for the KGB with equal dedication, for which she was amply rewarded financially. This very practical lady had her own savings account at the bank, which she filled up with all the fat honoraria from the KGB.

The examining magistrate, however, had come to the Neverovs' apartment for the first time, and therefore he introduced himself. "My name is Miroshnitchenko. I have been called by phone to speak with you about Irina Sokolova. Have you met her?"

Valentina sat down on a chair and replied, "Yes, we did meet in the Crimea."

"The Sokolov woman must have had conversations there with Nikitin. Did she talk, among other things, of the rape attempts; and did she mention anything about a pistol?"

Valentina looked at him in amazement. "A pistol, you say? No, I do not remember anything about that. But you know that I reported in writing everything that had happened in my encounters with the Sokolov woman. I handed all this written material to Siniszin, the KGB divisional head."

"Of course. Naturally," Miroshnitchenko quickly tried to reassure her, drumming on the arm of the sofa with his fingers. "I am aware of that, but could you have left something out?"

"Impossible," replied Valentina resolutely. "I have an excellent memory, and you can rely on that. Of course, I cannot retain things which have been said while I was absent."

Miroshnitchenko rose. He was relatively young, making his first attempts to serve in the field of jurisprudence. He examined the attractive young woman standing before him with a certain curiosity. For a moment a particular thought seemed to be going through his head, but he soon shook his head as if he wanted to rid himself of this thought, said good-bye and left.

Naturally Valentina could not know that her guest was a secret admirer of Solzhenitsyn or that he, hidden from all his relatives, read Solzhenitsyn's books, which one could obtain on the black market for large sums of money. Miroshnitchenko had received orders to imprison a number of Christians in the town, among them Valentina's husband. How blind the poor fool had to be!

Miroshnitchenko was all set to alert Neverov about his wife's true character. But he had to drop the idea when he realized that Neverov virtually idolized his wife and would hardly be willing to face reality.

After the investigating magistrate departed, Valentina resumed cleaning her home. She had hardly begun again when there was another knock on the door. She opened it. There stood a powerfully built man with greying hair. He asked to be allowed to enter so that he could discuss several things with her. Valentina assumed that he was a member of the KGB and let him in quickly so that her neighbors would not notice him.

The man whom she had let in behaved a bit strangely. He did not even say hello, but immediately began examining the walls of the home. Valentina wanted to speak, but the stranger held his hand over her mouth. Then he made a beeline for the large picture which hung in the living room. He lifted it off the wall and placed it on the floor. After that, he lifted off a corner of the wallpaper and soon held a listening device in his hand.

Valentina looked on wordlessly. She had known about the "bug," but her husband knew nothing about it. The stranger wiped the perspiration from his brow and asked, "Did you know about this?"

Valentina, still thinking that she had a KGB official before her, admitted openly that she did. "Of course; the meetings of the leaders of the congregation take place in this apartment."

The man sat on a chair and motioned for Valentina to sit down on the sofa. With the listening device on his lap he said, irritated, "What an old piece of junk! The people can't do anything decently! They could have put in one of these bugs from the United States. But no, they've got to go back to their own junk again and again. By the way, does your husband know anything about this?"

"No," she replied. Somehow all of this seemed rather unusual to her.

The man looked straight into her eyes and said, "Valentina, I want to help you. I am not here on behalf of the KGB."

Alarmed, Valentina jumped up. "Excuse me—what did you say?"

"Sit down again. And please, no hysterics. Not only do I wish to help you, but also someone very close to me."

"But who are you?" she cried.

He looked at her, sad-eyed, for a long time.

"Listen to me, Valentina," he finally said. "A very long time ago I worked in Kuibishev. Those were horrible years for our whole country. Not only were large numbers of believers thrown into prison, but also many Communists, scientists, and others. Once some others and I were given the job of arresting an evangelist named Serge Gratchov. His misdeed consisted of evangelizing even though this was prohibited by law. One of his 'spiritual brothers' had turned him in. We arrived at his home early in the morning, or perhaps it was even still night. We knocked on the door, and Gratchov's wife opened it up. When we asked whether her husband was home, she shook her head. She did not say 'no,' but merely shook her head. We were about to leave again when the 'brother' interjected, 'She is lying! I am absolutely certain that he is home.' Then he spoke to Gratchov's wife reproachfully, 'How can you lie like that, sister? And you a Christian!'

"He pushed her aside, stormed into the apartment and went toward the bedroom. But Gratchov was nowhere to be found, not even in the bedroom. I already had given the order to withdraw when the 'brother' darted under the bed and then to a closet. 'Aha!' he yelled, 'there he is! How can a Christian be so shameless and hide himself when he is brought to account for his misdeeds?' With that he dragged the man from the clothes closet.

"Gratchov apologized, then stepped over to embrace his weeping wife; and both proceeded to kneel down before our eyes. They prayed together and then said good-bye to each other. The good-bye turned out to be forever, since Gratchov died in prison. The 'brother' of whom I've just spoken continued a great career among the Christians. Not only did he achieve a reputation as a sincere preacher and wise leader hereabouts, but he also gained the trust of and exerted influence on people in foreign countries.

"You know, Valentina, I don't want to convict anyone too harshly when he betrays his friends in order to save his own skin. I can understand that if he was in danger he would tell the world lies and slander those close to him. But would you please tell me, dear Valentina, what forces you to be an informer? What is it that brings you to do that?"

Valentina had been uneasy the entire time, as if she were sitting on a bed of coals. "What business is it of yours?" she cried indignantly. "I am serving the Soviet Union! I am serving my fatherland!"

He looked calmly at her flushed face. Suddenly he asked, "Do you really love your husband?"

Valentina looked at him, startled. She said quietly, "Naturally."

"Do you believe in God?"

"Naturally. . . ."

"But how can you reconcile informing on your husband with the inspired Word of the New Testament?"

"Well, first of all, I am no informer, as you call me. I serve the Soviet people because the Soviet government has been put in place by God, and the New Testament requires all believers to obey their governments. So when our state views religion as the opiate of the people and enters into battle against the religious remnants in the country, then we must help with this fight. The apostle Paul, after all, did write that the government is a servant of God and that we must render it our complete obedience."

"And what happens when a government destroys whole people, as Hitler did with the Jews, for example, or Stalin with millions of people? Doesn't the church have to say, on the basis of the teaching of the New Testament, that this is wrong and, yes, inhuman?"

"No, under no circumstances should it do that! That is none of its business. If the government does this, then God has ordered it to be done this way."

Valentina did not acknowledge defeat easily.

"All right," said the stranger wearily, "then tell me why western churches are repenting at least in part for siding with fascism."

"Oh, that," smiled Valentina. "That's because the current government requires them to do it. In those countries there are almost more Communists today than we have here," she added venomously.

The stranger winced painfully. "But, Valentina, I'm not talking about that. Let me tell you something. 'Believers' like you have made it impossible for me to stand Christians anymore. There is nothing I despise more than religious hypocrisy or pious presumptuousness. These sometimes occur in tandem, and you are a perfect example of these traits. These are the things which have caused me to abhor everything which refers to itself as Christian. Because of them I have lost everything which gave my life meaning."

He said the last words softly and in an embittered tone. Then he arose to his full height, looked at Valentina penetratingly for a few moments and said, "This morning your husband was arrested. He is being accused of activities against the best interests of society." He fell silent again, then added, "This means that unlike you, Valentina, he did not function for the benefit of the Communist society of the future."

Valentina had turned pale. She stared at the man, unable to force out a single syllable. "It isn't true!" she finally managed to scream. "They promised me not to touch him!" She burst into tears.

He looked at the woman now wracked by despairing sobs. "What a fool you are," he growled. "What a miserable fool!" He left her standing there and walked out of the apartment.

Miroshnitchenko stood waiting for him at the street corner and asked excitedly, "Well, how did everything go?"

"Man, is she stupid!" said Sokolov, still shaking his head in disbelief. "You just can't understand it! Do you know, Grisha, my daughter once read to me from the Bible something that said, 'The sons of darkness are smarter than the sons of light.' But the Neverov woman actually has studied at the university!"

He handed the disconnected bug to Miroshnitchenko. Suddenly everything fell into place for Miroshnitchenko. He looked at the listening device more closely and scolded, "What a piece of junk! Just look at this! At Khrushchev's house they at least installed an American one. This one belongs on the junk heap."

Sokolov was silent. They entered their car and drove off. Sokolov said nothing more until they reached Minsk.

*   *   *

After Serov's burial Sokolov spoke with his widow. "What will you do now, Lyuba? You'll not suffer from any lack of funds. But if I know you, you won't be able to stand it without some work to do, especially now that the children are to be sent away." The KGB had arranged quickly for Serov's children to be placed in a boarding school for reorientation.

Lyuba gestured helplessly and replied, "I really have no idea. I haven't worked for so many years, playing the role of housewife and mother. Perhaps I'll go back to teaching. How I will live on without the children I have no way of knowing. But I know that by myself I never would be able to drive this Christian mishmash out of them."

She sighed.

"Where are they now?" Sokolov asked.

She shrugged her shoulders. "I don't know. They're probably by the river somewhere, praying. They're actually praying there every day now! I cannot fathom where something like this can come from." She sighed once more and added with gentle reproof in her voice, "That's the influence of your daughter, Yuri. Now they have no future before them whatever. No career, absolutely nothing pleasant, nothing but problems."

Sokolov looked out at the river from the window and quietly said, "The two of us have identical needs. My daughter became a Christian against my will, too, as your children did. Nothing can be achieved, however, by reproaching each other. We've got to concentrate on how we can aid our children."

At that moment the door flew open and the children stormed inside. They encircled their mother. Nina stroked her mother's hand gently and whispered, "Mama, they'll be here any minute now. Forgive us for bringing you so much sorrow." Tears spilled down her little face, and she pushed her head into her mother's lap.

"We will always pray for you, Mama," Alyosha said.

Svetlana laid her head on her mother's shoulder. "We will pray that everything will go well with you always."

Sokolov rose and stepped to the window. He simply could not stand these farewell scenes. He knew that Lyuba could restrain her tears only through sheer willpower and that her children's promises to pray for her cut even more deeply into her heart instead of consoling her.

Two Volga cars drove into the courtyard. One stopped in front of the door, the other under the window.

"They are here," Sokolov said.

Wordlessly the children embraced their mother. There was no loud weeping, and no resistance was shown by the children, which was something the authorities had not counted on. The officials put the children's suitcases into the cars and made two of the children get into each of the cars. The engines started.

Nina put her head out of the window and called, "Uncle Yuri, send Irina my regards, please, and tell her. . . ." Sokolov could understand nothing more. He put an arm around Lyuba and gently led her back into the house.

"Everything is upside down in the study," Lyuba complained. "The KGB took along everything, you know—documents, letters, everything that had belonged to my husband. And I simply haven't got the strength to put things back in order."

"May I do it for you?" suggested Yuri.

"Thank you, Yuri. I'm going to lie down for a little while now." She went off to the bedroom.

Yuri waited until she had closed the door behind her, then turned to the scattered papers, put them in some order and put them away inside the desk. The bookshelves, too, showed signs of having been hurriedly searched. Sokolov went to get himself a dustcloth and got to work. As he polished the bookshelves he took each book into his hand, dusted it off and replaced it in proper order. He was so engrossed in his activity that he was unaware evening had come. Only when a slip of paper fell out of a volume of Lenin's writings and he wanted to read what was written on it did he realize that he needed more light.

It was a letter. Sokolov could not overcome his curiosity. He sat down on an easy chair and began to read. The letter was addressed to one Nikolay Petrovich Lebedyev.

"My dear Nikolay," it said. "I've certainly written you five hundred letters but have still not had an answer to this day. So I will go to the Russian embassy this time, as my friends have suggested, and will hand them this letter to you. I am your wife, Varya, along with our sons, Ivan and Alexey. We are hale and hearty and have been living in Paris since 1945. When war broke out, the first bomb to hit the village fell on your brother's house. We were not in the house at the time, however, but were picking raspberries in the woods. After that we tried to make our way to Moscow but we were unsuccessful. Along the way we were all knocked unconscious by an exploding bomb, and all three of us awoke in a hospital. To our horror, this turned out to be a German hospital. It was our good fortune that the chief surgeon at the hospital, a Dr. Schaefer, was a Christian and, as we later discovered, belonged to a Baptist congregation. He felt sympathy for us and would have been happy to let us return to Moscow; yet it was wartime. Ivan had a serious concussion, and Dr. Schaefer said he needed rest. We were moved to the enemy's staging area, and this is how we came to Warsaw.

When the war ended we were in Paris, where some friendly people had put us up. Dr. Schaefer himself was shot at the end of the war at Hitler's orders because he had refused to work in a concentration camp where primarily Jews were kept. The Schaefer family introduced us to the Lord, and we have become Christians. Our two sons completed their education at the university. Ivan is at work in the nuclear industry, and Alexey continued his studies in Belgium at a Bible college. He finished that recently and now is working as a missionary in Ethiopia. Both of them are married. Ivan has three sons, and Alexey three daughters. If you receive this letter, please write to us right away, for we miss you a great deal. The two of us are old now, of course, in our seventies. We want so much to see you again. Are you still working as a prison guard, despite your age? With my kisses, Varya."

Sokolov turned the letter over in his hands and began to think hard. Lebedyev . . . Lebedyev . . . who could that be? Wasn't that old Lebedyev from Lefortovo? Miroshnitchenko had just told Sokolov of a man named Lebedyev who somehow succeeded in looking fifteen years younger than his actual age and who had been working in the prison since his eighteenth year. He apparently did not wish to retire because of some personal tragedy. No one knew what actually had occurred.

Sokolov pushed the letter into his jacket pocket and went to the telephone. He called Lyuba's sister. "I'd like to ask you to take Lyuba into your home, at least for a while," he said. "It is only a week since her husband was buried, and today her children were taken from her. She needs to be with people. I'm flying to Moscow tomorrow at ten o'clock and I am afraid to leave her here alone."

Lyuba's sister had a rapid consultation with her husband and responded, "It's all set. Tomorrow morning at seven we are coming to pick her up. Ask her to get herself ready."

Sokolov thanked them and hung up. He then walked to the bedroom in order to look after Lyuba. She was awake again and happy that her relatives were to come to get her. She immediately began packing her things.

*   *   *

Sokolov sat opposite old Lebedyev and waited until he had finished reading his wife's letter. The "white swan's" fingers were trembling. Tears rolled down the wrinkled face. He made no effort to wipe them away.

"Do you know that your son has been in our country twice on his firm's business?" asked Sokolov when the old man had completed reading the letter. "He made inquiries everywhere, but none of the officials wanted to help him."

Both were silent again. Finally Lebedyev asked, "Which one was here? Ivan?"

Sokolov nodded. Again they sat there, neither saying a word.

"This means that this letter has remained in Serov's book for more than a year?"

"That's right," Yuri confirmed, then added, "What I am about to tell you now you need to keep strictly confidential. Your son will be in Moscow again in a year. But you can't let this leak out under any circumstances, when you're drunk or something."

"I do not drink," said the old man in a hurt voice.

"All the better!" Sokolov smiled for the first time since they met.

"Tomorrow your daughter will be taken to Koshkin at the Serbian Institute for a medical appraisal," said "Grandfather White Swan."

"What? To that idiot?" Sokolov was beside himself.

Lebedyev squinted at Sokolov in amazement. "Everyone who was in Irina's group, including the Orthodox man, the Catholic, and the Pentecostal, have already been taken into the psychiatric clinic. Now it's her turn. I have not been told where her friends are located."

Yuri collapsed inwardly and sat silently for a long time. He knew full well what it meant when those who had fallen out of the Party's favor were sent to psychiatric clinics. He thought about General Grigorenko's fate and burst out, "You'll rue the day! Sticking my daughter into a nuthouse!"

"She hasn't been stuck into it yet," Lebedyev said calmly, "and you, as a psychiatrist, should know better than to make such a public display. Instead of helping your daughter, you may well actually wind up in a psychiatric clinic yourself."

That quickly restored Sokolov to his senses. That's also why Irina received her first illegal message from her father.

17 Freshman Prisoner

The first death camps were not set up by the Germans, but by the Soviets.

Mihailo Mihailov, Moscow Summer

Once again the prison was bursting at the seams. None of the prisoners knew what had caused this tidal wave of humanity, but there was such a flood of inmates that twenty people were shoehorned into a cell built to accommodate four. Here they awaited either their day in court or their shipment to a "corrections colony" or to a so-called free settlement.

The last kind had been established by the government for two reasons. First, the "all-knowing western press" indicated from time to time that two and one-half million persons in the Soviet Union were behind lock and key. The exact figure was, of course, not known to anyone; so the figure was occasionally referred to as "only" one and one-half million. Yet wasn't that also a rather staggering total? In any case, the interior ministry sought relief from this embarrassing problem and for this purpose invented the "free settlements." At rather regular intervals of two years, the ruling body of the Soviet Union issued exemptions by which prison inmates who had distinguished themselves by their good conduct were transferred to "free settlements." That is, they were put to work in the buildup of the Soviet economic system.

By this action two birds were caught in the same trap. The

prisons, full to overflowing, were relieved of some of their burden, a fact which also was not kept from the western press. But a second, much tougher objective was reached at the same time. The majority of Soviet youth refused to move to the inhospitable areas in the North to build new cities, establish new factories and mines, and lay down rails for new railroads. So the interior ministry simply transferred some prisoners into these zones. Only men whose prison behavior had proved them to be reliable workers were sent there. So for the remainder of their sentences, these "settlers" were put into harness to work at projects the state thought important. If someone there did something untoward, he was shipped back to a regular jail to serve the whole sentence to which he was "entitled."

These arrangements saved the state billions. No new jails had to be built, and the unpopulated zones were opened up and populated.

In the prison mentioned earlier, there were only 1,725 cells. The basement held those units designated for political prisoners or those to be executed by firing squads. In addition they contained a number of so-called detention rooms for prisoners who had somehow violated prison rules, as well as "type-eight" cells, which measured only eighty centimeters by eighty centimeters (thirty-two inches by thirty-two inches) and had no windows or other forms of ventilation. Customarily the jailer collected prisoners who had been caught sleeping during the day and placed eight of them together in one of these cells for an hour or two. The duration of the punishment generally depended on the soft heart of the jailer or on how quickly one of the prisoners lost consciousness because of lack of oxygen.

*   *   *

The jailer pushed Sasha into cell number 511. He had to give him quite a shove, for when the intolerable stench hit Sasha he took an involuntary step backward.

"Why the crab-walk, you stupid cow?" screamed the jailer, and pushed his enormous bunch of keys between Sasha's shoulder blades. Sasha stumbled head over heels into the cell and wound up in the arms of a huge fellow who in turn pushed him toward another group of prisoners who were playing dominoes. These men jumped up, took Sasha by the hands and flung him back toward the door. He hit the door hard, lost his balance and fell.

The gigantic fellow laughed uproariously and extended his hand to Sasha. "I'm Gniloy, and what's your name?" ("Gniloy" means "the decayed one.")

Sasha murmured an apology for having upset the dominoes game during his fall and introduced himself as Sasha Nikitin.

Gniloy howled with laughter. "Well, can you believe it? Your imperial highness Sah-sha Nih-kitin! Haven't you got a nickname?"

Sasha straightened out his tie and said softly, "I do, actually. They call me 'the Christian.'"

"What? The Christian?" Gniloy began to laugh unrestrainedly again until tears were rolling down his face. After that he calmed down, stepped toward Sasha and tore off his tie. "You don't wear ties in jail," he said, adopting a teacher's stance. "It reminds us too much of the Young Pioneers. They stink, as far as we're concerned." With his giant paw he grasped Sasha beneath the chin and examined his face as if to probe him, then whispered, "If you're a Christian, then you're certainly not a 'homo.' Brothers, shall we accept him into our community?" he asked, turning to the rest of the prisoners.

"Sure," growled the cell's inhabitants without enthusiasm. The attraction of a new arrival already had vanished, and they were no longer interested in him. A few of them resumed their game of dominoes, others simply crouched idly on the cots, on the floor, or on the single bench which offered the only seating surface in the cell.

Only one of them, a young fellow who had been one of the domino players, got up slowly and stepped toward Sasha. He looked at Sasha with cold, penetrating eyes for a long time, then snarled through his teeth, "Preacher, huh? Or to what role were you ordained?"

Sasha looked at him in surprise and replied, "I was ordained as a preacher."

The young man looked at him full of hate. "You people are nothing more than repulsive church rats," he spit out. Without any warning he struck Sasha squarely on the nose, returning to his former spot immediately. Sasha fell from the impact, struck the toilet pail and fell down headlong. Blood spurted from his nose, flowing down his shirt and over his suit.

Gniloy bent over him, lifting him up by his armpits. Then he gently led him to one of the beds after pushing off the prisoner who had been seated on it. He let Sasha sit on it, brought a towel and a piece of soap and then began to pound on the iron door with both fists in order to summon a jailer.

Sullen footsteps soon were heard outside. The jailer opened the cloth flap, stuck his head in and growled, "Well, what is it, you stupid cattle?"

"We just got through 'baptizing' the new man," explained Gniloy calmly. "He's covered with blood from top to bottom. He's got to go to the washroom to clean himself up."

"Listen," screamed the possessor of the cot at Sasha, "you're getting blood all over my bed, you scum!"

Gniloy's eyes narrowed, threatening trouble. "You're going to be nice and sleep on the floor, Mokry. Is that clear? You'll donate your bed to Sasha."

Mokry protested vehemently as the jailer proceeded to unlock the door, his keys clanging loudly. "Not a chance! I'm not handing over my bed to the new man! That would be something!"

Gniloy balled his hands into gigantic fists and advanced slowly on Mokry.

Mokry quickly stammered, "All right, all right," and retreated a few steps. "I'm doing it; I'm going to do whatever you want, Gniloy!"

"That's a lot better, Mokry," whispered Gniloy imperiously, "and remember this: one more word of protest and I'll pound you into mush."

"Hey you, listen!" the jailer yelled. "You start using your hands and I'll put you into the special detention cell!"

Sasha stepped out into the hallway. He held the towel to his nose, but the bleeding would not stop. The jailer locked the cell door again and ordered, "Straight ahead and then down the right-hand corridor."

"I really should go to a doctor," Sasha said softly.

"That's all we need, to take each one of you to the doctor after your 'baptism'! What did God give you fists for anyway? You're a cleric yourself; so get going. Take bigger steps, you stupid cow!"

The jailer jammed Sasha in the back so that he stumbled into the washroom. Sasha washed his face and began to put the cold towel on his neck. The jailer gave him all the time he needed, sauntering lazily down the corridor, looking into several of the peepholes as he passed. After a while Sasha was able to bring the bleeding under control. But his entire face was swollen, and his nose has bloomed into something that looked like a potato.

Meanwhile Gniloy turned to the young fellow who had struck Sasha.

"Why did you take care of him that way, Gander?"

Gander stared at Gniloy angrily. "What business is it of yours anyway? If I smacked him in the puss you can bet he earned it."

Gniloy was furious. "Who is this cell's oldest inhabitant—you or I?" he screamed.

"Aw go to—!" screamed Gander furiously, and went back to playing the game. Gniloy jumped toward him, grabbed him by his shirt, and lifted him off the floor. The buttons from Gander's shirt popped off and fell to the floor. He began to choke and gasped, "Let me down!"

Gniloy let the man slip very slowly back down to the floor, saying, "Well, are you going to explain everything to me now?"

Still fighting for breath, Gander squeezed out the words, "I'm not going to forget this! Never! If you absolutely have to know, I whacked this sanctimonious guy in the mouth because my old man is another Baptist cleric like him. And I've got reason to hate them all."

"You could have told me that right from the beginning," said Gniloy, his curiosity satisfied. "But don't you do something like this again. You see, I've spent time in work camps with Baptists like that, people like Vins, Khrapov, and Kosresov. I wasn't particularly close to any of them, but this much I saw: they really were men of God. Don't you touch that Nikitan again!"

"You don't have to tell me what I can and cannot do," snapped the furious Gander. "I'm in jail for the fourth time and I know what I'm doing."

Gniloy smiled, "And I've been in eight times, you greenhorn!"

At that moment the food flap was lifted. "Lunch!" screamed the man on duty. One by one the prisoners stepped to the door and each received his dish of rassolnik. This was a sour dish of barley, which on that occasion consisted of nothing besides barley and green, raw tomatoes. On good days the dish also included kidneys and mushrooms, sour pickles and sour cream. The prisoners slurped the soup, made a grimace and tossed the inedible tomatoes into the toilet bucket. Then they waited for the porridge. Today they would get "horse rice," which was the name prisoners gave to oatmeal. This was not brought to them until the soup had been distributed to all the cells.

Eventually Sasha returned. Gniloy handed him the dish of soup which he had put aside for him. But Sasha was unable to eat because his lips were swollen up and still bleeding.

Earlier, as the jailer had pushed Sasha into the cell, no one but Gniloy had noticed Sasha deftly sneaking a bag under the bed closest to the domino players.

It happened that the thoughtful Natasha, employing her best manners and her motherly, friendly ways, had bamboozled the militiamen into agreeing to give the bag to her son. Into this bag Natasha had packed twenty kilos of food, mainly dry bread and a big hard sausage. In addition, the militiamen had allowed her to exchange a few words with Sasha before he took him away.

"I don't know, my boy," she had told him, "whether prison habits have changed any since I spent time there myself, but let me give you this advice anyway. As soon as you step into that cell, put that bag under somebody's bed when nobody is watching. After your 'baptism' you can play the generous host to the other prisoners with what you'll find in that bag. If they discover it before your 'baptism' they will most likely take it away from you, and they won't leave a single crumb for you! Of course, each prison has its own unwritten laws. You'll discover that all by yourself." She had kept herself under control and had not wept, but instead smiled pleasantly and laid it on his heart to pray regularly.

Now Sasha was really happy to have followed his mother's advice. He reached for his bag and untied it. Everyone's eyes were fixed on him expectantly.

"Fellows, why don't you help yourselves," Sasha said softly.

In an instant the whole mob hurled itself at Sasha's magnificent hoard. In a few moments there would have been nothing left for him. But Gniloy made a lightning-like leap to place himself between the hoard and the rest of the prisoners, then pushed them all aside.

"Hold it, hold it, comrades!" he called, pulling the bag out of their reach. "It may have been touching of you to do this, good soul, but there's no point in letting these devils gobble up everything at once." He threw the bag on his bed and ordered, "Get your dishes of porridge first."

They had not noticed that the jailer was already in the process of doling out the porridge through the food flap. So, grumbling, each man picked up his allotment of porridge. After that, Gniloy threw a few slices of sausage into each man's dish. "That's to give it good taste, brothers," he said tenderly. Only Gander refused the sausage. He sat down in the corner with his dish and looked at Sasha warily.

The cell was terribly crowded. There were four cots, and on the floor were several mattresses which during the day were rolled up to serve as seating surfaces for the twelve prisoners. Sasha counted the number of prisoners once again and thought, *What the people from the committee for human rights said was right.* Then he fell asleep. No one saw the jailer entering.

"You there! Get over here!" the jailer shouted in Sasha's direction. Sasha stood up, tottering, but was too sleepy to realize what was going on.

"What's the matter, natchalnik?" Gniloy objected. "Why don't you leave the guy alone?"

"Shut your trap!" yelled the jailer. He grabbed Sasha's hand and dragged him out of the cell. The steel door clanged shut. Sasha was barely able to understand what was going on. He was indifferent to it all. Inside his head he felt as if a cauldron were bubbling.

The jailer dragged him down the steps with him. Five prisoners already occupied the basement cell where he was taken. The jailer took Sasha to them and told him to wait. Sasha had more or less awakened, and he examined his fellow sufferers a bit more closely. A man with an unnaturally bloated body attracted his attention.

"Well, my brother, what did you do to get beat up like that?" one of the prisoners asked him.

Sasha presented a really pitiful sight. His face had swollen beyond recognition, and he had a huge blood clot under one eye.

"My 'baptism,'" Sasha murmured.

"I see," the other one said, "but that doesn't happen in every cell. It depends on the 'contingent.'"

"What do you mean by 'contingent'?"

"Oh, the particular reason the men were sent to jail in the first place. And also their age category." But Sasha's weary brain was unable to comprehend it. He desperately sought to recall where he had encountered the bloated man before, but he simply could not remember.

"Why are we being detained in here?" he asked.

"The jailer caught all of us asleep. We're being put into the 'type-eight' cell."

"What is a 'type-eight' cell? Why are they sticking us in there?"

Someone laughed sardonically. "Just wait; you'll see for yourself. We're waiting for two more unlucky guys."

Suddenly it came to him! It was crystal clear! Excitedly Sasha stumbled toward the enormously bloated man, who looked at him uncomprehendingly.

"Silitch!" Sasha whispered, his heart beating rapidly. "Silitch, how did you get here? You were working with Professor Kuznetsov, weren't you?"

The man stared speechlessly at Sasha.

"Yes," he finally said, "I worked with him. I was with him as recently as six months ago. But now I'm in prison here."

"I remember you very well, Silitch," continued Sasha eagerly, "and you actually should remember me, too. I was the preacher of the Baptist congregation. Your sister Antonina was one of our members."

"You're Nikitin?" Silitch exclaimed in amazement. "My God, but your face is unrecognizable!"

"And what's wrong with you, Silitch? Are you sick? You must get to a doctor!"

"I've been there already," Silitch answered resignedly, "but the head doctor of this prison is actually a veterinarian's assistant. That's not even the worst of it. The guy happens to work hand in glove with the KGB! A couple of days ago he snapped at me, 'Well, Silitch, do you still want to go to the land of your forebears? You're clearly ready for the heavenly Jerusalem! Get out of here, you Jewface!' With that he simply threw me out of his office. There's absolutely no point in going to him a second time."

Sasha shook his head speechlessly. Another prisoner was brought into the cell. Silitch resumed, "I suffer from edema and angina pectoris."

The jailer reappeared. "All right," he announced, "you have all violated prison rules. If you are asked to remain awake during the day and to sleep during the night, then it is your duty to obey! As punishment for your disobedience we are going to put you into our education cell. Aha! Here comes one more! So we've finally reached the quorum. If we had failed to get eight of you together, we would have been forced to cancel visits by your loved ones." He grinned wickedly. "Unfortunately, I don't have a physician on staff here; so I will be forced to personally guard the state of your health."

He swung open the heavy steel door and ordered, "Silitch, forward march! You get in first."

Silitch stepped across the cell's doorsill and recoiled. "It's cold and wet in here!" he whined like a child. The jailer unceremoniously pushed him inside. Then he and the corporal who acted as his assistant began to push the rest of the prisoners into the cell. Sasha was the last to be jammed in. The tiny chamber was so overcrowded that it was almost impossible to close the heavy door. The jailer and the corporal had to force it shut. Finally the lock clicked. Now those outside could hear neither screams nor groans even if they walked right by the cell.

The lack of oxygen became apparent in just a few minutes. Silitch was the first to lose consciousness. The rest groaned and cursed in their agony. Sasha attempted to pray, but he also quickly lost consciousness.

When the door was reopened the men tumbled out like wet burlap sacks. That is what they looked like, too, lying one on top of the other. Silitch's body lay halfway inside the cell, across the others' legs. The jailers brought buckets of water and poured it over the unconscious inmates' heads. After this "therapy" six of the men revived and were taken back to their cells. They had emerged alive from the ordeal. All of them were new to the prison and did not know that there was a way to sleep during the day without getting caught.

Silitch and Sasha, however, were not as well off as the rest. The jailers dragged the two unconscious men upstairs. Sasha heard someone say as he was coming to, "This one will survive, but the other one is not likely to make it."

With a start Sasha raised himself up. He saw only strange faces around him. He was in a different cell from before. Eight pairs of inquisitive eyes followed his every move.

"Well, my fellow countryman, the type-eight cell didn't seem to be a good place for you, did it?" inquired an old man who introduced himself as Perepyolka, or "Quail."

They certainly have droll nicknames in this place, Sasha thought. Later, however, he was to learn that this was the man's real name.

Silitch lay beside Sasha, trying to open his eyes but unable to do so. His entire body was sopping wet.

Sasha pulled himself together and went to work. First he removed Silitch's wet and bloody clothing. Perepyolka handed him Silitch's duffel bag, which the jailer had just brought inside. He removed Silitch's underwear from the bag and handed it to Sasha. Sasha smiled gratefully. The other inmates began to join in. They massaged Silitch's bloated body with ice-cold water and put fresh clothing on him. Silitch smiled as if he were in seventh heaven and whispered to Sasha, "There's a family photograph in the duffel bag. Would you please hand it to me?"

Sasha rummaged around inside the bag and found the photo. He handed it to Silitch.

"Listen to me," whispered Silitch, "the picture is made up of two separate layers. Would you try to carefully pry them apart?"

Perepyolka took the photo from his hands and began to turn it around so that he could inspect all of its edges. Finally he discovered the tiny ending of a thread. He pulled on it, and the second layer began to separate from the photograph.

"How about that? What a smart Jew!" Perepyolka said admiringly. Everyone looked in amazement at the marvelous view of the city of Jerusalem. On the back of the photograph of Silitch's family there was a Hebrew text.

Silitch held both of the layers in his trembling hands. For a long time he gazed on the family picture, from which his wife and children were smiling happily. Silitch kissed the family picture tenderly and then looked at the view of Jerusalem for a long time. Then he read the verses out loud. Sasha, who had studied Hebrew for three years with Silitch's sister, translated the text into the Russian language.

"We sat by the waters of Babylon and wept when we thought of Zion. We hung our harps from the willows in that country. For those who had held us there as prisoners told us to sing and to be happy in the midst of our tears: 'Sing us a song of Zion!' But how could we sing the song of the Lord in that foreign land? If I forget you, Jerusalem, my right arm will wither away...." Tears were coursing down Silitch's face. "My tongue shall cleave to my palate," he continued, "if I do not remember you...."

He allowed his head to fall down on the padded cotton jacket they had put underneath his head as a pillow, and repeated in Russian, "My tongue shall cleave to my palate if I do not remember you, Jerusalem!" He looked searchingly into the faces of his fellow prisoners, who were in a circle around him. He grasped Sasha's hand and almost inaudibly requested, "Man of God, pray with me!"

The eight prisoners stared at Sasha and Silitch with bated breath as Sasha softly said the prayer, "Lord receive this man into Your kingdom!"

"Hallelujah!" breathed Silitch. He took one more deep breath and died.

No one had noticed that the jailer had quietly stepped inside the cell and had stood there witnessing everything.

18 The Interloper

The two sons of the old jailer Lebedyev had taken their wives' family names when they married. Their mother, however, kept her married name.

Pyotr had learned of Lebedyev's fate through one of the many secret channels of communication between Russia and the outside world. He had then gotten in touch with the sons, and now he was to meet Alexey Lebedyev in Basel.

Alexey had held occasional talks with the Marxist partisans in Eritrea and had become deeply disturbed at what he had learned through them. He badly wanted to discuss with Pyotr the status of Christians within Marxist-oriented societies, since Pyotr had gained a rather good idea of this relationship while in the Soviet Union.

Tanned by the African sun and bubbling with the joy of life, Alexey sat opposite Pyotr at a table in one of Basel's better restaurants. First he wanted to know as much as possible about his father. That done, and recognizing that they could be open with each other, Alexey began to talk about himself.

He had been in Eritrea for ten years as a missionary and had started many new congregations there. During all those years he had kept on writing to the foreign ministry in Moscow, inquiring about the fate of his father. Usually he received no reply whatsoever. Once in a while he received a reply saying that nothing was known about the whereabouts and fate of his father. His mother, in fact, had been told by the Soviet embassy in Paris that Lebedyev had disappeared during the war. But the old lady knew the government apparatus well enough to lend no real credence to this report. She kept right on sending letter after letter to their old home address. Unfortunately these letters consistently were "lost in transit."

"So neither I nor my relatives trusted those Soviet sources," Alexey stated. "We intuitively suspected that something must be going on behind all this secrecy. We thought that perhaps father had fallen victim to one of the purges Stalin and Beria staged. Yet the authorities would have known about that. My wife and I concluded our studies at the Bible school in Saint Chrishona, were married, and were then sent to Eritrea by a mission organization. Every four years we have returned home for our furlough. Financially we were always very hard up, since the group which supported our mission was quite small. We often found ourselves in great need.

"When we returned to our mission station after our most recent furlough, I prepared to visit each one of the congregations I had founded. I had traveled quite some distance from our base station when I heard someone behind me calling me by my old name, Alexey Lebedyev. Since I was completely alone, I was startled. There was nothing but miles and miles of endless steppe around me. What increased my concern was that my name had been pronounced in accent-free Russian. I stopped and abruptly whirled around.

"Hurrying toward me was a European supported by a walking stick. When he finally caught up with me he smiled warmly and put out his hand in greeting. He exclaimed, 'Well, it's certainly great to run into you here! What a wonderful act of providence.'

"Excitedly I squeezed his hand and asked, 'Who are you?' My heart was pounding as though it would break, and I had the peculiar feeling that my knees were shaking. The stranger ignored my question and said instead, 'I have brought news about your father. Can we sit down in the grass? I am terribly tired.'

"Question upon question ran through my mind. Naturally I was curious as well. The stranger spoke flawless Russian; and I, in turn, had a tough time with Russian, since we spoke French at home. At any rate I sat down in the grass alongside the stranger.

"'Well, isn't that absolutely amazing! Finally I receive news of my father right in the middle of Eritrea!'

"I was naive enough to believe that he would hand me a letter or at least a slip of paper with my father's handwriting on it. But the unidentified man said, 'Your father sends his greetings and has asked me to tell you that he is really homesick for you. I am here as part of a group of Soviet scientists who are undertaking some anthropological studies. We are to remain here for a few weeks at the behest of the foreign ministry. I am to transmit to you the news that your father is hale and hearty. However, he is sad that you have taken another name instead of your Russian one.'

"The stranger had a disarming smile and was exceptionally cordial and friendly, so that I ultimately abandoned all my suspicions. Believing that he was indeed nothing more than a scientist, I invited him to our home. He accepted immediately but told me that he had left his all-purpose vehicle in the nearby village. He suggested that if we both walked there we could proceed to my mission station by car. I agreed, and within an hour we were seated at our table drinking tea with my wife and little daughters. Our girls were totally carried away by the stranger. Soon they were all over him, jumping on and off his lap while he stroked their heads gently.

"Our guest spoke French with my wife. He and she quickly became good friends. Not suspecting anything, my wife told him that we were having many difficulties with the Marxist partisans who were terrorizing the nationals. The stranger, who urged us to call him Yevgeny, responded, 'Oh, really, my dear ones, the partisans here have a totally different understanding of Marxism than the one we have in the Soviet Union. Our government views the activities of these murderers with great concern.'

"Already by then these Ethiopian Marxists were causing us many problems. They had read in Marx that 'religion is the opiate of the masses' and sincerely believed that they were performing good deeds on behalf of communism when they murdered many of the best Ethiopian preachers.

"After tea we withdrew to our covered veranda and continued our conversation. My wife had to do various things inside the house; so the guest and I spoke alone. He told me many things about Russia, painting everything in the most glorious colors. As a result, I became so homesick that tears rose in my eyes.

"'Lebedyev,' he said suddenly, 'I see that we have a joint enemy in this country which we ought to fight. I think we should work together.'

"'Who is this enemy you talk about?' I asked, surprised. But he gave me no answer and began to say his good-byes.

"'But you don't want to leave us this soon, do you?' said my wife, disappointed.

"He consoled her by saying, 'If you have nothing against it, I would like to come for another visit.'

"'But of course, please come as often as you wish. It makes us very happy!'

"The stranger smiled charmingly, hurried to his vehicle, and returned with a rolled-up package. 'There you are,' he said. 'This is especially for you!'

"My wife blushed and stuttered, 'Th-thank you; that wasn't really necessary.' The stranger raised his arm in greeting once more, stepped into his vehicle, and sped off.

"We looked after him for a long time. Then we unpacked his gift. It was three thousand dollars! I was bewildered. My wife began to cry and laugh at the same time, exclaiming over and over again, 'Praise God!' I should tell you that the two of us had just decided to send our eldest daughter to a boarding school in France, which would cost us a great deal of money. All in all we needed exactly three thousand dollars."

"But why didn't you send your children to the school for missionary children?" asked Pyotr.

"That will require some explaining. I will tell you about that later," Lebedyev replied. "At any rate we had asked the Lord again and again to send us the money we lacked. We needed the money for the airline ticket so our daughter could fly to France. But no money came. Yet this unexpected three thousand dollars made me extremely uneasy.

" 'Marie,' I said to my wife, 'we will return the money.'

"But she wanted to hear nothing of that. 'How can you even *say* such a thing?' she shouted at me with tears in her eyes. 'Under no circumstances will we return that money! I would not think of it! This very morning I asked the Lord for a sign. If no money were received in the mail today, we would accept this as a message not to send Michelle to boarding school. But you see, the mail hasn't even arrived yet, and the Lord has already sent us the money!' I went to my study totally crushed. I felt like crying.

"The Marxist partisans operated mostly in the mountainous regions. We heard their guns so frequently that we had become used to them. They had all their hiding places in the villages. We knew them all. They did not pay any attention to us because they knew we were concerned only about spreading the Gospel. They usually killed preachers who belonged to their people, leaving us foreigners alone, for the present at least.

"The strange visitor showed up at our home again a few days later, unfortunately while I was not at home. When I returned I saw his car standing in front of our house. When he spotted me he was suddenly in a big hurry, said his good-byes and drove off. Marie was simply glowing. Yevgeny was a very attractive human being, she told me, and a very knowledgeable one besides. Bit by bit it became apparent that he had questioned her about the partisans and that she had told him everything she knew.

"He turned up once more and announced that he was going to Paris and, from there, home. Again I was not present. My wife gave him her parents' address, asking him to pay them a visit, give them our greetings, and take them a few small gifts from us."

Lebedyev fell silent. The waitress wordlessly removed the plates with the steaks and left for the kitchen. Pyotr looked after her in amusement and winked at Alexey, who laughed. While the steaks were being warmed up again, Alexey resumed his story.

"I could not feel at peace for a long time after these visits by 'Yevgeny.' In fact, I had learned from my daughter that he had left with my wife another five thousand dollars which my daughter was to take to Paris on the way to her boarding school. As earlier, Marie considered this man a messenger from heaven and living proof of the fact that Christians in Russia had complete freedom to spread the Gospel in the Soviet Union. But I began to notice that my work was no longer being blessed as it had been in the past. Something stood between me and the Lord. I began to fast and to implore the Lord to reveal to me as soon as possible what lay behind this strange series of circumstances.

"I did not have to wait long for an answer. One day a young Coptic priest named Abdullah paid a visit to our mission station. He brought us cordial greetings from 'Yevgeny' and asked us to give him further reports about the Marxist partisans. I was incensed by that and asked him, 'Why do you need this information?'

" 'We Christians must fight for Marxism,' replied Abdullah, 'since God has urged us to live together in brotherhood, equality, and freedom. But these partisans interpret Marxism the wrong way and cause it much harm. That is why we must fight against them.'

"I was so angry that I had difficulty controlling myself. 'I am a missionary and not a spy!' I said. 'It is my life's work to preach the Gospel to Marxists as well as non-Marxists and to lead them toward belief in Jesus Christ.'

"At this Abdullah smiled indulgently and replied, 'I, too, am a Christian, my dear man, and I believe in Christ no less firmly than you do. But the practical liberation of man comes through Marxism.'

" 'Indeed,' I snarled. 'According to you Marx is our savior and not Christ?'

"At this point Abdullah showed me a photograph of my father near his residence. Of course I cannot remember my father any longer. So Abdullah said to me, 'This is your father. If you refuse to work with us, it will go badly for him.' Then he brought out yet another photograph. On this one I could see my wife accepting money from 'Yevgeny.'

"Would you believe, Pyotr, that I had only just received some money? A family had discovered that we were in financial difficulty and had promptly transmitted twenty thousand dollars to us toward the education of our daughter. Isn't that ironic? My wife did not know, either, that some people from the United States who had just paid us a visit had left behind nine thousand dollars so we would be able to pay for the boarding school.

"I took a look at both of the photographs, then rose and went to my study. It so happened that a Christian national had been waiting there to speak with me. I asked him to take my camera and take a few pictures of me and Abdullah. He was not to worry about using up the remainder of the film in the camera. Then I took eight thousand dollars from my desk drawer and went back to Abdullah.

" 'Here is the money which "Yevgeny," or whatever his real name is, gave my wife,' I said to the astounded priest. 'Count it and then get out! I don't ever wish to see you on my property again!' He stood there, indecisive, holding the money while my black friend was busy shooting picture after picture. Then Abdullah beat a hasty retreat.

"My wife had watched the entire episode and was appalled. But when it became clear to her that we had been within a hair of becoming spies for the KGB, she wept brokenheartedly and begged me to forgive her."

* * *

The waitress returned with the warmed-up steaks. She said, "Well, how about it? Do you want to eat now or not?"

As if they had rehearsed it, Pyotr and Lebedyev said in unison, "Yes, absolutely! Many thanks!"

They remained in the comfortable atmosphere of the restaurant for a while. Pyotr told Lebedyev of Irina and her friends, who still were incarcerated in psychiatric hospitals, and that through them contacts with Alexey first had been established.

"So it is true, eh?" said Lebedyev. "And I couldn't believe it. I always believed that the partisans were up to something. These fellows kept telling me again and again, 'Go on, keep on preaching! When we come to power you'll all be in institutions anyway. Only crazy people could work themselves up enough to get involved in religion. Those are delusions, that's all.' So that's what it is. Whoever has an opinion differing from theirs must of necessity be insane. Why, that's diabolical!"

Lebedyev insisted on speaking with a representative of the Soviet Baptists or with someone from the patriarch's office in Geneva. He and Pyotr called them and asked to be connected with one of the responsible people. Yet not a single member of the delegation indicated any desire to talk with Lebedyev about Russia's Christians and their fate.

19 In Temptation's Crucible

In the society of the future, which is the society of harmony and freedom, there will be neither courts nor prisons. Instead of this, those afflicted by sick passions will be conducted to hospitals, and the incurable cases will be isolated in special colonies on islands.

One of Karl Marx's teachers

It was cold in Tshernyakhovsk when Vassiley Kuznetsov, Semyon Anakin, and Valentin Relin alighted from the Black Maria.

There had been no trial, no investigation for them. Instead they had been "evaluated" by a psychiatrist. The diagnosis was schizophrenia.

Dr. Koshkin looked Kuznetsov over from top to bottom and asked casually, as if something trivial were under discussion, "Do you really believe there is a God?"

With dignity Vassiley responded, "Yes, I do believe that."

That was it as far as the evaluation was concerned. Koshkin merely shrugged his shoulders and left the room. Vassiley was returned to his cell.

A woman doctor spoke with Semyon Anakin and Valentin Relin.

"What do you think of religion?" she asked cautiously. She observed Anakin's reaction closely.

He looked straight at her and replied, "I believe in God and consequently also in a supernatural world. It is my conviction that man's life continues even after his earthly existence."

"And you want to convince the government that your ideas should be propagated freely throughout Russia?"

"Not *my* ideas, but the Gospel of Jesus Christ as it is given to us in the Bible."

There were no further questions. Anakin was conducted back to his cell.

The same woman spoke with Relin. "The Bible is nothing more than a collection of fairy tales which originated among the oppressed masses. Do you believe in the teachings of this book?"

"Yes," answered Relin laconically.

She abruptly began to question him about his childhood, his education, and his professional training. When Relin informed her that he had studied medicine she interrupted, "How do you manage to reconcile medicine with religion?"

Relin attempted to explain it to her. "Jesus Christ asks us in His Gospel to serve God and man. For this reason I find that my work in medicine presents an excellent way to initiate service to mankind. Yet I have not been able to find a position in a hospital because of my religious convictions."

She continued to question him, taking notes of his answers. "Don't you feel a certain splitting of your personality when you go about trying to bring your scientific thinking into line with your religious thoughts?"

"Not in the least," said Relin calmly, "because if that were the case, even the Nobel Prize winner Pavlov would have had to suffer from schizophrenia. He was well known as a sincere and upright Christian."

"That may have been possible," she smiled. "It may have been possible."

Relin was taken back to his cell.

The physician on duty in the special psychiatric clinic of Tshernyakhovsk received them without saying a word. There were no questions. He looked through their personal dossiers and disappeared from the room for a while. Eventually he returned and ordered them to be conducted to their cells.

Vassiley entered his semidark cell and saw a huge fellow lying on a bed. He lay on his side and inspected Vassiley with raised eyebrows.

"Good day!" Vassiley said.

No answer.

He walked over to his bed and sat down on it. *So I am now a mentally ill person,* he said to himself. He shuddered when he realized that it might be many years before he was released from this place. He began to say a silent prayer. Suddenly his roommate began to speak.

"Does someone like God really exist?" he asked, still flat on his bed.

Somewhat annoyed, Vassiley raised his head and responded, "Without a doubt."

"If there is a God, then why are we here, you and I?" The man sat up and faced Vassiley.

"God has not disclosed His plan to me," Vassiley replied, "but I am certain that His reasons will become clear to me later."

From out of the blue, a heavy blow knocked Vassiley off his bed. Screaming and cursing, his roommate started toward him. It all happened so quickly that Vassiley wondered if he had been put into the same room with a truly sick person. *I've got to calm him!* he thought.

He seized one of his roommate's legs and tugged at it with all his might. The man fell backwards onto the floor and started screaming, "Help! Murder!"

The cell doors immediately opened, and several hospital orderlies raced into the room and hurled themselves at Vassiley. They pinned his arms to his back and began to drag him from the cell. The "doctor" on duty hastened toward him.

"What's going on here?" he asked the supervisor.

"He's having a fit and started beating up his roommate."

The doctor grinned and commented, "One cleric beating up

another! That's really something! Put him into the pacification chamber!"

Vassiley was led to the cellar. By now it was obvious to him that any resistance would be senseless. The attendants began to beat him up, working him over from head to foot. He took it all with resignation. As they put the straitjacket on him, one of the attendants jeered, "Around this place you'll soon forget that God of yours!"

The straitjacket was made of a fabric which began to shrink when water was poured over it. The shrinking squeezed the victim's body so much that he lost consciousness in a short while. The use of these jackets was permitted only in the presence of a physician and the officer on duty.

Once in the straitjacket Vassiley was picked up and hung from a hook attached to the ceiling. Then the attendants began to spray water on him from a hose. The jacket began to contract around his chest cavity, and he began to suffocate.

The "physician" stepped toward him and commented, "Kuznetsov, let's see whether that God of yours will help you now!"

The attendants ceased running water over him. Vassiley gasped, "May God forgive you your evildoing!"

The "physician" snickered, "Poluchkin started out saying things like that, too!"

Vassiley was taken back to his cell and thrown on the bed. It took a long time for him to come to.

"I felt as if there were a thick fog inside my head," he would explain later, "and I could not concentrate on anything. Then suddenly the words of Jesus came to me from my memory, '. . . Whosoever shall smite thee on the right cheek, turn to him the other also.' After that I resolved to offer no further resistance. Nothing they might do made any difference to me from then on. If it had been decided that I was to die, then I was ready for that also."

He received an injection, and his body relaxed completely. His mind was no longer capable of understanding anything.

He became totally indifferent to everything for the time being.

Night came. His cellmate, Poluchkin, could not sleep; and Vassiley could not fall asleep either. He rose and walked over to the toilet bowl. When he returned to bed Poluchkin asked him, "Do you know Koshkin?"

"Yes," replied Vassiley. He could move only slowly. Every bone and muscle in his body hurt. He lay down, forced his eyes shut and murmured, "How peculiar. How extraordinary!"

"What is peculiar?" Poluchkin wanted to know.

Vassiley kept on speaking as if he were talking to himself. "We, the shepherds of the church of Jesus Christ, have the responsibility to keep the peace and to extend our love to all mankind no matter what mischief they cause us. Instead we beat each other up."

Poluchkin realized that it was he who was being referred to. "Do you have any idea how long I have been detained in this godforsaken place?" he said in an attempt to justify himself. "Can you imagine the situation? My own wife published a libelous article against me in a newspaper and then married someone else. And my little ones, my twins, have been placed in a boarding school!"

Vassiley did not answer him. Instead, he continued thinking out loud. "Some years back I knew a man named Poluchkin. He worked for some time with a certain priest, Abdullah. Abdullah was a member of the Coptic Church in Egypt. We were told that this man was a fanatical Marxist. I did not believe that of him at the time. Abdullah was so honest and so good. He wished nothing less than the very best for everyone. Poluchkin spent a lot of time in Abdullah's company. A few times he actually traveled to foreign countries with him. Then all of a sudden Poluchkin vanished. It was rumored that the KGB had stuck him in a loony bin."

Loud screams and groaning interrupted Vassiley's story. He raised his head from the pillow and listened. There were hurried footsteps in the corridor, angry outbursts from orderlies, screams and outcries from the "sick" patients. Vassiley recoiled in horror. On the other hand Poluchkin, who apparently had become used to these sounds, seemed to notice nothing. He sat up on his bed, staring at Vassiley.

"Tell me, are you actually the same Kuznetsov?" he asked in a voice which betrayed amazement.

"What do you mean by 'the same'?" inquired Vassiley, squinting across the room.

"Would you believe this: while I was still operating as a sort of liaison between the KGB and the foreign section of the patriarchate, my boss, Major Leftov, often mentioned your name. He was very angry about your religious activities."

"Oh yes?" grinned Vassiley. "He was angry, was he? That's good. Let him be angry. But what did *you* do to get sent to this place?"

"Well, you know that new reports about church persecutions in the USSR are being circulated in western countries. I was given the task of ridding the world of these rumors. In response to orders from the KGB I invited a number of leaders of churches in foreign countries to our country. This was to let them convince themselves that these rumors were fabrications. We had brilliant success on this assignment. But when our plan to recruit an American bishop ended in failure, we felt we had to neutralize him. To achieve this we arranged to put a beautiful young woman into his bed."

Vassiley raised his eyebrows. "That's really stupid. But tell me more about it. Give me some more details." He sat up in his bed and began to listen closely to what Poluchkin was saying.

"All right. As I told you, the bishop refused to work with the KGB. This put us into a tricky situation. You see, the bishop might bring the entire thing out in the open. Can you believe what trouble that would have started? All we could do was put a sedative into his food. Then we employed a lovely maiden and photographed them in bed in a close embrace. Then we showed the bishop the pictures and demanded that he keep his mouth shut or we would publicize these 'evidences of his immoral conduct.' He traveled back to his homeland, and I soon learned that he had died.

"In the meantime my wife apparently learned of my activities from a brother who worked in the patriarchate. She was indignant and demanded an explanation from me. I beat her up. In desperation she went to the Baptist preacher and told him everything. He soothed her and invited her to become a member of his congregation. There she expressed the wish to dedicate her life totally to the Lord's service.

"She was the mother of our twins. Because of that, I went to my boss, Major Leftov, and told him that I was no longer prepared to live a lie and to conduct a double life. He asked me what I meant by a 'double life.' I replied that I meant serving the church while working for the KGB.

"He then smiled a nasty smile and suggested, 'You are quite right when you say that you are living a double life. It is quite obvious that you are schizoid.' I've been here ever since. I have never again seen my family." He halted, bitterness distorting his face.

"Your wife searched for you for a long time," said Vassiley gently, "but to no avail. When the newspaper article you mentioned appeared against her wishes—the article which attributed to her a statement that her husband was mentally ill—she had a heart attack that resulted in her death."

Poluchkin jumped from his bed. "But I was told that she had remarried!"

"Those were lies, nothing but lies. But if you will permit me to counsel you, Poluchkin, please keep quiet about that. No more attacks of frenzy, no more letters of complaint to your patriarch. Your letters don't go any further than to the KGB, you know that. Keep your emotions under control. Your children are waiting for you. In fact, they are not in a boarding school but with their grandmother."

"How is it that you know all of this?" asked Poluchkin excitedly.

A key began to rattle in the door. Poluchkin and Vassiley hurriedly slid beneath their covers. Vassiley pretended to be fast asleep. An officer and a medical auxiliary entered the cell.

"This one won't wake up quickly with the haloperidol we gave him," said the medic as he gestured toward Vassiley.

The officer inspected Vassiley's face closely and asked, "Who had him put into this cell?"

"The duty officer," replied the medic.

"Stupid jackass!" the officer thundered. "Give him another shot so that he sleeps through until tomorrow morning and has no chance to recognize his cellmate. And give the other one the same shot." He snapped the last instructions while he was already on the way out. He disappeared, still cursing.

When the door clanged shut again Vassilley whispered, "Poluchkin, remain steadfast! Don't offer any resistance. I know how much damage these medicines and injections can do, but hold fast. Remain steadfast for God and for your children. Tomorrow they certainly will separate us."

The door squeaked open again, and four medics entered. They administered the injections in a hurry, wondering why Poluchkin remained calm throughout when he normally would have offered angry resistance, swearing at the medics like a trooper. Both Poluchkin and Vassiley fell into a trance-like sleep. They did not exchange another word until the next morning.

The next day Vassiley was moved to a cell occupied by a man who had murdered the secretary of a district commissar.

*   *   *

Old Lebedyev filed his application for retirement. No one in the interior ministry was surprised by this. He had been a reliable employee and his supervisors knew they could trust him. He had seen a great deal, but they were certain he would remain silent about it.

Lebedyev stepped into Irina's cell and told her, "Your father sends you his regards. You are to keep calm and not to hang your head." With those words he departed again.

A short while later Irina was picked up by a medic and taken to Koshkin. He was sitting behind his desk leafing through Irina's personal dossier.

"Your sex drive is too powerful, Sokolova," he casually announced, motioning to her to sit down on the chair opposite him.

Irina was already acquainted with this method of interrogation. The KGB had prepared their diagnosis in advance. The dossier contained photos of Koslov kissing her. But she was shocked when she also saw pictures which must have been taken in the Crimea. She and Sasha Nikitin had gone swimming in the Black Sea together. The photographs showed her swimming away from Sasha while he attempted to pursue her. She suddenly recalled a comment by the leader of her congregation that she should repent for swimming in the company of a young man. This was unacceptable for a virgin. Astonished, she had asked him whether he did not have confidence in her. He had merely muttered, "Well, we'll see; we will just see."

She was so preoccupied with other matters at the time that she had not paid any more attention to the preacher's words. Now, suddenly, everything was clear to her. They had rigged this "case" for her long ago, she decided. But why hadn't he, as a servant of the church, said something to her?

While these thoughts whirled through Irina's mind, Koshkin was examining other photographs, shaking his head in disapproval. "Here, look at this," he said as he held up a picture of her in the company of Vassiley Kuznetsov. At the time, Vassiley apparently had tugged at her ear playfully as a "punishment" for something or other. On another picture she could be seen with Victor, who was the son of the first secretary of the district committee. She was still a student at the time. Victor had waylaid her in the Institute's lobby and had covered her with kisses in full view of everyone. Someone had taken her photo at that time, too. She had, in fact, massaged Victor's face with quite a "love tap" immediately after the photo was taken; but apparently no picture was taken of this.

Koshkin allowed the photographs to slide through his fingers. "Based on this I feel safe in assuming that you are no longer a virgin."

"That is not true," said Irina.

"Well, then why not?" asked Koshkin, giving her a perplexed glance.

"A medical examination could contradict this garbage with no trouble whatever," said Irina, motioning toward the photographs.

"You don't say!" Koshkin said, astonished.

But why should I explain anything to him? Irina thought. As a KGB physician he knew perfectly well all this evidence was manufactured.

Koshkin pushed the photographs to one side and fixed his eyes on Irina.

"Would you believe it? I have spoken with your father. I did not know that he is a psychiatrist, too. How could such a split personality develop in the presence of such an educated man? On one side she is a future scientist, on the other a Christian! What a paradox!" muttered Koshkin as if addressing himself.

Irina's father had warned her that such situations could be extremely dangerous and that one had to be extremely careful not to supply the KGB physician with a pretext for declaring the "patient" a schizophrenic.

Abruptly Koshkin got up from his chair and walked to the telephone. He dialed a number and said into the mouthpiece, "I have Sokolova here with me right now. Would you like to speak with her?" He turned to Irina. "Somebody wants to talk to you on the telephone."

She walked over to the telephone and picked it up in hopes

that her father might be at the other end. Her voice wavered a
bit as she gave her name.

"Great, Irina," the voice said at the other end. "This is
Koslov!"

Irina's eyes filled with tears as she turned to look out the
nearby window. "What do you want?" she asked coolly.

"Irina, come to your senses! Let this silly religion of yours
go! They are going to stick you into a loony bin for the rest of
your days! Change your mind now, Irina; I still love you."

Revolted, Irina slammed the telephone down.

"I see," Koshkin remarked sarcastically. "Along with everything else you have very little self-control."

He is only trying to make me lose my composure, Irina thought
irritatedly. She sat down on one of the chairs without replying and began to pray quietly.

Koshkin made another phone call. After that he ordered
that she be taken away.

That's how Irina, too, was committed to a psychiatric
clinic.

20 The Card Game

After three weeks in solitary confinement Sasha was moved to another cell. Once more he wound up in the company of Gander, who had beaten him up in cell number 511. Sasha resembled a walking skeleton after his ordeal.

"Why did they stick you into solitary, little brother?" inquired the thief Sokol, who was serving his seventh stretch in prison for thievery.

"When Silitch the Jew lay dying he asked me to pray with him," Sasha explained, "and that's what I did."

This cell was not as overcrowded as the others. There were only twelve prisoners for the eight cots. In deference to Sasha, Sokol offered him his cot so that he could recuperate from the rigors of solitary confinement.

Sasha was exhausted to the point of collapse; so he thankfully stretched out on the cot while the others kept a weather eye out for the guards so Sasha would not be caught sleeping. Sasha's stubble, which had begun to grey, was in sharp contrast to the color of his face. He was already considered a "veteran." He possessed authority, and the other prisoners trusted him. Only Gander, out of all of them, made every imaginable effort to stay out of his way.

The duffel bag Sasha had left in cell number 511 was returned to him without the hard sausage, which had been consumed by this time. Yet with all that, oh wonder of wonders, they had left him his reserve of dry bread! Thoroughly starved, he lay on the cot and nibbled contentedly on a crust of bread, urging the others to help themselves as well.

The cell door swung open a great many times during the day. The inhabitants of the cells constantly had to be on their toes. Now and again someone was picked up for interrogation. At other times the prison administrator made a tour of inspection. Twice everyone was taken to the bathroom. On several occasions a special commission turned up to receive complaints or to share the news of a sentence or a court decision with the inmates. Despite these interruptions the prisoners managed to play a secret game of cards. And in a corner of the cell, a powerful Tshifir tea was brewed. The prisoners even smuggled in money and hashish.

"Move it! Get up, Sasha!" Sokol cried. Sasha jumped off the bed. Already the warden was turning the key in the lock. The door flew open and Bublik was shoved inside. The men could hardly believe it, the man was actually glowing. A victorious smile played on his lips.

The door closed abruptly behind him. The inhabitants of the cell surrounded Bublik and asked for the outcome of the court's deliberations.

"How much time in jail are they going to give you, buddy?" Gander inquired.

Bublik screwed up his forehead, thought for a brief moment and then declared, "They're definitely going to hand me ten years in stir, maybe even more. I've got five kilograms of hashish hanging over me like a sword!" He squinted toward Sokol and winked conspiratorially. "Well, how about it? Are we going into business together?"

"Have you got any?" asked Sokol, his voice wavering.

"Naturally! Watch the door. Keep a lookout for the jailer, somebody!" Bublik opened his mouth and began to fumble around in it. Finally he grasped the end of a thread fastened to one of his teeth and began to pull at it. After some tugging and choking, a cellophane bag filled with hashish popped up. He had swallowed it during his mother's visit. He was able to endure the choking only because of his great self-control.

That string in his mouth and gullet must have been very bothersome.

Sokol reached for the bag of hashish and immediately hid it.

"We can use this stuff only during the night," Bublik grinned. "And that isn't even all I have!"

He shifted his gaze toward the men on lookout, then started to take off his trousers. He told Sokol, "On my buttock you will see a bandage. There is a thread under it. Pull it hard."

Soon Sokol was rinsing off a small capsule. Bublik smiled the smile of a victor.

Sokol unpacked the contents and complained, "Aw, come on! There's a religious book in here!"

"What's that?" Bublik exclaimed angrily. "Are you trying to tell me that my devout mother talked herself into getting a Gospel from Father Dudko and substituted it for the thousand rubles promised me?"

"The money's here too," said Sokol to calm him. "Several hundred-ruble bills."

Bublik lost his money in the card game. The veterans in the jails played "seventeen and four" in this cell, a game strictly forbidden. Anyone caught playing it was punished severely.

Sasha had no idea how the inmates were able to smuggle playing cards into the jail, but they managed somehow. If six of them played, the remaining men stood watch by the door.

Sokol won Bublik's thousand rubles from him. Possession of such personal funds was also strictly forbidden, and the money was confiscated when found. But for these hardened veterans of the jails, the regime's rules and regulations existed only on paper.

It was really miserable to play and wind up with nothing more to play with. The stakes could include almost everything from one's toothbrush to the very last pair of shorts. A good many notorious card players had lost every stitch of their clothing and thus lost the ability to pay their debts. This type of loser was abused by the rest of the group in homosexual relationships. Or they were simply killed. Another punishment was to force one of them to eliminate another man, perhaps an informer.

Bublik examined the small Gospel of Saint Mark, printed on extremely thin, expensive paper from a foreign country. Sasha was in the midst of greedily devouring the first page while looking over Bublik's shoulder when Gander tore the small booklet out of Bublik's hands.

"Why don't you throw this rubbish in the toilet, you idiot?" he screamed. He had already raised the cover when Sokol quickly moved him to the side and gave him a powerful shove in the ribs that sent him sprawling in the corner.

"If you do that I'll tear you to ribbons on the spot!" With that Sokol tore the booklet from Gander's hands.

At that moment the door opened again.

"Sasha Nikitin! Get ready for interrogation!" the jailer yelled.

But how was Sasha to "get ready"? He could not iron his rumpled suit or shirt anywhere. He walked through the door as he was and soon found himself in the interrogation chamber. A man and a woman were sitting on chairs opposite Sasha. When Sasha entered, both of them rose and introduced themselves.

Sasha knew that somewhere he had relatives on his real mother's side, but he had never met them. For that reason he could not possibly know that the man opposite him was his uncle. He originally had been a preacher but now worked in the KGB's ideological section. This couple was respected by everyone who came into contact with them because of their warmhearted generosity.

Sasha's uncle gave him a searching look. Then he began the conversation. "You've gotten thin, Sasha. Of course you wouldn't know me. But I'm the brother of your mother, Lena, and this is my wife, Nina."

Sasha looked at these unusual persons and did not know what to say.

Nina became aware of his confusion and said, smiling sweetly, "Of course you must be amazed to see us here. Didn't your father tell you about us?" She had a sweet, gentle voice. There was an aura of understated sophistication about her.

All of a sudden Sasha had the feeling of being back home again. It was as if the calm of a home had again enveloped him; and he seemed to have only one wish, to put his head on his uncle's shoulder and cry away his misery. He was so exhausted, and his body so weak! His whole inner being implored his relatives, *Get me out of here! Get me out of this house of horrors!*

"They're not being very nice to you here, I'm told," his uncle said in a resonant bass voice. Siniszin patted Sasha's shorn skull and sighed.

It would not have taken much to make Sasha cry. But he pulled himself together. *Not nice? I, as a servant of God, am unable to intercede for others! They take away the very air I breathe! Not nice, indeed! Don't you know what is going on around here?* Yet Sasha swallowed his pain and said nothing.

"Sasha, you've been in prison for only a month and they've really banged you up already," his uncle went on. "Isn't it time for you to come to your senses and return to your former activities as part of the officially recognized church? Stop doing foolish things!"

The memory of the Bible study groups Sasha had started surfaced in his mind. "Back to the Source," these groups had been called. How difficult it had been to persuade Christians from various persuasions to sit down together around the Bible! What battles had to be fought against every imaginable misconception! Yet in return the Lord had poured a wealth of blessing on these small cells of prayer and Bible study. And these are now supposed to have been "foolish things"? What kind of people could possibly consider these foolishness?

Sasha wearily raised his head and fixed his eyes squarely on Siniszin.

"I'm truly glad to meet my late mother's close relatives," he said with some difficulty, "but I haven't done any foolish things, as you call them, Uncle Misha. I have had no controversy whatever with the preachers of the official church. On the contrary, I've always maintained excellent contacts with them. To this day I don't know why I was arrested."

Siniszin, who had risen and walked around for a moment, sat down next to his wife again. Lost in his thoughts, he said, "I still can recall when I was a preacher myself, trying to win the whole world for Christ and His message. When people in droves were brought to the Lord by my sermons I told my future wife, 'If all human beings were to serve God sincerely, then everything—exploitation, swindling, oppression of every kind, problems of race and so forth—would cease. Then peace would reign among mankind and people would deal with one another in love.' In a word, Sasha, this would be the realization of the communism of the messianic nation as it appeared in Jewish prophecy. I preached the crucified Christ with such conviction and fiery zeal that even convinced atheists sought me out. I thought those Christians who are faithful to Christ's Word should be ready to go to their death for each other—with a song on their lips. I hoped that through the sufferings of the believing Christians, millions of unbelievers would come to appreciate the beauty of Christ's teachings. My spiritual father and mentor had taught me that, and I believed it.

"Then came those terrible years of 1937 and 1939. A half million innocent human beings were slaughtered. And who do you think turned me in to the security people? Why, my teacher! Yes, Sasha, it was my teacher who loved to preach about faith in Christ! This so embittered me that I betrayed all of my brother-preachers while I was in solitary! Well, I have survived it all, but others did not. And neither did my beloved sister, Lena.

"Sasha, believe me, all Christian leaders are opportunists, traitors, and adventurers. I know whereof I speak. Are you listening to me? I run into them every day in my work in the

ideological section of the Central Committee. What you are
taking upon yourself is not worth the pain, believe me!"

Siniszin really believed what he was saying. His voice
showed so much emotion that it touched Sasha's heart. What
is more, he had to admit that his uncle was right in many of
the points he had made.

"You could very well be right, Uncle Misha. But don't you
see, the fact that you were betrayed and that you betrayed
others has not altered any of Christ's teaching. God still
remains the same," he stated quietly.

Nina rose and walked to the window. "I used to sing in the
choir in the old days," she stated. "I even conducted it. For a
time I was profoundly involved in the problems of religion.
And I can assure you that those involved in religious matters
are nothing more than tiny screws in the political machinery
of the state. That is the way it is everywhere. They're all used
as instruments of politics, and that is the way it is always
going to be. I am in touch with many people in foreign
countries who are involved in religious activities. Believe me,
Sasha, to them their pastorates are not a matter of personal
calling but a means of getting involved in politics and drumming up funds for their own adventurous purposes. To them
Christ is nothing more than a character from a fairytale and a
means of getting hold of some money."

"But you cannot possibly toss them all into the same pot,"
said Sasha, interrupting his aunt.

"That may be," she said, wrinkling her nose, "but those to
whom Christ is their Savior and the way to heaven have no
authority within the congregations. The remainder of the
community of the saints sees religion as nothing more than
an instrument to gain power."

"But I don't have anything to do with this excrement!"
Sasha broke in.

Siniszin allowed that he might be right. "It is correct that
you, Sasha, have nothing in common with such types. But,
dear nephew, we are here to talk to you because we don't

want you to remain in prison and die here. We have been telling you the truth, that much you know. If you didn't happen to be the only son of my favorite sister, I wouldn't dream of trying to get you out of here. Who will be concerned about you after you die?"

"It is not necessary for people to remember me," said Sasha quietly.

Siniszin shook his head and looked down into the prison yard from the window. "Down there Russia's favorite sons have walked their rounds. Not a single one of them, however, has left here alive. We've got our people in key positions in every religious group throughout the world. And they are working for us, don't you understand? They exert their influence in their congregations on our behalf. You and those like you will inevitably fall victim to our policies! I would like to know where God's eyes have been! What kind of God is it who stands by, placidly observing the suffering of His children? And where is there a church that is truly a church, that turns its ideas of shepherding the flock and serving one's neighbor into practice?

"There's no such thing, no such church! Do you hear, Sasha? Shake off your religious convictions. Rid yourself of all of this Christian rubbish and become a citizen who lives in freedom! The young woman you love, Irina Sokolova, is in a psychiatric clinic in Dniepopetrovsk—or is it Leningrad? I'm not certain which. But one thing I do know is that all your Christian friends must not waste their lives among mentally ill people. Do you, too, my one and only nephew, want to disappear into that hell forever?"

Sasha looked closely at his uncle's face, which showed so much suffering, and began suddenly to feel great compassion for him. He took him by his hand.

"Look, Uncle Misha, a servant of God who permitted himself to be compromised betrayed you. This disappointed you so much that you lost whatever faith in God you might have had. And now you fight a pitched battle against religion here in our country as well as in foreign countries. If I, too, were to renounce my faith, how many people would be so disappointed that they, too, would renounce their faith in Christ and become what you are? First you urged me to return penitently to the lap of the official church. But now you implore me to renounce my belief in Christ altogether. No, Uncle Misha, I do believe in Jesus and His teaching and am resolved to bear witness to that not only with my words but with my deeds."

"But you will perish, my dear nephew," lamented his uncle. "You will be wiped out and not a soul will weep at your death. Your pastors don't know how to live for others and how to tolerate human frailty in love. Instead of assisting their brethren to gain spiritual maturity by teaching them to stand on both feet they revile them, cause them to look like fools in the eyes of others, and spread false rumors about them."

Sasha shook his head, aghast at what he had just heard. "Poor Uncle Misha. How you must have suffered! I am ashamed of my brothers in Christ."

He turned away and walked rapidly toward the door. A prison guard opened in response to his knocking. He looked at Siniszin's face, which had become quite pale, and asked curtly, "Take him back to his cell?"

Siniszin nodded.

Later Sasha heard that not long after this conversation Siniszin suffered a heart attack, was taken to a hospital, and died that same night. Before he died he was said to have told his wife, who sat by his deathbed, "Ninotshka, do everything in your power to prevent Sasha's being killed in prison. I swore to Lena that I would care for her son for the rest of my life. May God forgive us."

*   *   *

Gander and Bublik were having a violent argument when Sasha was returned to his cell. From what he could understand of their shouting, he gathered that Gander had lost everything down to his bare skin and had nothing left to pay his debts. Meanwhile a "troika"* consisting of Sokol, Golov, and an inmate with the gorgeous nickname of "Lenin" was deliberating about the punishment to be meted out to Gander.

Soon Sokol rose and announced, "Gander, first of all you cheated while playing the game. Secondly, you knew that you had nothing with which to pay, and thus you have played yourself out. This, then, is our verdict. Either you stab a 'hen' to death, if you are able to find one anywhere; or we will make you serve us as our 'bride.' Otherwise one of us will somehow put you out of your misery altogether.

"You are no longer entitled to a get-even game because you were so impudent. That's that. You have until tomorrow to select your form of punishment. Someone else could take your guilt upon himself and play a get-even game on your behalf, but you yourself have forfeited your right to one."

Sasha was so astonished by this turn of events that he was unable to speak. Gander squatted on his bed in deep depression. Soon no one took any further notice of him and life inside the cell went back to normal.

Sasha was unable to sleep that night. The events of the day weighed him down spiritually like a ten-ton load. Peaceful snoring emanated from all quarters. Only he and Gander lay wide awake on their cots. Gander was preoccupied with the selection of his punishment. Sasha constantly had to think about his uncle and could not get peace. He began to pray for him.

Suddenly Sasha began to hear stifled sobbing. He turned to his side and looked in the direction of Gander, whose cot stood next to his. Gander had buried his head deep in his pillow and was weeping heartbrokenly.

Sasha extended his arm and cautiously stroked Gander's

*An allusion to the KGB Troika, a committee of three which has the power to sentence without a jury trial.

shorn head. "Don't cry, my friend," he whispered. "Go on; tell me something about yourself."

Gander stopped sobbing, but he kept his head buried in the pillow for a long while.

Sasha waited. Then he said, "I understand that your father is a servant of the church, too. Please tell me about him."

Gander sat up abruptly, looked wildly at Sasha, and almost gagged as he forced out, "I'd like to strangle that poisonous snake if I could! With my own hands!"

"But really, why?" Sasha whispered, startled.

That night Sasha learned the truth about Gander's father. He actually was a preacher. Gander was his oldest son and formerly went to his father's worship services. He also played the old piano which had been donated to the congregation by a Jewish family.

Then came the years when the government forced the church leaders to begin a drive against the active participation of young people in congregational activities. Gander's father (whose name was Gussev, from which his son's nickname originated) felt that it was his duty to observe the decrees issued by the Soviet legal body against religious movements. He therefore prohibited participation by young people in all activities involving the Bible, and also forbade the young people to meet together. They were also told not to sing in the choir any longer. No one below the age of eighteen was permitted to attend the worship services.

Gussev's son Nikolay, who later was to receive the nickname of Gander in prison, was then below the age of eighteen. For that reason he was no longer to attend the services. He was so ashamed of his father's behavior that he wished the ground would swallow him up. Whenever representatives of the ministry for religious affairs were seen in his home, Nikolay eavesdropped on his father's conversations with the officials. His father really believed he was obeying the Bible's commandment to obey one's superiors when he followed their instructions.

It was quite obvious to Nikolay that there was a terrible contradiction in this position. On one hand his father had a touching concern for the members of his congregation. But on the other hand he told the government's lackeys whatever they asked him about the people he was called to serve. This included even those things entrusted to him in the secrecy of the confessional. The young man attempted to argue with his father, but he kept putting him off with phrases like, "My dear Son, you are still too young. You will understand your father when you have grown up."

But this seventeen-year-old no longer wanted to understand his father at all. He was ashamed of him and began to warn the members of the congregation, urging them not to talk to his father any longer.

When the father got wind of that, he lost control of himself and thrashed the young man. Nikolay ran into the street crying loudly and disappeared into the first bar he could find. He became so drunk that he was no longer able to stand on his own feet. Then he tottered to the building which housed the executive committee of the Communist Party, where the local representative of the ministry for religious affairs had his offices. He set about breaking all their windows. The militia started looking for him, but they did not catch up with him until he had broken the windows of his own father's house and had turned himself in.

They played "fifth corner" with him at the precinct station. He was so badly battered that it took him a long time to recover.

Since then things had gone downhill for Nikolay. At that time he had been sentenced to five years in prison. Now he was already serving his fourth stretch in jail.

"I could have choked my father to death with my own hands, do you understand?" Nikolay hissed through his teeth.

"I can understand you," Sasha murmured thoughtfully, "but you shouldn't talk like that. This man is your father, after all. Whether good or bad, he is still your father. These times we are living in are very difficult. Who doesn't make a mistake in times like these?"

Gander stared at him uncomprehendingly. His face expressed utter contempt, and so Sasha stopped talking. He spent the remainder of the night in prayer, mulling over a great many things.

After being awakened, the prisoners were led to the bathrooms. After washing himself in cold water, Sasha went over to Sokol.

"I am assuming Gander's gambling debts," he announced.

Sokol's eyes rolled in horror at this, and he began to stutter. "Y-y-ou are a B-b-aptist pastor—have you lost all your marbles? Say that again! You want to play this jackass's get-even game? You're risking your head, you know!"

They were prodded back to the cell. When they got there Sasha reiterated, "I have announced that I will assume Gander's debts and that I will play in his stead."

Eleven men gawked wordlessly at Sasha. Gander acted as if he had been turned into a statue and was unable to get out a single word.

"And what happens if you lose?" growled the angry Sokol. "You think we'll show you leniency just because you're a cleric?"

"That won't be necessary," replied Sasha in quiet but resolute tones. "Jesus Christ took on the debts of the whole world. And God did not allow Him to be dishonored. He will not allow me to be put to shame either. I will pay for Gander."

Until time for roll call, not another word was spoken inside the cell. In fact, silence prevailed until breakfast. After that, six men moved toward one of the cell's corners while the remainder posted themselves around them so that the players could not be seen over their backs.

They agreed to play "seventeen and four." Sokol was dealer. Sasha reached for his card.

If I lose now, my life is over, he thought, *and there'll be no more future for me.* He shook off those thoughts and looked at the card he had drawn. It was a jack, or two points.

"Deal me the next card," he said calmly.

Sokol clenched his lips. He had no intention of showing the slightest mercy to Sasha. Sokol was famous for never losing a game in the correctional institutions. Even the experts were afraid of him.

Time seemed to stand still within the cell. It would have been possible to hear a needle drop. The tension mounted until it became intolerable.

"Let me have the next card, Sokol," Sasha repeated. A queen—good for three points. In other words, he had a total of five points.

"The next one," Sasha ordered. A king. Four points for a total of nine.

"The next one."

The next card turned out to be a tenner. He had a total of nineteen points. Sasha pondered his next move. To ask for yet another card would border on insanity. In human terms, he did not have the slightest chance of receiving a jack. Any other card meant inevitable defeat.

Sasha looked up and said softly, "Sokol, is it all right with you if I take one more card? I'm staking everything on this card—the money which Gander has gambled away, the possessions, everything."

"You fool," hissed Sokol through his teeth. "You've got nineteen points. You've got enough cards. Let me draw my cards now. The next card means your certain death!"

"The card!" demand Sasha. "I'll stake everything on it."

The veins of Sokol's neck stood out. Bublik licked his dry lips with his tongue. No one could have known what number of points Sasha had drawn. Yet Sokol had some sort of sixth sense where cards were concerned. He knew intuitively how many points his opponent had in his hand.

"Agreed, you idiot!" cursed Sokol. He drew the next card

and threw it, face up, toward Sasha. It was a JACK! Two points! TWENTY-ONE in all!

Sokol stared at the card in disbelief and murmured, "But I was absolutely certain that the next one was a king!"

Sasha arose as if he were in a daze. Suddenly he broke into laughter. "Folks, of course I knew that God would hear my prayer! It was a matter of life and death!" he added in a low voice.

Gander broke into tears. Sokol stayed as if he had been tied to his chair and examined the cards in bewilderment. "Never in my life have I ever been wrong," he muttered. He turned up the next card and saw that it was a king. Four points. In excitement he must have pushed the jack aside and sensed that the king was next. But he had been correct; he had dealt the card which was next. He had dealt the jack honestly.

The lives of Sasha and Gander were spared.

Sasha went over to Gander and put his arm on his shoulder. "You see, Nikolay, this is just what Christ has done for us all. He took our sins upon Himself and assumed our punishment. Whoever surrenders his life to Him and places himself in His service, honestly and without compromise, will live in a new world—in Jesus Christ's world. You must understand that it is not the one who mouths the name of our Lord who is a Christian. But it is that person who surrenders himself to Him without reservation. Everything else is hypocrisy."

Nikolay stopped crying, wiped his face and softly said, "Sasha, from this moment on I place myself completely at God's disposal. And I ask to be forgiven by Him."

Sasha listened to Gander's prayer. Then he laid his hands on him and said, "Father, forgive me, too, for accepting such a risk. But I relied on You totally. Accept this soul into Your community."

Sokol did not utter another syllable for the entire day.

After lunch Bublik handed Sasha the Gospel of Mark and asked him to explain its contents to him. Sasha's heart leaped with joy. The fatigue and dejection vanished as if they had been blown away. By evening, three prisoners had already expressed their desire to serve the Lord.

After dinner, which consisted of a plate of watery soup, Sokol walked over to the toilet bowl and burned his cards. "You have the victory," his lips whispered. "You have won." After that he walked over to Sasha and declared, "I want to serve the Lord."

Sokol then told Sasha about meeting a man in one of the labor camps who had told him, "I will pray for you until you will find God." Many other prisoners had had to suffer much because of Sokol's skill at cards.

One week after that, Sasha baptized the men in his cell. How he was able to accomplish this from a technical standpoint he never disclosed to anyone. The new believers merely stated that they had been baptized in the name of Jesus Christ and would not say another word. No one needed to be concerned about whether or not the baptismal method Sasha had used conformed to biblical teaching.

Five days later Sasha was transferred to another prison.

21 Unexpected Encounters

Yuri Sokolov looked dejectedly down on the high fence which surrounded the Serbian Institute. He was unable to explain to himself exactly what had drawn him back to this place. The fact was that Irina was no longer there and had not been there for a long time. He had learned that her friends were in Tshernyakhovsk; but where his own daughter had been placed was kept secret by the KGB, mainly so that he could not find out where she was.

Did Irina have the privilege of a trial in court? If so, what actually took place? Thoughts of all the things that could have occurred during such a court proceeding tortured him. Naturally the KGB made all such arrangements behind closed doors. And even if he had discovered where and how such a proceeding took place, he would not have been admitted to it anyway.

A taxi suddenly came to a screeching halt alongside Sokolov. Someone called his name. He whirled around in surprise. Coughing, his father stepped out of the taxi and greeted him, "Hello, my Son! I'm glad to see you again!"

"But Father, what brings you all this distance so suddenly? And what about your health?" Yuri gently chided his father as he kissed the old man.

With his bushy white beard and piercing eyes, Vladimir Sokolov still looked quite imposing despite his slightly sickly appearance. He put his arm around his son's shoulders and drew him into the taxi with him. "Sit down, sit down," he stated and pushed Yuri down on the back seat. Then he plunked down next to him.

269

"I looked for you everywhere. After I discovered that you had come to Moscow for the fifth time, I made it my business to find you at all costs. The hotel told me that you intended to leave this evening. So I decided that you certainly would make one more trip to the Serbian Institute to say good-bye. So I'm here now to discuss a few things with you."

With a movement of his head Yuri warned his father of the presence of the taxi driver.

"I knew you probably would not recognize him again!" laughed the father. "Take a close look at him!"

The driver looked at the two of them and smiled. Then he said earnestly, "We've got to get away from here. Two KGB men in that Volga car over there are watching us."

"Tell me, Yuri, where did you hide Koslov's pistol?" the old man inquired after the driver, still unrecognized by Yuri, had started up the engine again.

Yuri scowled. The mere memory of that event was enough to give him stomach cramps. "I hid it inside a tree," he growled, "and I can't recall whether it was a beech tree or an oak. I haven't checked to see whether it is still there or not."

The elderly gentleman smiled. "We must return it to Koslov. The gun does not belong to him but to one of his relatives. You can probably understand how difficult it could become for him if he doesn't get the thing back. And of course he will resort to any dirty trick to get his pistol back."

Abruptly the driver slowed down and turned into an adjacent narrow lane. He drove through a courtyard and then entered another narrow street. Old Sokolov was hurled on top of his son, who desperately tried to restrain his father with one hand and to hold himself upright with the other. He turned and saw that the KGB's Volga was hard on their trail. Once again the taxi turned into a side street. At that very moment a troop of little boys stormed from an adjacent courtyard and filled the entire side of the street. The children romped laughingly along. The driver of the taxi braked one more time, then steered sharply to his right; and with his right-hand wheels on the sidewalk he skirted alongside the troop of children. Hooting, the children began to run after the taxi. At that very moment, the Volga turned the corner but was forced to brake sharply because of the crowd of children. The kids spread across the whole width of the street and kept on running. Risking everyone's neck, the taxi driver made one more turn into a side street, drove into a larger street, then raced into the yard of a large building, where he finally brought the car to a halt.

"Hurry, hurry! Get into that car over there," insisted the driver, pointing to a Moskwitch which already had another driver seated behind the wheel, evidently waiting for them. Father and son made a lightning-like switch to the Moskwitch. The next moment the taxi vanished as if it had disappeared from the face of the earth.

(Later Yuri was forced to listen to the story that he did not even recognize his own nephew as the daring driver of the taxi. The nephew had to spend two weeks in jail for this adventure and was dismissed from his job on top of that.)

A half hour later father and son sat in the apartment of a university professor named Nikiforoff. Two foreign reporters were also present. They viewed the elder Sokolov with curiosity and Yuri with certain suspicion. They already had learned from Nikiforoff about Yuri's former KGB activities.

Nadyeshda, the professor's attractive wife, served tea. "Please excuse me, but coffee is so expensive that we cannot afford to have any." She turned to the elder Sokolov. "Would you perhaps prefer some Russian tea?" She happened to know that he did not like black tea.

"But of course," grunted the old man. "Naturally I would prefer kwass to this rat poison."

Everyone laughed.

His glass of kwass in his hand, the old gentleman told the reporter the following, occasionally sipping a bit from his glass. "As I mentioned to you the last time, these young people who were just tossed into psychiatric institutions tried to convince the government that the Christians preach a social order in which justice, honesty, and truth reign. This, however, could be realized only under the total lordship of Jesus Christ who, as is stated in the New Testament, will come again and bring His own people with Him to reign over the peoples of the world in truth and justice. According to the New Testament's teaching, anyone who surrenders himself to God already resides in God's kingdom. But they say that only when a Christian has committed himself fully to Christ in all areas of his life will he become a healing element within his own family. And through the witness and the spiritual perfection of an intact Christian family all society will be healed."

Everyone listened with interest; yet no one offered any comment. Nadyeshda poured everyone a second glass of tea and refilled Vladimir Sokolov's glass of kwass. He drank another vigorous swallow from this and continued, "It is deplorable, but so far we have had to experience a kind of Christendom whose members rarely or never had any thought of being here for the purpose of demonstrating the grandeur of God's kingdom through their personal testimony. This is why Christianity failed to become a principle of life and instead became simply one religion among many.

"We are not opposed to the Party's propagating its idea of a Communist society without a God. But at the same time it ought to allow us the right to proclaim the Gospel of Jesus Christ and of the kingdom of God. You see, only if the government declares its agreement to such an ideological contest will it be possible to avoid the destruction of millions more innocent victims.

"So this, in broad strokes, is their concept. I have warned the greenhorns and told them that the Communist Party will never give up the battle against religion for the simple reason that true Christianity as it was lived in the days of the apostles would signify the end of communism. The 'Christianity' tinged by Marxism with its 'gospel of liberation through revolution' still is tolerated by the Communists. This is because they can utilize it as a tool for expanding their power. But in places where the Marxists actually gain power, these Marxist-Christians will be shoved into prison before they know it—unless they have already been shot."

"And what is your position vis-à-vis European communism?" asked one of the American reporters.

The elderly Sokolov pondered this for a few moments. "Well, my friend, you need only to examine Lenin's writings," he said after a pause. "Think of the promises which he linked to the freedom to make religious propaganda. You will discover immediately that he failed to keep his word. In western countries, power is also achieved by means of an electoral contest. But everyone knows that most candidates do not stick by promises made in the heat of battle.

"There are few real differences between Europe's Communists and those of Soviet Russia. Their political aims are the same. If things went the way they would like them to go, then the Chinese, Soviet and European Communists would stretch out their hands in brotherhood toward each other and go on to conquer the entire world. Our young people who sought the dialogue understood that, and they set themselves the objective of achieving the peaceful coexistence of Christian and Communist ideologies. But the KGB wasn't born yesterday, either. They immediately perceived the great danger communism would face if such an idea were permitted. You see, we in Russia have grown tired of communism. It has taken too many victims. So the younger generation is turning toward God and Christ with renewed interest."

Yuri paid close attention to his father's presentation. After Irina's arrest he had, in his loneliness, read several books by Solzhenitsyn which Lebedyev, who had been pensioned in the meantime, had lent to him. To Lebedyev's great joy he was able to establish contact with his loved ones in Paris. Ever since then, emissaries appeared at his home who "as a coincidence" happened to bring books by Russian authors published abroad.

Yuri was particularly touched by Solzhenitsyn. His heart

was deeply moved by descriptions of suffering which the Russian people were enduring. These books also led him to begin thinking about the possibility of the existence of God. When Irina had still been at home he had had no time for such reflections. He was obliged to concentrate on protecting Irina from the KGB. How many nights had he remained awake, racking his brain about what he might do to save her from going to prison. But all that had been in vain.

His powerlessness caused him untold suffering. This vigorous and courageous man, accustomed to acting decisively, perceived it as especially frustrating and humiliating that he was now unable to do anything to keep Irina protected from the outrages of a "special psychiatric clinic." As a psychiatrist he had no illusions about the consequences of the "therapeutic procedures" employed in such an institution.

Often he suffered such spiritual agony that he was driven to whisper—without actually being aware of it—such things as, "O God, if there is someone like You, then do protect my child." On one occasion he noticed Irina's Bible lying there and opened it. "In the day of your need, call out to Me," he read in profound amazement, "and I will save you, and you shall praise Me." These words were seared into his brain. He had to think of them again and again.

When he learned that Sasha Nikitin had been arrested, too, Yuri was overcome by concerns about Natasha. He often was unable to sleep at night. Once when his inner sufferings became nearly intolerable he knelt down, lifted his hands and began to pray, "Jesus Christ, if You really exist, then return Natasha and Irina to me! I promise to serve You faithfully as they do. Grant me my wish!"

Was he actually aware of what he had promised? Was it nothing more than an act of despair? That might be. But after speaking even the first few words he felt an unusual calm. A peace which he had never before known settled about him. Yuri lay down on his bed again and fell into deep sleep. On the following day, everything outside of him seemed to be as before, but within dwelt an inexplicable hope which even he did not understand.

*   *   *

Old man Sokolov was just in the process of playing the cassette tape which contained the sounds of the struggle between Irina and Koslov. The reporters asked him for a copy. Nikiforoff walked to his study in order to make a tape transfer. At the same time, Vladimir Sokolov pulled a whole stack of photographs from his pocket and spread them out before the reporters.

Yuri looked at him in amazement. "Where in the world did you get hold of these pictures?" he asked his father.

"That should remain a secret," said the elderly gentleman with a broad grin, "but I am able to tell you. I recently ran into Valentina Neverova. She had just learned of her husband's imprisonment. After her conversation with you, Yuri, she became totally disillusioned with her friends in the KGB. She went to them and told them that she would no longer be willing to work on their behalf now that her husband was under arrest, that they had deceived her, and whatever else one talks about in such a case. She was reassured and told that everything was only half as serious as it seemed, that things were not always as they appeared, that they merely wanted to shed light on some matters connected with her husband's work, and that they would subsequently let him go free again. Then these photographs were given to her and she was urged to spread the rumor of Irina's turn to an immoral lifestyle. Of course I attempted to use the opportunity to try to set Valentina's head straight. And I arranged for the photographs to accompany me."

Sokolov gave a self-satisfied smile.

"And what about Neverov himself?" Yuri inquired.

"The poor man has to sit in jail. In the holding cells he happened to run across Sasha Nikitin, who explained his

276

wife's activities to him. That was a crushing blow for the poor man, as you can understand. Natasha Nikitina, Sasha's mother . . ." (the elderly gentleman looked searchingly into his son's eyes at the mention of Natasha's name) ". . . had succeeded in receiving permission to pay a visit to her son. On this occasion Sasha urged her to visit the Neverov woman and to talk with her as long as necessary to bring about her repentance."

"You say 'repentance,' do you?" Yuri laughed. "I still can hear her pompous words, 'I am a servant of the Soviet Union! I am serving my people!' If someone belongs in the loony bin, it must be she and not my perfectly healthy daughter!"

The doorbell rang. Everyone was startled. The reporters got ready to make their departure through the back door. But the lady of the house said that everything was perfectly in order and attended to the door.

It was hastily arranged with the reporters that nothing of the material they had been given was to be published until Nikiforoff had given them the green light for that. The two Americans did make use of the back door, which led into a small vegetable garden, and departed from the house this way.

Yuri was in the process of pouring himself some tea when a woman of approximately the same age as he entered the room. She glanced around the room, saw those who were present, and greeted them quietly. How her voice inspired trust! Yuri forgot to respond to the greeting and stared at the recently arrived person. Two beautiful deep-blue eyes countered his gaze. They were the most beautiful eyes in the world—the eyes of his daughter. At first he actually did have the impression that his own daughter stood in front of him, matured and about twenty years older. His thoughts ran together in confusion. He was actually on the brink of saying, "Dear Daughter, what have they done with you? . . ." when he finally recognized her.

Nikiforoff, Nadyeshda, and old Sokolov quietly stole out

of the room one after the other and vanished to the kitchen. Natasha Nikitina looked after them, confused. Why were they leaving her alone with this stranger without introducing him to her? *Who is this man?* She examined him once again. He was rather rough-hewn, with graying hair. *Who could he be? Why is he looking at me so longingly? How uncomfortable! Oh no, now he even weeps, this strange creature. Tears are rolling down his cheeks and dripping on his tie.*

Natasha caught herself counting the tears which were striking Sokolov's tie. Suddenly her cheeks began to flush beneath his ardent glance. It seemed as if she were still a young woman. She wanted to ask the man who stood before her who he was and why he was crying, but she could not say a single word.

"Natasha, . . ." Sokolov said in a low voice.

It was all so confusing! She raised her eyebrows as if she were a child thinking hard about something. Those grey eyes . . . that penetrating glance. And then memories began to crowd into her mind. The blockade of Leningrad. . . .

"Don't you recognize me, Natasha?"

All at once she began to sway. The floor seemed to fall from beneath her feet. Sokolov caught her and carried her to an easy chair. "It is only a slight fainting spell," he muttered. "She'll come to in just a moment." Yet somehow he was afraid that she would pass out of his life again after he had finally discovered her once more.

The color began to return to her cheeks. "Where am I? What happened?" she asked in confusion.

"I longed for you for such a long time, Natasha," said Sokolov.

She looked into his eyes and broke into tears. "But the child—our daughter—I couldn't save her. She is dead. She died right after she was born."

He stroked her hand wordlessly. Suddenly she gave a start and asked anxiously, "You're still working there? I mean for the KGB?"

"No, Natasha. Your imprisonment ended my career with the KGB. I became a doctor."

He stood up and poured her a cup of tea. They talked and talked, forgetting about dinner. Yuri had booked a flight home for that evening, but he forgot about that, too.

Nadyeshda finally emerged from the kitchen and interrupted their eager conversation. "All right, you young folks, now we're going to eat something! May I ask you to come to the table?"

"Young folks!" repeated Yuri.

They had dinner in the kitchen. The old man threw inquiring glances toward his son. Natasha appeared to enjoy the whole thing immensely.

"Now only Irina is missing," Nadyeshda interjected cautiously. "Then the family would be united and bliss complete."

Natasha looked at Yuri probingly. "Irina? Is that the same Irina about whom Sasha keeps enthusing? Is that perhaps your daughter, Yuri?"

Even though she and Sasha had lived very close to Vladimir Sokolov, Natasha had never connected her former fiancé with the old gentleman and his grandchild. The events of recent days—her husband's death, Sasha's arrest—had so preoccupied her that she had no time to think about the past.

She looked inquiringly at Yuri and suddenly felt sorrow rising within her. *So he is married and has a daughter,* she thought. But then she had to feel ashamed. What indeed was wrong with her? She also had married. Still the thought of it all lodged inside her heart like a thorn. She forced herself to look at her plate, pretending that she was concentrating completely on her meal. *What business is this of mine?* Thoughts such as that raced through her mind. *His daughter is a Christian, but he surely is not.* Sasha and Irina had, after all, prayed on one occasion for her father to be saved; Natasha remembered that. Oh well—nonsense! All this was in the past for her anyway. You cannot bring back the past.

Yuri looked at his father inquiringly. "After dinner," the old gentleman said softly.

The lady of the house told of some funny incident. The professor listened attentively to his wife. The two Sokolovs and Natasha nodded in agreement on occasion but actually did not hear much of the story. After dinner the woman of the house began to wash the dishes. The professor was called away to a meeting at the Institute. Old Sokolov, Yuri, and Natasha sat down on the living room couch together.

Guardedly old Sokolov began, "I've got to confess something to you, Natasha." He allowed her time to prepare herself for the unexpected. "I am at fault," he continued very gently, "for your loss of your daughter in those days." Natasha looked at him in amazement. "I ask you now, Natasha, to be very strong. . . ."

Oh, what weighty words these had to be! How could he let the words cross his lips? How could he say, "Natasha, your daughter is not dead; she is alive"?

*   *   *

In the transfer prison, Sasha was unexpectedly taken from his cell and shown into the administration building. A major received him there and invited him to take a seat at a table. Then he disappeared through a side door, through which Koslov entered a few minutes later.

"Alexander Nikitin?" he inquired. Sasha stood up without a word and bowed.

"Well, did you lose your tongue at meeting a fellow university student?" Koslov thought he was being very funny and laughed goodnaturedly. "Do sit down, Nikitin. Or should we perhaps use more familiar terms?"

"As you wish," retorted Sasha coolly.

Koslov came to the point immediately. "Alexander, what is your relationship with Irina Sokolova?"

Sasha shrugged and said, "She is my fiancée."

Koslov stared at him with his eyes wide open and then broke into wild guffaws. "That's the biggest joke of the century! Fiancée? Isn't marriage between a brother and a sister forbidden to you Baptists?"

Sasha looked at him uncomprehendingly. "What do you mean by that?"

"What do I mean? Well, how about *that?*" Koslov actually shouted with glee. "Well, didn't your immediate relatives inform you that your mother had twins? You and Irina? Irina was subsequently adopted by Sokolov, a KGB employee."

Sasha had the sensation that the rug was being pulled out from under his feet. His insides were in an uproar. All at once he tried to remember—how did the prison doctor say it back then? His mother had died as she was having a daughter. Or was he confusing that with Irina's mother now? There was a flaw in his reasoning capacity. But his father never had mentioned that. At the end he seemed to have wanted to tell him something just before his death. But probably not the whole story even then.

Sasha sat there stunned. This news had struck him as if he had been hit by a club. Yet he had the feeling that something did not make complete sense. He would have to ask Siniszin. Too bad he had interrupted his conversation with him! With great effort he forced himself to come back to the present. He became aware again that he was seated in the major's office. This fellow had just told him Irina was his twin sister. His thinking processes had become sluggish.

"I am grateful to you," he stated with an effort. "Now I know that Irina is my sister."

If I could be back in my cell right now, he thought. *If I could forget everything for a few moments. . . .*

Koslov handed him several photographs; Sasha reached mechanically for one of them. He looked at it a little more carefully and was incredulous at what he saw—Irina on the floor, half naked, Koslov on top of her, covering her with kisses.

Sasha began to feel sick to his stomach. He returned the snapshots to Koslov without a word and pushed the remainder of the photos away. As if from a great distance he heard Koslov babbling, "Well, don't you see, Alexander? You had a romance with your own sister! Isn't it funny? I must tell you this woman can't get enough sex! Her actions stem from a sexual illness. For that reason I did not marry her. . . ."

Sasha did not allow him to finish. He rose and said, full of revulsion, "Koslov, none of that is of interest to me. At any rate, these photos are insufficient cause to put my sister into a special psychiatric clinic."

"Wait, Nikitin, that isn't all! You have no right to go that quickly as long as I have not given my permission!" Koslov's voice broke in his fury.

Sasha was clear about one thing. Here he had no rights whatever. So he sat down on the chair again and closed his eyes. He didn't even listen as Koslov ranted excitedly at him.

It was only when Koslov lost control of himself completely, yelling, "You are mentally disturbed yourself!" that Sasha reopened his eyes and calmly asked, "Do you always scream to your former fellow students that way? If you insist on raving like this, then I've got to ask what the actual purpose of this visit is. What do you wish—or what do you have to achieve with me?"

Koslov rose abruptly and silently stalked out through the side door. A woman's voice with a distinctly German accent piped through the door, "My dear, should I perhaps talk to him?"

"Aw, leave that—." Koslov let loose some choice language.

The major reentered the room and looked at Sasha, trying to guess what his thoughts were.

"Come on, I will return you to your cell," he said in an almost friendly manner. As he stepped forward he made a painful grimace. He had lost a leg in the war.

*   *   *

Natasha cried softly. She did not know which of her feelings was stronger: joy at the fact that her daughter was alive or bitterness at the fact that the truth—and her own child—had been withheld from her for so long.

Yuri spoke gently to her. "Natasha, try to understand my position, too. In the beginning my father was afraid—I knew nothing of any of this; I was, after all, at the front—that the child would not be able to survive life in the concentration camp. In addition, this child would have to be raised in different surroundings. And then, when the child was finally here, we could not go our separate ways. To me the child was a part of you."

Natasha made an effort to understand the two men's reasoning. Yet the grandfather had become a Christian. Should he not have spoken with her?

As she tried hard to comprehend everything, Yuri's voice became audible again. "I had lost you. But I had loved you so much that I never was capable of loving another woman. Never! Occasionally I ran across a woman who appealed to me; but when I began to compare her to you, I lost the desire to try to establish a stronger relationship with that person. If I had lost my daughter on top of everything else, it would have been the end of me. You had your Sasha; you had your husband. But I had no one besides Irina. Forgive me. I will give everything back to you. Natasha, if—"

She did not respond. Yuri remained silent in his sorrow. What more should he say? Yet all of a sudden Natasha smiled her sunny smile through her tears.

"Yuri, now you will have a wife, a daughter, and a son-in-law all at once!"

Yuri took Natasha in his arms and whirled her around the room. "Natasha! Natasha!" he shouted so loudly that he could be heard through doors and windows.

Abruptly he put Natasha down again. "Goodness!" he called out excitedly. "I promised it to Him!"

Natasha, startled, looked up and asked him, "What was it? To whom?"

With his voice expressing deep emotion he said, "I promised God that if He restored you and Irina to me I would obey Him and serve Him!"

"That is wonderful, indeed!" said Nadyeshda from the kitchen doorway.

Old Sokolov stumbled inside and could not restrain himself from making a joke in his happiness. "Well, Natasha, you have not yet asked me for my son's hand!" Everyone laughed.

"What's going on here?" exclaimed Professor Nikiforoff as he entered his home. His wife told him the news, and he rejoiced with the others.

"Isn't it marvelous," the professor said, "how the Lord has led like this? It's absolutely astonishing. I believe we should thank Him right now!"

They all knelt. Yuri's prayer was offered in an unsteady voice. It was only the second prayer of his life, and the first said in the presence of others. His prayer was, "Lord, Creator of the whole universe, I praise You and thank You for becoming man so that we might become the children of God. Forgive me for not wanting to acknowledge You for such a long time. Now I wish to dedicate myself completely to Your service. Help me in that. Amen."

Each prayed in turn, with the elder Sokolov closing the session in prayer. He prayed especially for Irina, for Sasha, and for his grandchild's other friends who were in prisons or psychiatric clinics. Then they sat together until early dawn, exchanging ideas about ways in which they might effect the release of these young people.

"By the way, Valentina Neverova has confessed everything to her husband and has repented for her work with the KGB," Natasha related. "She wants to return all the money they gave her!"

The elder Sokolov said, "I've learned from someone in one of the prisons that Neverov spoke to Sasha and told him, 'Pray for me so that God will give me the strength to live with such a woman after my release.' I can understand how Neverov must feel. That is really a tough personal trial."

Yuri raised his eyebrows. He said, "All right, at least she has admitted that she is a traitor. But how many people continue to be traitors even after they confess it?"

* * *

Two months after this memorable gathering, Natasha gained the right to visit Sasha in prison. This was clearly a serious error of the otherwise smoothly operating KGB apparatus. Koslov was furious when he discovered it and had two of his best people dismissed.

Sasha's first question was, "What have you heard about Irina?"

"She's still in a special psychiatric clinic for criminals," replied Natasha, "but no one seems to know which one."

"Mother, did you know that Irina is my sister?"

"What do you mean by your 'sister'? Do you mean your sister in the Spirit?"

"No, Mother, my bodily sister. My mother had twins when I was born. Irina was given to Sokolov, and I was given to you. It is a good thing everything has finally been cleared up. Can you imagine what would have happened if we had married and only then discovered that we were twins?"

"What kind of nonsense is this, my Son?"

"That isn't nonsense, Mother; it is the truth. Koslov recently clarified our relationship."

For a long time Natasha looked at him with real compassion. Finally she asked softly, "Tell me, you don't really have any doubts about the fact that you are Lena's son and that I nursed you, do you?"

"Of course not."

"That's good. Now listen closely. *Irina is my daughter.* I brought her into the world. But Sokolov raised her because he is her actual father. Do you understand that? I became pregnant with his child before I accepted the Lord."

"Is that really the truth?" cried Sasha, totally beside himself with joy.

The other prisoners and their visitors stared at them. Then Natasha began to tell what had occurred in Nikiforoff's apartment. Sasha hung on every word. Everyone else in the room also heard it with great interest and sympathy. When Natasha finished her story, Sasha rubbed his eyes hard and exclaimed, "That's simply unbelievable! The things that happen in this old world! If you only knew what I endured after Koslov's visit!"

"Visiting hours are over! All visitors will leave the room and line up at the checkpoint!" announced the guard on duty.

22 Psychiatric Treatment Soviet Style

"**I** don't understand what is happening around me. I only know that they have stuck me in here along with the mentally ill. What do You wish me to do here, Lord?"

The medic read these words written on the wall by one of three women who had been detained there earlier. For some reason he laughed and then left the room. The medic, Mladenov, was a giant of a man. His fiery-red hair was carefully combed. His watery blue eyes bulged out of an already ugly face that struck terror among patients of the special psychiatric clinic. Whenever he spoke his long nose nearly touched his upper lip, his ears wiggled back and forth, and his eyes wandered restlessly from one object to another. Occasionally the clinic director said, "Never in my entire life have I seen such an ugly human being. But he is irreplaceable to us as a medical orderly!"

Mladenov had just gone off duty and was on his way out of the clinic building. When he reached the yard he looked up at the detention cells with curiosity. Their windows were protected by wooden planks. He himself had spent an entire year in detention there pending trial. After that he was sentenced to six years in prison and was moved to Vladimirskaya prison.

Mladenov had had bad luck throughout his life, all because of his distorted face. His grandmother, who had raised him, attended an Orthodox church in Leningrad but took her grandchild along only on rare occasions. She could not stand the mocking glances of people around her. When Mladenov grew up he fell in love with a young student, but she quickly let him go. He was unable to understand why girls avoided him.

"Look, little Grandchild. You just came into the world as an ugly person," his grandmother said one day, "and you will just have to accept it."

His grandmother's words struck him like a bolt of lightning out of the blue. For the first time ever, he carefully inspected his face in a mirror. What he saw there explained everything to him. He was overcome by a terrible sense of despair. All of a sudden he felt such a terrible hatred for the old woman who had filled the role of mother for him that he beat her to death. As he stood in the courtroom later, he could not explain his behavior. After the investigation the KGB became interested in him. They removed him from jail and turned him into a clever stool pigeon. And after he was released from prison, the KGB offered him a spot as a medical orderly in the special psychiatric clinic.

Soki's voice broke into Mladenov's reverie. "Please report to my study, Mladenov," he ordered.

"I am off today, and I don't want to get to the movie too late," said Mladenov cautiously.

"Oh, you can go to the movies another day. We've got somebody here who will interest you," Soki asserted, his voice full of promise.

They entered Soki's study together.

"We've caught an interesting little bird here," Soki said. "We can't hold her too long because she is a foreigner. But she certainly will provide some fun for you."

Soki rang for the supervisor on duty. A few minutes later the female supervisor brought in a young blonde woman who looked very frightened.

Mladenov sat down in a rather dark corner and listened in on the conversation which examining magistrate Soki had with the young woman.

Valya was an American. As a small child she had lost her Russian parents and was adopted by an Armenian couple. She was a Christian and intended to become a missionary.

After she had attended a Bible school for four years, she learned from an emigrant from Russia that she had an uncle in the Soviet Union who lived in total isolation in Minsk. She wrote to him, received an answer, and then traveled to Minsk as a tourist. But she failed to get to her uncle before he died.

She could never have anticipated the implications for her of her uncle's life, about which she had known nothing. He had been a preacher in the Soviet Union and had spent ten years in jail. After his release he found that his wife had died while he was in prison. He moved to Minsk and lived there totally alone. Off and on he visited the local Baptist house of worship, usually on important religious holidays. He spent the remainder of his time at work in a factory, earning much overtime pay.

He had become disillusioned by the behavior of his fellow Christians, especially by the church itself. But he had retained his belief in God. Each day he spent many hours in prayer. But when he found that the government was interfering more and more in the internal affairs of the church, he resigned from it and virtually never attended another gathering of the congregation.

His honesty and diligence drew the attention of Irina Sokolova, who was employed in the factory's research center. She obtained permission for him to come to work with her in the research section, and she invited him to join her Bible study group. He received new courage from that, and a new life seemed to begin for him. But when Irina was arrested, the KGB began to bring him in each night for interrogation as well.

At that point he received his American niece's letter. In his answer he shared some of his plight. He, of course, had no idea that the KGB would examine all his letters and that as a result both he and his niece were in danger.

After the final interrogation he was forced to endure, he

fell to his knees in front of his bed and wept and prayed exceptionally loudly. A neighbor heard this and knocked on his door. The old man stopped his loud crying and praying. Since the door was ajar, the neighbor stepped inside to see what was going on. He found the praying man lying half on and half off his bed. He was dead.

Valya later learned all this from that neighbor. At that point she made a mistake: she gave the neighbor all the things she had brought along for her uncle—a tape recorder, a radio, a pair of binoculars, and a camera. She was arrested for this.

Mladenov now observed the American woman's behavior. She insisted that her arrest be reported to the United States consul.

Soki, the examinining magistrate, smiled, "Certainly we'll do that! But you are being accused of spying. For that reason your consul will not be allowed to come to see you."

"At least permit me to write my fiancé a letter. He teaches at the Bible school."

"You will be able to put your arms around your fiancé in a week," countered Soki, "if you will accept our suggestion."

(A few years later, Valya, then a missionary in Africa with her husband, personally reported this incident and gave permission for it to be made public.)

An attempt was made to recruit Valya for the following purpose: she and her intended husband were to work with one of the western missionary organizations. They were to keep the KGB continually informed about the working methods of these missionary groups and about their relations with Russia's Christians. At the same time, she was handed compromising "documents" about the leading personages of a number of missionary organizations, documents which she was to make public at a certain time.

Valya quickly and decisively rejected this proposition.

Meanwhile Soki had received instructions to terminate her case as quickly as possible and to set her free so that the western press would not get wind of the so-called project. Soki resolved to try to catch her with her guard down by using a trick on her.

"All right, fine, Valya," he began. "You refuse to work with us in a peaceful manner. I will leave you alone in the company of this man." He pointed to Mladenov and walked out of the room.

Valya stared into the corner where Mladenov was crouching. He did not immediately understand what was expected of him, and he remained there for a while.

Mladenov was a homosexual. His hatred of women stemmed from the fact that all women other than his grandmother had consistently avoided him and treated him with contempt. It was common knowledge in the clinic that when Mladenov shut himself inside a room with a patient he was raping another unfortunate victim.

At long last he rose and slowly ambled toward the table. "Is it true, American girl, that western girls lose their innocence by the age of thirteen?" he asked with genuine curiosity.

Mladenov's ugliness had robbed Valya of her ability to speak. Eventually, though, she stuttered, "What do you mean by 'losing one's innocence'? What are you up to?"

Mladenov laughed uproariously, grabbed for her blouse, pulled her up from her chair and pushed a finger at her. Valya slapped him hard on his hand and pulled away from him.

"Aren't you ashamed? You're a citizen of a Communist country and you allow yourself to do things like that? Where is your Communist morality?"

Mladenov laughed even louder. "Communist morality? You stupid goat, you want to have morality! All methods are all right when used against the enemies of our social order!"

"But I am no enemy of your social order," gasped Valya, panic-stricken.

Suddenly Mladenov appeared to calm down. He asked her,

"Suppose I belonged to your Christian group. Would you marry me then?"

What's that supposed to mean now? Valya asked herself. She quickly got hold of herself and replied, "But of course, if this were God's will. God is never scornful of anyone. He loves every human being. Why shouldn't I, as a Christian, be able to love you too?"

Mladenov was deeply touched by this. He was suddenly very confused. Never before had he heard anything like that. No one had ever spoken to him in that way. But at that instant he saw Soki's threatening fist in the partially open door. Mladenov pulled himself together.

"Take your pants off!" he ordered Valya. "You've got your nerve, wearing pants and driving us men crazy. In our country only prostitutes wear pants, in order to better advertise their main attraction. Pull 'em down, I say!"

The color drained from Valya's face and she didn't know what to do. Mladenov seized her by the waistband and pulled her pants down to around her knees. Valya broke into tears, pushed him away from her and began to call for help. He punched her stomach with his fist until she buckled over with pain. Then Mladenov held her body against his. A few minutes later he released her, sat down in perplexity, and looked at his victim.

Soki entered the room again and asked, "Well, what's going on now?"

"It didn't work out," stuttered Mladenov helplessly. "It's the first time in my whole life, word of honor! I can't understand it. She kept blubbering and praying, 'Lord, don't let this happen! Don't let it happen!' I just couldn't go through with it!"

"Makes no difference!" Soki laughed. "You can go now, Mladenov. I took a few snapshots of the two of you," he said, turning to Valya.

Mladenov retreated, completely bewildered. Valya dragged herself up from the floor, hastily pulled up her pants and zipped herself back up. "May God forgive your evil deed!" she managed to get out.

During the minutes of her struggle with Mladenov she actually had prayed from the bottom of her heart and in faith for the first time in her life. Obviously, to her, her encounter was a victory of God's might over a perverted human being. She rejoiced and praised God. "It didn't work out!"—a human being actually admitted his defeat in an area where he had never encountered defeat before. Yet for a fraction of a second she became aware that she was in the hands of people who were capable of anything. For the first time in her life everything—simply everything—was at stake. Either her faith would be lost or it would grow deep and strong, sinking deep roots in her heart. What a victory this had been! To her, God was now a present reality, close enough to touch. And what would have happened had He permitted it after all? That question did not even cross her mind.

*   *   *

During the days of her imprisonment, Irina shared prison cells with a variety of people. Large numbers of perfectly healthy people were treated with electroshock therapy and with psychopharmacological medications at the instigation of the chief of the security police, Andropov.

Irina shuddered as one day her cellmate was dragged back into the room from Mladenov's duty room and tossed on her bed, near collapse. Irina realized that the same thing could happen to her one day as well.

Mother Yevdokia—her cellmate—was a nun. She had been held inside institutions of this kind for several years because when released from prison in 1965 she again attended church regularly and again read to her many nephews and nieces from the Bible. This time when she was arrested, she was placed into the "psychiatric clinic" instead of another prison.

Dirty, disheveled, and only half conscious, she lay on her bed. Her lips were murmuring a prayer in old Slavonic. Irina sat down beside her on the bed and stroked the old woman to calm her. Suddenly Mother Yevdokia began to weep loudly. She had preserved her innocence throughout her life, and this shame simply broke her heart.

"They robbed me of my honor, these ... these, ..." she complained like an aggrieved child. "Whatever did I do to them?" She could not seem to calm down. Irina stroked her back gently and said a quiet prayer. She was fully aware that many people would never emerge from this living hell.

Irina was still busy calming down Mother Yevdokia when she noticed that a medic named Lyoma had entered the cell. "Well, won't the old lady accept her fate?" he asked calmly. He, too, was a former prisoner and currently a henchman for the KGB. Irina shrugged her shoulders and walked to her bed.

Lyoma brought in a handful of pills and a glass of water, forced open Mother Yevdokia's mouth, and compelled her to swallow the pills. She resisted, and he struck her hard on the mouth. Blood began to trickle from her lips. Yevdokia swallowed the wrong way and began to cough violently. The three other women in the cell began to mutter indignantly, whereupon Lyoma gave them an evil, steady look. They quickly fell silent.

When Lyoma finished with Yevdokia he stepped over to Maria, a young student, and barked, "Come with me!"

Maria shook her head. Lyoma grabbed her elbow and bodily threw her out of the cell.

Irina sat on her cot. These women needed her help. She simply had to do something for them. But what could she do? How could she bring them any consolation? She herself could be dragged into the duty room tomorrow, and some pervert might rob her of her virginity as well.

How would she react? *O God, help me get out of this hell!* But why had He not helped Mother Yevdokia. Had He caused them all to be delivered to this place? Had He forgotten them? Was there no sense in praying in this underworld? Had they already been discarded?

Then she heard the words, "Irina Sokolova! You are to see

the department chief!" She shuddered but stood up and did as she was told.

Dr. Osinnik, the department chief, greeted Irina very politely. She looked at him pensively and asked him, "Comrade Osinnik, did you know that Maria is the daughter of a ship captain who makes trips to foreign countries, too?"

Osinnik looked at her in astonishment. "What business could that possibly be of mine? I didn't send her to this place, and neither did you. Maria has to suffer for having praised the American way of life too much among her student friends. Her father is equally guilty, and we will have to treat him also when he returns."

Irina could only shake her head. "Well, really!"

Osinnik showed her a place to sit down at a table, sat down across from her, and began to leaf through her file.

"You know, Sokolova, I don't know what to think when I view your personal file and your treatment record."

"Comrade Osinnik," Irina retorted gently, "I can understand that the director of this clinic, who happens to be a dermatologist and has no idea of psychiatric practice, would have difficulty with that. But you are a specialist in this field! You should be able to recognize at first glance that this entire treatment record and my personal file consist of fabrications put together by the KGB and that I am being detained in this clinic even though I am perfectly healthy. Why is that?"

Osinnik shrugged his shoulders and responded, "But how else can one explain this crazy idea of a dialogue, for example? I beg you, Sokolova, I am trying to understand you. I do not intend to create difficulties for you. But there are so many unrealistic, even fantastic ideas in your record that a Soviet doctor really finds it difficult to declare you mentally healthy. When the leaders of western religious movements conduct such a dialogue with the Communists in Europe, and when they actually try to flirt with us—like the World Council of Churches and the leadership of the Baptist Church in the West—then this is obviously nothing more than an act of desperation. There are no other alternatives open to them.

Western theologians know quite well that religion has no future and that it has proved itself to be a failure in all areas of life. So they grasp for the last straw available to them and attempt to ingratiate themselves with communism. The purpose is to have a warm place to escape to for the future. These are egotists, believe me, Irina—perfectly obvious and repulsive egotists who, since they find themselves on a ship that is sinking, think only of how to save their own skins and how they might preserve their personal authority and their own families! To them, religion is merely a springboard for their manipulation of others and at the same time a job with which to earn their keep. We can understand that kind. But as for you, we want to meet you halfway so as to liberate you from your befuddled state.

"What you actually want are the same rights to propagate your religious activities as Communists! But that's a paradox, when you think about it! That's Utopian thinking! That's really monstrous! This can never, ever happen! We grant concessions to the theologians and admittedly delay the death process of religion by that. But we do it only when this strategy does not entail any drawbacks for our own ideology and when it makes it possible for us to deliver, when the time comes, a more accurate death blow to these remainders of the past. That is what religion is, after all—a relic from the past."

Deep in thought, Irina shook her head and said, "Tell me, Comrade Osinnik, what are we Christians to do when you pursue such aims—which I was aware of before you stated them?"

"Listen well, Sokolova! Sooner or later we will kill this anachronism! You must get away from it, and better today than tomorrow!" He became more and more insistent and spoke with a passion which could sweep one away.

"Well, all right," indicated Irina, unmoved by all this, "but what, in your opinion, is to become of the more than fifty million Christians who live in the Soviet Union?"

"We will treat their sickness! We will cure them by means of ideological persuasion! And where this does not suffice, we will be forced to resort to reprisals. But believe me, Sokolova, this will be the most extreme measure only, when nothing else works! It is our actual purpose to persuade every Christian to move in the same direction as ours because of his convictions and to concede the rightness of the Communist ideology with his whole heart! He is to love it! He is to be willing to fight for it! He is to place his entire life solely at the disposal of the Communist ideals. When we have achieved that state with all Christians, they will no longer have a need for their God! For this reason our constitution allowed for the freedom of individual religious conviction, naturally only when it does not contradict Communist ideology. This gives us the ability to put an end to religion in a humane way. A Christian who has adopted our ideology will forget the supernatural world. For this reason I urge you, Sokolova, detach yourself from this mad idea. Then you will be released immediately."

Irina persevered, "And what will you do with those who despite your treatments and despite the Communist ideology continue to believe in God?"

Osinnik grimaced. "I guarantee you that these will be only isolated instances, and these we will put in psychiatric clinics."

There was a knock on the door.

"Come in!" called Osinnik.

"The Yevdokia woman is dead. Lyoma fed her some pills and probably did too much of a good thing," the doctor on duty reported.

"Has she been removed from the cell?"

"Yes."

The doctor walked toward the door.

Osinnik began pacing up and down in his office. The telephone rang. He picked up the receiver.

"The examining magistrate Soki wants to speak with you," he said to Irina.

Soki was seated behind a table smilingly examining some snapshots when Irina entered the room.

"Aha, Sokolova! Please sit down," he said without actually looking up at her. He waved to the prison guard indicating that he could go. Irina's personal file lay on the table.

Abruptly Soki asked her, "What do you know about Sasha Nikitin?"

"He is my fiancé and friend," Irina replied. "In addition, he happens to be a Christian, too."

"Hmmm! Tell me, does your faith permit marriage between brother and sister?"

"He is not my brother," Irina explained, "by which I mean that we are not related to each other."

Soki handed her a letter. "Here, read this."

It was a letter from Siniszin's wife. She wrote, "Dear Soki: I want to ask you urgently to care for the welfare of Irina Sokolova, as she is the niece of my deceased husband. My husband's sister, Lena, died in childbirth during the war. The twins to whom she had given birth remained alive. The son was placed into the care of his father, who was serving a prison term at the time. Natasha Borisova nursed the little one, then married the child's father, who has since died. The daughter was given to Vladimir Sokolov, who entrusted the child's care to his son after the war ended. These facts leave no doubt that Irina Sokolova is my relative, and I would be deeply obliged if you were to take good care of her. With best regards, Siniszina."

Irina put the letter down on the table. She was so confused that she was unable to get out a single word. But Soki would not allow her time to think.

"You are here, Sokolova," he stated, "because, judging by these photos, you have a pathologically overdeveloped sex drive. What's more, think about this: we had to imprison an American missionary woman in recent days, also because of a perverted sex drive. Is this characteristic of all religious fanatics, or do just a few of you have this inclination?"

Irina turned red and replied, "Citizen examining magistrate, I have not had sexual relations with a single man in my entire life. Any doctor can confirm this with great ease."

"Oh yes?" the examining magistrate growled. "But how do you account for these documents?"

He threw her the snapshots which she had seen so frequently by then. Included was the picture which showed the American girl with Mladenov. Irina examined the picture carefully and said with compassion, "Mladenov apparently did not do his assigned homework! You poor atheists! May God have mercy on you!"

"What? Where? What are you looking at?" Soki tore the photo out of her hand and looked at it closely. Now he understood everything. . . .

"Mladenov!" he screamed. Mladenov was already standing outside the door and came in immediately. "Teach this religionist her P's and Q's, will you? I'm going outside for a breath of air." Seething with anger, Soki left the room.

Irina smiled at Mladenov and told him in a friendly way, "Now listen closely to me. You are well aware of the fact that I am a Christian and have broken no laws. I'm being held in this hellhole for no reason whatsoever. You, in turn, are being used by the government people to do their dirty work. And when they no longer have need of you, they will also get rid of you."

"Shut your trap, you—," cursed Mladenov, continuing to stare at the picture with him on it.

Irina persevered, unperturbed, "I know how you suffer because you are not a good-looking man. However, we Christians are not concerned with how good one looks on the outside, but how good one's heart is. If you give your life to Jesus Christ and serve Him, you will certainly find a Christian woman who will grow fond of you from her heart and will become a good life's companion for you."

Mladenov stared at Irina with his watery eyes and, like a robot, ordered, "Take off the dress."

Irina merely smiled and said, "Why don't you stop, Mladenov? It won't work this time, either. Do you really want to fight against God? He who is inside us is stronger than he who is in the world. Do you want to strike out against a thorn? You will die miserably, Mladenov. . . ."

He was not to be dissuaded and grabbed her by both

shoulders. A quick second later he was lying flat on the floor staring wildly up at Irina.

Calmly she sat down at the table and looked into his eyes. "Listen to me, Mladenov! The Word of God says that he who calls on the name of the Lord will be saved. Whoever has Jesus has life; whoever does not have Jesus does not have life. He who is not for Him is against Him. Your conscience still tortures you because you killed your grandmother merely because she told you the truth. You are afraid because you are ugly, and you have forgotten in all this that it is the inner man who is decisive. Repent of all your crimes, Mladenov, and accept Jesus Christ as your personal Savior. Do it in the detestable situation in which you find yourself at this moment. The KGB will take you to your grave. You are its victim; you are a puppet in the hands of satanic powers. Think about it! God holds out His hand to you and wishes to help you."

She rose, walked over to Mladenov, and extended her hand to him. "Come, get up! Forgive me for dealing you such a clumsy blow. You are probably in great pain."

Something inexplicable was taking place inside of Mladenov. If anyone on this earth was unable to understand what was happening to him, it had to be he. It was as if a giant block of ice was melting within him. *What's going on inside me?* he wondered. He took Irina's hand. Her firm, friendly handclasp and her confident voice brought him back to reality.

He straightened himself up and suddenly broke into tears. Irina put her hand on his shoulder and said, "Yes, do cry! Tears are a good thing. Don't be ashamed in front of me. God wants your heart. He will make a happy man out of you."

As he stepped back into the room, the examining magistrate stopped as if he had been turned to stone. He could not believe his eyes! Irina and Mladenov were kneeling together, praying. When they rose, Irina said, "Now you are my brother, Mladenov! I am proud and happy to have such a brother!"

23 Epilogue

Ilya Orlov, a member of the foreign department of the All-Union, was delivering a sermon in the Baptist house of worship. Lyuba Serova and her four children, whom she had recently picked up from the boarding school, were in the audience. Her children had persuaded their mother to go with them to this worship service, during which Orlov was to report about his experiences in western countries. His official journeys often took him to foreign countries. Everyone now listened attentively to his report.

"Under the leadership of our Communist Party our country is taking giant strides toward a wonderful future," said Orlov, working himself into a lather. "In recent decades our Party has been able to turn the loftiest ideals into reality—ideals which are of the greatest significance for all humanity, ideals which Jesus taught. While western Christianity certainly is promoting Christian ethics and ideals, it actually labors against them in practice. Meanwhile, our Communist Party is constructing a society which conforms to God's Kingdom in every aspect of life!"

Svetlana Serova nudged her brother Igor and whispered in his ear, "Man, if the same kind of regime rules in the kingdom of God as that which rules in the Soviet Union, I would much rather fry in hell's fires!"

"S-s-sh!" hissed Igor, and turned to look at his mother. She sat immobile, but a slight smile was playing around the corners of her mouth.

Orlov continued preaching, "Step by step the Soviet Union is making the eternal verities a reality. Mankind is being liberated from exploitation by his fellow human beings. Each man receives each day that which he needs.

"In the capitalistic countries men live just like wolves. But in our country everyone is everyone else's friend. He is a brother among brothers. All men are equals here.

"Deceitful rumors about us are being spread in western countries. These rumors include the lie that our government puts perfectly healthy people into psychiatric clinics and that Christians are persecuted for proclaiming the Gospel.

"It is our sacred duty to attack these lies with all the strength at our command. Millions of people in the West already understand that these are infamous lies. They place their confidence in us and will do everything to expose those individuals who put such lies into circulation. They will unmask them everywhere. Never has a human being had to spend time in prison in the Soviet Union because he is a Christian. Always it has been those acts which contradicted the spirit of Marxism and the progress of socialism that earned men the punishment of a jail sentence.

"We are citizens of a glorious country, and we are proud of it! We will fight with all our might so that everyone in our country can follow the ideals of communism in complete unity—ideals which are being promoted by our glorious Party!"

Alyosha Serov stood up quietly and tiptoed toward the exit. His mother's eyes followed him. The KGB major seated next to Lyuba bent over to her and whispered, "It looks as if your children are being reeducated even more quickly here than in the boarding school!" But when the young boy did not return immediately he announced, "I'm going to see what Alyosha is doing."

Alyosha's mind was in an uproar as he left the church. His father's words still rang in his ears, "We have sacrificed four million lives in order to turn our Party's policies into reality, and we will have to continue to sacrifice men and women. But the question remains, was it worth sacrificing those millions of lives after all? This question will be answered only by a generation which will live in the very distant future."

Unexpectedly Alyosha burst into sobs. The pain he felt in his heart could find expression only in this way.

Someone put an arm on his shoulder and kissed him on the forehead. He looked up and through his tears saw Irina Sokolova standing in front of him.

"Irina!" Alyosha shouted, overjoyed.

Whether from the great joy of seeing her again or the deep sorrow her imprisonment had caused him—on top of his horror at the "sermon" he had just heard—he turned toward her, buried his young face in her jacket and sobbed even harder.

"Dearest Irina," he stammered through his tears, "these aren't shepherds! They are wolves!"

"Who are you speaking about, Alyosha?" Irina asked. She quickly took him by the arm and pulled him around the corner with her.

"The man who just stepped out of the house of worship is a KGB officer," she said. "I saw him once at your father's house. It would not be good if we were to run into him!"

They turned into a side street. Irina gave her handkerchief to her companion. "You have to understand, Alyosha, that I was just released from the psychiatric institute this very morning," she explained. "The first thing I meant to do was to worship God, but evidently I haven't succeeded. So that's how I ran into you! Quick, tell me how all of you are."

Alyosha gave her a brief report of his father's death. Irina listened, shocked. Then she inquired about the well-being of his mother and his brother and sisters.

Right in the middle of his account Alyosha suddenly stopped, gave her an astonished look, and said "I think you have become even more beautiful in prison, Irina."

Irina laughed indulgently. "That's only what *you* think because you cannot really make such comparisons yet. Not long ago you didn't even have an eye for such things. Now, though, you are on the way to becoming a young man and are beginning to discover whether girls are pretty or not."

"Alyosha, where are you?" a child's voice cried out.

Irina was startled. "Could that be Svetlana?" she asked.

Alyosha nodded.

"All right, Alyosha," Irina said, "you had better go back now. I will grab a taxi and rush to my father's. Could you all come to my house tomorrow? That would be nice!"

She kissed him on the cheek and disappeared into a side street. Alyosha ran back to the house of worship.

Why Sasha Nikitin, Irina and all her friends were unexpectedly released from detention was a mystery. Could it have had something to do with the fact that material proving that perfectly healthy people were being imprisoned and sent to psychiatric clinics had been confiscated from a German family at a checkpoint at Brest-Litovsk—evidence which might already have found its way into western countries? Yuri Sokolov's notes about his daughter and Sasha Nikitin were among the papers confiscated.

Or did it have something to do with Siniszina? Perhaps she had kept her word, given to her husband before his death, to see to it that nothing happened to his nephew. No one was able to answer this question.

* * *

"Sasha Nikitin! Get your things together and pack up!" the prison guard yelled through the flap over the prison cell peephole.

"Well, little brother, now you'll finally go to the prison camp," said one of the prisoners. For six months Sasha had been shunted from one temporary detention cell to another.

His transfer to a permanent "rehabilitation camp" had been delayed for some reason.

Shortly thereafter the door was pulled open abruptly. The guard bellowed, "Outside!"

Sasha said his good-byes to the one hundred prisoners who had been jammed into this cell. "So long, folks! I hope we'll meet again in the prison camp!"

The guard led Sasha to a special section, where its supervisor already was waiting for him.

"Nikitin, please sign this release certificate!"

He handed Sasha the court decision and pointed to the place where Sasha was to sign it. Sasha was so surprised he didn't know what to say, and he silently signed his name.

"What is your relationship to Mrs. Siniszin?" the supervisor asked with deliberate casualness, as if something unimportant were at stake.

"She is the wife of my uncle," replied Sasha, still unclear about what to make of the whole thing.

"I see," muttered the official in a tentative way. "Do you have any sort of complaints against the prison leadership?"

"No," said Sasha hastily.

"Then please sign here, too."

He handed Sasha a second sheet of paper. On it he, Alexander Nikitin, was to indicate that he had no complaint whatever against the prison management and to obligate himself to remain silent about everything he had encountered during his time in prison.

Sasha suddenly remembered Silitch and quickly added the following sentence to the text on the sheet. "I agree to remain silent about everything which I encountered in the prisons only if the government agrees to pardon Silitch posthumously and to furnish his widow and children the appropriate financial support." Then he signed his name.

The supervisor took the paper from his hands, scanned its contents quickly, and disappeared from the room. About twenty minutes later his august majesty the colonel, head of the entire prison, appeared in person. Sasha knew this man was Jewish—something the colonel tried desperately to hide. But prisoners generally know much more about their supervisors than vice versa.

"Tell me, Nikitin, have you lost your senses?" the colonel screamed. "What did you write here? Do you want to go back into your cell?"

"Comrade colonel," Sasha replied calmly, "I have already signed my release document. Please allow me to go now."

"I'm going to throw you back into your cell," the colonel stormed.

"Comrade colonel, there are four healthy children growing up in your home. One of them hopes to go to Israel someday. Silitch's widow also has children—five—who have lost their father. She herself is unable to find work. All this only because they expressed the desire to emigrate to Israel, the land of their forefathers."

Sasha said no more, since the colonel suddenly had become very quiet and withdrawn. Without saying another word he turned on his heel and left the room.

The special section's supervisor reappeared wordlessly, handed Sasha his papers, and conducted him to the exit's checkpoint.

Suddenly a song rang through the prison corridor. "I am free! Praise be to You, O Lord! I am free! Praise be to You, O Lord! I am free and now I am going home!"

Singing the hymn were Sasha's cellmates, those who filled this humid, dirty cell of the transit prison to bursting. Men who still had to wait to be transported to a camp where they were to be "permitted" to build up socialism were singing for fortunate Sasha! Dozens of eyes followed him with overwhelming homesickness and undisguised envy.

About one-half the prisoners knew they were not in prison because they had committed any sort of crime. Often the offenses they were guilty of were so insignificant that in other countries they would simply have been subject to a public reprimand, certainly not imprisonment. These men knew that they were the victims of Russia's Five Year Plan, that they were a part of a cheap army of laborers whose job it was to fulfill the Five Year Plan before its term.

Someone called, "Sasha!" Sasha turned around, but by this time someone already was embracing him, lifting him high off the ground and swinging him around in a circle.

"Gander!" cried Sasha, full of joy.

Gussev had finished his term before Sasha and had been released. He said he had gotten out of his fourth term in jail with nothing more than a scare.

"How did you know that I was to be released today?" asked the amazed Sasha.

"We-e-ll, one has to have connections, you know," indicated Nikolay. "The special section's chief has a driver who is a trustee. I happened to run into him by accident near the prison director's office, and he told me about you. We were in jail together in Taishet."

"Let me tell my mother quickly," Sasha interjected.

"I've already sent her a telegram. I told her that you will arrive by plane tomorrow. I've even got your airplane tickets!"

"Airplane tickets?" Sasha was simply unable to suppress his surprise.

"I'm going to accompany you, Sasha. I've just gotten fired again," said Gussev happily, "and that is why I can go with you."

Gratefully Sasha embraced his brother in Christ, who had now also become a friend. He put his arm on his shoulder, and together they cast one glance toward the prison complex. A fence four yards high hid the prisoners' barracks from the eyes of passersby.

Sasha sighed. "None of this would happen," he said, "if our government were ready to give up this ideology which brings nothing but misfortune to humanity."

* * *

Professor Kuznetsov and his wife, Nora, waited at the gate of the psychiatric clinic of Tshernyakhovsk. The evening before, a highly placed official had telephoned the professor and informed him that his son was to be allowed to go free. The professor's concession had been that he would guarantee with his signature that his son would remain silent about everything the officials had forced him to endure.

They were becoming impatient waiting for Vassiley. The gate was opened, and three young men stepped toward freedom: Vassiley, Semyon Anakin, and Valentin Relin. Vassiley walked toward his parents and greeted them. His father embraced him in silence, his eyes moist. Nora wept quietly. Vassiley took his mother's arm.

"You look so different, Mama," he whispered in her ear.

"Well, many things have changed," she replied, her eyes radiating joy.

Vassiley motioned toward his friends. "I've presented them to you once before."

The two stepped forward and extended their hands to the Kuznetsovs.

Vassiley turned around once more and gazed at the barracks where the mentally ill were kept. "How many perfectly normal people are incarcerated forever in this hellhole!" he said. "And no one does anything about it! At the very least, the patriarchate ought to raise its objections in the name of justice against such lawlessness, which cries out toward heaven! But no! They all tremble in fear and hold their tongues."

"Yet your patriarchate is not afraid to protest against racial discrimination in the United States," said his mother grimly. "In addition they now channel money to western Marxists to aid them in preparing for revolution!"

"Well, what do you know?" said Vassiley, astonished at his well-informed mother. At one time she had shown no interest in such matters.

"Come on, my dears, let's get in." His father gestured

toward a nearby automobile. "I came in the government car," he explained, noticing his son's inquiring glance. Vassiley knew that his father disliked driving an automobile.

"Poluchkin is dead," Vassiley muttered after the car had started on its way. "They poisoned him, those sadists." Everyone looked inquiringly at him, since no one in the car had known Poluchkin. But Vassiley volunteered no more information.

*   *   *

The closer the taxi came to her father's house, the more excited Irina became. She had spent an entire year in the psychiatric clinic and during that time had had no contact with her father. She did not even know how he was. He had been unable to secure a visitor's permit.

Irina stuffed her last ten-ruble note into the taxi driver's hand and ran to the house. The courtyard had been swept clean, but no one was to be seen anywhere.

Irina knocked on the door. No answer. She thought for a moment, smiled, and then ran toward the shed. There, at the agreed-upon hiding place between the roof beams, was the key. They had always kept a reserve key there in the event one of them misplaced or lost a key.

She unlocked the door, her heart beating rapidly, and stepped into the foyer. Her heart was in her throat. She opened the door to the kitchen. On the table she saw *pelmyeni*, bite-sized morsels of noodle batter, ready to be cooked in hot water. She gently closed the door again and on tiptoes stole into her room. It was neat as a pin, the bed made and her Bible lying on the night table.

Suddenly she heard a sound and quickly hid behind the door. Through the crack in the door she saw her father walking into the kitchen.

She actually had planned to surprise her father. She wanted to wait until he had cooked his dinner and sat down to eat. But she simply couldn't stand waiting so long! She yanked open the door, ran into the kitchen and threw her arms around her father's neck. "Father! Dearest Father! I missed you so much!"

He reacted as if struck by lightning. For a few seconds he stood motionless. Then he pulled Irina up and whirled her around the room just as he had done when she was still a small girl.

"How grey your hair has turned, Papa!"

"But you haven't changed in the least. No, you actually look better." They chattered and chattered and did not notice the time passing.

"Wait a minute," Sokolov said abruptly, looking at his watch. "We've got visitors coming in half an hour, and lunch isn't even ready yet!"

"Oh? You expect visitors? Papa, I'll help you!"

Irina's excitement grew. What a joy it would be to receive visitors! Everything was in the past now. Irina felt as if she were in seventh heaven.

But all at once she thought of it again and a knife seemed to go through her heart. It was as if someone had shut off the warm sunlight for a moment. Suddenly she shuddered.

"I've got to ask you about something, Papa." She could not wait any longer.

Sokolov looked at her questioningly. "What is it?"

"Why didn't you ever tell me that you are not my real father?"

All right. Now it was out in the open, but Irina felt miserable!

Her father looked keenly at her. "Come, let's go into my study." He held her by the shoulder and pulled her along with him. This was important. The *pelmyeni* would have to wait.

"What have people told you, Irina? Tell me all of it before the guests arrive."

Irina told him about the letter from Mrs. Siniszin.

Sokolov listened carefully, then laughed bitterly and commented, "What they must have done to you in the loony bin to cause you to ask me a question like that! Look, the Siniszin woman could not possibly have written such a letter. The KGB people apparently wanted to confuse you. They have told you a lie, my child. Not only am I your bodily father, but your mother is also still alive."

At this Irina's eyes popped open wide. This was almost too much at once.

"Don't you want to tell me the complete truth, Papa? Please tell me everything; keep nothing from me!"

Yuri told her about Natasha. Tears were streaming from her eyes as she listened with bated breath. She said nothing for a long time.

"This means," she eventually said in a voice so low it was almost inaudible, "that Sasha isn't my brother after all? And that his mother is really my mother?" Her whole body trembled with excitement. Her father laid a calming hand on her shoulder.

"It sounds outlandish, Irina, but that is precisely the way things are," he said. But he did not have the nerve to tell her that Natasha and Sasha would soon be standing at the entrance. And sure enough, someone was already making a racket at the front door. Natasha, Sasha, and Gander entered the house chattering happily.

Natasha screamed, "Irina has been released!" and stormed into the study. Irina jumped up from the sofa. The two women stood facing each other. Natasha extended her trembling hands toward her daughter. Irina flew into her arms. "Mother, my dearest Mother!"

Sasha and Yuri guided the two to the sofa. Yuri quickly administered an injection to Natasha, since she was nearly fainting. He constantly had to compare the two women, mother and daughter. How closely they resembled each other! He could not understand how Natasha, who had seen Irina several times, had not guessed at the truth.

Irina silently stroked her mother's hands.

Natasha was better after the injection. She embraced her daughter. The men had left the room; it was high time to see to the *pelmyeni*.

Yuri looked out of the window. He left the housework to the young men. Only when lunch was ready and the table set did Yuri return to the women. They sat next to each other, alternately chattering excitedly and weeping. They appeared to have forgotten where they were. There were so many things to be told to each other. So much had happened—so many good things, important things, but also painful things. How could they possibly have lived so long without each other? A giant dam had broken, it seemed. The flood of pent-up feelings bore them along with it.

For a few moments Yuri stood irresolutely and listened. Then he sat down next to them, coughed politely, and said to Irina, "Dear Daughter, may I ask you for the hand of your mother? I would like for her to become my wife."

He managed to get it all out, though a bit clumsily, did good old Yuri.

Irina went completely out of control. Again she embraced him eagerly.

"I'll never, never let either of you go again, do you hear?" She was in a state of utter bliss.

Her father touched her back to calm her and said, "Today we are behaving like children, yet we should be thanking God for bringing us together."

Irina felt as if her heart had stopped. "Am I to assume that you have become a Christian, father?"

"Yes, my young one, you can express it that way. Sasha is going to baptize me in the Ptitch River this evening."

Ardent thanks went heavenward from Sokolov's house. Those gathered there gave thanks to God for bringing them to one another again and for all His grace in leading them in the past. And they asked for His blessings in the future.

The *pelmyeni* had gotten cold long ago, but no one appeared to be hungry. Only the ringing of the telephone reminded them that it was really time to eat lunch.

"It's for you, Irina," said Yuri. Irina went to the telephone and picked it up.

"Sokolova," she said, identifying herself.

"Irina, this is Mladenov," said the voice at the other end. "I heard that you had been allowed to go free and determined to get in touch with you."

"Where did you wind up, Mladenov? I asked all the medics about you."

"After I repented and turned to the Lord, they wanted to stick me right back into a psychiatric hospital again. After all, I know too much about their methods. They ordered me to renounce my faith, but I cannot do that. So I asked a preacher for advice. He advised me to pretend I was renouncing my beliefs, but to continue in the faith in my heart. But you know I cannot do such a thing!"

"Wow, that's enough to make one cry!" Irina blurted out. "What kind of an idiot of a preacher gave you *that* kind of stupid advice? You saw many Christians being tortured to death with your own eyes. And despite that they remained true to the Lord to the very end! Listen, Mladenov, where are you right now?"

"I'm in Minsk, hiding out with a woman acquaintance of mine. She is a telephone operator and is working right now. She is a hopeless case, since she earns extra money for herself by being a prostitute," explained Mladenov.

"Give me your address!" demanded Irina with authority. She was back to being her old self, the active and energetic Irina.

His address in hand, she reported to her family on Mladenov's status. Her father slowly nodded and said, "You go ahead and pray for Mladenov now. I'll get on my motorcycle and pick him up."

"Dad, they haven't been tapping your telephone, have they?"

Yuri raced off as if the devil himself were on his tracks. To shorten the distance, he raced through Minsk's narrow little streets. He prayed that the police would not stop him for violating speeding regulations. Just as he pulled into the courtyard of a huge apartment house, he noticed a Volga automobile pulling out of the opposite entrance.

Yuri hurried inside the building and ran up the stairs. As he arrived at the apartment he threw himself against the door. It yielded to his weight, opened and caused him to fall inside headfirst. He pulled himself together and jumped inside the room—but recoiled in horror. Before him dangled the legs of Mladenov. Sokolov grabbed the legs and lifted the body. To his relief he remembered that he had brought along a pocketknife. With one arm he supported Mladenov's body, and with the remaining hand he searched his pockets for the knife. There it was! He pulled the blade out of the handle with his teeth and cut the laundry rope from which Mladenov was hanging. Then he carefully put the poor young man down on the floor.

He felt Mladenov's pulse and examined the slipknot. He smiled. *These fools, they couldn't do anything right!* In their haste they had anesthetized the man and had tied the slipknot without taking out an existing knot.

Sokolov stepped over to the door and warily checked both sides of the hallway. Not a person in sight. He closed the door again and set himself to the task of reviving Mladenov. When Mladenov finally reopened his eyes, he was helped up by Sokolov, who sat him down on a chair.

"You've had some incredibly good fortune, Mladenov. In the crucial spot, the laundry line had a knot. This made it impossible for the knot to tighten on you. Besides, who would hang himself like you did, with the rope on top of your uniform collar?"

"They hung me," Mladenov gasped, "after they forced me to sign this nonsense." He fished a slip of paper out of his pocket.

Yuri read, "Irina, I have decided to depart from life. I know that you could never love such an ugly man. Your Mladenov."

Yuri pocketed the slip of paper and pulled the staggering

Mladenov out of the apartment. They left the door ajar in the event that his hostess were to return home soon. He helped Mladenov onto his motorcycle, tied him to himself, and drove off.

*　　*　　*

A large group of people had gathered in the new house, in a suburb of Odessa, to which the Sokolovs had moved a few months after Irina's release. The family was to have a great celebration. Irina was to marry Sasha Nikitin; and Irina's father was to marry Natasha Nikitina, born Borisova. The Baptist preacher named Klim, from Siberia, was to perform the ceremony. All the other ministers present were to bless the unions of the two pairs of newlyweds by the laying on of hands.

Vassiley Kuznetsov and his parents, Polevoy from Siberia, Professor Nikiforoff and his wife, Nadyeshda, old man Lupa, Yelena Lobova (the former secretary of the Komsomol's management, who had turned to the Lord along with her fiancé)—all these and others were seated at a long table, quietly chatting and waiting for the festivities to begin.

Vladimir Sokolov, the elderly gentleman, looked wan. But the old fire was burning in his eyes, and it was easy to see that he was overjoyed. He sat at the head of the table with his wife, Pelagea. He did not speak. Either he was not strong enough to do so or he had the feeling that he had done enough talking. He looked around as if to say, "Now it's your turn! Somebody say something sensible!"

Mladenov felt as if he were in seventh heaven. At last he was accepted and treated as an equal among equals. No one moved away from him; no one treated him condescendingly. Again and again someone in the group made an effort to include him in the conversation.

An engineer named Boyko talked in subdued tones with Professor Kuznetsov. Poor Neverov sat there looking melancholy, his wife next to him. She had decided to make a break with the KGB but had run into difficulties she could not surmount. The KGB had "convinced" her that the Christians had not been harmed by her activities. Thus she eventually had reached the conclusion that she was fulfilling the biblical injunction to obey the government when she informed on the church. As a result of her "change of mind," her husband was released from prison. But the poor man suffered unspeakably because of her traitorous behavior.

At last Yuri Sokolov and Natasha arrived, followed by Nina and Alyosha Serov. Everyone rose and sang a happy wedding song, during which Sasha and Irina entered the room. Svetlana and Igor Serov carried the bridal veil. Vladimir Sokolov wiped away a few tears.

Klim then asked those present to take their seats and made a few brief remarks. He spoke a few words of admonition to the two couples and asked them to kneel. Then he asked all ministers present to step forward. Vassiley Kuznetsov, Polevoy, Relin, and Semyon Anakin came to the front.

"I would also like to ask Grandfather Sokolov and our brother Lupa to join us here," said Klim.

All of them laid hands on the two wedding couples and each said a brief prayer. Old Sokolov and Lupa wept. After this, Klim let the two couples rise and announced, "Before all these witnesses I declare you, Yuri Sokolov and Natasha Nikitina, to be husband and wife. What God hath joined, let no man put asunder. Likewise I declare you, Sasha Nikitin and Irina Sokolova, husband and wife. I now ask the relatives and friends of the newlyweds to congratulate them!"

The celebration lasted late into the night. Many stories were told, sad ones as well as happy ones, for the recent painful events were not easily wiped off the slate. One thing was clear in everyone's mind—the dialogue between Christians and Communists could not happen.

Among other things Vassiley said, "Jesus Christ did not commission His followers to carry on a dialogue with the

Gospel's enemies, but to proclaim the good news. This proclamation survived the dark ages as well as national socialism. It also will survive atheistic communism. We must remain faithful. This may, of course, mean that we will have to go back into psychiatric clinics or jails again. *But so what?* We must be willing to give up our lives in the name of Jesus. So let us sing the beautiful song, 'For faith in the Gospel, for Jesus Christ will we stand . . . to follow His example, always forward, behind Him!' Those who are for Christ and His kingdom, rise and join me in singing this hymn!"

Dear Valentina Neverova found herself in an embarrassing situation. What was she to do? Finally she, too, pulled herself together, rose with the rest of them, and sang with her head raised high. Lyuba Serova sang along with them, too, with tears in her eyes. Mladenov sang loudest of all, greatly inspired. The Christians held one another's hands while they sang.

The windows were wide open, and the winds carried their song far away into the night. Those who passed by stopped to listen.

Other True Stories from Bethany House Publishers

HELP ME REMEMBER, HELP ME FORGET by Robert Sadler with Marie Chapian

The powerful story of a man who was sold as a slave in the Twentieth Century but eventually found the true meaning of freedom.

THE DIRK'S ESCAPE by C. Brandon Rimmer

The World War II escape from Naziism and eventual conversion of the man who is the father of the modern computer.

CHARLA'S CHILDREN by James Scheer

An ordinary Southern California homemaker with a great love for children and a great faith in God, and her remarkable south-of-the-border adventures with homeless children.

GONE THE GOLDEN DREAM by Jan Markell

From the terrors of Russia to the ghettos of New York—three generations of a Jewish family in search of a dream.

MIRACLE IN THE MIRROR by Mark Buntain

The dramatic story of a lovely Asian girl and her physical and emotional healing from total paralysis.

OF WHOM THE WORLD WAS NOT WORTHY by Marie Chapian

A Yugoslavian family's remarkable survival under the boots of Naziism and Communism.

ONE WOMAN AGAINST THE REICH by Helmut Ziefle

A Christian mother's struggle to keep her family together and true to God during the horrors of Hitler's regime.

WHAT'S THE MATTER WITH CHRISTY? by Ruth Allen

A rural community in the Midwest, a pastor's family, a teenage daughter in trouble—a mother's prayer journal during this difficult journey through pain and anger to forgiveness and hope.

WHERE DOES A MOTHER GO TO RESIGN? by Barbara Johnson

A wife and mother learns to cope with the crippling of her husband, the death of two sons, and the homosexuality of a third.

HALFWAY TO HEAVEN by Max Sinclair

A tragic accident, a broken neck, and a nearly hopeless medical prognosis. But the doctors reckoned without God. . . .

MAURY/Wednesday's Child by Maury Blair

An illegitimate boy's incredible suffering at the hands of a brutal stepfather, and his ultimate triumph when he becomes a child of God.